NewsBiscuit

'Real Fake News'

15 Years of Typos

Foreword by John O'Farrell

All contributors have given their time for free to this project and all royalties from the sale of this of this book go straight to charity. NewsBiscuit is proud to support the award-winning mentoring charity and support network Arts Emergency (arts-emergency.org) and English Pen - one of the world's oldest human rights organisations, championing the freedom to write and read around the world. (englishpen.org), with each charity receiving 50% of the royalties from this edition of the book.

CHAPTERS

Foreword

This is a collection of some of the best stories from Britain's original online news satire site going back over the last one hundred and fifty years from when it was first launched by Isambard Kingdom Brunel.

Although NewsBiscuit remains proud to have been Britain's first daily news satire website, I am forced to admit that in the years that followed, others may have come along and managed to achieve more hits and recognition with the same basic template. Yeah, those bastards totally copied my idea of copying The Onion.

However, the central ambition with the site was always to create a forum for new comedy writing online, and what remained unique about NewsBiscuit was the interactive submissions board, where aspiring writers could submit potential front pages, rate each other's work, suggest improvements or learn that hot Asian girls were in their area right now.

Back in the 1980s, I had got my first big break writing on Radio 4's Week Ending, which was open to anyone who wanted to send in a sketch or turn up at their weekly open meetings. So, when I came up with the idea for a British news satire website, I tried imagining an online writers' room. How would you recreate the smell of body odour and stale nicotine? How would we talk loudly over the solitary woman offering up her ideas?

The other problem was that all the topical shows I had worked on had usually been swamped with mad submissions in green ink, claiming that all BBC producers were satanic shape-shifters with lizard heads (when in reality only a few of them were). But now the Internet could provide the technology where readers of the site did all the sifting for us.

The star rating system allowed the cream to rise to the top and gave anonymous trolls the chance to give just one star to any story that was funnier than theirs (i.e. all of them). Fellow writers were encouraged to comment constructively on submissions, to suggest possible improvements or point out that this was not the place to sell your complete set of 'The World at War' on VHS.

Being on the World-Wide-Net-Web meant that this 21st century writers' room was open to anyone, just as those Week Ending writers' meetings had been open to everyone who was a male middle-class graduate in their twenties. In that sense, the site has been a huge success, providing an outlet and mutually-supportive development lab for aspiring scribes all over the world.

Many comedy writers who first gained some confidence on NewsBiscuit have since gone on to greater things; getting their material broadcast or professionally published. Others have gone on to create satire websites of their own. Occasionally our jokes would get taken literally and tweeted around the world in outrage by people who thought the stories were real, and so our comedy writers would discover they had written the actual news in Ghana or somewhere.

Now nearly 15 years old, NewsBiscuit has racked up over 5,000 front pages and 10,000 other funny news stories, making it the single most powerful satirical force in the world and the main reason that the British Conservatives were swept from power and have now dwindled into total political obscurity.

All of this is thanks to the huge pool of comedy talent that has always been out there. It is the hundreds of writers down the years who have made NewsBiscuit an enduring success, and without all that talent and enthusiasm, without people writing up and sharing their funny ideas simply for the love of it, the site would have ceased to exist years ago.

This book is a tribute to their talents, and to the current team of editors of the site who keep the show on the road and have pulled together this old fashioned 'book' thing. I can't take any of the credit for this publication – my lawyers have asked me to make that very clear.

When the funny writers stop turning up to our site or when the submissions board ceases to have enough decent stuff to put on the front page, it will be time to wind up the site. But as so far that has never looked like being the case, so NewsBiscuit looks set to continue for as long as there is enough mad news for us all to laugh at. And that particular well does not look like it is drying up any time soon...

John O'Farrell - 2020

CHAPTER ONE

Water found on Mars; Tories privatise it (and other UK News)

Police step up hunt for pensioner's missing sock

Bristol police have intensified the hunt for a missing sock belonging to pensioner Bill Smith, 72. Police say the sock is 'blue and shaped like a foot' and went missing while in transit between Smith's laundry basket and his washing machine. Smith himself believes 'someone walked off' with it.

An Avon police spokesman said that the force took all crime seriously. 'A missing sock might not matter to a one-legged man,' the spokesman said, 'but it matters to the ordinary Bristolian and we're determined to locate its whereabouts.' However, criminologists have pointed to holes in that argument, and have pointed out that sock theft has increased dramatically since police stopped patrolling in pairs.

Scientists confirm clown pubes match their hair

Research has revealed that the one thing scarier than a deranged clown is a huge mass of multi-coloured pubic hair bursting out of your pants. Scientists have spent five years studying the contents of fairground shower plugholes and now vouch that clown 'collars match their cuffs' - even the ones with two tufts of hair and a bald section in the middle.

Explained one circus historian: 'Rodeo clowns have been known to enrage bulls, by flashing their garishly coloured genitals, while circus clowns will clumsily pratfall over their own painted knob. Yet, there is nothing more family friendly than a nylon rainbow pube thatch.'

Stephen King immortalised clown genitals in his sequel to 'It', called 'Thingamabob'. In the story, a child becomes trapped in a storm drain with a particularly wiry clump of discarded clown hair - which would later go on to become two-thirds of Boris Johnson.

Some beauticians refuse to wax clowns. One said: 'When I removed his trousers, all I could see was a soft rubber skin-coloured cap. It was pretty off-putting, as every time I inadvertently touched his privates, they made a honking noise and squirted in my eye.'

Fear of Brummie epidemic as accent spreads beyond city

Concern is growing that Brummie is spreading much faster than originally estimated and colonising many of the dialects that once distinguished surrounding towns and rural districts.

'We have started an emergency inoculation programme for high-risk groups, including pregnant women, who can protect their unborn children from developing Brummie in the womb,' said Paul Jackson, professor of sociolinguistics at Walsall University, who is working on a vaccine, known locally as TamiFlow.

'We would like to reassure the general public that the vaccine is completely safe, although you may experience a slight Black Country inflection for a few days after the jab.'

A spokesman for Birmingham City Council then read a prepared statement, but no-one understood what he was saying.

Cannabis farm wins regional tourism award

A cannabis farm in mid-Wales has received a coveted five-star award from Welsh tourism chiefs for its contribution to the regional economy.

Weed World, which was established in 2011 by a consortium of specialist farming enthusiasts after a trip to Amsterdam, expanded its enterprise by introducing family-friendly activities, such as a miniature railway, elaborate water bongs and cake baking sessions.

'Everything is geared up towards making people feel welcome and really, really mellow,' said founder James Wellington-Henry. 'Our visitors now leave on a real high as some of the comments in the visitors book prove, if you can make out what they wrote. Plus, the tuck shop does a roaring trade.'

The farm has further plans to undertake outreach activities in schools and on street corners, including a red, gold and green-coloured 'magic bus', which will feature roll-up demonstrations by costumed guides. '

We totally applaud local initiatives like this,' said a spokesman for the Welsh Tourist Board. 'With family tickets starting at £7.00 an ounce, this is unreal stuff, a real intense buzz.'

Large car driven by twat has oversized poppy on it

The presence of a poppy on the radiator grille of a car clearly indicates that the owner is a much better person than everyone else, because he not only has a bigger car but clearly also cares far more than anyone else about honouring the soldiers who died in two world wars, it has emerged.

'Lest we forget,' said massive twat Nigel Walker, using the subjunctive tense for the first time in his life. 'I've kept this very large polypropylene flower in my garage since 1997 and I bring it out for three weeks each year leading up to Remembrance Day or once someone else's poppy reminds me, whichever happens first.

'Two generations of young British men went to war for our freedom to drive around in flash cars intimidating people in smaller cars before parking them across two spaces at Sainsbury's,' continued Walker, solemnly. 'It's the least I can do.'

The ghost of Private Sidney Dobson of the Royal Fusiliers, who drowned in a cesspit at the Battle of Ypres when he slipped over while trying to escape mustard gas, said: 'Well, I'm still lying in the ground with bits of mud stuck to my bones, though naturally I'm happy it wasn't in vain and you lot can spend your free time arguing on typewriters about who has the best poppy.

'Actually, not. Now f*ck off and let me Rest in Peace like you keep saying you want me to.'

Dave Lamb provides comedy voice-over for family Christmas row

A potentially disastrous situation was narrowly averted at the Ellington family's Christmas Day lunch in Redditch when actor Dave Lamb burst in off the street to provide a camp and amusing comedy voice-over straight from 'Come Dine with Me'.

The Ellington get-together followed a traumatic year, during which Chris Ellington had an affair with a work colleague, his wife Elaine had stopped speaking to her mother after a row over her late father's will and their hitherto engaging younger daughter, Jessica, had turned into a sullen, moody teenager.

'Elaine had badly underestimated the time needed to cook the turkey and Chris got narked with her,' said Chris's depressive brother, John. 'She said "I'll have to give it another hour" and he just glared at her with an evil look on his face. Then suddenly, an oddly familiar voice piped up from the spare room, saying "An hour? That's about as long as I'd give their marriage".'

Ten minutes after this, when pervy Great Uncle Charles' hands started to wander towards the Ellingtons' older daughter's knee, Lamb popped up to say 'Looks like Charles missed out on his holiday in Thailand this year,' and he backed away a split second before his face would have been slapped. Shortly afterwards, Lamb's wise advice to Chris's mother: 'No second sherry this year, Audrey. The vicar's barely recovered from last Christmas,' also stopped potential embarrassment in its tracks.

'Things were still simmering when Elaine finally brought the turkey to the table at 2 o'clock,' said John Ellington. 'It could have gone either way, but when Elaine hesitantly asked who liked pigs in blankets, Dave piped up with "Well, Chris certainly does. Have you seen the size of that woman he was knocking off?" We all high-fived each other, Chris went chasing Dave down the street with the carving knife, screaming, and we didn't see him again all day. Best Christmas ever!'

Dildo batteries are essential items, say lockdown experts

Following desperate calls for dildo batteries to be added to the list of essential items during the current lockdown, the Government has made a U-turn. They will now be categorised as being as essential as milk, bread and Werther's Originals.

'I'm so relieved,' said Yvonne Hand from Woking. 'I only do a clothes-wash once a week so my rinse cycle stick-on has been my only pleasure and I've even had to put it on an extra spin.'

Ms Hand is no longer worrying about her extended isolation. 'I've now been out to the shops and managed to get hold of a 48 pack which will luckily provide me with enough juice to power up my Rampant Rabbit vibrator with its 12-speed clitoral stimulus for a good week. I forgot to get any milk though.'

Daily Mail marks April Fool's Day with true stories

The Daily Mail announced today that it has chosen to mark April Fool's Day this year by printing only stories that are true and not misleading in any way. For one day only, it will only be offering cancer remedies supported by medical evidence. Moreover, it will stress that, while lifestyle changes and 'superfoods' can certainly affect your risk level, they are not in any sense a miracle cure.

The Mail will also admit that the price of your house is determined entirely by its size, location and condition, and is really not worth obsessing about anyway since you only sell it when you're buying another one. Also, the EU isn't the reason those roadworks in your high street are taking so long.

Early signs are that Daily Mail readers are not pleased with this temporary change. 'Iss the fin end of the wedge, innit,' said Dave Chambers from Basildon. 'Whatever 'appened to the good old

Great British 'ysterical panic abaaht nuffink? I got frough my full English this morning wivaaht choking on it once.'

Garden furniture refusing to come out for Spring

'I'm staying put in the shed,' said grumpy rattan chair Kevin Wilkins after refusing a plea from its owner, you, to come out at the end of April. 'I was designed for Mediterranean al fresco dining, not Barnsley with hot soup.

'If you reckon it's spring, then why don't you try sitting naked on a mouldy patio for whole day?' Wilkins continued. 'Look, we had an agreement: I create the illusion that you're a sophisticated homeowner and you stop the cat from pissing on my leg. But my whole 'holiday in Crete' vibe is ruined when there's a snowman on the lawn.

'I've spoken to the picnic table and none of us are coming out any time soon. And don't try your usual tricks, with fake plastic topiary, spray-on tan and a trail of breadcrumbs,' Wilkins said.

'Oh, and Steve the George Foreman Grill said to forget it, he's still traumatised from his only outing last year. And nobody's fooled by you wearing shorts, when your kneecaps are still blue.'

One in ten firefighters 'not fit enough' to be novelty strippers

Hen parties throughout the UK have been put at risk by the paucity of fit firefighters, with many displaying allergies to baby oil, thongs and Velcro, it has emerged.

The Scottish Fire and Rescue Service (SFRS), whose motto is 'Tease, not sleaze', is one of the worst offenders for fitness. It has reportedly been trying to fob customers off with a novelty gorilla-gram covered in whipped cream and a petulant dwarf in a kilt.

One disappointed bride said: 'We called 999 in response to a bonfire getting out of control. When the crew arrived, they just extinguished the flames. At no point did they remove their clothing or rub their genitals on my face.'

An SFRS spokesman said: 'If our members want to continue to show their members, they need to buff up. Public safety can only be guaranteed if we quickly tackle fires and fire our tackle off quickly. We need to return to our proud roots as sensuous, well-built strippers with an intimidatingly large hose.'

Scottish Widows lady told: 'Get over it'

Morag McGafferty, the attractive lady who has been dressed in black in the Scottish Widows adverts for the past couple of decades has been told to get over her husband's death and move on.

Friends told her: 'Will you nae put on some brighter clothes and come out for a wee drink, girl?' 'Och, no,' she is reported to have replied. 'My late husband Hamish would not have wanted me frittering away our savings like that.'

The friends pointed out that McGafferty had been a Scottish widow for longer than she was married and there must be more to life than wearing a black-hooded cape and standing around on the hills looking enigmatic.

Attempts to get Morag to eat a Flake in a field of poppies or invite round the dishy bloke next door for a cup of Gold Blend have all failed. Instead, she pulled up her hood and spoke wistfully of how Hamish would have admired the Flexible Options Bond and PEP transfers now available to cautious investors. Morag's friends pledged to call on her again in another couple of years, before going off to spend all their hard-earned investment money down the pub.

Queen honours Stephen Hawking with English accent

In a moving ceremony at Buckingham Palace, world-renowned physicist Professor Stephen Hawking has finally been granted the right to speak like a member of the Royal Family. His synthesiser was ceremonially re-programmed so that he sounded like he was from his native England and not a cheap 1950s American sci-fi movie.

'One has finally arrived,' Hawking said proudly through his new synthesiser, in cut-glass syllables that would put Camilla Parker-Bowles to shame.

However, it soon became clear he found it hard to conceal his bitterness at being overlooked for the past 20 years. 'One feels one would have achieved greater recognition if one didn't have to address conferences on cosmology with the accent of a Bronx taxi driver,' he complained.

Eddie Redmayne, who recently played Hawking in the hit film 'The Theory of Everything', was said to be distraught at the news. 'I spent ages trying to get that American robot accent just right but this new one's impossible. I can do Ray Winstone. How about reprogramming it to that, until after the Oscars?'

Post-Brexit deportation fears for elderly Wimbledon Common residents

Several elderly Wimbledon Common residents without proof of residential status are living in fear of removal from the UK after the 31 December 2020 Brexit deadline. Madame Cholet, 85, who insists that she is British by birth, has lived and worked as a cook in the Wimbledon area since the 1960s.

Cholet is now appealing to the Home Office for leniency in the absence of the relevant paperwork, which she said was lost in a spring clean in the 1970s. 'It is a very frightening time pour moi,' said the elderly pensioner. 'I 'ave lived 'ere for many years, but maintenant I feel like I am very unwelcome.'

A close neighbour, affectionately known locally as 'Uncle' Bulgaria, says he too feels under threat. 'I've been cleaning up the local Common for over 40 years, so this is a complete and utter travesty.

'Under the new immigration points-system I will be classed as an unskilled worker and I'd be totally buggered in Bulgaria because I don't know anyone there. My nephew Orinoco, who really is a work-shy benefits scrounger, will have no chance.'

Inventor and local engineer Tobermory has promised to give what help he can, but said: 'When Scotland gets its independence, I'll be back up there in a shot. Then, if the worst comes to the worst they can come and live with me.'

One local resident said he feared the residents might be forced to go underground 'or overground' - in the manner of their friend Tomsk, who disappeared after being exposed as a Soviet spy in the 1970s.

Satire now Britain's only growth industry

Satire could account for over 30% of GDP by 2022 and most new jobs, according to a few quinoa-scoffing metropolitan elitists or 'expert analysts', depending on which way you look at it.

'The last five years have been an amazing rollercoaster,' said Nigel Walker, an all-purpose, generic, cliché-spouting idiot from Lincolnshire who appears on numerous satirical news websites.

'It seems like every day someone gets me to make up a quote about something I don't really know anything about, then a couple of months later a cheque for about £35 comes through the post.'

Britain originally started the Industrial Revolution and spread free trade across the world, usually via gunboat, and it still remains the fifth, sorry sixth, no make that seventh largest economy in the world. Now, Britain is looking to a boom in derivative piss-taking to launch it into a bright new future.

'This is only going to grow,' said satirical news website editor Johnny Farrow. 'The great thing about satire as an industry is that self-sustaining clusters form naturally because half of them don't even know they are in the industry: angry men in pubs who say they are 'backing Britain', people who think tomatoes are about to start tasting the same way they did in 1972, Jacob Rees-Mogg ... pure comedy gold, all of them. Rule Britannia. I'm so proud.'

Spontaneous combustion threat to elderly this winter

Thousands of Britain's elderly could die this winter through spontaneous combustion brought on by overheating their homes, according to the Government.

'When you're wearing as much knitwear and tweed as some pensioners, just turning the central heating up a notch too high can easily spell disaster,' said a spokesman. 'Their dry, wrinkly skin is like paper – they go up in seconds.'

Government ministers believe that the overheating of homes every winter by the elderly needs to be tackled. 'Just because we give people £200 is no excuse to go mad with the heating,' said the Minister for the Environment. 'I've been in some of their homes – they'd be better off spending the money on fans.'

The Government has therefore suggested that if an elderly person does spontaneously combust, others should gather round to warm themselves by the fire while it lasts.

Stonehenge to be fitted with sprinklers

'English Heritage and the National Trust have fitted sprinklers in properties that are only visited by a handful of pensioners every year,' said a Stonehenge spokesman. 'We get millions of visitors. It's a shame the Stone Age builders didn't build a couple more henges, because that would have helped with demand.'

The spokesman claimed that there was still some confusion about whether the 'stone cladding' was acceptable. 'We've looked for a kitemark everywhere, but can't find any evidence of the structure being built to an acceptable standard. It may have to be pulled down if we can't find suitable documentary evidence.'

'Never mind the travel distances, who checked the footings?' asked one building inspector. 'I'm concerned that one of the lintels will topple off in the wind.'

Stonehenge trustees are confident that the structural components are up to scratch and point out that in reality only a small fraction of the annual visitors are allowed in the monument these days. 'Ageing bloody Druid hippies,' pointed out one trustee. 'If a lintel fell on them it would do us all a bloody favour.'

Traces of meat found in poor people's diets, admits DWP

Minute traces of meat have been found in some meals consumed by poor people, according to the Department of Work and Pensions secretary Iain Duncan Smith. Duncan Smith said he had long suspected that the poor were spending money on food instead of on bus fares, bicycle maintenance or telephone calls looking for work.

'If you give some people living in poverty more money, they'll just squander it on more food for themselves and their children,' he said. 'Some families are even buying meat. No-one is going to get into the world of work while sitting at home around the kitchen table eating and drinking.

'Next thing you know they'll be smiling or even laughing, forming meaningful relationships with other poor people, and expecting to be given Christmas Day off work, if they ever do any.'

Duncan Smith is said to be planning a visit to North Korea to see how Pyongyang has cured people of addiction to food and drink.

Metropolitan Police 'still discriminating against clowns'

A large-scale enquiry has revealed that years after promises were made to tackle widespread discrimination against clowns in the Metropolitan police, clownist attitudes remain ingrained among the force. Members of London's clown population are twice as likely as non-clowns to be stopped and searched or have a custard pie flung into their faces.

One clown spoke today of his experiences facing daily coulrophobia from London's police. 'When I said my name was 'Coco', he asked if I was trying to be funny,' he complained.

'It's such a stereotype, assuming that we're all trying to be funny, just because we might have big red noses and enormous false smiles. Though to be fair, squirting him with my plastic flower buttonhole can't have helped.'

Another clown said: 'So, I stop at the traffic lights, and quite innocently my car collapses in a spectacular heap, with the wheels falling outwards, the chassis slumping to the tarmac, leaving me standing there holding the steering wheel. Suddenly there's coppers everywhere, as if I'm some kind of menace.'

Metropolitan Police chief Sir Paul Stephenson denied the allegations. 'My men have no interest whatsoever in harassing the innocent clown in the street,' he insisted. 'We're far more committed to tracking down the ringmasters. In fact, some of my best friends are clowns, as indeed are many of my officers.'

Birthday boy just happy to 'hit stuff'

Parents Jacob and Zara Thomas have been disappointed to discover that their three-year old son was uninterested in their gift of a toy espresso machine, with matching child-sized Aga, but more elated with the cardboard box it came in. Sadly, Zac's interpretation of imaginative play had little to do with the lute and pottery workshop they had arranged for him, but everything to do with being a 'death robot'.

Four years in the planning, this birthday event was to be in part a celebration of Zac's life, but primarily a shining tribute to the parenting skills and exquisite taste of Jacob and Zara. Yet, as adult guests marvelled at the Renaissance ice sculptures on display – all in the style of Botticelli - Zac and his pals just licked the ice.

The present list, published in 'Town & Country', clearly informed guests that all artisan gifts should be in an Art Deco theme, which is why it was so disappointing for everyone to see Zac armed with a stick, chasing the cat.

With a budget of thousands, Jacob and Zara had provided an ergonomic bouncy-castle, organically sourced jelly, with an exquisite orchid and willow branch centre-piece - which Zac promptly stuck up his nose.

Woman gives birth and raises child in IKEA queue

Expectant mum Helena Churchill and partner David Lomax from Darleston are thought to be the first couple to give birth and raise their child in IKEA.

After loading their shopping trolley with their bargain Sniglar Cot and heading to the checkout, the couple were surprised to see 15 aisles each with an average of 125 customers waiting to pay. Just a few minutes after joining the queue, Helena's waters broke. Some ten hours later she delivered a bouncing nine-pound baby boy in the line for till eight.

'The staff tried to help with the birth but kept insisting Helena had definitely got all the bits necessary for a baby, when it was obvious we were short of a leg and a foot,' explained David.

'The manager wanted us to come back for those later but I wasn't making another bloody trip. Eventually an assistant found what we were looking for, after a quick root around in Helena's Fäni.'

Now, almost ten months later, the child is taking his first steps towards the checkout. 'He's developing very quickly,' said Helena.

'He's got a lovely collection of Klappar Cirkus toys, and we've been able to assemble his own little nursery right here in the queue. We're a bit concerned about his diet, though. I'm not sure Godis Skum marshmallows and chicken meatballs for every meal is ideal for a toddler.'

Woman returns husband to M&S as 'not fit for purpose'

A woman who found her husband in Marks & Spencer has returned him to the store under its refund or exchange guarantee.

Mavis Adams, 49, from Luton, met husband-to-be Bert in her local M&S while buying a shepherd's pie ready meal for one, and marriage was on the cards soon after he proposed a ready meal for two instead.

However, once she got Bert home, she discovered he didn't fit properly and soon started to unravel, prompting her decision to take him back to the shop as not fit for purpose.

'Although I didn't have a receipt, they were very nice about it' said Mavis. 'The girl suggested I look round the aisles for a replacement, but I couldn't see anything I fancied that afternoon so I settled for a year's supply of ready meal shepherd's pie for one and a credit note.'

Airport expansion: Additional Costa Coffee at Luton approved

The decision to approve a new branch of Costa Coffee at Luton airport has ended years of wrangling over the future of air travel.

'Thank f*ck that's over,' said the pro-third runway at Heathrow campaign. 'We've been waiting for this decision for so long that if we never hear the name "Heathrow" again, it'll be too soon. A nice toffee nut latte somewhere else entirely sounds great, thanks.'

The Prime Minister told the Commons: 'Our guiding principle is how to help our air industry reflect the strength and ambition of our economy. Of course, now we're all as poor as pig shit since Brexit, we couldn't afford to build a runway even if you lot could afford to use it.

'So, a nice new coffee shop at Luton is pretty much all we can manage, although they won't be able to import any nice Danish pastries without paying 45% import duties, so don't get your hopes up. Airport expansion means airport expansion, and we're going to make a Brexit of it.'

Man 'left with no choice' but to leave family home

Bob Evans, 34, revealed today that he was taking a leaf out of the Royal Family's book and leaving his family home. 'My mother is upset, of course, but I have to do this for the sanity of my family,' he said, clutching his baby son Tyler closely.

'If he feels he has to move to Stockport to start a new life, so be it,' Evans' mother said. 'However, his wish to remain an active member of the family isn't going to happen,' she added, pointing to Bob's desire to continue chipping in to the family Lotto ticket every week.

'If he thinks he can up sticks and take my grandson with him, yet share our fortune when the EuroMillions comes our way, then he can swivel.'

Evans' girlfriend is just glad to be leaving. 'Living with the in-laws, getting all that constant attention and putting up with creepy Uncle Andrew is too much. Stockport here I come.'

His father, however, was circumspect. 'Stockport's not that far away. A number eight and change for the number three at Sale,' he said. 'Half an hour tops, no idea what the fuss is all about.'

Evans is 741,324th in line to the throne.

Soldiers to be protected with armour made from grandfathers' pocket watches

The Ministry of Defence has swooped on antique shops across Britain after discovering that most Great War survivors had been saved by a future heirloom in their pocket, usually a fob watch or cigarette case, deflecting a Jerry bullet.

Mass purchase of vintage timepieces, Zippo lighters and other knick-knacks to fashion into body armour for the modern-day soldier has created a shortage, forcing MOD procurement officers to compromise, in some cases issuing non-critical troops with grandfather clocks instead.

'The typical long-case grandfather clock provides ample cover for the modern soldier,' claimed General George McCartney, pointing out that the pendulum would probably stop a bullet. 'But I would advise troops using one to avoid going out on stealth missions on the hour, half-hour, or in certain cases, the quarter hour.'

Soldiers who complete a tour of duty with a standard issue grandfather clock will be in line for a gong.

Northerners to be trained in Tube etiquette

Following a spate of incidents involving Northerners chatting to random strangers on the London Underground, the British Transport Police (BTP) have launched a poster campaign to dissuade them.

'We had some seriously scary moments last week', explained a BTP officer. 'Last Thursday this guy from Leeds told a complete stranger his name, his business, everything. Even worse, he was called Alan, and people thought he was saying something about 'Allah' and legged it down the carriage.

'The next day there were these two chaps from Warrington who wouldn't stop chatting to strangers. By the time we got there they'd been beaten to death by the mob. Perfectly understandable. These people need to realise that a conversation isn't our natural habitat, so we get stressed and lash out.'

The poster, to be displayed on all underground trains, depicts a young Asian man with a bomb strapped to his chest trying to avoid conversation with an overweight man eating a pie with a whippet and flat cap who is prodding him cheerfully in the chest and obviously trying to chat. The caption reads: 'You're not in the North now. We'd rather sit next to the bomber.'

The BTP official added: 'I'm sure you're a fascinating person, so tell it to somebody who gives a shit. Here's a clue, they don't live in London.'

RNLI criticised for 'taking so bloody long'

Thrill seekers up and down the country have condemned the RNLI crews who took 'ages' to rescue them in the middle of Storm Ciara.

'All I did was surf in storm force conditions. I took all the proper precautions - I even had a packet of condoms ready inside my waterproof jacket in case I was rescued by a really hot lifeboat woman,' said one complainant.

'How bloody hard is it to launch a boat in gale force winds?' asked another. 'I launched my li-lo in seconds and found myself halfway to Ireland in minutes. If it wasn't for the Government's custom boundary running down the middle of the Irish Sea, I'd be voting Sinn Fein by now.'

All of the rescued people agreed at how grumpy the lifeboat men and women appeared. 'A bit of public service training wouldn't go amiss,' said one of the rescued people, before catching a train to

Scotland. 'They're forecasting avalanches - I wonder what those look like from below.'

SAS soldiers to experience raw horror of female beauty regimes

The recent landmark decision by the Ministry of Defence to allow female personnel to occupy all positions within the armed forces has left Britain's elite soldiers filled with dread.

Major Steve McCabe of the SAS explained: 'I've been there: Afghanistan, Iraq, Newcastle, you name it - I've seen horrors beyond imagination, but there's nothing that can prepare a soldier for the sight of a comrade using a pencil to draw lines inside her own eye.'

Although men and women of all ranks will engage in combat alongside each other, they will initially be kept apart in grooming areas.

McCabe added: 'After a training exercise, a lady soldier once gave me a dollop of gritty paste to remove camo paint. It stung like jellyfish jam and took the top layer of skin clean off my face. Never again!

'And the self-punishment of hair should be against the Geneva Convention. Steaming-hot batons straightening the hair because it's curly, then curling it because it's straight. Try explaining the rationale behind this to a shaven-headed squaddie.'

Sergeant Julia Hampton added: 'Some of the soldiers mixing with female recruits will be young lads, it's too early for them to see what the little scissors are used for just yet.'

'I was forced into marmalade smuggling,' says bear

A small bear who was arrested at a London railway station yesterday said he was 'coerced' into smuggling marmalade in small containers into Britain from South America. The bear, who was seized as he got off the Heathrow Express, has not yet been identified.

A police spokesman said: 'When we asked the bear his name, he looked up and the first thing he saw was the station name, which he gave as his own. Oldest trick in the book. We are in the interim calling him Pooh Bear, after where he allegedly hid the marmalade.'

Camelot urged to produce thinner lottery winners

The Government has urged Camelot to find fewer lardbucket winners in the National Lottery. Statistics show that fat couples in council houses are more likely to win the lottery, leading to speculation that the lottery is weighted towards the overweight.

'It's often quite difficult to get the publicity pictures,' admitted Camelot head of PR Mike Newby. 'Tiny houses, enormous cheques, fat, dazed looking couples and jeroboams of champagne – talk about a 'rollover'. All too often we have to make do with photographing them in their garden, or in some cases the local park.'

Agreeing that the body image of lottery winners is a concern, a senior treasury minister said: 'If all the winners appear overweight and under-educated, people might somehow get the impression that the lottery is simply a tax on the poor and stupid.

'Which is why we're urging Camelot to come up with some thin posh looking winners. Or we will just parade the wife of some banker who just got a massive bonus and be a bit vague about where her millions came from.'

Full UK rebuild advised after storm damage

In the aftermath of Storm Ciara's trail of devastation and destruction across the country at the weekend, experts have surveyed the damage and concluded that it would be cheaper to knock the UK down and do a total rebuild.

'With a blank canvas to work with, there are a number of improvements we could make', said one. 'The favourite is for four separate islands. England, Scotland, Wales, and Northern Ireland, which will be situated in the North Sea. The Isle of Wight will be attached to England in an attempt to drag it into the 20th century.'

Motorist accepts parking ticket without complaint

'It was my own fault,' said David Jackson from Bromsgrove shortly after becoming the first person in the UK ever to not kick off about getting a parking ticket. 'I knew I only had two hours, but I lost track of time. The traffic warden was only doing his job, and I have only myself to blame.

'I was briefly tempted when my neighbour told me the Daily Mail would pay me a shedload of money for the story and a couple of sad-face photos of me holding the ticket. But then I thought better of it. I have my pride and the value of my house is nobody's business but mine.'

Countryside Alliance furious at ban on badger fisting

The Countryside Alliance has reacted with fury to Parliament's decision to end one of rural England's oldest traditions. The ban on badger fisting comes into effect immediately, following the passing of the Badgers (Manual Penetration) Act, which makes it an offence to knowingly fist or assist in the fisting of a badger.

The little-known country pursuit apparently dates back to the 13th century, when hungry peasants would thrust their arms deep into badger setts to retrieve tender young cubs for the table.

Over the centuries the tradition of fisting badgers evolved from this seasonal hunt. For many years in late March and early April, country folk have paraded through hamlet and village with live adult badgers impaled upon each arm, all the while singing the traditional folk ballad 'O brock, thy sphincter doth squeeze me so, but my true heart lies with Mary-o.'

Mary, portrayed by a golden-haired girl of 12, is carried through the streets in a wicker cage of badger form. The celebrations continue throughout the day, with the climax at sunset, when the badgers are allowed to hobble back to their setts and families. Lilting voices carry the final strains of the traditional Badger Song across the air 'Oh merry beast of twilit earth, who joy brings to our land e-oh, go now in peace and joy and love, while I go wash my hand e-oh.'

A DEFRA spokesman confirmed that the ban will be strictly enforced, and said that the tradition was barbaric and should have been stopped years ago. However, the Countryside Alliance has planned a rally in Hyde Park next week to protest against the blatant destruction of historic rural traditions.

'Fisting badgers is part of the way of life in the English countryside,' said an angry Jethro Finnegan from Shropshire. 'City folk have no understanding of rural ways. Next they'll be saying we're not allowed to fellate the otter.'

Edinburgh 'regrets having tattoo'

Scottish pensioner Edinburgh, known as Edina to her friends, has admitted her regret at ever agreeing to have a tattoo. 'I was young and impressionable,' she said, 'and when this group of manly soldiers suggested I had one to please them, I thought why not?'

Edina said that she was intoxicated by heady thoughts of rebellion and making herself attractive to those red-blooded fighters. 'I had the first tattoo in a back street near the castle,' she said. 'It was quite small, fairly tasteful and not really painful at all.'

'But every year more of these guys would come along and persuade me to do it again and make it bigger, and before you know it, I was left with this monstrosity that I can't cover up with my fringe.'

Edinburgh now fears that any tattoo removal is now going to require a laser the size of Leith.

Bus companies warn of travel chaos if passengers return

The UK's bus service operators have slammed the Government's decision to ease coronavirus restrictions to allow wider use of public transport, saying it will cause timetable chaos if their vehicles have to stop to pick up more than two passengers again.

'For months now our fleets have been running like clockwork,' said Mike Lewisham, managing director of First Bus. 'Buses sailed serene and empty through the quiet streets, breaking punctuality records week after week. Now it seems those glory days are over.'

Train operators have different fears for the week ahead. 'Yeah, sure, our trains have been running on time, well mostly,' said TransPennine Depresse CEO Sam Sunderland. 'Punctuality improvements, blah blah blah. Who cares about that stuff? Since

March we've saved £142.57 in performance fines, but lost £93 million in fares.

'To tempt customers back, I can reveal that a train - but I'm not saying which one! - now has a toilet with working flush, plenty of toilet paper, running water and working hand dryer. So, get back on the train and you might get to experience that. Although it'll probably be out of order by Wednesday so act now.'

Homeless men cruelly taunted Cambridge student

A group of homeless men have been convicted of laughing in the face of a Cambridge University student after he approached them lying on a park bench outside a convenience store. Giles Bartley-Atkins, 21, a member of Cambridge University Conservative Association, asked the group if they could spare him some loose change as he needed it for a parking meter.

Video footage showed one of the homeless men mockingly waving a 10p piece in front of his Porsche Macan, while another put the coin back in his pocket and urinated on it through his trousers, before falling over and fighting himself.

Bartley-Atkins told the judge all he had in his pocket was three or four thousand pounds in £50 notes. At first, one of the men offered him a drink from his bottle of Tennent's Super, but then it turned ugly and another of them tied the Porsche to the parking meter with a string from around his dog's neck.

Ordering the men to be admitted to a clinic for treatment for alcohol dependency, Judge James Digby said: 'You are fortunate I am sparing you from a custodial sentence this time. Mr Bartley-Atkins was cold and hungry, having driven through ten miles of heavy traffic with the top down on his Porsche. To treat him in this manner knowing his table was waiting was heartless and cruel.'

A friend of Bartley-Atkins criticised the sentence as too lenient: 'These people don't realise just how difficult it is to find a parking spot outside a Michelin star restaurant at night,' he said. 'There are no end of park benches in Cambridge for them to choose from - they don't know just how lucky they are.'

Yorkshire guests at Lancashire wedding 'charming and self-deprecating'

Fears of confrontation at a cross-Pennine wedding on Saturday were averted when the groom's family and friends failed to brag about Yorkshire or the concept of 'Yorkshireness' at all.

The service and reception at the prestigious Blackburn House Hotel passed uneventfully, with conspicuously absent topics of conversation during the festivities including respective abilities at cricket, strength of tea, thrift, honesty - including 'speaking as I find' and 'calling a spade a spade' - and the relative importance of birth place and upbringing.

'To be honest, when our Maggie said she was marrying a Yorkshireman from Skipton, my heart sank,' said the bride's father, John Haythornthwaite, 'but Richard has been delightful from the word go. Nonetheless, the thought of a contingent of Yorkshire's finest on the wedding day did give me some sleepless nights.'

Maggie's mother Catherine described her disbelief when the Yorkshire guests all arrived wearing red roses, the symbol of Lancashire. 'Richard's parents said the white roses hadn't been up to much, and anyway the thought of perpetuating an ancient rivalry between two branches of the Plantagenet royal family hadn't even crossed their minds.'

'Aye, we had a grand day', said Richard's father, Geoffrey Arkwright. 'And we didn't pay a penny towards it. Lancashire? Wankershire, more like.'

IN OTHER RELATED NEWS:

Optimistic borehole digger augers well

Tampon tax to be reviewed every four weeks

Downing Street cat resigns after admitting to historical catnip use

Man wins 'Who Wants to be a Millionaire' by phoning his friend Alexa

Duke of Edinburgh to retire from stand-up

Cocaine 'deeply regrets' being up Michael Gove's nose

Tim Peake 'over the moon' to be included in honours' list

Prince Charles contracting COVID-19 'probably Meghan's fault', confirms Daily Mail.

'Is my 'Support the NHS' banner tax-deductible?' asks Tory voter

Annual round of applause to replace pay increases for nurses, says Matt Hancock

Government to deter immigrants by telling them what Britain's actually like

The post-war years called, they want their grim hopelessness back

No statues for slave-traders, but the Pyramids are fine

Norfolk man loses wife, sister and cousin in accident; her funeral is next week

Escaped North Korean soldier hired as Brexit consultant

London Book Fair - 'tickets cheaper on Amazon'

Government's latest game-changer replaces chess with Scrabble

Government to avoid second wave of coronavirus by ensuring first wave never ends

Twitter finally bans Hitler after 80 years of racist tweets

English Cricket Board apologises for playing 2020 Cricket before 2020

Loft extension visible from space

British engineer wins World's Filthiest Mug accolade

Government slashes waiting times for unemployment

Parents going to extreme lengths to secure children's places in top teenage gangs

'Self-service' security checks to begin at UK airports

CHAPTER TWO

'Twelve Angry Non-Gender-Specific People' heads for West End (and other Arts stories)

Tate Modern stages retrospective of Clip Art

Renowned as one the twentieth century's most influential artists, Claus Von Clip is being honoured with a four-week exhibition of his pixelated bitmaps. The London gallery will be presenting hundreds of home-made greeting cards and whimsical pictures of puppies to a public too lazy to use Google Images.

An Art Historian explained: 'Von Clip was devoted to garish colours, poor resolution and an ironic sense that he couldn't be bothered. Who can forget 'Slice of cake with candle', 'Bubbling pint of beer' or the romantically titled 'JPEG45576'?'

To this day, Von Clip's work adorns thousands of emailed party invites and last-minute PowerPoint presentations. Not so much ahead of his time, but lagging fifty years behind, his experimental GIF years alienated many 'one-dimensional' purists. Sadly, Von Clip himself died penniless, having given away most of his art for free.

One of his models reminisced: 'Claus spent hours in his garret experimenting with Microsoft Paint. He could take a landscape by Turner and reduce it down to its essence – that of a big smiley face with a light bulb over his head. My lasting impression of Claus is that he was the reason my printer kept running out of coloured ink.'

Verona social services slammed over under-age abduction of Juliet

Social services in Verona have come under fire following the alleged abduction of a 13-year-old girl by a notorious local teenage hoodlum. Government ministers have warned that heads will literally roll if negligence is proved.

'It's disgraceful,' sobbed the distraught girl's mother. 'Everyone knows what a load of villains those Montagues are. First, someone sprayed 'Juliet iz well fit n i want 2 shag her 100% true' on the walls of our castle and then that little thug, Romeo, starts sniffing round my baby girl. I told social services what would happen, but they didn't want to know.'

Neither of the pair has been seen in the 72 hours since Montague was caught on CCTV cameras riding his mountain bike up and down the road outside a first-floor balcony window at the Capulet home. The authorities are increasingly fearful for the wellbeing of Juliet and have warned local chemists not to dispense the morning-after-pill or poison until further notice. An all-points notice has been put out for a missing friar.

A police spokesman added: 'We understand that Juliet is mature for her age and she speaks in iambic pentameter. However, the fact is that she is still below the age of consent and we will not tolerate paedophiles in this community. Besides, her family want to marry her off to the son of one of their friends when she is 15.'

Man seeks restraining order against his Narrator

Dave Sanders, 34, of Stevenage, began legal proceedings today seeking a restraining order against his Narrator, saying that his life had been made intolerable by the constant banal and intrusive commentary.

Sanders said he first noticed the voice-over to his life after becoming a devotee of documentaries and reality shows, but it gradually took on a life of its own. 'It started as an occasional voice in my head, generally making an obvious statement followed by a meaningless rhetorical question, such as: "Dave really needs a cup of tea, but will he remember where he left the teabags?".'

After a while Dave began to feel he was being watched, and then other people started to hear the voice too. 'I'd be like talking to my boss and the voice over would say "Dave is trying to impress the new Head of Human Resources – but did she notice him glance at her cleavage?"'

Things then took a further turn for the worse when he invaded Dave's social life. 'I was never that confident telling jokes,' said Dave, 'so I was a bit miffed when the Narrator appeared in the pub next to me and my mates saying "Dave is about to deliver the punch-line, but will he cock it up like he did last week?" The final straw was when he materialised while I was in bed with my girlfriend, saying: "Dave is ready to come now, but will he be able to hold off until Lisa is satisfied?"'

Sanders said that he was confident that his legal application will succeed, at which point a voice continued '...but is that confidence really justified?'

Physicists riot at pantomime after unfeasible balloon gag

'I like a joke as much as the next man and I'm prepared to suspend disbelief for a night at the theatre,' said one theatre attendee, while being treated for injuries sustained at his local pantomime.

'But when you see a man being handed a balloon filled with air and he subsequently begins to levitate, that really is beyond the pale of scientific feasibility.'

A physics lecturer in the cheap seats began booing first and witnesses say the barracking was mostly good-natured. However, the situation escalated when the illogical 'air lighter than air' stunt was repeated.

'It all kicked off when the audience asserted that this occurrence was scientifically impossible. The dame kept shouting "Oh no it isn't!" If that wasn't bad enough, she and the principal boy managed to rally the crowd round to their side.'

It was at this stage that punches were exchanged, and pretty soon conical flasks and mercury filled thermometers were raining down on the stage. Last night police were trying to calm tensions and have promised to appoint an officer with an understanding of Boyle's law and physical principles.

Scandinavian detective upbeat despite series of personal tragedies

Scandinavian TV detective Fred Blomqvist is in no way downcast after falling victim to the latest in a series of personal and work-related traumas, it has emerged.

Having your six-year-old daughter chopped into pieces and fed to piranha by Sweden's self-styled 'Aquarium killer' would be enough to make even the most battle-hardened detectives consider their future, but Blomqvist insisted he is rolling with the punches.

'Yeah, I'll hold my hands up - the daughter thing was a setback,' admitted the 53-year-old divorcee from his converted Uppsala farmhouse, which overlooks acres of bleak agricultural landscape. 'But I'm refusing to react to it. I won't take the bait,' he added, with a cheeky wink and a playful nudge to the ribs.

Blomqvist is legendary for his almost supernatural ability to take everything in his stride and is credited with the introduction of a

'You don't have to be mad to work here, but it helps' poster in the foyer of the police HQ.

The interview was interrupted by Blomqvist's distinctive ringtone. When the call was over, Blomqvist's voice cracked momentarily. 'That was the son from my first-marriage with Linda, who was killed when a tractor reversed over her in a one-way street in broad daylight,' he said.

'Well, it's not such great news about his leukaemia, but on the plus side it's looking like the jackdaw he found by the roadside with a broken wing is going to pull through. Isn't that just fantastic? Aww heck, pass me a tissue will you - I've got something in my eye.'

Violinists to have extreme facial expressions curbed

Frontline musicians are on the brink of a historic agreement to regulate the excesses of grimaces, lip biting, hair-tossing and excessive nostril use commonly deployed to express spurious musical emotion.

'This is very much like the controversy of the grunting tennis player,' explained one gurning harpsichord player. 'We've seen fake tears, faces screwed into paroxysms of concentration, anguish, agony, manic nodding and occasionally downright orgasm. It can confuse and occasionally mislead audiences into thinking the performance is more intense than is really the case.'

Musicians will now be limited to four basic and easily identifiable expressions: lament, ecstasy, whimsy and concentration. Artificial aids like onions and Viagra will be expressly banned.

Art world admits: 'We just like tits'

Ever since Mona Lisa refused to go topless, there has been a tension between artists and their libido. All art students will have casually doodled a cock in their sketchpad, and the only reason to attend a life-drawing class, is for a bit of 'nipple action'.

One art critic explained: 'It's important to note that even the cultural elite love the sight of a cracking pair of jugs. Who can forget David Hockney's 'The Big Tit' or his follow-up 'The Even Bigger Tit'? And I don't need to remind you about Pablo Picasso's 'The Fallen Madonna with the Big Boobies'.'

Fetching $170.4 million at auction, Modigliani's 'Reclining Nude' has proven to be one of history's most expensive pieces of pornography. Tragically, Modigliani himself, a renowned peeping tom, masturbated himself to death at the early age of 35.

One aspiring sculptor declared: 'I plan to create one big row of tits out of marble. I call it 'The Tory Frontbench'.'

Alton Towers closes Emotional Rollercoaster

'We were trying to give people a mental as well as a physical thrill,' said Peter Brindall, manager of the Alton Towers theme park, which has just closed its increasingly unpopular emotional rollercoaster.

'What's wrong with seeing placards saying "Stuart Williams; your mum's about to die!" or "It's OK, Stu, she suddenly pulled through!" as you twist and turn about? It's not as if we didn't warn them.'

One visitor complained: 'To be honest, it wasn't the ride promising major lottery wins, rapid promotions or a rare bone marrow disease. The problem I had was being kidnapped at gunpoint during one of the loop-the-loops, then being held hostage by terrorists. Only it turned out they weren't terrorists, the leader pulled off his mask and it was Simon Cowell to tell me I'd actually made the final of The X Factor. Not.'

With many customers subsequently complaining of deep feelings of emptiness and depression, the Staffordshire Emotional Health and Safety Inspectorate told the ride's designer the devastating news that his life's work has all been for nothing.

They then added: 'It's not really closing - we were just joshing. The ride is actually going to be copied all over the world, making you a billionaire. No, actually, we are closing it.'

Mock the Week team rejoice at Abu Hamza passport appeal success

Champagne corks flew and high-fives have been exchanged at 'Mock the Week' in reaction to the news that the Special Immigration Appeals Commission has ruled that Hamza could keep his British passport, and therefore can still be regarded as a valid topical reference for the show's writers who provide the panel members with their off-the-cuff remarks about the radical cleric and tabloid hate figure.

Perennial 'Mock the Week' makeweight Andy Parsons said: 'This is the most relieved I've been since I heard Abu Hamza wasn't going to do my prostate exam.'

Host Dara Ó Briain echoed the thoughts of the entire team, saying: 'Thank God he's back in the news and staying in the UK - without Abu Hamza, the material for our show would have been about as rough as Abu Hamza's iPhone screen... Points all round!'

Hamilton audience discover hip hop for the first time

Fans of musical theatre have completely lost their shit after being exposed to contemporary sounds and the notion of ethnic diversity. Many audience members are reported to have been astonished by something as edgy as a story from the 18th century. 'It was like Dr Seuss but with drums!' one said.

Cleaning up at the Olivier Awards, Hamilton won the award for the 'Best musical, thankfully not involving Andrew Lloyd Webber', 'Best revival of a sound from the 1980s' and 'Best civics lecture on an obscure piece of American History you really didn't care about'.

One UK producer is confident that rap can work in the West End: 'I'm hoping to push a few musical boundaries, by getting John Barnes to reprise Terry Wogan's 'Floral Dance'.'

Comments on X-Factor must now meet the five Canons of Rhetoric

Poorly constructed judges' comments on 'The X-Factor' will no longer be tolerated, an independent review concluded today. Nearly all the judges' comments were found to be derivative and dull, with the exception of Simon Cowell's wise words, particularly his iconic 'I didn't like it, I loved it.'

'A classic of the genre,' gushed Plato, from consultancy firm 'It's All Greek to Me', who conducted the review. 'Enhanced by years of repetition and delivered with an increasingly mischievous sense of irony. Going forward, it's mission critical that all judges now develop the bandwidth to reach Simon's benchmark level.'

'Listen, I found these guys surprisingly persuasive,' admitted Cowell. 'Although they could start an argument in an empty room. They also suggested some sort of shaming for poor oration, like you used to see in Ancient Greece. I told them not to worry on this count, as public humiliation was already written into the DNA of the show.'

Dame Judi Dench retrains as scaffolder

Following the Chancellor's advice that those in the arts should consider new careers, it appears that many of Britain's top actors have done just that.

'I was amazed,' exclaimed labourer John Wiggins. 'We were on site waiting for the scaffolders to arrive, and who should turn up but only bloody M from those Bond films. She did a pretty good job to be fair, she certainly knows her way round a 48.3mm tube clamp. And not a bad arse either for an 85-year-old.'

Not everyone in the building trade was as pleased. Plumber Alf Maynard was one of many warning about the effects a swathe of newly butt-cleavaged thespians might have on his livelihood.

'It was bad enough when all those Polish lads came over and started undercutting me with their quality workmanship and reasonable pricing structures. But now I've got to cope with this as well. Take the other day - I got called out to fix a dodgy ballcock only to find Mark Rylance there already, elbow deep in the U-bend.

'Then I popped in to Screwfix and that Sir Ian McKellen was in buying their entire stock of thermostatic mixing valves from right under my bloody nose. Honestly, it's a nightmare.'

TV first as 'last time' and 'next time' fill entire episode

Television history was made last night when the middle episode of a three-part drama contained no new footage at all but consisted entirely of a summary of the story from the first episode and some pointers as to what would happen in the last.

The latest three-episode story opened a new series of the popular drama 'Silent but Deadly', which features maverick cop DI Rebecca Long, a mature single woman with a chaotic love life, and rugged, brooding, flatulent forensic pathologist Dave Strahan.

Producer Kurt Angstrom explained: 'With a detailed recap of what happened last time, many viewers start to understand the plot and get much more out of it. Similarly, a full preview of the next episode makes it feel nice and familiar when they get to it and enables them to make sense of closing plot twists that would otherwise leave them frustrated.

'Actually, the second half of the first episode is a preview of the second episode, while the first half of the third is a condensed recap of the first two, so basically we only have to provide one hour of drama,' admitted Angstrom.

'With the title sequence, credits and adverts, we reckon on getting it down to 45 minutes of original material for three episodes – less if we insert flashback sequences from previous series.'

TV producers are hoping to take things a step further with the next series of Downton Abbey, which will cover ten years of family history and will be shot in a single afternoon.

COBRA to meet as terror grips nation over Genesis reunion

Alarm has spread at the thought of 1970s Prog Rock group Genesis getting together again. An ashen-faced Prime Minister said: 'Although we do not wish to alarm the general public, nevertheless we must take immediate and decisive action now to put contingency plans in place in case this worrying threat spreads.

'Measures will include a two-week isolation period for anyone who hears even so much as a strain of Phil Collins singing 'Invisible Touch'. And please do not heed these scaremongering stories circulating on social media, that the band is to record a new 5-CD concept album. They are simply untrue. Rest assured - our priority is to ensure Britain remains Prog-Free.'

Derbyshire destroyed as romantic hero smoulders a bit too much

According to unofficial reports, most of Derbyshire was destroyed by fire yesterday following an incident that began in the grounds of Pemberley House, near Lambton.

It appears that the owner, Mr Fitzwilliam Darcy, an extremely handsome gentleman with a fortune of £9,000 per year, began to brood out of control when taking a turn in the gardens with Miss Elizabeth Bennett, the demure yet witty daughter of an impoverished local gentleman.

'With hindsight, Mr Darcy was an accident waiting to happen,' said Commander Ray Walker of the Peak District Fire Brigade. 'Such was the ardour of his unspoken passion that his breeches had spontaneously combusted several times before. Apparently, this once forced him to dive into a lake in the grounds. Several young ladies who witnessed him climb out were later found reduced to ashes and damp petticoats.'

Architectural historians are lamenting the loss of Pemberley House, which had long ravished the refined sensibilities of all the gentry who saw it. They are now calling for restrictions on the movements of rich, mysterious, romantic yet dangerous men with dark secrets, before more disasters take place. However, the move is being fiercely opposed by young ladies.

'His eyes met mine so keen and fierce, I started; and then he seemed to smile,' said Catherine Earnshaw, 22, from the Yorkshire Dales. 'I could not think him dead: but his face and throat were washed with rain; the bed-clothes dripped, and he was perfectly still. The lattice, flapping to and fro, had grazed one hand that rested on the sill … sorry, what was the question again?'

Man stuns friends by watching gig with eyes not phone

A man has come in for much ridicule after suggesting a live gig is better if watched with the naked eye instead of on a tiny smartphone screen.

'I was peering at Coldplay on my phone just like the thousands of others at the O2, when the battery suddenly died. I was stumped and just looked directly towards the stage. It was absolutely incredible – or at least by Coldplay standards,' said Gary Stewart from Twickenham.

'Suddenly I felt that I was actually right there experiencing the show first-hand. Almost as if I was in the audience. I know that sounds crazy but believe me I really did. I had somehow become part of the gig.'

Stewart's friend Tim Barnett was not convinced, however. 'OK, so Gaz reckons he enjoyed watching the band without using his phone, but he's gotta ask himself this: how's he going to relive the experience of Chris Martin's piano being lifted high above the stage during 'Yellow'?

39

'He won't have his own really crappy quality video with horribly distorted sound to remind him of it, will he? … What? He can buy the official tour DVD with perfect sound and HD picture quality when it comes out? Nah, that's hardly the same thing at all really.'

Nigel Farage to star in 'Love Thy Brexit'

'Love Thy Brexit', a newly-created humorous and affectionate take on modern Britain against the backdrop of our withdrawal from the EU, will see much-loved comedy actor Nigel Farage playing a jobbing frog-impersonator living next door to a family of Eastern Europeans who make his life a misery just by their very existence.

Farage told reporters: 'A lot of the humour comes from me just simply hurling abuse at them. The head of their household is named Bogdan, but I call him Bog Roll.'

'It's hilarious because, even though he's a senior registrar at the local cardiology department saving thousands of British lives, I just ignore that because, let's face it, there'd be no scope for mildly racist gags there. Instead I insist that he's a dole-scrounger and him and his family are only here to cheat Britain out of benefits. "Your lot will all be gone come December 31st!" is one of my catchphrases.

'There's an episode where I suffer a heart attack when I go ballistic because he's disrupting my summer barbecue. You see he's also out in his garden cooking some bloody awful smelly foreign muck at the same time.

'He saves my life by jumping over the fence and performing emergency CPR, but what about this … even as I'm being taken off in the ambulance, I'm hectoring him and demanding he gets rid of the bloody stink. Hahaha! It's going to be fantastic. Full of good old-fashioned British humour.'

Sarcastic heavy metal tribute band 'delighted' to be touring tiny venues

Ironic Maiden, the UK's premier sarcastic metal tribute band, have reassured their 'fragrant' fans that the 'Ironics' have no plans to split. The rumour is believed to have started when lead singer Brusque Dickinson told a crowd: 'We'll see you next year, Daventry!' in a more sardonic than usual tone.

Internet chatrooms were ablaze with speculation that the band were fed up with the lack of mainstream success in such an otherwise rather over-literal musical sub-genre.

'Why would we want to split up?' hissed Dickinson rhetorically, while addressing the tiny press conference. 'The Frog and Drainpipe in Daventry is exactly the sort of venue we love to play. Ironic Maiden is not about the millionaire lifestyle, the groupies or the stadium gigs - we just want to bring our music to very small audiences of balding distribution managers. Now excuse me, I need to put on some quizzical eyebrow makeup.'

Cartoonists stumped for way to illustrate 'Puppet President'

'Everyone is describing this new guy as a puppet,' said one illustrator of the new US President. 'What on Earth are we supposed to do with that? They're saying that someone will still be pulling all the strings, a puppet master of this new puppet Government. I mean I just have no idea how I could possibly illustrate such a thing.

'I could draw a great big dinosaur, with the head of the President – but that sort of suggests a political dinosaur. How about I draw him playing Monopoly? No, that only works if we're looking to express his monopoly on power.

'In the end I decided to abandon the whole puppet Government thing and go for the 'Death of Infant Democracy' angle. So, I drew the Grim Reaper pointing his finger to a small cot with 'Democracy' written on the side. I might write 'Death' on the back of the Grim Reaper, just to make it extra clear. Clever huh?'

'The Science' is the new Science

A new Punk Rock band, 'The Science', is to perform an outdoor satellite link concert for the NHS backed by The Cure, The Doctor & The Medics and the The The. Other guests will include sixties soul singer PPE Arnold, and of course the ubiquitous The WHO.

Under lockdown, 'The Science' is popping up everywhere, rewriting the curriculum to include The Geography, The Latin (Somerset Schools only) and, of course, The 'The Science'.

A reporter from the The New Musical Express said that the support for 'The Science' was astonishing: 'All the leading Cabinet ministers are following 'The Science' now.'

Films for Lockdown

- No Close Encounters of Any Kind
- When Harry Couldn't Meet Sally
- Apocalypse Right Now
- Schindler's Shopping List
- Harry's Pottering Around
- Home and Very Alone
- Unemployed Taxi Driver
- A Zoom with a View
- Bugsy Alone
- Four Funerals and no Wedding

- One Flu over the Cuckoo's Nest
- 2020 - A Confined Space Odyssey
- The Postman Always Rings Twice Then Does A Runner
- Brief Infectious Encounter
- The Third Man (That's Two Too Many)
- Porn on the 4th of July, and on the 5th and 6th...
- A Fistful of Sanitising Gel

'Orange flute band must win X Factor or no deal', say DUP

DUP Leader Arlene Foster has one non-negotiable red line if she is to deliver her party's support to prop up Boris Johnson's minority Tory Government and continue the terms of the deal they cut with his predecessor Theresa May.

'The PM must award Simon Cowell a knighthood and ensure the 10th Ballymena Loyal Orange Lodge Flute Band triumphs in this year's upcoming X Factor competition, or there will be no support forthcoming,' said Mrs Foster.

A show insider, who did not want to be identified, said: 'It's true. We've been told we are to go through the motions of staging heats but the 'Kick-the-Pope' band is to win.'

Foster added: 'The band's cover of 'Uptown Funk' is going to be the soundtrack to autumn, so it is. It'll be fantastic, so it will.'

There is now further speculation that, buoyed-up by having secured one concession, she might now insist that the men from Ballymena go on to represent what's left of the United Kingdom in next year's Eurovision Song Contest.

Warning! Flash photography can also occur in real life

The BBC has cautioned its audience that it is 'powerless' to protect people from flash photography that occurs off air. A new documentary called 'Warning, Flash Photography' will alert people to the dangers of red eye, annoying uncles and clicky noises. It will contain bad language and flash photography 'from the f*cking start.'

By contrast, news reports now feature coverage in which the flash photography has been meticulously edited out, with reporters saying 'flash!' and occasionally 'flash flash flash!' at exactly the right moments to preserve standards of accuracy.

Meanwhile, a campaign is under way to persuade photographers to consider alternatives to flash photography, like exquisitely executed line drawings or one thousand words.

'We built this city on boar terrine' fails to reach Xmas Number 1

Jacob Rees-Mogg's Christmas single, 'We built this city on boar terrine', with absolutely none of the proceeds going to charity, is thought to be the first of a number of releases planned over the coming months, despite not making the coveted Christmas number one. Many are expected to have a Brexit-related theme, including 'We Owe You Nothing', a reworking of the Bros hit, and Queen's 'Don't (Back) Stop Me Now.'

'It's a shame that we haven't reached the top of the hit parade,' said the disappointed Tory MP, outside the south wing of his Somerset mansion.

'But I hope people will take heed of the important messages in the song nonetheless. There are some less than subtle digs in there at those people who only marinade their boar for a couple of hours, and who accompany the meal with a 1984 rather than a 1978 Bordeaux.'

International super-villain defends murder of British agent 007

Megalomaniac villain Ernest Blofeld has responded vigorously to claims of unsportsmanlike conduct in his execution of a British secret serviceman who was captured in his lair under a volcano in Iceland. The man has been unofficially identified as James Bond 007.

'This man was a menace,' Blofeld told reporters. 'Despite being armed with only a service revolver, he somehow tunnelled into my base using a helicopter that converted itself into a submarine and got within 50 yards of the clock that was counting down the seconds until I launch nuclear warheads at the world's capitals.

'He killed seven of my henchmen. Do you know how much henchmen cost in Iceland?' asked the scarred Germanic egotist. 'What was I meant to do? Rig him up to some Heath Robinson contraption he could easily get out of? Give him a guided tour of my lair and explain my world domination scheme to him?'

Blofeld and his team briefly considered leaving Bond in the custody of his sulky blonde girlfriend, who was wandering around the base in a bikini. However, after a debate during which those who advocated this course were fed to piranhas, the decision was taken to kill him without delay.

Blofeld has admitted that personal animus towards the British upper classes played a role in his decision. 'I hate the supercilious smirks on those public schoolboys' faces. "Do you expect me to talk?" he says. Well, I told him straight "No, Mr Bond, I expect you to die" and blew his brains out on the spot. Now nothing can stop me taking over the world – oh sod it, that bloody cat has pissed all over my lap again.'

A&E waiting rooms to screen '24 Hours in A&E' around the clock

Patients hoping to be treated on the NHS one day will be able to watch Channel 4's '24 Hours in A&E' non-stop on the waiting room TV, while they spend 24 hours, if not more, in A&E.

The Health secretary told survivors' groups: 'If you're waiting for NHS treatment, there's no better show to take your mind off things. It shows how a small group of dedicated medically trained junior care assistants cope with the steady flow of people, many of them immigrants on benefits hoping to assault a consultant before they die of injuries caused by obesity, drink and drug abuse.'

Now though, E4 is to launch a new live show, '24 Hours in A&E Waiting Rooms', which depicts the tension and drama of life in the waiting room of a number of A&E departments, where arguments, fights, arrests, gun battles and deaths are commonplace.

Patients waiting to get into the crowded waiting rooms at A&E will be able to watch the new show in the fresh air through the windows of A&E waiting rooms, provided they don't breathe too hard on the windows.

Berlusconi to play Dame in Aladdin at Redditch

The Redditch Players pantomime has been given an added boost this year by the surprise booking of former Italian Prime Minister and definite non-crook Silvio Berlusconi to play Widow Twankey.

'We wanted a high-profile 'resting' politician but finding one near to home was impossible,' explained director Leon Stirling. 'Tony Blair's fee was just ridiculous, even though several Middle Eastern countries offered assistance with it, and Anne Widdecombe was already committed to her one-woman comedy stand-up tour.'

At first, Berlusconi was reluctant to commit, but once Stirling explained about the levels of crudity, innuendo and cross-dressing, he became much more enthusiastic.

All that remains now is to iron out the details of his contract. Stirling said: 'We have ensured that all the chorus girls will be teenage Moroccans, but we still draw the line at the personal fluffer. After all, this is a family show.'

Claim that Venus of Urbino reclines on a DFS sofa sparks conflict

Professor Massimo Taglia of Florence's Uffizi gallery has sparked controversy with claims that Titian's nude of a young woman was part of an early DFS advertising campaign.

'On a visit to Britain in about 1537, Titian stayed at Tunbridge Wells, the believed site of an early DFS store, where he bought this fetching sofa and fold-out bed,' he explained. 'We have also established that the visit was probably around the New Year, in time for the sales.'

Rival sofa store Furniture Village has hit back. Professor Jan de Riejter of Holland's Rijksmuseum, said: 'There can be no doubt that the sofa in Titian's painting is a Furniture Village recliner - currently on special offer at £599 with four years' interest-free credit and pay nothing for the first year.'

Meanwhile, Margaret Lovegrove, 26, from Luton, said that she was the original model. 'I don't do nudes anymore. But if I were to recline stark bollock naked and with my hand over my pubes, you'd soon see the resemblance between me and the Venus of Wotsit.'

Prog Rock to be decriminalised

The news that possession of Prog Rock albums for personal use will no longer be a criminal offence has been welcomed by dope-smoking daydreamers the length and breadth of the land.

A tearful 'Moorglade Mover', from Bolton, said: 'Wow! Like this is so amazing, to think I'll be able to order 'Tales from Topographic Oceans' and not get raided by the fuzz is really mind-blowing. Well it would be if my mind wasn't already totally blown.'

Following the emergence of punk rock, it became illegal to own or even hum a bar of progressive rock music. Illicit trading in material has been driven into back streets and more recently the dark web. Recently a copy of Caravan's 'In the Land of Grey and Pink' was being offered for £3,500.

Iconic keyboardist Rick Wakeman said: 'I'm already planning a two-month residency at Wembley Arena with a 55-piece orchestra, full choir and ice skaters, performing my new concept album, 'The Wooden Horse of Troy'.'

Meanwhile the scourge of Prog, John Lydon, was unavailable for comment. His management told us: 'John's at a secret location shooting this year's John Lewis Christmas TV ad.'

TV cop fails to have dinner interrupted by murder

In a scene from a forthcoming episode of a police drama, DCI Jason Beesley walks into the canteen, orders a pasta bake with broccoli, and for dessert an apple and rhubarb crumble with custard, topped off with a tea and two sugars - and 28 minutes later, puts the last morsel into his mouth and contemplates the weekend.

Beesley then returns his dirty cutlery and dishes to the kitchen station, wipes custard from his chin, lets out a loud belch and checks his phone.

However, there is still nothing and it is not until he has nearly reached his desk that his phone starts ringing. Poised to rush to the scene of the ritualistic murder of a surprisingly attractive young prostitute, he is then disappointed to discover it was a wrong number.

Literary historian discovers Lewis Carroll sequel 'Alice in Sunderland'

A follow-up to Lewis Carroll's classic children's tales has been unearthed, this time set in the north-east of England.

The action once again begins with the young heroine lazing by a river one summer afternoon. Only this time Alice is a teenager and she's spread-eagled on a bench beside the River Wear, her soporific state explained by the two dozen empty bottles of WKD and vodka, labelled DRINK ME – which, for Sunderland, is a redundant instruction.

With the air of unreality common to all of Carroll's novels, Alice is then led into a strange and beguiling place, Sunderland town centre, by an oddly-dressed white rabbit. This is in fact her classmate Chantelle, who is late for her shift as a bunny girl at the Blu Bambu nightclub.

Here, she witnesses all sorts of bizarre goings on, including men wearing short sleeves in January, people urinating in shop doorways and, in celebration of the city's victory over Middlesbrough in the local derby, sporadic outbreaks of singing and violence.

After accepting a mushroom from a stranger in a bar, Alice then meets a host of mythical creatures, including a miner and a shipbuilder with whom she forms such a strong bond in the High Street in the early hours of the morning that all three are arrested on public decency charges.

'Alice in Sunderland is very much like the original novels,' said Professor Terry Eagleton. 'Just grittier and racier. Not unlike Alice Through The Looking Glass, which describes a hen weekend in Gateshead.'

Calais migrant camp to host new music festival

Having seen the misery and degradation encountered at music festivals, surveyors have concluded that all that Calais is missing is a few low-rent indie bands.

Levels of typhus and dysentery are now on a par with Glastonbury 2005, the year Coldplay headlined - although later analysis of the vomiting outbreak found that peak levels were reached when the audience had time to digest Chris Martin's lyrics.

While levels of frustration and violence across the camp have been rising steadily as conditions worsen, they remain far less volatile than when The Fall were invited to play T in the Park. However, some migrants say that conditions are bad enough without being woken up at 4 a.m. by somebody in an Arctic Monkeys T-shirt urinating against their tents.

According to the festival organiser, the site's latrine has great potential as a corporate bar area. 'Somebody who has handed over their life-savings to an international people-trafficking ring will think nothing of paying £8 for an undercooked veggie burger,' she said.

Residents delighted as graffiti vandal scrawls over unwanted Banksy

Local people celebrated with an impromptu street party after a Banksy that appeared in their area recently was defaced by graffiti. Some said that as the artwork was now worthless, there would be no coachloads of pretentious art graduates taking selfies with it.

Remarked a local decorator, pouring himself a Prosecco: 'I appreciate the vandal's irony, wit and incorporation of elements of surrealism. He's allowed his vision to remain fresh and the choice of bright day-glo pink coupled with the word "wanker" really works.'

One local resident added: 'A blank wall is always going to present an opportunity for mindless art from the likes of Banksy. Luckily the heroic actions of a real vandal have put our minds at rest. We can't thank him enough. Banksy should just f*ck off to Stonehenge and give it an undercoat or something.'

Heaven 'a kitsch nightmare propped up by vulgar columns', says critic

Renowned and recently deceased art critic Brian Sewell has launched an uncompromising verbal attack on the afterlife, calling it 'meritless - a kind of memorial garden for the death of beauty.'

Sewell went on to describe the pearly gates as 'clearly knocked up by a five-year-old', angelic choirs as 'unlistenable caterwauling' and the throne of God as 'something one might see in a Croydon second-hand store on a dreary Sunday afternoon.'

Upon entry to heaven, the critic was greeted with a swiftly curated exhibition of new paintings by long dead classical artists, mixed in with several contemporary pieces.

'If this God fellow is omnipotent, it's hard to see how He could have presided over the creation of something so aesthetically nauseous,' wrote Sewell in the Evening Standard.

'It looks to the educated eye more like the submitted work of GCSE students. If this is Heaven, give me Hell - where at least one may gaze upon sights reminiscent of the triptychs of Bosch or Bacon.'

Families of gorgeous Bollywood couple happily accept their relationship

Ravinder Khotra and Priti Kumar, a fabulously wealthy and attractive engaged couple from Mumbai, have expressed relief that their extended families are both entirely supportive of their relationship. The pair had feared that one or both families would disapprove, causing them anguish that could only be expiated in song over the course of many hours.

'I am delighted for them,' said Khotra's corpulent and ridiculous but fundamentally decent father, Vijay. 'What's not to like? Priti is stunningly beautiful and on the few dozen occasions she has accidentally got her sari wet, I could certainly see why my handsome, if somewhat headstrong, son might fall for her!'

Khotra's irascible and controlling mother, Ameera, admitted that she was surprised by the speed of the engagement - the couple only met two weeks ago, while foiling a gang of jewel thieves in a high-speed motorcycle chase - and would have hoped to have had a part to play in choosing her son's bride. However, she added, times are changing and their happiness is the main thing.

Following consultations with astrologers, the wedding has been scheduled for early April and both the couple and their families are hoping that there will be no comical slip-ups between now and then to derail their plans.

'But if there are, that's just karma,' said Kumar. 'In which case I'll just have to spend four hours singing out of tune in various exotic locations I've never been to in my life.'

Stuntman working from home causes huge damage to his house

Emergency services were called out to a property in St Albans last night, following reports of a small explosion and fire. They arrived on the scene to find a man jumping from an upstairs window, covered in flames and rolling around on the front lawn.

The man turned out to be Joe Mee, 43, a professional stuntman with dozens of film and TV credits to his name, including the famous, if controversial, car chase scenes in 'Downton Abbey' and 'Call The Midwife.'

'The lockdown's clearly putting him under a lot of strain' said a neighbour. 'The fire brigade used to be here two or three times a year, now it's twice a week.

'Joe's a bit of a nutter at the best of times. After work, he drives his car at ninety miles an hour down the road and crashes it sideways through his front gates most evenings. Even before the quarantine he jumped over our fence in full combat gear and blew up the greenhouse with a hand grenade.'

A fire brigade spokesman agreed there had been a small surge in call-outs to the property, but as Mee was complying with social distancing measures and had given him an autographed photo of Hugh Bonneville, they were happy to keep coming out.

Top ten most unsuccessful movie sequels

- Pretty Woman 2: Back on the Boulevard
- Aladdin 2: Rise of the Caliphate
- Definitely No Mohicans Now
- Planes, Trains and Congestion Charges
- Star War-Crimes Tribunal
- Titanic 2: Brexit
- Oh Look, There's Red October!
- Oh! What a Lovely Proxy-War
- Educating Lolita
- The Fast & The Furious 40: Slower and Mellower

Shakespeare to remain authentically boring

The board of Shakespeare's Globe are looking for a new artistic director, saying he should be someone in keeping with the Renaissance Period - preferably an apothecary with typhoid. Any applicant must come with a ruff, a small goatee and a pathological distrust of the Spanish navy

The successful candidate will be expected to produce shows of 'mind-numbing tweeness', purposely designed to send your average GCSE English Literature student into a spiral of self-harm. They will also need to manage the bear-baiting pit and the 'Potato Museum of Wonder'.

The board expect the new director to adhere to a life expectancy of 40, have a rat as a pet, and to ban all actors who menstruate. One scholar explained: 'The fear is, that by making Shakespeare contemporary and relevant, you might actually make Shakespeare contemporary and relevant. And the last thing we want are ordinary people comprehending theatre or even, God forbid, enjoying it.'

IN OTHER RELATED NEWS:

Radio Four guest tries to interrupt interviewer's interruption
Hamlet undecided about using soft or hard pencil
Islamic State to be referred to as 'The Artist Formerly Known as IS'
'Batman v Super-Gonorrhoea' begins filming
Lesbians furious about being left out of BGT
That Guy who played That Guy in That Guy Movie, dies
Supermarket Sweep upgraded from light entertainment to documentary
Studies find the key to liking Prog Rock is to give it 7/8 time
Panini rumoured to be in studio working on difficult second album
Streaming service offers hay fever
Edinburgh Fringe cut
Samuel Beckett 'wrote Brexit'
Home-brewed morphine to replace Saturday night TV
Glastonbury sells out on news that 'there will be face-painting'
Shock as female newsreader paired with a man of an appropriate age
Arriving at prom night in dad's Vauxhall Vectra was 'post-modern irony'
Screaming fans mob tabletop wargames championship
Listening out for dark, incidental music could prevent crime and save lives, say Police
New 'Banksy' hailed after discovery of yellow lines on road
Sergeant Pepper disqualified from all-time Top 100 Albums after testing positive for drugs
Children in Need rocked by bear-blinding scandal
Susan Sarandon and Tim Robbins fight for custody of liberal conscience
Damien Hurst to spend a year in formaldehyde for tax reasons
Man Booker Prize may go to penalty shoot-out
Circus world in turmoil as lions conquer fear of chairs
Mapmakers thank musicians for putting town on map

CHAPTER THREE

Murdoch says you can vote now (and other Politics stories)

Report accuses Tories of 'persistent right-wing bias'

An independent report has concluded that the Conservative Party is still prone to a pernicious right-wing bias in its attitudes, extending to the highest levels of the party.

This has been a blow for the leader of the party, who last year proudly declared to the party conference: 'Let's have no more of this 'right-of-centre' nonsense; from now on our policies will be driven by three things: common sense, the bleedin' obvious and that's it.'

The leader is said to be deeply concerned by the allegations and will be instituting a full root and branch review, just as soon as he has signed off the current policy document: 'It's for their own good: Sustainable strategies for reclaiming India.'

Blair flattered by new war memorial for war criminals

Former PM Tony Blair has been appreciative of a new war memorial for war criminals, which has been funded by The Sun's patriotic campaign - 'Support our soldiers. Just don't question the war.'

The jagged monolith is deliberately carved out of rough-hewn Portland stone to symbolise the fact that you cannot polish a turd. There will also be an empty plinth, to represent Iraq's Weapons of Mass Destruction.

An MoD spokeswoman remarked: 'These brave soldiers gave their lives upholding British values – sorry, I meant to say upholding the value of shares in the arms industry. Thankfully the three wars in the Middle East have brought peace and prosperity to the region, making the world a safer place,' said Blair's official spokesman. 'Let us not forget why we fought these great conflicts … um … er … why was it again?'

MPs filmed offering 'services for votes'

Westminster was rocked by further scandal today after several former Labour ministers and other MPs were filmed approaching their constituents and offering to lobby the Government on their behalf in return for their vote.

The allegations centre on Stephen Byers, Patricia Hewitt and 644 other MPs who are reported to have held secret public meetings where they promised to influence policy 'however the voters wanted them to.' Senior Government figures condemned them.

'It's not our place as politicians to listen to the ordinary public,' said the Prime Minister. 'And certainly not to promise that we'll do whatever they want us to do. Otherwise what sort of a mess do you think we'd be in? Messy wars, economy down the tubes, worsening social mobility, incompetent Government - it just doesn't bear thinking about.'

Personal injury claims causing 'soaring' cost of S&M, claim MPs

The price of S&M services has 'gone through the roof' in recent years, a cross-party Parliamentary committee has found. The committee has blamed a steep rise in the large number of companies encouraging punters to make spurious personal injury claims.

'The cost of an evening's humiliation has doubled in the last few years,' remarked one MP. 'And the second I get home afterwards, there's always a call from some shifty insurance company or other asking me if I have suffered any whiplash injuries. What damn fool kind of question is that? Of course I have - that's what I've just paid for.'

The Association of British Insurers has agreed that radical reform was desirable. 'We would like to act more decisively on this one,' explained a spokesman, 'but unfortunately our hands are tied.'

Cabinet 'too nervous' to tell Thatcher she's dead

Coalition cabinet members have privately admitted that no-one has yet told Lady Thatcher that she has died.

One nervous minister said: 'I don't think she'll take it very well. I met her a couple of years ago and asked if she missed being PM and I got ten minutes of ranting followed by a shout of "Release the flying monkeys!" Luckily, they turned out to be cats with cardboard wings, so I was able to escape.'

It is understood that Michael Heseltine was later called in to slip a note into Lady Thatcher's coffin.

PM deals with 'anti-homeless spikes'

A crack squad of Indian fakirs has been flown in to the UK to teach the homeless how to have a good night's sleep on the two-inch-long metal spikes which have sprung up all over London to deter rough sleeping in doorways.

'I read about this and decided to get to grips with the root of the homelessness problem immediately,' said the Prime Minister, after calling an emergency meeting of COBRA.

'Homeless people will now be able to enjoy a good night's sleep, despite being tucked up in stinking sleeping bags and sodden cardboard, while drunken yobs urinate on them.'

Speaking through interpreters at the launch, Swami Yogesh said he was impressed by how quickly rough sleepers in London were adapting to the spikes using fakir techniques.

'They're naturals,' he said. 'We fakirs don't eat or wash for years on end either. The only difference is, we choose to do it, they are forced into it by the fakirs who rule them.'

Jeremy Vine now in a state of perpetual election arousal

Jeremy Vine has been kept in a cruel and artificial state of pre-election arousal for nearly three weeks, human rights campaigners have claimed. Usually after an election, Vine is brought to a 'soft landing' by sharing a thermos of tea and a chat about 80s hits with Ken Bruce.

However, with the Brexit referendum coming hard on the heels of council elections, the presenter's state of excitement has been artificially extended by a team of 'fluffers', who maintain Vine's election readiness by teasing him with statistics from exit polls.

'Given the short timescales, powering him down with a game of Scrabble then re-arousing him using images of Edwina Currie doesn't make sense', said a BBC producer.

'In an emergency we can show Jeremy a documentary about the 1886 Ashton-Under-Lyme by-election,' continued the producer. 'It's the only one where the top two parties polled exactly the same number of votes. The 'money shot' is when the returning officer takes matters into his own hands and makes the casting vote, but we'd only show Jeremy that ending in an emergency. It puts too much of a strain on his swingometer.'

Clegg to play with tiny steering wheel during PMQs

Deputy Prime Minister Nick Clegg is to be given a toy plastic steering wheel while David Cameron is answering Prime Minister's Questions.

'The wheel was a crucial part of the coalition agreement,' said Cameron. 'It is great to think that while I am up at the despatch box dealing with important matters of state, Nick can sit behind me with his steering wheel and still feel part of the action.'

'It gives me a real sense of power, because I can turn left and turn right in accordance with prevailing Government policy,' said an excited Clegg. 'It even has a little horn which I can honk, but only if Dave says it is safe to do so.'

Clegg will unveil his new steering wheel at the next PMQs. 'This Government is all about giving power back to the people,' he said. 'I want everyone to feel the same sense of power as I do when I honk my little horn.'

Sacked librarians going feral

Thousands of librarians sacked as part of Operation Austerity are creating havoc on the streets of Britain. Incidents typically start with aggressive tutting, but quickly escalate into a frenzy of violence and sexual excess. Police officers are attending up to 50 incidents every week involving humping librarians on bus shelter roofs.

'What the Government didn't realise was that they've read everything' said a police officer. 'Yes, they're bookish and middle-aged, but they've absorbed decades of military manuals, unarmed combat, karate, kung fu, you name it. It's a bit like The Matrix. I haven't actually seen one dissolve into ones and noughts yet, but it's surely only a matter of time.

'They've got no respect for our laws. They live by the Dewey decimal system, which demands total obedience, silence, and the timely return of borrowed items. Seven branches of Waterstones have been torched in the last month, and a vicar was subjected to what I can only describe as a horrific incident involving jam and a swarm of bees.'

One million gather for Alan Milburn's 'message of hope'

They came from all over Britain. Young and old, black and white, Christians, Jews and Muslims; arm in arm, united by Alan Milburn's message of hope and his 27-point plan for urban renewal. In a speech that will go down in the annals with 'I have a dream', the Labour leadership hopeful brought tears to the eyes of young idealists with his vision of business/community partnerships.

'Yes! Yes! Yes!' wept 22-year old Hannah Campbell, who had travelled from Cornwall to attend. 'This is what we felt with a passion but couldn't put into words.

'Regional business councils, voluntary groups working with the private sector, local councils empowering stakeholders in neighbourhood enterprise zones – I never dared hope that we might see all this in my lifetime.'

'People's consumer councils, community transport champions, maybe even Internet business advice forums – it feels like a whole new society is now possible,' said one lifelong activist.

'I wish my father had been alive to hear this speech. And just imagine the dream ticket of Alan Milburn as Prime Minister with Peter Hain as deputy!? Bliss was it in that dawn to be alive...'

Labour set to unveil the iCorbyn™

To the delight of technology fans and beard-wearers, the Labour Party is planning to launch a new device that will revolutionise the way we think of revolutions. This simple hand-held socialist will come in a retro 1980 shell, an expanded memory that includes references to Nye Bevan and with one button, which is mysteriously labelled 'panic'.

Some have complained that the iCorbyn™ will have a bad reception in parts of southern England, but admit that it cannot be worse than Vodafone's. Regardless, the new phone will have a range of apps, guaranteed to customise as well as nationalise.

In response, the Tories plan to launch the 'Chocolate Boris', but early concerns are that it is a bit of a brick, with a ring tone that sounds a deflating space hopper. By contrast, the iCorbyn™ has an inbuilt virtual assistant, voiced by the late Tony Benn, which will instantly provide directions to the user - provided all those directions are 'turn left'.

Owen Smith mania reaches frenzy point

Holidaymakers are reporting gridlock on the roads and all forms of coitus have ground to a halt, as people take to the streets in support of Owen Smith. Lately, Smith groupies have packed out anime conventions, in numbers upwards of three, bursting into tears at the mere sight of their idol. Handmade t-shirts publicly advertise their love with the phrase 'I'm With Stupid'.

Bunting lines the streets and nothing can stop his propulsion - once it actually begins. Explained one Owenite: 'Many people are asking - who is this man of mystery running in the election? Or maybe they said – it's a mystery why he's running. Either way, voters have Owen on their lips - or it might be a cold sore.'

MPs now only embarrassed by the 'sound of pooing'

After decades of embezzlement, corruption and world-class douchebaggery, the House of Commons has managed to eliminate shame in all circumstances, including being caught masturbating in the Cabinet Office and calling a male teacher 'Dad'. Only an unexpectedly noisy act of defecation in a public toilet still tugs at their sense of shame.

'It's a gradual deadening of the moral sense - like laughing at James Corden,' explained a psychologist. 'Most MPs have learned to accept their skeleton in a cupboard. Even if that skeleton is wearing a gimp suit, with an orange stuffed in its mouth and the PM's tax returns rammed up its bony arse.'

Fury as man adds 'further ado'

A Conservative party meeting in the sleepy Buckinghamshire town of Steeple Claydon was thrown into chaos as Raymond Bingley, 61, added 'further ado'.

About to confirm that the meeting was to close the party secretary said, 'Thank you everyone and without further ado, let's head to the...', only to be interrupted by Bingley, saying he had further ado.

Bingley went on to talk about parking privileges with regards to proximity to the wine bar where the after-meeting drinks would be held.

People were stunned as the 'ado' carried on for three and a half minutes, culminating in a demand for a fixed spot. An item about raising further ado has already been added to the next meeting's agenda.

House of Lords to be replaced by panel from The Voice

In a major constitutional change aimed at raising public levels of interest in parliamentary proceedings, the House of Lords is to be replaced by a new second chamber consisting of the panel from The Voice.

Panellists will listen to all proposed Bills with their chairs turned away. If one or more of the judges likes the sound of the legislation, they can press a button causing their chair to spin round and automatically triggering a round of applause and a Second Reading.

If it navigates the early stages, the Bill is then brought before a public phone vote. Calls cost 25p per minute. Please ask the bill-payer's permission before enacting legislation.

Once a Bill has successfully passed the phone vote stage it will then achieve Royal Assent, a ceremonial process in which Sir Tom presents the new Act of Parliament before the Queen and she throws a pair of gold lamé knickers at him, so bringing it into law and completely bypassing the views of the 'commons'.

Shadow cabinet downgraded to cupboard

In a shock move by the political credit ratings agencies, the Shadow Cabinet has now become the Shadow Cupboard. Now that Labour no longer has enough MPs ready to serve in it, said Moody & Poor's, 'we think that a smaller cupboard, perhaps the one under the sink where you keep scouring pads and washing-up liquid, would be a more appropriate fit for the remaining members.'

The move follows desperate attempts by Labour to preserve their Shadow Cabinet status, including offering to fill the spaces in it with brandy and Scotch. However, the agency declined the move, leaving Labour relegated to political minnows alongside that bloke who stands around in clown make-up at the counts for by-elections, though their rating still remains some way above the Liberal Democrats.

PM to repeal the repeal of the Corn Laws

The PM is to use the Queen's Speech to remove workers' rights and return us to a golden age of indentured servitude by repealing the repeal of the Corn Laws.

A Number Ten official explained: 'We've been mollycoddled by EU bureaucrats with their five-day weeks and straight bananas. There's no sight more heart-warming than a small child ensnared on a Spinning Jenny.'

Dark, satanic mills are expected to pop up on every street corner, while the minimum working age will be lowered to the third trimester. Said one MP: 'My ancestors didn't come all the way over from Normandy to be governed by Europeans. We need to bring back feudalism and fornication with beasts of the field. Although admittedly, that last one never really went away.'

List of stations to wait for delayed HS2 trains announced

The Government has unveiled details of the next phase of the HS2 high-speed rail network, revealing which stations rail passengers in Northern England will be left waiting at while faster trains than we currently have are delayed.

The line is due to be opened by 2032 (expected 2047, due to signal failures). Passengers in Manchester, Nottingham, Sheffield and Leeds will then be stranded on platforms, waiting impatiently for a very fast train to arrive.

Retailers are looking into the possibility of opening-up new stores on the platforms of the HS2 stations to serve increasing numbers of passengers with time on their hands while they wait for a replacement bus service. In response, Amazon is exploring options to deliver to stations and put the new stores out of business.

Parliament to consider permanent switch to Hammer Time

As British Summer Time draws to a close, the Government is to conduct an analysis of the costs and benefits of adopting the highly controversial Standard Hammer Time throughout the UK.

The concept of Hammer Time was introduced in the early 1990s by the recording artist MC Hammer on his top-selling 'Please Hammer – Don't Hurt 'Em'. Although highly regarded at the time, its popularity waned after a series of poor-selling follow up albums.

The National Farmers' Union in Scotland remain vehemently opposed. NFU spokesman Andy MacDonald said: 'Without wanting to diss Hammer Time, many of our members are uneasy about having to tend sheep on dark winter mornings wearing large trousers, raybans and lots of bling. Things right now are tough enough for farmers as it is.'

If the new system is adopted, businesses will be required to provide employees with regular Hammer Time intervals, which are to be spent well away from their workstations in areas where they will be encouraged to 'break it down'.

IN OTHER RELATED NEWS:

Ed Miliband to receive BAFTA for Inner Monologue

Nigel Farage fears 'rivers of congestion'

Maybot fails Turing test

Fisherman told Green Party membership now at sustainable levels

SNP to replace daylight savings with 'borrowed time'

Chilcot: 'Blair is a lying bastard, I'm not sure I can be any clearer?'

Lib Dem Party Conference survives ban on large gatherings

Labour to go Corbyn-neutral

'Populism is bad' say MPs as they form unpopular party

EU flies its flag upside down as signal of distress

Arlene Foster judged 'Borderline insane'

Facebook recruits Nick Clegg so it can't influence elections

SNP: Second Bannockburn 'inevitable'

Ken Livingstone banned from PC World

Last known Lib Dem dies in captivity

Wild optimist asks for intelligent and considered political response to terrorism

Rocking horse shit more abundant than good Government decision-making

It's not casual racism – it's carefully orchestrated, insists Cummings

New data loss scandal as civil servant 'left on train'

Tony Blair to do 'You Can't Handle the Truth' speech at Iraq Inquiry

Coalition in crisis over where to spend Christmas Day

Clegg 'in tears' after Cameron reveals truth about Santa

Chancellor reveals fluffy kittens from budget briefcase

British Intelligence launch subscription surveillance service, GCHQ+

CHAPTER FOUR

Celibate Kama Sutra Enthusiasts enjoy the juxta position (and more Lifestyle news)

CAPOZZOLA.

'Manspread' to replace butter

An unconventional low-fat spread, which involves collecting a watery emulsion from the inner thighs of a hirsute man, has proved a wildly popular alternative to butter.

Manspread can be found on any public transport, where the spread has encroached on other seats, leaving a distinctive sticky residue, combined with the heady aroma of a festering jockstrap.

The origins of Manspread date back to the Napoleonic era, when aroused Frenchmen would regularly ferment cream in the folds of their nether regions. Subsequently, it has proved very popular among dieters, who claim that calorie intake is significantly reduced when food is smeared in unappetising man juice.

One food critic commented: 'A cottage industry has sprung up where you will regularly see men on their daily commute, legs spread apart, churning their own milk. This is a non-dairy spread, which ironically has also led to a lot more cottaging.'

As yet, a non-salted version is not available, but there is an almost unlimited supply of man-dripping, particularly on hot days.

Architects just hate people

The Royal Institute of British Architects has revealed that its mission is to 'erode the human spirit through the abuse of concrete'. De-programmed RIBA members have described secret meetings where architects plot the destruction of the human soul through the design of individual buildings, public spaces and entire neighbourhoods which drive people 'closer to despair'

'It takes over your life, architecture. You don't realise what you're doing to people, everybody thinks the same thoughts, believes the same lies,' admitted former RIBA member 'Eric', who now earns a living selling crystal meth to schoolchildren.

'Now I look back and I'm ashamed, really ashamed. At least with the crystal meth I'm only killing people one at a time, know what I mean? I'm not taking out an entire generation. And the kids probably wouldn't need drugs if they lived somewhere nice.

'It was really hard being there, cos the place had sash windows. We weren't allowed to even think the words 'sash window', if they caught you thinking about them it was electric shocks, rats on your genitals, everything. So, we drew straws when a window needed opening.

Eric strode towards the sash window and shuddered before throwing it open: 'I can do this now. Whenever I please. Sash window. Sash window. S – a – a – a – a –sh window. I've written a song all about sash windows and cornicing. Do you want to hear it?'

Anti-nanny-state campaign flounders as public asks 'What's a nanny?'

'No to Nasty Nanny Oversight!' (NNNO!), a multi-million-pound campaign to roll back the so-called 'nanny state', has been pulled after only two weeks, following extensive market research showing that the proud British public had no idea who or what a 'nanny' was, or indeed why it was such a bad idea to have them running the country.

'I used to have a nana and a grandad, they were nice. But I don't think that's the same is it?' mused Clare Roper from Crawley. 'I think nannies might have been big in Victorian England. Didn't they help children take medicine or something?'

The findings were initially met with shock by the founders of NNNO! 'It turns out that most of our target audience – the B/C1/C2/D/Es - have rather different child-rearing traditions to ours.' explained NNNO! founder Rupert Harrington-Berkshire.

'Apparently, they use one or more of the natural biological parents to rear the child, with occasional help from friends and relatives. Crazy! I have a son at boarding school. Or is it two? Can't remember.'

Cauliflower 'steak' actually just cauliflower

Fashionable London restaurants are still pretending that the vegetarian alternative to a juicy bit of sirloin is a cauliflower 'steak', even though it is basically semi-raw brassica.

Chef Miles Hess said: 'Cauliflower is barely food. We used to serve it in bowls of nameless generic vegetables - because people pretend not to just want chips - and even then, we had to cover it with carrots and broccoli, so people didn't think we had blocked drains.

'Then some genius thought if you call it a 'steak' and actually cut a massive wedge of that crap, fry it in a butter, you sell it as a main course. Good luck with that, I thought.

'But people are clearly just weird. Now, for £15 you can watch idiots eat cavity wall insulation on a wooden skillet. WTF? Even supermarkets got in on the act. Packet it up with a sachet of lemon aioli - cha-ching!'

One customer said: 'The wife ordered it. It was like eating an oily shoe. I'm going to sneak out for a Big Mac later.'

Shock as woman correctly diagnoses 'funny noise' in car

A Basingstoke woman has left her husband devastated after her car started making what she initially described as 'a funny noise'. Debbie Simmonds was immediately asked by her husband Brian, 'What kind of 'funny noise'?', clearly expecting the traditionally terse reply 'I don't know what kind of funny noise, it's just a funny noise, alright?'

However, while Brian was mentally preparing himself for the customary argument about the difference between a squeak and a squeal, Debbie described a low but persistent rumbling sound that appeared to be coming from the front of the vehicle.

71

'It seems worse at higher speeds and it's there whenever the car is moving,' said Debbie. 'And it's definitely part of the running gear as it varies with the car's speed rather than the engine speed.'

A visibly shaken Brian stutteringly began, 'Well, I suppose it could be ...' but he was interrupted by his wife, who said: 'Wheel bearing, near side front I reckon.'

'I nearly filed for divorce on the spot when I spun that wheel and heard the noise,' said Brian, during his subsequent investigation. 'Cars that make funny noises provide a time-honoured battleground for couples and I wondered where it had all gone wrong.'

Audi smashes two-metre land speed record

A tinted-windowed white Audi A8 has been recorded by a speed camera on Manchester Road, in Manchester, travelling at 76 mph in congested traffic over a space provisionally estimated at 2.3 metres, thus breaking its own world record.

Onlooker, Tim Fenton, commented: 'I heard a growl coming from a car in a queue of traffic. The growl turned into a roar as a slight gap opened up. Before I could blink, the Audi had blasted forward six feet and stopped dead millimetres from the tiny Chevrolet Dinkum in front.

'The noise from the Audi's turbo popping, the blinding flash from the speed camera mixed with inhaling plumes of smoke from the driver's-window weed exhaust was an assault on the senses. More so for the petrified Dinkum driver who had braced for impact and clearly soiled himself.'

The successful Audi driver has escaped a driving penalty for violating speed limits due to the number plate being one of the snide ones that scatters light, which also means the driver cannot be recognised in the Guinness Book of Records. The record beats the previously held record by the same vehicle of 75.8 mph thirty seconds before.

Brexit time capsule discovered buried underneath Cameron's shed

Workmen employed to move David Cameron's shed two feet to the left have discovered a time capsule buried under the left-hand rear wheel.

'We thought it might be important,' said the site foreman, 'so we opened the capsule. It contained a handful of empty promises, a half-arsed negotiation paper and what looks like a lock of Boris Johnson's pubic hair.'

Time capsules are meant to reflect the aspirations of society at the time and are expected to stay buried for hundreds of years or until a trade agreement is negotiated. When they are opened a little early, it is usual to add a few pertinent items and rebury them for a future find.

'I stuck my P45 in there, Bill found a vial of bile and nestled it in with the pubic hairs and Geoff dropped a turd in,' the foreman said. 'It wasn't a political message; the Camerons didn't let us have access to the loo and he was busting.'

Contents of shopping list confirm couple's romance dead

A casual review of the items contained on the shopping list of late thirty-something couple Dan Lewis and Jane Moran revealed their seven-year relationship had finally shed any last vestiges of its original passion.

Lewis admitted that the couple were less like lovers and more like flatmates, 'but without the underlying sexual tension'.

'I just happened to be looking over the list of mundane domestic items when it suddenly struck me how much it had changed since we first got together and it left me wondering: had the romance and mystery gone out of our relationship?' explained the 38-year-old carpenter.

'I think I got my answer when Jane appeared to tell me I needed to add Canesten Duo to the list. Especially as I was in the middle of having a dump at the time.'

Lewis reflected that when the pair had first cohabited, trips to the supermarket had been all about buying champagne and treats, luxurious breakfast goods to be enjoyed in bed on lazy weekend mornings.

'That opened the floodgates,' he acknowledged. 'Before I knew it, we weren't so much writing a shopping list as compiling a schedule of potential programme sponsors for the Spa of Embarrassing Illnesses.'

However, Lewis is hopeful their relationship could soon be back on track. 'I found a new list Jane had left lying around reminding her to pop into La Senza for some new undies, and to get a new Gillette Venus and some condoms from Boots.

'So maybe after she comes back from this weekend work conference, she's planning to put in a bit more effort,' he said, 'although it must be so long since we had sex she's actually forgotten I had that vasectomy, the dozy bint.'

Girlfriend 'struck off' after admitting not always saying what she meant

A woman from Berkshire has been struck off the National Register of Girlfriends after admitting 'not always saying exactly what she meant' in at least two previous relationships. Sarah Crosby, 26, from Newbury, told a tribunal in London that she had not intended to bring womankind into disrepute.

'I know it's wrong to say one thing and mean another,' she said at the hearing. 'But I justified it by telling myself that all women did it, especially ones with husbands or boyfriends.'

She admitted insincerity in a string of statements made to her ex-boyfriends such as 'No, you watch the rugby, I can always see EastEnders on catch-up later' and 'I'd much prefer to eat at McDonalds, Italian food is too expensive' and 'Yeah, that's my favourite position too'.

Goths looking forward to Hallowe'en night at ordinary dress party

A group of Goths in the Bath area are said to be 'mildly excited' in anticipation of their Hallowe'en ordinary dress party where they all plan to kit themselves out in outrageously conventional costumes, celebrate until gone half past eleven on a Saturday night and 'really get their hair sensibly combed.'

'We had one last year and it was just a blast,' said Ravyn Voltaire, a 31-year-old tattoo artist. 'Without all the black and white make-up and piercings it was impossible to recognise anyone, and it led to all sorts of daring conversations about getting a better rate on a mortgage, or what happened on last night's Coronation Street, without a single mention of visiting Bram Stoker's grave to recite necromantic spells.'

Party host Morpheus admitted: 'I've also got wacky prizes, like Jennifer Aniston romantic comedy box-sets for the dullest costumes.' He will himself be foregoing his usual Victorian aristocratic Vampire garb to greet guests in the casual slacks and V-neck sweater combo of a moderately successful architect.

'I just hope everybody makes the effort, and we don't have a repeat of last year when everybody turned up in their usual leather and bondage get-up and claimed to have come as Tory MPs at home on the weekend.'

Man does thing without being asked to complete a survey about it

A man was left shocked and insulted after completing an activity without a request to 'evaluate his experience' online for a chance to win something.

'I really enjoy filling in surveys, as you do all the time after doing anything nowadays, so I was gobsmacked not to be asked to spend a few minutes telling somebody what I thought of my experience,' said Bryan Wilson of Basingstoke, male, married, home-owner, father of two, age 40-49, administrator/senior manager, reads Daily Express, drives Ford Mondeo, one foreign holiday in the last twelve months.

Wilson is reluctant to release details of his upsetting experience in order to protect others from being similarly snubbed. However, it is understood that the activity for which no survey exists is nothing to do with eating at a restaurant, shopping in a supermarket, ordering something online, getting a car serviced, staying at a hotel, being a member of an organisation, hiring a car, visiting a tourist attraction or buying something from a shop.

Worst-dressed man award won by 'all cyclists'

'We congratulate the cycling community for winning, but this award is partly for the designers of cycling accessories,' announced Tim Ryan, chair of the panel that has just awarded the annual 'worst dressed man' award to all cyclists.

'They have convinced a gullible public to wear ever more outrageous outfits simply by using words such as hi-vis and personal safety,' Ryan added, looking resplendent in a skin-tight luminous green number.

The progress made since the days of cyclists looking a little bit silly due to putting on one bicycle clip or stuffing the bottom of one trouser leg into their sock has been spectacular.

The judges were particularly impressed with those bright jerseys which are stupidly short at the front with large pockets for energy drinks strategically placed just out of reach at the bottom of the stupidly long back.

Due consideration was also given to the use of outlandish wrap-around safety glasses and those absurd shoes that force cyclists to walk with an inelegant, flat-footed, waddling gait – not forgetting of course, that absolutely no-one looks good in a cycling helmet.

Families struggling with post-Christmas leftover cheese/biscuit balance

Across the nation, households are struggling to finish up the stockpiles of cheese and biscuits bought for the festive season without being left with too much cheese for the remaining biscuits, or too many biscuits for the remaining cheese.

For most families left with too many biscuits, all that is left from the original four different boxes of biscuits for cheese assortments are the really boring, rock-hard water biscuits and those strange-tasting, thick, crumbly, green ones that were possibly made by Winalot.

In many of the cases of excess cheese, all the interesting ones have gone, leaving just two dozen of those tasteless little rubbery Dutch mini-snacks and that huge slab of Stilton that may be out of date but is too expensive to throw away and is just cheese that's gone off anyway.

Supermarkets are said to be perpetuating the cycle by discounting their own excess stocks of cheese selection packs and large tins of biscuits for cheese. One woman who complained to her local Morrisons about having too much cheese left over claimed: 'It's sending me crackers.'

Man starts affair with Tesco automatic self-service checkout

'I'd been working late and had just popped into the store to get something for my supper and used the self-service checkout to dodge the queues,' said Dave Headworth, an account manager from Norwich who has recently begun a steamy liaison with self-checkout number three at his local Tesco.

'I wasn't taking much notice until a sultry voice said "Do you have a Clubcard?" and my pulse starting racing immediately. I knew straight away she was the one for me.'

Dave admits that conversation is limited but puts that down to No.3's shyness. 'Sometimes I tease her and remove my shopping too early. Quick as a flash she retorts by saying something hilarious like "Item has been removed from the bagging area". Well, actually, that's what she always says. But it's still very funny.'

Dave's problem is how to take the romance to the next stage. 'No.3 has been non-committal when it comes to developing our relationship and she has not agreed to come out with me yet.'

However, he remains optimistic. 'I think it is only a matter of time, I bought a packet of condoms yesterday evening and she didn't raise any objections. She's a wonderful lady and I do so want to put an unexpected item in her bagging area.'

Rock dad in hiding after not playing Stairway to Heaven in guitar shop

Finance manager Derek Sanders of Bromsgrove is reported to be in hiding following a humiliating visit to a guitar shop with his son Matt, 17.

'When we got to the shop, I picked up a Stratocaster,' explained Matt. 'Dad said it was a 'great axe', but it wouldn't play anything and was useless compared to Guitar Hero 5, where I'm already on expert level. So, Dad said he'd have a go.'

Derek then strummed a couple of chords and said it seemed fine, but the assistant said Derek had to 'do the tune'. He played the riff from 'Smoke on the Water' and handed the guitar back with a smile, but the assistant refused to take it. By then the shop had fallen silent and all eyes were on him.

'It dawned on me that I had to play the introduction to 'Stairway to Heaven', like everyone else in the shop,' said Derek. 'But I'd never quite picked it up. I always played rhythm when I was in a band, not lead. I couldn't even manage the first four notes. I had to beg the assistant to play it for me before we were allowed to leave.'

A Musicians' Union spokesman said it was widely known that doing the tune was obligatory when buying a guitar, and there was no excuse for what had been one of the worst incidents of its kind since The Edge had to get a roadie to play it for him in 1987.

Woman ostracised after finishing reading group book

Vikki Stone, 43, is slowly coming to terms with the fact that her friends in a local book group are not speaking to her after she read the book set by her best friend Sue Stevens for their monthly meeting.

'I started to discuss the plot and characterisation and the atmosphere soured as if I'd committed a war crime,' said Vikki. 'Then Sue just started shrieking: "You're not supposed to read the bloody thing, Vikki. The idea is we all get together with a few bottles of Andrew's Cloudy Bay and we slag off anyone who isn't here." I didn't know where to look. Nobody else had read it.

'I felt so low I went home and sat in the kitchen till David came home from work, so we could talk about 'Ulysses', a book he's always going on about and which I'd just finished. He just laughed and said he'd never got beyond the first hundred pages, but it made an excellent doorstop.'

Naked fries 'essentially chips' confirms café owner

The naked fries listed on the food board at £7.25 for a small container are, when it boils down to it, effectively chips, the manager at a hipster food outlet has begrudgingly admitted.

The news was revealed by Michael O'Mahoney, 'content creator and executive chef' at the Tuber and Tonic on Hoxton High Street, amidst repeated questioning by hungry and confused diners sitting on Formica school chairs, studying menus printed on artificially yellowing paper, gratuitously clipped onto oak-effect clipboards.

'If you're being pedantic, 'Pipers, quadruple cooked, and finished with coarse incisions designed to decant hints of peat' could be taken to mean chipped potatoes,' accepted O'Mahoney, stroking his beard while rolling his eyes upwards towards some dark, exposed beams.

'And yes, I guess 'Artisan loaded skins' might be referred to as jacket spuds with a choice of one or two fillings, if you really want to socially deconstruct the whole thing.

'Some people just don't get what we're aiming for here', sighed O'Mahoney, taking a leak into a urinal reclaimed from a derelict Victorian prison in the gents' toilets, before returning to standing at his botanicals station.

'Could you curate four Old Skool Corn Syrup shots for Table 4?' O'Mahoney shouted out to Pete, his 'gastronomic requirement scribe', before clarifying that yes, those were made by pressing the 'Coke' button on the mixer gun behind the bar and adding some ice.

'One it always was' quits due to stress

Harold Robson, 57, from Penge, has quit his job as making true the popular observation that 'There's always one, isn't there?' He blamed stress and exhaustion from overwork after a frantic career of being the annoying exception to a broadly benevolent rule.

'From speeding to cut in at the front of a queue of traffic at a roadworks so I could make it to a wedding to photobomb the pictures and still have time to take my dog for a walk and hang up a bag of poo right next to the dedicated waste bin, it was a 24/7 job,' said a visibly drained Robson, speaking from his seat in front of the sightscreen at The Oval.

'The pressure was relentless,' he confessed. 'The trouble was there really was always only one – me. No chance of a holiday – that was my busiest time. Do you know how much the small change needed to pay for a return flight to Magaluf in cash weighs? And the one litre bottle of Scotch in my hand luggage?'

However, not everyone was pleased at his decision to retire. 'What with pension shortfalls and retirement ages going up, we've got to keep our noses to the grindstone,' said Sidney Jones of Littlehampton. 'But there's always one, isn't there?'

Middle class man 'low' on conversation starters with kitchen fitters

Fears are growing for a Nantwich teacher after it was revealed that he was down to his last available anecdote to help him bond with the workmen fitting his new kitchen.

'Things started well,' reflected Peter Steel, 43. 'On Day One, I noted Mike and Roachy's hot drinks preferences, and topped them up regularly. They seemed genuinely interested that I'd had an agency job for a day as a student making Formica kitchen units in a factory in Peterlee.

'By Day Three, however, I'd used up my supply of references to England's left midfield problem and I had repeated three times my story about plumbing in my own washing machine in my first house. I hated myself for it. I don't think they like me.'

With at least three more days of fitting to go, Steel looks set to ask whether Mike and Roachy watched the World Final of the darts on TV, having established through extensive Google searches over the weekend that the pair both play darts for their local pub. 'I'd wanted to save that interaction until I was writing them their cheque, but needs must,' he admitted.

'Nice bloke, that Mr Steel,' said Roachy, while sipping his tea with five sugars. 'Bit odd when he's tried to sit with us in the front of our van when we have our lunch, but he's the boss.'

Kitchen bin still not full, man confirms

The pedal bin in the kitchen still does not need emptying yet, a Leicester man has announced.

'Room for a few more things in there, and then the binmen come on Friday so I might as well take it out then,' said Peter Jones, 46, in a tone designed to cut off any challenge, while simultaneously trying to hold back a retch after getting a whiff of four-day-old chicken carcass.

Privately, Jones is thought to be harbouring concerns, having deployed a two-handed compression technique to squeeze in a load of mouldy fridge items into the already crammed bin a couple of days ago. He is thought to be preparing for the worst, resorting to wedging the base of the bin between his two feet while trying to extract the bin bag by the couple of millimetres of material that remains visible at the top.

'It's a perfect storm,' said Jones' wife, in an exasperated tone. 'Cheap Asda binbags. Rips in the side from when he put a tin can in earlier this week. Already seepage of some unknown liquid into the base. God help whoever empties this one. And, yes, it will definitely be Peter.'

Average length of UK dog lead 'now 50 yards', says Kennel Club

'It's a God-send,' said rotund dog owner Bob Beesley, revelling in his elongated dog lead, a type that is now of barely above average length according to a Kennel Club report.

'It means Alfie can poop outside at least another five more houses in our street and I don't even have to move off the sofa. On Friday I sat outside Wetherspoons all day and he was able to drop eggs outside every shop in the high street. Nobody had a clue he was mine. Ha!'

The report also revealed that if you tied all the dog leads in the UK together it would go round the world 14 times. 'But that still wouldn't be long enough for some f*cking dog owners,' snarled a pedestrian, nursing a sprained ankle after his morning walk.

Man at crowded bar waving £20 note 'really helpful', confirm staff

'Without the guys at the back of an impatient scrum holding up £20 notes, I'd have no idea who was next to be served,' confirmed Jenny Cotton, a barmaid working on a zero hours contract at a local Wetherspoons.

'His rather obvious attempts to strike up a dialogue as I'm pulling the pint for the person at least two in front of him in the queue gives me a further helpful clue that it must actually be his turn next, and I'm also grateful for his views on who I should serve after him.'

'The same people also help us to keep active in a long shift,' noted Pete Caldwell, one of Cotton's colleagues. 'Letting us get the first drink in their order from the fridge, before asking for a Coke from the dispenser at the other end of the bar, then asking for two spirit-based drinks one by one. Helps get my steps up. And then having the foresight to ask right at the end for a pint of Guinness to give us a natural rest break...'

Man sentences pan to yet another cycle in the dishwasher

Paul McBride, 43, has ordered a pan to go through his dishwasher for a sixth time, after noticing that the piece of crockery had failed to come out totally clean again, still containing significant debris from a chilli-con-carne meal four days ago.

The pan will join a couple of cups, a random knife and a horizontally placed baking tray which blocks everything from the water blade, in a seemingly endless long-term cleaning programme.

Critics, including McBride's wife, have argued vociferously that such a punitive approach does not address the root cause of the problem, and why can't he add some f*cking rinse aid and clean the filter once in a while.

'It hurts, it works,' said McBride, after meting out the punishment to the burnt orange ten-inch Le Creuset pan, in front of his wife and crying children.

'And you'll have plenty of time to bloody well think about why you're still not ready for release back into the cupboard during the super-hot four-hour 80-degree cycle I'm going to put you on,' he concluded, with a slam of the door.

Couple totally persuaded by IKEA product names

A Retford couple have totally bought into the optimism, vitality and practicality suggested by Ikea product names at their local store, it has been revealed. Kevin Anderson and his wife made unanticipated purchases totalling £845.46, alongside the modest Bestå drawer unit they originally went to buy.

'This Sensuëll frying pan – probably great for frying meatballs really lightly?' noted Anderson to his wife as they wandered round the store. 'And those Komplement kitchen organisers will go with some of our decor, or maybe none of it, who cares?'

Ikea's product names have a complex genealogy, created by dyslexic founder Ingvar Kamprad, who wanted to avoid a labelling system that relied on numbers. That, plus he saw an opportunity to exploit the fact that customers will automatically assume that tea lights are dead good if they are called Glimma.

'Look at how those Swedish book titles and simply styled children's toys fit snugly under that Storå bed frame. Coincidentally, the name almost suggests as much,' noted Anderson, towards the end of their five-hour visit. 'Just one item left to find. Where can I find a Tówtall Bjellend?'

Man tricked again into thinking 114.9 pence per litre is 114 pence

A Colchester driver has had the wool pulled over his eyes again by ingenious global petroleum companies, through their clever use of fractions of pence in their pricing, it has been revealed.

Steve Vickers subconsciously made the assessment that 114.9 pence per litre was 'significantly less' than 115 pence per litre and therefore excellent value for money as he filled up his Ford Focus at his local Esso station.

'Petrol is still pretty reasonable, isn't it,' remarked Vickers to his wife Samantha. 'At 115p a litre, Big Oil would really be taking the piss out of us, through their cartel-like practices. But it's good to see them trying to look after their customers – they've got my loyalty with that gesture alone.'

Vickers expressed surprise, however, that he was unable to dispense exactly four litres and pay £4.596 for his fuel. 'I guess they must round the total bill down, in line with their strategy of trying to look after Joe Public,' he said.

'Some might argue that using 0.9 rather than a full penny is no longer an effective way of getting consumers in, when petrol costs over a pound a litre, or roughly a penny per tablespoon,' noted Vickers. 'But, as they say, every tenth of a penny counts.'

Scepticism about 'perfect result' after one cycle in pop-up toaster

A Pease Pottage man claims still to be 'gobsmacked' after he put two slices of bread in the toaster for a tasty beans on toast lunch and the bread popped up perfectly toasted after just one cycle.

Dave Ryan told reporters: 'I'd already grated the Cheddar and figured by the time the bread popped up for the second time the beans would be nicely up to temperature.'

His claims of what happened have been roundly pooh-poohed by domestic scientists as risible, but Ryan insists his bread was done to a perfect, even golden-brown on both sides after the first pass, meaning his beans were not even nearly ready and his lunch was ruined.

One leading kitchen gadget expert was emphatically dismissive. 'This is either a hoax or a clumsy publicity stunt by the toaster manufacturer,' he stressed.

'The first cycle of toasters hardly marks the bread meaning you have to repeat the process at least once more, unless in a foolish attempt to trick the machine you turn the element up higher than halfway. And everyone knows this inevitably ends up setting off your smoke alarm and produces two twisted slices of smouldering charcoal.'

Chat room member wins argument with strategic use of CAPS LOCK

A chat room frequenter has created thousands of converts to his opinion with the judicious use of the CAPS LOCK key and unprovoked personal abuse.

'I simply told them that if they didn't agree with what I was saying they were a DAILY MAIL-READING IDIOT,' said the man, who went on to illustrate his point with a series of personal anecdotes and unverifiable claims. 'A couple put up some resistance, but when I told them THAT'S WHAT HITLER WOULD HAVE SAID, they threw the towel in pretty quick.'

Chat room experts have previously labelled such tactics as risky and liable to backfire, but now agree that targeted profanity and use of the CAPS LOCK can, in the right circumstances, persuade fellow debaters of the error of their ways.

'And don't listen to anyone who says otherwise,' said one, 'because THEY ARE RIGHT WING TWATS!!!' Researchers are now exploring whether the edge can be taken off upsetting news by use of the Comic Sans font.

Photos show devastating effect of reading Daily Mail

A shocking series of 'before and after' photos released by the police shows the mortifying effects of Daily Mail addiction.

The horrific premature ageing of addicts is clearly demonstrated even after just a few weeks of surfing the headlines: a lowered brow, massive worry lines and torch-bearing burn marks. Ordinary lower middle-class readers, enticed by free offers of spring tulip bulbs, are then forced to buy the paper while they collect enough tokens to take advantage of the promotion.

Many move on to other seemingly harmless practices, like dipping into the sports column and football news. But these recreational hits seem to whet the user's appetite for something stronger and they move on to harder stuff. From here the escalation is rapid, with mainlining Richard Littlejohn the last stage before they descend into the sidebar of shame.

Black and white photos 'not actually more arty'

A retrospective of the work of Armand de l'Apres-Midi, telling the story of the dark underbelly of modern urban life, the forgotten, the overlooked, the left behind, has led art's many observers to conclude that taking photos in black and white is not necessarily any good.

'What's so clever about taking a photo of some graffiti or an abandoned bike in a crappy part of town and whacking up the contrast in Photoshop to make everything look harsher?' asked account manager Brian Wilkins, speaking quietly so he wouldn't be overheard by the newish girlfriend who'd persuaded him to come.

'And anyway, what's all this about urban decay and desperation? That one's quite near where I live in Brockley. It's quite posh these days, we've got an M&S Simply Food.'

Middle class London couple buys Yorkshire

'We'd been thinking for a while we needed more space, what with a second child on the way,' said Annabel Williamson, a marketing consultant from Hoxton, who has just returned from buying Yorkshire. 'And a garden would be nice for the dogs.

'So, when we were on holiday in the Dales, out of curiosity, we asked what we could get up here if we sold the flat. I was surprised to learn the answer to that was all three of the Ridings, whatever they are.'

As yet it is uncertain whether the Williamsons will live in one of the existing houses or build something of their own, or what they will do with the existing population.

'Cripes, that's a thought,' said husband Simon. 'I suppose they could pay us rent? Rent's pretty cheap up here, after all. Or they could always be homeless in London. There's a chap who sits outside our local Tube station, he could probably show them the ropes.'

Man admits to buying small car to compensate for enormous penis

Generously endowed John 'Holmes' Harrison initially has told acquaintances that he bought his 2008 Ford Ka for its road-handling, unique design features and ability to park in tight spots, but friends quickly saw through the story.

'John has always been insecure about his huge hampton,' said his girlfriend, 'and no amount of hyperbole about power-assisted steering could conceal his longcomings.'

Harrison's admission has drawn criticism from TV personality Jeremy Clarkson. 'This guy is a sad loser who needs to get a life and deal with his penis issues,' spat the Top Gear frontman before roaring off in his whopping twin-turbocharged, 670 brake horsepower, 6.0 litre SL.

Woman's cat 'no better than boyfriend it replaced'

Independent woman Michelle Lancashire, 32, has revealed her heartbreak after her beloved cat gradually morphed from surrogate baby into her former boyfriend, Steve.

'Kasper was such an attentive and loving kitten,' she recalled. 'He was there for me when Steve and I split up, and always happy to spend time together. But over time he became less communicative. He started wandering in late, eating the dinner I had lovingly prepared without so much as a 'thanks', and then falling asleep on the sofa.'

Things finally came to a head when Kasper failed to turn up for a romantic microwave meal for two, only to be later found curled up by the outside bins eating a day-old kebab. 'It was Steve all over again,' she sobbed. 'I just can't believe Kasper was seeing that cow from the kebab shop as well.'

Man converses with newsagent after 14 years of buying milk

Gerald Trantor from Camden today accidentally initiated a conversation with Atif Dasu, the owner of the corner shop he has used for 14 years. It is the first time they have exchanged any words besides 'Eighty-nine pence please' or 'Sorry, I've got no change'.

'I saw the story about the floods on all the front pages and, before I knew it, I'd asked if he was from Pakistan. It turns out his family is, but their village is on a hill so they're okay. Then we had a brief conversation on the necessity of making do in difficult situations.'

Trantor is now concerned that he will have to engage in conversation on future visits to the newsagent. 'But we won't be able to talk about the floods forever. Maybe I'll start going to the corner shop two minutes further down the road.'

Burglars demand 'more clarity' on Facebook users' holiday plans

A spokesman for the burglar community has said that he appreciates that most Facebook users are 'admirably candid' about when the entire contents of their house are there for the taking but added that a stubborn minority is still vague about the details of their travel plans.

'Usually, you can have the whole place cleaned out while they're still at the airport arguing with Ryanair staff about baggage restrictions,' said housebreaker Jeremy Quinn from Birmingham.

'But when they don't give enough details, it's costing burglars an estimated £20 million a year in lost earnings.

'People should be franker about the true value of their belongings. I get the impulse to boast and fib, but honesty is the best policy. I can tell you that the 'Cartier' watch Greg Morgan in Peterborough has been bragging about is nothing but a pathetic Chinese knock-off.'

Lancashire folk group pens song about the future

Traditional Lancashire folk group The Ferret's Hot Pot has surprised experts by releasing a song which does not hark back to the good old days of cotton mills, TB, coal mine disasters, slavery or asbestosis, but instead appears to focus on the future.

The song, named simply 'We Can't Wait for HS2', focuses on the development of the future high-speed rail link between the north and south of England.

'Like the title says, we can't wait for HS2,' said lead singer Bert Thumpbrush. 'After all we love our southern cousins, and if they can make it up to Lancashire a bit quicker so we can share a glass of cold lager with them, then all the better.

'And if we can encourage Michel Roux to open a new restaurant in Rochdale, then we can all enjoy some haute cuisine, so long as the 15 courses are particularly small and expensive, otherwise the locals will start moaning.'

Thumpbrush confirmed that the band's new song also has an ecological twist, playing with the prospect of the storage of the fuel required to make HS2 travel at over 200 miles per hour.

'After all, storing enough coal and water to complete the journey is pretty much unimaginable, which is why our lyric refers to a stop at Stoke-on-Trent to take on extra supplies and put some torn-up newspapers down the loos.'

Applying both Lynx and Impulse creates 'perfect sexual null point'

Medical researchers at the prestigious Edinburgh University have made a breakthrough in the fight against overly attractive people after discovering that simultaneously applying popular deodorants Lynx and Impulse renders the wearer completely unattractive to both sexes, thus creating what scientists term a sexual null point.

According to lead researcher Professor Soren Lorensen, his team were surprised at how this simple solution worked. 'The Lynx effect is a long-established phenomenon that drives women mad with desire, while it is well known that men can't help acting on Impulse.

'Bringing two such efficacious compounds together should have created a formidable aphrodisiac, but in fact it's exactly the opposite – the two deodorants actually cancel each other out, forming a pheromonal vacuum.'

Sorensen recently revealed his motivation for unattractiveness: 'Being a tall, blonde Scandinavian who works out regularly is a major hindrance when it comes to the serious world of medical science – have you ever tried searching for a cure for cancer when all your assistants keep swooning at you? Now I can get on with my important work without having to fend off awkward misunderstandings from Barry in genetics.'

New swearword launches tonight

The British Expletive Board is poised to launch a brand-new swearword this evening, in a move calculated to counter the growing familiarity and apathy towards established expletives. According to BEB spokesman Trevor McCorkindale, tonight's launch will reignite Britain's flagging indignation at such four-letter-words.

'At one time the C-word was the sole preserve of rapists and perverts, but now everyone uses it. And no-one bats an eyelid at the F-word nowadays - it might as well be taught in primary schools for all the good it'd do. This new word will be a shot in the arm for our cursing and insulting prowess.'

In order to maximise its effect, details of the new swearword have been kept a closely guarded secret. 'An expert panel of linguists, etymologists and religious representatives have worked for months on the word. We wouldn't want to diminish its profoundly upsetting and abhorrent impact by giving the game away too soon,' McCorkingdale said.

Viewers will be able to hear the new swearword in a special bulletin at 6:50 this evening on the CBeebies channel, just after 'In the Night Garden'.

Unborn babies can distinguish good wine from plonk, study finds

Having proved that light to moderate drinking during pregnancy has no detrimental effect on the foetus, doctors now also believe that a mother's occasional glass of wine can help her unborn child develop a sophisticated wine-tasting palate, which will stand them in good stead in later life.

The findings are based on a long-term experiment in which foetuses were separated into groups and plied - via their mothers - with alcohol of varying quality and strength.

Group A were given a perky Sauvignon purchased from a local independent wine retailer able to offer advice on acidity and soil; Group B were given a £3.99 Blossom Hill Chardonnay from the off-licence that came with a watercolour of a vineyard on the label and the instruction 'Serve with Fish'; and Group C was a 'control', meaning the embryos went a full nine months without a drink.

The study has received a warm welcome from many thirsty middle-class mothers. 'I've known all along that the odd bottle of wine wouldn't do my little darling any harm,' said Tamsin Forsdike.

'And as I kept telling doctors, it all depends what you mean by light to moderate drinking. I'm just so relieved my cravings for Chenin Blanc mean our Amy has grown up to drink Pinot Grigio in the park, and not those hideous alcopops like the rest of her Brownie group.'

Bloke you meet in office kitchen sapping your will to live

A bloke you keep meeting in the office kitchen on the mid-afternoon tea round is beginning to take its toll on your *joie de vivre*. You have now run out of silly expressions to pull when you meet him, have no more small talk to make and it's becoming quite an issue.

'He's nearly always there every sodding day! It's becoming more awkward every time it happens, and it nearly ended in total disaster on Tuesday,' you said.

'We were waiting for the kettle to boil when I sneezed and inadvertently dropped a silent fart at the same time. As the foul aroma of my lunch-break egg and onion sarnies rose up and enveloped us, it was touch and go I can tell you,' you added.

Meanwhile, the bloke said: 'I keep seeing this same chap in the kitchen. It's driving me bonkers. He keeps pulling bloody stupid faces, like he's having a seizure every time he sees me. But worse than that, I thought the dirty bastard had shat himself on Tuesday. If we can't somehow break this vicious cycle, I'm thinking of getting a new job.'

IN OTHER RELATED NEWS:

Möbius strip artist ends up still wearing clothes
Fears for the lonely as PPI calls stop
Gyms hope to restart charging people for not going soon
Brexiters going for an Indian agree no daal is better than a bad daal
Drug dealers complain of political correctness gone mad as Scotland bans smack
Surveys are made up to get publicity says INSERT MESSAGE FROM PR CLIENT HERE
New trendy craft beer to be made from hip hop
Secret condiment maker refuses to name his sauces
Supermarket Sweep upgraded from light entertainment to gritty documentary
Ban on fellatio 'a huge blow' to sex industry
Man given the moon on a stick complains about length, colour and quality of stick
EU court classifies parenthood as a taxi service
White supremacists now required to carry proof of supremacy
Arachnophobes shun new web-based help forum
Roads to avoid on the Bank Holiday: Anything beginning with an A, B, C or M
Man finds smartphone emoticons have greater emotional range than he does
Tube Chat badges succeed in getting Londoners to say 'F*ck off' to each other
Man who had full penis transplant wakes with Audi driver in his trousers
Wife blames husband for losing no blame divorce papers
Most depressing words in English are 'According to a recent study' says research
Sacked baggage handler reinstated after case is dropped
Wheelbarrow shortage as people realise where the pound will be next month
This is not just a lazy joke about job losses, it is a lazy joke about M&S job losses
Mask industry faces change

CHAPTER FIVE

Stock exchange 'has got too commercial' (and other Business news)

High-speed spinning jenny 'needed to boost North'

A high-speed spinning jenny shared between Manchester and Leeds could help create a 'global northern powerhouse', the Chancellor of the Exchequer has said. Modern technology meant that a cotton mill hand could work over 120 spindles at once.

Labour accused the Government of 'cruelly raising false hopes amongst northern lads and lasses' to try and win votes, but the Government is determined to press on with the plan and that of building a high-speed locomotion link between Manchester and Leeds.

'It will be a high-speed version of Stephenson's Rocket with its innovative 0-2-2 wheel arrangement,' the Chancellor said. 'Speeding between the two great northern cities will come at a cost, but this Government is prepared to stump-up the £5,059.02 investment if it helps create a global northern powerhouse and engine-shedfuls of votes.'

Ikea launches new range of flat-pack coffins

Meatball giant and furniture retailer Ikea has launched a range of coffins for the budget-conscious bereaved. The Krøke range contains over 2,300 separate components, packed into 13 boxes, and can be rapidly assembled by a team of six people, using a range of industrial power tools, in just ten days.

The company said that the new range is already selling well throughout the UK, as people struggle to keep pace with Coronavirus. And, at a time when funerals are limited to five attendees anyway, many newly bereaved families can no longer see the point in going the whole hog with brass handles and all that.

Each Krøke coffin comes with a lifetime, or ten-year, guarantee, whichever is the shorter. Customers can add internal bookshelves and an Alexa speaker to customise their purchase.

Reviews have been good so far, although customer Mark Kelly from Streatham in South London did say: 'The 120-page instruction manual in Japanese was useless and Uncle Reg fell out the bottom when we were coming down the stairs. Still, at £49.99, I suppose I can't grumble.'

Libraries to start lending money

In its latest bid to kick-start the nation's ailing economy, the Government has announced that from today, customers borrowing books from public libraries will also be able to take out financial loans for a period of three weeks, though it may be possible to renew the terms of these agreements provided no other customer is waiting to borrow the cash.

'Libraries are ideally placed for this transition,' argued the Chancellor. 'Just one look at their modern dynamic workforce and state-of-the-art equipment should reassure even the most hardened sceptic that their proven track record in bookkeeping will make this scheme a resounding success.'

Tight financial control suggested by guidelines will limit borrowers to no more than six loans at a time on a single library card, enforced by a zero-tolerance culture which will see any failure to return a loan by the date stamped on the cash punished by a fine of 5p a day up to a limit of £5. Persistent breaches of loan conditions will result in a chastening stare from the beady-eyed old lady on the checkout desk.

However, some critics have questioned the credentials of the public libraries to operate such a scheme. A number of branches needed massive Government bailouts after announcements of enormous hikes in gas prices saw a pre-winter run on Jeffrey Archer novels. Further attempts to explain the new system ended abruptly, however, when Government advisors around the library said 'Shhh!'

One dead, two pregnant, five sacked in 'best ever Christmas party'

Employees at an office supply firm in Leatherhead are celebrating after their annual Christmas party topped their previous record for fatalities, colleague impregnation and sackings.

'There's always a certain pressure to make each year's Christmas do better than the last,' said Emma Kirkwood, junior sales assistant at Deskatronic and this year's party organiser. 'All we could manage last year was a paperweight-induced head injury and two temps having their contracts ended for arson.'

This year, the five-man sales team were all summarily dismissed after listing all the office chairs, desks and IT equipment on eBay in a bid to hit their December sales targets. Tragedy followed when logistics manager Alan Rogers was electrocuted while sitting on the photocopier with his trousers round his ankles after spilling his beer on the Xerox.

'At least we have one hundred A3 copies of Alan's arse to remember him by', said managing director Keith Shah. 'It's what he would have wanted.'

The celebrations were completed when an ambulance crew came to deal with Alan's body. Thinking they were strip-a-grams, Tamsin and Shreeti from marketing undressed the paramedics and took them on a tour of the stationery cupboard.

'Something to do with hole-punching, I think,' added Shah. 'Anyway, they've both said they won't be around for next year's bash and have asked for Mothercare vouchers this Christmas.'

Workers must wear nappies to boost efficiency

Trade unions have reacted angrily to plans to make people wear nappies at work in a bid to boost productivity. It is believed toilet breaks cost the economy up to £11 billion a year in lost production.

Captains of British industry have commissioned specially designed adult nappies that allow employees to work non-stop and just 'let it all go' when they feel the urge. Already available to order are:

- 'Execu-Dump 2000' by Calvin Klein
- 'Diaper-Power Max' by Clinique for Men
- 'Squeeze n' Go' by Paco Rabanne
- Pampers and Huggies (for factory and shop workers)
- Bicycle-Clips (for apprentices, interns and under 25s)

The proposal has had mixed reaction from employees. One receptionist in Bradford said 'I've been using an Execu-Dump nappy all day and already I feel ten feet taller.'

A customer in a restaurant in Luton was somewhat more lukewarm, however, noting: 'It's disconcerting to see your waitress clench her teeth and go red in the face. But hey-ho, you can't stop progress.'

Argos till staff pushing houses as well as extended warranties

There are concerns that retailers who have had a tough year may be trying to boost their sales by suggesting all manner of additional products that customers might like to purchase.

'The assistant told me that the exercise bike needed batteries, and asked if I'd like to buy some,' said one Argos shopper. 'I said no and also declined the warranty, but then she suggested a car to get it home in.

'Apparently, they had a special offer on a Renault Megane at the moment. When I told her I already had a car, she then asked if I needed a three-bedroom semi-detached house to put it in.'

A spokesman for Argos has defended the policy of trying to sell 'complementary' goods, but it has annoyed some customers. 'I was stood there for 25 minutes rejecting all sorts of suggestions before I finally got my exercise bike. It was ridiculous, though I do quite like the pony that I bought with it.'

BHS bidders advised to keep receipt if sale goes through

Administrators looking to sell BHS have warned potential bidders that there can't be any returns 'unless they've got the original receipt.' Whilst they are optimistic that they will find a buyer, they are cautious about buyers not considering the 'fit' of the outfit with their existing organisations.

'It's fair to say the colour might not suit,' observed one administrator, concerned that there was 'way too much green' in the stores, 'although one bidder had enquired about 'doing a deal' on the pension obligations. At least I think that's what he meant, that he could buy one and get one free.'

Potential bidders have been advised that they will need to provide their own bags if they are successful in their bid, in line with current legislation, 'or we can sell them a bag for life for 5p, if they don't mind doubling their cash investment.'

'Boots on the ground' in Syria problematic, say pharmacists

The prospect of the UK putting 'Boots on the ground' in Syria has once again been on the agenda after the UK's recent participation in US air strikes. However, experts have questioned whether the pharmacist and general store's winning formula could be successfully translated from high street to war zone.

'The military situation in Syria is highly complex, with multiple factions and warring ideologies at play,' said Jane Ramsey of the British Pharmacologists Association.

'We have to look at what Boots' role would be. Could they take on a role in conflict resolution? Or do Assad's army just need a reliable place they can get some sun cream and a packet of paracetamol? You've got to sort these things out before committing yourself to action.'

David Dickinson accidentally sold at auction

Antiques expert and 'cheap as chips' television presenter, David Dickinson, was accidentally sold at an antiques auction yesterday after the auction house staff mistook him for an ornately carved teak bookend.

The buyers, Carole and Bobby Dazzler, were quite surprised to have won the lot admitting that they hadn't planned to bid but had suffered a bout of auction fever and just couldn't resist.

'I said I'd go up to £35,' Carole told a reporter. 'But something came over me and I just had to have it. I couldn't believe it when we won him. He's worth every penny of the £49 we paid for him.'

It is understood that Dickinson will take pride of place in the Dazzlers' front room, among the china dogs, Great War thimbles and Lady Diana plates.

A spokesman for the auctioneers said: 'This is quite a rare find and for it to go so cheap is unheard of. The last time something similar happened was in 1978 when a Barnsley couple paid £87 for Arthur Negus, which later turned out to be a fake.'

Greggs vegan sausage rolls 'made from actual vegans'

When Greggs recently launched its vegan sausage rolls, it received an unexpected boost to the bottom. However, rumours in the City of London seem to suggest that the number of donor vegans is drying up.

'When we started, there was only a small demand for products made from vegans, so we assumed that the relatively short supply chain would be adequate,' said a spokesman.

Some commentators are suggesting that the core material for the vegan sausage rolls might include vegetarians and the 'odd omnivore' to bulk it out, a charge Greggs denies.

'We only use natural vegans in our vegan range but the supply chain is getting overtaken by the demand for this product,' said the spokesman. The share price did rise slightly when the company announced it was launching a Brexit politician sausage roll. 'May contain nuts,' cautioned the spokesman.

Man buys fishing waders instead of milk from Aldi

When he entered his local Aldi, Dave Wells from Hatfield had every intention of fulfilling the basic instruction from wife Cheryl to purchase milk. However, the overwhelming allure of the 'middle aisle' proved too much and he ended up buying fishing waders instead.

'I walked in repeating to myself milk, milk, milk – but then I looked up and it was just, f*ck me, are those fishing waders? I'd heard about the middle aisle of Aldi but it's nothing compared to being actually confronted by it - completely mind-blowing. Where else can you buy a snail-shaped doormat and a Viking helmet-shaped coffee mug?

'I ended up settling on the fishing waders, but it was a tough call between those, the six-step aluminium ladder with built-in radio and a polyester Nehru-style jacket.

'I got home totally buzzing, then I saw Cheryl just standing there in the kitchen with her arms crossed – and I remembered I'd forgotten the milk. She nearly sent me back to Aldi in the waders, which I would have been totally up for, to be honest.'

Cheryl said: 'Obviously, I couldn't trust him, so I went myself. I returned with a Disney Princess yoga mat. B*llocks!'

Man imprisoned for failing to provide an Amazon review

Billy Askew, 24, from Winsford, has been sentenced to three months in prison for failing to review a set of toenail clippers he bought on Amazon. 'We must have sent him four emails asking for a review, but he just ignored them,' said an Amazon spokesman. 'He hadn't marked the product as a gift, so there was no excuse.'

Judge Gordon Roberts commented that it is every online shopper's civic duty to provide a review 'even if it's clearly horseshit'. A shaken Askew mumbled as he was taken down from the dock: 'They cut my toe-ails, what more is there to say?'

The Amazon spokesman defended referring Askew to the authorities: 'Everybody provides reviews these days, even HMRC gave our tax return a review. One star, a bit harsh,' he added, while confirming that if Askew had been an Amazon Prime member, 'we'd probably have written the review for him.'

Askew has clearly seen the error of his ways, as he posted a one-star review of his cell at HMP Long Lartin on TripAdvisor. 'Smaller than advertised, has an all-pervading smell of wee and can you believe it - no spare key!'

West Coast Mainline to provide replacement bus service until 2026

Passenger groups reacted angrily last night after closer examination of First Group's successful bid to run the West Coast Mainline franchise will mean replacement bus services operating the entire line until at least 2026. First Group has assured customers that it will be able to meet demand through its minibus subcontractor, Jim's Coaches of Brentford.

Board member Susie Butcher said: 'When people book their train tickets, they aren't worried about minor details like what the rails are made from or if there are actually any trains. Without making these sensible efficiencies we simply can't keep price rises under 63% per year.'

The chairman of the UK Train Passengers' Association, Phil Carson, said: 'It's bad enough that people have to travel to places like Wolverhampton and Stoke without being forced to travel there by coach. And have you ever tried to wee in a coach toilet? It's next to impossible.'

A Virgin spokesperson was unable to comment as they were stuck just outside of Coventry in a quiet carriage and said they couldn't talk now.

Ninjas to be trained in stealth by parcel delivery guys

A troop of British parcel delivery men has been sent to Japan to train their ninjas in the art of approaching buildings without being detected.

Japan's ninjas are renowned for their stealth and their silent killing techniques. However, in a test set up by the Ministry of Defence, parcel delivery guys performed better than them, the British SAS and the American Delta Force in a task of silently approaching a building and inserting a card through the door.

'There are many scenarios where special forces operatives have to approach a building without being spotted,' said one expert. 'Surveillance, planting explosives, silent entry, hostage rescue – it's one of the trickiest roles they have to carry out.

'We asked instructors to stay home all day and listen out for anybody in their garden. Several of the homes had yappy dogs. Thirty percent of them had alarm systems. They all had doorbells.

'To our surprise, the parcel delivery guys were able to put a card through every door without being heard or seen. They didn't even show up on CCTV or infrared cameras. Their camouflage and panther-crawling techniques are awesome.

'They only marred their performance at the end of each sortie by throwing fragile objects over the gate. Apparently, in their culture this is a great achievement.'

Paranoid Ryanair passenger demands answers

Dave Dubbs, a certified paranoid pedant and grammarian, has demanded answers to the following questions after sweating through his latest flight with Ryanair.

'When they announce that it is the "Last and final call for the flight to BerGAmo", does this mean there is a last, then a final call followed by a last and final call, or just the one, a call which leaves all the Italians on the flight wondering – do they mean BERgamo?

'In the safety announcement, why are we only told about SOME of the safety features on the aircraft? – how many others are there and why are we not being told about them?

'We are told, "In the unlikely event of a landing on water..." - but if calculations have been made about how likely this event is, could they not give us a percentage probability – 0.05% would be reassuring but 25% less so.

'Finally, could it be made clear, before the flight attendant sets off down the aisle calling "Garbage, garbage!", that at this point it is what is being collected rather than offered for sale?'

Supermarkets launch 'Donate to Landfill' scheme

In an initiative to help their customers during the Coronavirus pandemic, supermarkets have begun displaying 'Donate to Landfill' collection boxes. Instead of queuing up to strip the shelves in person, anxious shoppers can simply put money in the collection boxes.

Dedicated volunteers then use the money to buy essential goods, such as flour, cheese and milk, and take it straight to landfill sites. There is no need to find cupboard or fridge space, and the service is entirely free of charge.

'This saves people the trouble of queueing,' said Help the Aged volunteer Susan Speyers, explaining that her national team of volunteers makes a vital contribution by doing all the panic buying at off-peak times, when most people are at home holding in utility companies' telephone queues, or trying to log on for a home delivery slot.

'Last week, it was mostly toilet rolls, hand sanitisers and eggs. This week, it's flour and cheese. We're very responsive to public demand and we're proud of our efficiency. When did you last see a packet of yeast?'

Three Little Pigs' planning permission rejected

Oldham Council Planning Committee has once again rejected an application for planning permission from Pig, Pig & Pig Builders. Councillor B.B. Wolfe, responding for the committee, pointed out that previous applications have been rejected for not following building regulations and being built prior to permission being approved.

'The first one was erected predominantly from straw,' said Wolfe, noting that there were exceptional circumstances where wattle and daub construction can be approved, usually for preserving traditional listed buildings, 'but not as a modern three-up, two-down detached. They didn't even consider sprinklers, for goodness sake,' he said.

'Then there were the premises constructed from sticks. A gazebo, yes, maybe, but a residence with a mezzanine and loft extension - not on my watch. And, this latest monstrosity. OK, traditional and conventional brick construction - tick. But that's it.

'No attempt at drainage, footings minimal, no separation of cooking, eating and other living areas. I inspected the premises and, to be honest, it looks like a pigsty. They say they'll address the issues, but with their track record I doubt it and let's face it - they tell porkies,' he said, licking his lips.

Unpaid overtime 'balanced out by people doing sod all'

In response to TUC claims that UK workers racked up almost two billion hours of unpaid overtime every year, the CBI has published their own report, showing that this is more than balanced out by the amount of people who do absolutely nothing every day.

According to the TUC's figures, 5.3 million workers regularly work an average of 7.2 hours of unpaid overtime a week. CBI figures, however, show that over ten million workers often spend up to 30 hours per week dicking about on the internet, checking Facebook on their phone, or just having a bit of a chat, while desperately trying to look busy.

'These people may be hung-over, having personal problems outside of work that stop them concentrating, or may just be work-shy gits,' said a spokesman.

'There are a variety of factors that contribute to it, and employers need to be empathetic, understanding, and tolerant, without compromising the viability of their business. But something certainly needs to be done.

'Now, if you'll excuse me, I was just in the middle of a game of poker on Facebook.'

Workplaces to get screaming supporters

With Britain's Olympic medal winners attributing their success to the lift given by the home crowd, Government ministers hope that the flagging economy can be boosted by having people work in front of thousands of noisy fans.

Early trials are showing positive results with productivity at one sandwich factory up 20% when 5,000 spectators were sent in to 'ooh' and 'aah' - increasing the possibility that the scheme could be rolled out across the country.

'The crowd were like a few extra keys on my keyboard,' said exhausted writer Erica Corbett, moments after completing a thirty-page radio script in a new personal best of 53 minutes and 18 seconds in front of 70,000 fans at Twickenham Stadium. 'Or maybe a few extra fingers.'

Meanwhile, James Eaton, a newly qualified surgeon, echoed the thoughts of many others. 'The noise is amazing,' he said. 'It meant so much to know they were all behind me. Obviously, I'm disappointed the operation didn't go too well, but the fans were brilliant.'

Bank of England 'can't remember' how to put up interest rates

Interest rates are set to remain at their historic low of 0.5% after the Governor of the Bank of England, Mark Carney, revealed today that no-one at the bank could remember how to raise them because it has been so long since the last time.

'There was a CD-ROM thingy that I was given on my first day that explained it all, but I'm buggered if I can find it,' Carney said. 'The last I saw of it was in the bottom drawer of my desk where I keep my stash of caramel wafers and that VHS tape explaining Windows 95.'

This latest embarrassing revelation comes only two months after a 16-year old schoolboy on work experience increased the rate of inflation by mistake while the Monetary Policy Committee were out for their Christmas lunch.

'Interest rates will stay the same until the growth forecast improves,' Carney told reporters. 'Or until we can raise them manually with a big crank handle and a shitload of WD40.'

Anti-capitalist protester starts anti-capitalist events company

An anti-capitalist protester camping outside St Paul's Cathedral in London confirmed today that the experience has inspired him to start ProtestEx, the world's first event management company dedicated to 'making sure your bid to overthrow the status quo goes without a hitch'.

'The people running this one have done brilliantly,' said Christopher James of Kingham, Oxfordshire. 'It's a great central location, near Starbucks and Pizza Express, and there's plenty of opportunities for a few sherbets in the evening.

'That said, all the organisers are hippies and unemployed, so they had some time on their hands, and that got me thinking – what if you wanted to start a protest but couldn't fit the destruction of the entire bourgeois rentier system into your busy working schedule? You'd need an events manager – just like if you were planning to get married.

'What we want is to make sure your big day goes off without a hitch,' James continued. 'You can't have just anyone turning up, so we've negotiated favourable security rates with G4. The last thing you want when demonstrating to save the world is a bunch of selfish people only worried about their own needs. We'll stop them for you – for a fee.'

Dr Rowan Williams dropped as face of Pepsi

PepsiCo have announced today that they are terminating the current contract with Dr Rowan Williams, Archbishop of Canterbury, as the face of Pepsi Cola. The brand will now be moving away from the centrist Church of England image, in which Pepsi drinkers were portrayed reflecting upon difficult spiritual matters as the product is remarketed 'in more of a hip-hop direction towards youth and music'.

The Rowan Williams Pepsi campaign had been blighted by controversy since its inception. The advert, a two minute 'Thought for the Day' style monologue, which first aired during Superbowl XLII, gave Williams the opportunity to reach millions worldwide with his views that we should all try to save water, use our cars only when truly necessary, and remember that Jesus Christ died for our sins.

The strapline 'And in many ways that reminds us of our relationship with God', spoken at the end of each advert before the archbishop swigged from a can of Pepsi, became a staple of television humourists, most notably on Saturday Night Live.

Dr Williams was reported to be 'saddened but not surprised' but said he would pray for PepsiCo's marketing executives. The drinks giant was apparently determined to terminate the celebrity endorsement, even after a desperate last-minute offer from the Archbishop to start wearing a backwards baseball cap and baggy gangsta clothes.

Men demand multiple orgasms in exchange for equitable pay

Men have said they are willing to concede ground on pay differentials provided they are compensated from traditional areas of female monopoly, such as extended lifespan, wardrobe space and 'knee trembling' duration. They want greater transparency when it comes to shoe-allowances and just as much right to pout in a cute way.

The disparity in the length of climax is but one of several areas of injustice impacting on men who, for far too long, have had limited hairstyle options.

One male executive admitted: 'Yes, we've been guilty of a few thousand years of discrimination, but it's not all been one-way traffic – and don't get me started on car insurance. *La petite mort* needs to be more *grande*!'

Banks now refusing to lend pens

The ongoing lending crisis has escalated despite a Government bailout which saw the Treasury giving the banks millions and millions of ballpoints.

'We went through all the drawers at 11 Downing Street, trying out all the old biros to see if they had any ink in them,' explained the Chancellor. 'We even gave them those free ones you get from the charities to make you feel guilty.'

'During the current economic climate, we cannot be expected to sanction the loan of biros without guarantees of adequate security,' said a bank spokesperson.

Complained one customer: 'The guy behind the desk said I could borrow a biro if I filled out the six-page form Lf/20b 'Application for a Ballpoint Loan.' But I couldn't fill out the form because he didn't have a pen.'

Budget airline to allow bombs for £5 surcharge

By allowing bombs on board, no-frills airline BudgetAir hopes to increase passenger numbers, particularly among members of the extremist militant communities who claim they are currently made to feel unwelcome by many other airlines. The airline will of course also benefit financially from the charges made for allowing small bombs in hand luggage.

'Obviously we have no intention of letting terrorists detonate these bombs and kill hundreds of innocent passengers,' said a spokesperson for BudgetAir. 'We would want much more than a fiver for that.'

The ban on nail scissors and bottled water remains in place.

Account executives fail to make key worker list

As Coronavirus continues to tighten its inexorable grip on society and sanity, several professions have failed to prove their worth, not least of which include tired TV producers, HR departments and people who shake hands for a living.

'It just doesn't seem fair or logical, according to this diagram I have just made up and scribbled on this flip chart,' said a management consultant from the company ThrustNow! 'Who will be advising companies to sack - sorry, I mean 'right size' - for short-term shareholder gains?'

To their own surprise, telephone sanitisers have made it onto the list for the first time.

Female Dr Who suffers work-based harassment from aliens

'I've been chased all over the galaxy, primarily by male aliens - all with wandering hands and tentacles,' complained Jodie Whittaker, the first female Dr Who. 'Time and space should be a safe working environment for women. Instead, I'm on 40% less Gallifreyan dollars than my previous incarnations and the Tardis is only fitted out with urinals.'

Constant inappropriate banter from Daleks, waving their proboscises in a provocative fashion, have made things uncomfortable, coupled with snide comments from androids that only doctors and 'cybers' can be men. Ironically, now that she has male companions, the Doctor is still expected to save the Earth and then tidy up afterwards.

Brexit included in Black Friday offer

Much to the surprise of shoppers, the UK has reduced the price of Brexit by 70%, making it similar to a discounted Belgium or a top-end electric toothbrush.

This Friday, trade deals will be available for a fraction of their original cost, with consumers expected to rush out to buy a 55-inch Smart TV or a Boris Johnson – '76-inches of dumb'.

One consumer watchdog warned: 'Investors should be wary of budget economies and panic buying. Normally Black Friday ends at midnight, but I suspect the UK will be cut-price for years to come.'

The Prime Minister is offering large portions of the economy to anyone with store credit or a plan to win the next election. Those with Amazon Prime or who are watching 'The Walking Dead', can experience Brexit a full year before everyone else.

Ten ways to get a meeting done in ten minutes

- Conduct all meetings while standing. On hot coals
- Swap the conference room for the lion enclosure at Longleat
- Add Russian roulette as an agenda item
- Invite that guy from IT to all meetings - you know, the guy with the questionable personal hygiene regime
- Conduct all meetings during free-fall parachute jumps
- Only allow laxative refreshments to be served
- Attendees have to clean and jerk 25% of own body weight for duration of meeting
- Next person to use a word with a vowel has to leave the meeting
- Don't invite Marketing
- Don't have a meeting, they're a waste of time anyway (to be discussed at next meeting)

48 trillion Nectar points to be put into the economy to boost recovery

In an announcement that will delight shoppers and the city alike, a fourteen-figure sum of Nectar points will be released into the economy. Eight billion air miles will also be created, enough for a family of four to travel to RAF Northolt and back (terms and conditions apply), while Boots Advantage Card owners will get a free nail care kit.

'"Generous" is a loaded term in these difficult times,' said Junior Trade Minister Sally Jones. 'But we feel that this recovery package will stimulate consumer confidence, tend the green shoots of economic recovery and ensure no-one misses out on double points when you spend over a tenner on personal hygiene products.'

'The Nectar deal alone is thought to be worth the value of one 200-gram box of unbranded cereal for every man, woman and child in the south east of England,' she continued.

'And Air Miles collectors with more than 10,000 miles will be entitled to a packet of cheesy biscuits on selected flights, provided they travel on the fourth Tuesday of the month in Class Y674 when Saturn is rising in the House of Aquarius.'

Sceptics have criticised the scheme, but Jones countered that: 'With the increase in loyalty points put in place, there's never been a better time to buy a full colour printer and a range of coloured inks. So, get down to Argos.'

Leech claims it is a 'blood creator'

Medical research normally endorses the careful removal of a parasite, but some leeches are of the opinion that if it was not for them, no blood would ever be produced. In fact, many leeches have threatened to leave our bodies altogether, in the event of income tax, a lack of good parking spaces in Knightsbridge or a whiff of socialism.

A recently ennobled leech commented: 'It's very simple, when I suck your blood, I force you to make more blood. That in turn means you have to work twice as hard, just to keep up with the level of plasma draining from your body. If I leave, how would you know how to make your own blood?'

London-based leeches have threatened to take their business elsewhere, setting up on the rump of an Irish Setter. They denied transferring profits to an offshore blood bank.

'We are vital to the economy, blood just won't siphon itself, you know. If you compare us to Richard Branson, I think it's fair to say that one of us is a parasitic worm sponging off the nation and the rest of us are just leeches.'

Government to kick-start economy by promising 'terms and conditions won't apply'

The Government has unveiled plans to boost the flagging British economy by promising British consumers a 'disclaimer holiday'. For one month, terms and conditions will not apply, all rights will not be reserved, and nothing will be subject to status.

'It's the big left-field idea that everyone has been hoping for,' said the Chancellor. 'By temporarily freeing consumers from the worry of all those phrases you hear rattled off at the end of every advert, we will restore confidence to British consumers.'

Sales of power tools, crossbows and fireworks have all risen dramatically now that manufacturers are accepting all liability for injury or loss resulting from use. 'We've also done away with the "Investments can go down as well as up" strapline. Er, because now they only go down.'

Video conferencing spike matches dislike of magnolia backdrop

As Britain's workforce moves further towards more virtual meetings, it has become alarmingly apparent how dull the nation's interior walls are, with the sheer beige-ness of it all.

Complained one worker: 'I'm so bored staring at the same faded pastel print or the gurning smile of your husband on your wedding day. Just mix it up, will you! Oh, and f*ck off with your kids' finger-paintings, you know they'd be in the bin if you didn't think you might need a kidney one day.'

An IT expert observed: 'Appearing in front of a fake library fools no one and casually leaving musical instruments strewn in the background just makes you look a like medieval bard.'

Meanwhile, one bold executive took the decision to plaster his wall with black and white stills of Mussolini, Katie Hopkins and a movie poster of 'Jaws, The Revenge', saying: 'Not only is it eclectic, but it creates a sense of unease in the viewer and sympathy for sharks.'

New charges will only apply to 'poor, stupid people' says bank

First Debit Bank today defended its new costs for current account customers explaining that the monthly £10 charge will only apply to people who are already completely skint and have wasted their money on 'stupid rubbish'.

'Most customers will continue to enjoy all the benefits of free banking,' said CEO Mike Collins. 'But if you are spending what little cash you have on unnecessarily large plasma TV screens, chunky gold rings from the Argos catalogue, and crisps and fizzy drinks from Lidl, then the new bank charges will apply.'

As predicted, a number of other banks have quickly followed First Debit Bank's lead of increased charges for the poor. Today the World Bank announced it would be introducing current account charges of $89 trillion to any country with a 'z' in its name.

Business celebrates best ever year for corporate bullshit

Business leaders across the country should be proud of their prodigious output of meaningless twaddle last year, according to the CBI. 'The last year has seen a huge increase in the productivity of techniques such as alliteration, with several slogans synergising the strategic sustainability of stakeholders,' said CBI spokesman Piers Collingwood-Hancock.

From snappy soundbites like 'integrated governance' and 'value creation', to long 'mission statements', with lots of awkward nested sub-clauses which make them difficult to read and include words such as 'leveraging' and 'internationalization' - the latter spelled with a 'z', as if making it look American somehow gives it more credibility - while saying absolutely nothing at all, it has been a bumper year for many of Britain's top bullshitters.

Companies will need to continue to work hard going forward, according to Collingwood-Hancock. 'They must enhance their output while embracing the unique ethos of their employer and the esteemed heritage of the company,' he said.

'Otherwise they could face the possibility of widespread examination and re-evaluation of core competencies, followed by supply chain management optimisation and product portfolio rationalisation. Or getting laid off, as it used to be known.'

Sports Direct profits fall linked to having no staff at tills

Market analysts suspect that the 60% reduction in profits at Sports Direct may be related to them having no employees actually dealing with shoppers. Studies have shown that the skeleton staff are instead employed to stand on very tall ladders putting replica Premiership football shirts out of reach, and fold up piles of T-shirts for the public to unfold again.

Retail gurus have especially noticed a drop in profits from footwear sales, despite an increase in the number of people seen standing in stores with one shoe off holding a bright green football boot in the air, desperately looking for assistance.

'We did hear about one shop where there was reportedly a member of staff behind a till at one point,' explained Brian Wilson, senior market analyst at Hill-Brown Capital.

'But we understand that the employee was just trying to explain the company's "No Refunds Under Any Circumstances Whatsoever" policy to a disgruntled customer who had somehow managed to buy something.'

Yellow Pages rebrands as Yellow Page

Yellow Pages has decided that the time has come for a rebranding, to fit in with its contemporary slimline look - and will henceforth be known as 'Yellow Page'. Once a breezeblock sized tome and the chief source of information, the publication has been steadily shrinking ever since the dawn of the Internet.

As well as cheaper production costs, the new Yellow Page will be much easier to fit through a letterbox, and also much easier to tear up, allowing 95% of the UK population to be able to claim that they are incredibly strong.

'Inevitably with our move to one side of A4 we have to sacrifice some of the text,' says Yellow Page's CEO Ruth Jones, 'so the plan is simply to put the address of our website in 36 point and leave it at that.'

Shock as everything goes in 'Everything must go' sale

History was made in Exeter High Street yesterday morning, when Avis Bentley purchased the final item of stock in Edinburgh Woollen Mill's 'Mega everything must go sale'.

Bentley made the final purchase, a fuchsia cashmere cardigan, on a visit with friends from the Tiverton Women's Institute. 'We popped in there on our way to visit the cathedral and grabbed the last few items left,' she told a BBC news team. 'My friend Mavis had the last box of Highland shortbreads and I got the cardie.'

'It was like a plague of grey-haired locusts descending upon the place,' said shop manager Irene Wilson. 'We've had all sorts of sales in the past: stocktaking sales, refit sales and, of course, 'Everything must go' sales, but we always had plenty of stock left over, which we put into store ready for the following sale a week or two later. Perhaps really getting rid of the lot was down to the use of the word 'Mega'.

'Deep dive' actually a Google search

One of your colleagues, who had indicated that they had undertaken a 'deep dive' to fully investigate a topic, has basically done some rudimentary cut and pasting from the first few entries from a Google search, it has emerged.

Mike Jones, 44, head of regional pricing strategy at your company, highlighted in a recent team 'pulse' meeting the need for a thorough analysis of potential price points for the new KP216 model or whatever it is you are launching next month, and immediately took ownership of the deliverable, arguing he was well suited to 'ride herd'.

'It was the right seat on the bus for me, and I've swept the shed,' Jones confirmed to you and assembled colleagues in the follow-up meeting today. 'I've peeled the onion right back and done a full meta-analysis. You can see from the swim lanes in this Excel sheet how this will now play out.'

'Time for everyone to paddle on both sides now,' continued Jones, as your team shuffled out of the meeting room. 'There'll be a few rooster calls over the coming days, and we'll all be eating Al Desko for the foreseeable.'

Northern Rail reduced to one stationary 5,000-carriage train

Northern Rail has revealed radical plans to deal with timetable disruption today, with the announcement that it will now just place a single, completely stationary 5,000-carriage train on the tracks between Preston and the Lake District, leaving commuters to walk through the train themselves to get to their ultimate destination.

'You can get on at your usual station and stroll through the carriages at your leisure, enjoying the excellent scenery and the interiors of our classic 1970s rolling stock,' said a spokesperson.

'We won't actually need any drivers, but we are pledging to employ staff to sell customers Kit Kats and cups of tea. They'll be in carriage 1842 which is located just outside Oxenholme.'

'Journey times will inevitably increase by a few minutes,' admitted the spokesperson. 'Preston to Lancaster will take approximately five hours for a reasonably fit 30-year-old woman walking at a brisk pace, rising to 35 hours for a clinically obese 55-year-old man, as he will have to edge through the carriages sideways-on.

'Unfortunately, since the trains are stationary, passengers will not be able to use the toilets at all,' he continued. 'However, since this has been the default for Northern Rail commuters for many years now anyway, we don't anticipate any problems.'

IN OTHER RELATED NEWS:

Religious right to reject 'sinful' moneylending, capitalism to end
Panic buying as stocks of common sense run out
Commemorative 50p coin now worth 49p
UK credit rating lowered to 'Clueless'
Bank of England Governor praised for Sterling work
Highly qualified migrants to be reclassified as 'offshore investments'
Greendale no longer has its own postman, Royal Mail confirm
UK Steel returns to the Iron Age
HMRC relocates to Panama
Chancellor owes Littlewoods catalogue £25 billion
Greek credit rating identified as new pen
'This is not a drill,' trainee B&Q staff told
Cuadrilla furious that they've chosen to dig in an earthquake zone
Camelot £3 million fine rolls over for another week
Yorkshire-only merger of eBay and Gumtree creates eBay-Gum
Black Friday 'was dry run for Zombie Apocalypse'
Lion counter has pride in his job
Publishing of exponential graphs grows exponentially
Banksy asks for bailout before he goes to the wall
Decision to move Marmite HQ to Netherlands polarising opinion
East Coast Railway franchise found on Ebay
Interest rate falls as public show record lack of interest in Budget
Dyslexic millionaire donates his celery to charity
China warns not using Huawei transmitters 'would send a very bad signal'
Oxfam cancel contract with Durex - split inevitable
'Happy Days' actor charged over multi-million dollar Fonzi scheme
Swiss travel company slammed for not explaining 'refreshing euthanasia breaks'
UK credit rating reduced to 'Pay As You Go'
Striking male prostitutes to down tools
Greek cheesemakers say Euro bailout a 'feta compli'
Dignitas vows revenge on man who left bad review on Tripadvisor
Financial crisis deepens - AA Milne downgraded to just A

CHAPTER SIX:

James Corden asked to fake his own death (and other Celebrity news)

Various Artists, world's biggest album-selling band, to split

Dave Dee, Dozy, Beaky, Mick, Titch, Stills, Crosby, Hall, Oates, Emerson, Lake, Palmer, McGuiness Flint, Ernst, Young Gifted and Black and White Minstrels are to split, closely followed by the Isley Brothers, the Pointer Sisters, the Carter Family and Bachman Turner Overdrive.

Known in the music business simply as 'Various Artists', the supergroup boasts more album releases than any other band. Some members will fragment to form solicitors' practices, while others will retire together.

'We just became too big,' said band leader Dave of Dave Dee, Dozy etc. 'It became increasingly hard to define our style. At one point we tried to decide on a single name, but The Jackson Five insisted it should be The Jackson Five, and as there were 327 of us at that time, we couldn't agree.

'We only toured once, in the seventies, and even back then we routinely outnumbered our audiences. At the end of each gig, the bit where each artist got a namecheck and took a bow went on till the following day.'

Vanilla Ice regrets 20-year backlog after boasting 'If you've got a problem, I'll solve it'

It has emerged that rap star Vanilla Ice has spent decades problem-solving after a rash promise made in his Number 1 hit 'Ice Ice Baby', left him snowed under with requests. Complained Vanilla: 'At first I thought it was a joke when a little girl wanted me to find her cat. I told her to scram, but then she came back with a lawyer. It's been non-stop ever since.'

While most of the problems he has been called upon to solve have been minor, Ice has been thrust into international affairs, most notably in the aftermath of the Iraq war in 2003.

'The White House called, saying, "We've got this Iraqi army and we don't know what their loyalties are. We heard you solve problems. Solve this one." I just said, "Hell, just disband the army and let 'em keep the guns. What could go wrong?" They weren't happy but part of the deal legally is they have to follow the advice so, you know, that happened.'

Ice did try to make money from the promise, selling merchandise under the brand 'Ice'll Fix It' and offering big metal badges to those that he helped, until 2011 when he unaccountably stopped using it.

Journalist trapped inside Adele's anus

At least one member of the music press and upwards of a dozen photographers are thought to have gone too far in trying to ingratiate themselves with international pop star Adele, and may have disappeared up her awarding-winning rectum. Friends fear that they may have inadvertently entrapped themselves with a series of fawning interviews cunningly disguised as suppositories.

One journalist declared, as he emerged bleary-eyed from Adele's lower intestine: 'It was hellish. All I asked was: did she think she was the greatest human being of all time? And the next thing I know, I'm up to my neck in poorly digested ballads and covered in sweetcorn.'

Missing for sixty days, presumed dead, the journalists will have to adjust to life outside of the UK's most successful female recording artist. For some, it may be difficult to relinquish their sycophantic ways and the comfort of her derrière.

There have also been concerns that James Corden might decide to interview Adele, but fortunately 'he was too busy' disappearing up his own arse.

Thomas the Tank Engine slams Ringo in tetchy rant

Speaking from the sidings at Sodor, Thomas the Tank Engine has expressed his anger at Ringo Starr's knighthood: 'I did all the bloody hard work on that show, being a good little engine. All he had to do was turn up and read off a script. It's only because he was in The Beatles he got the gig in the first place.'

The news is set to rub further salt into the wounds for Thomas, who in recent years had to watch fellow characters Percy and Gordon enjoy considerable post-show career success with appearances on 'Strictly Come Chugging' and 'I'm an Engine, Get me Out of Here'.

The iconic engine went on to complain bitterly of multiple retakes on set as the Octopus's Garden star repeatedly fluffed his lines and took interminable drug-induced 'comfort breaks' during shooting. This follows the award of an OBE to author Reverend W. Awdry, known by everyone as 'The Fourth Engine'. Thomas saw this as a kick in the buffer-stops.

Prince Harry to split with Tequila

Following weeks of speculation, Buckingham Palace has announced that Prince Harry has split with long-time partner Tequila. Over the past few years Tequila has been a constant companion for the young royal, despite claims that the glamorous Mexican brought out the worst in him.

Rumours that Harry had slept with Tequila seemed to be confirmed when they were snapped lying motionless in a gutter together. But the pressure of always being in the public eye obviously put a strain on the relationship as Harry found himself constantly being expected to walk in a straight line or just stand up.

After one last night with Tequila, Prince Harry was said to be suffering from a powerful headache, dehydration and intense nausea, and asked to be left alone, as he swore that he and Tequila were definitely finished.

An anonymous source from Highgrove commented: 'He always says never again in the morning, but then he remembers all the good times. They'll be back together before the pubs close.'

North Korea behind all one-star reviews

North Korea has decided to undermine Western civilisation by leaving bitchy reviews for all media products. To his own people the Supreme Leader Kim Jong-un is known as the 'One Star Fairy', which is not a slight on his lack of military experience.

With a series of snarky comments, Pyongyang has unfairly reduced Michael Bay's 'Transformers' movies to: 'A cacophonous blend of mind-numbing explosions, computer-generated nonsense and clumsy racial stereotypes', completely misrepresenting a series of subtle Edwardian dramas, exploring the bittersweet nature of the human condition, through a series of metallic groans and thuds.

A spokesman for the CIA said: 'Not every bad review is down to North Korea, as James Corden's agent will confirm. In fact, the majority of negative comments about 'One Direction' can now be attributed to Taylor Swift and a 13-year-old from Slough, called Kim.'

Gandhi and Mandela come to blows over hypothetical ideal dinner party

Police were called to a hypothetical dinner party last night, after Gandhi and Nelson Mandela resumed hostilities. Tensions continue to run high between the two top guests on the ideal dinner party guest circuit.

'It was the usual story,' said Oscar Wilde. 'Everyone was exchanging profound, witty and entertaining insights around the dinner table in a three-bed Barratt Home in Tewkesbury, when it became obvious that Mohandas had sunk one Merlot too many.

'He starts winding Nelson right up for using the wrong dessert spoon; next thing the racial slurs and insinuations about their mothers' sexual promiscuity are flying around. Elvis tried to hold Nelson back, but he smacks Gandhi right on the slaphead.

'Shakespeare and Mae West tried to diffuse the situation with a game of Spin the Bottle, but it was too late. Let's hope another night in the cells straightens them out before tomorrow's fondue in Dundee, and Nelson spares us all the usual histrionics when he's released on bail.'

Sting admitted to pretentiousness rehab clinic

Diminutive Geordie megastar Sting has been undergoing emergency rehab. Fears began building when he announced his next project was to be a ten-disc CD set of tone poems intended as an homage to James Joyce's 'Ulysses', with one piece being a forty-minute orchestral suite in three movements.

Dr Marvin Schultz, an expert in Acute Advanced Pretentiousness, said: 'AAP is a complex disorder and should be nipped in the bud. Look no further than Bono or Kanye for proof of what it can lead to if not treated early.

'We're hopeful that once Sting's treatment is complete, and even though he's still adamant about going into the studio, thankfully it will be just to make a regular album ... well, 'thankfully' is probably not the word, but trust me, it could be worse.'

Statue of Margaret Thatcher to be pre-vandalised

A broken child-sized milk bottle in one hand, a Hitler moustache and a tiny Michael Gove peeping out of her handbag, crying his eyes out. These are just some of the ideas that have emerged in a competition to 'pre-vandalise' a controversial statue, to be erected in Grantham, Lincolnshire, in unironic honour of the Iron Lady.

Sculptor Jenny Smythe said that pre-vandalisation was the only way to deter people from adding their own adjustments to the statue.

'The council has discussed a barbed wire fence round the statue, or a permanent detail of the police officer from the West Yorkshire force who acted as her political cadre during the miner's strike,' said Smythe, who has also sculpted Robert Mugabe, the Kray Twins, Harold Shipman and Simon Cowell.

Smythe said her favourite idea was to show Mrs Thatcher covered in human excrement, but it's understood there was an objection from Conservative HQ, saying that even after her death 'The lady's not for turding'.

Bruce Forsyth: 'I was an MI6 agent - an MI6 agent, I was'

It has long been rumoured that veteran entertainer Sir Bruce Forsyth has led a double life and this was officially confirmed today. 'You don't think he got that gong for his fumbled autocued ad libs, do you?' asked an espionage expert today.

'He travelled extensively, then passed messages back to British Intelligence on mainstream TV using carefully constructed code phrases,' alleges a former MI6 operative.

'"Nice to see you, to see you..." was a message to indicate that he'd left information in a dead letter box. "Let's meet the eight who want to generate" was code for "There's a dead Russian agent in my dressing room, neck snapped with my bare hands" and "Good game, good game" was his way of playing for time while he worked out how to unzip Anthea Redfern's dress using his magnetic watch.'

Critics point out Forsyth's penchant for snappy dressing as evidence that the allegations are untrue. 'Who can believe someone wearing a tuxedo and attracting improbably beautiful women could be a British agent?' asked one doubter. 'And his propensity to hang around card games - surely no British spy would be foolish enough to draw that kind of attention to himself?'

Hostage negotiators strike deal to free X-Factor contestants

'We've reached a deal with the British Government to release the X-Factor contestants from their contractual obligations,' Simon Cowell's chief henchman has confirmed. 'They were never held against their will and we do this as a gesture of goodwill.'

The contestants emerged from a blacked-out windowed bus, blinking and cowed, and rushed into the arms of their awaiting loved ones. It is thought the deal let Cowell keep Dermot O'Leary. At present Olly Murs has disappeared – but nobody really cares.

'It was a living hell,' said one. 'Cowell would have us singing and dancing for 18 hours a day with little breaks. He even kept our toenail clippings and urine for some reason. If we didn't do what he told us, he said he would make us work with Cheryl or bring back Louis Walsh. We were terrified.'

The selection criteria for next year's venue will focus on improving X-Factor's human rights record. Top of the list is North Korea.

LBC replace Farage with Romanian/Bulgarian immigrant double act

'The Ivanka and Alexandru Show', a phone-in where callers are encouraged to share positive experiences of multiculturalism, will take the slot on LBC previously filled by former UKIP leader Nigel Farage, who is expected to explode at the news.

'We're excited about this new direction for the weekday evening show, although there is a very real danger that the first caller may be Nigel himself to complain,' said an LBC Radio spokeswoman.

'If that does happen, then we've told Ivanka and Alexandru to just talk loudly over the top of whatever he's trying to say and then cut him off. I'm sure he'll respect that technique.'

Shock as celebrity names son 'John'

An as yet unidentified celebrity has caused amazement by calling his newborn son. John, it has emerged. Had the baby been a girl, it would reportedly have been called Doreen.

'At first, we were going for Marshmallow, Kilimanjaro or Pelham 123, but we wanted something a bit unusual,' the celebrity said. 'Then out of the blue we thought: "Why not John or Doreen?" It was a really exciting moment, a sort of epiphany. We liked the name Epiphany too, by the way. I just hope people don't think we're being pretentious.'

Victoria and David Beckham are said to be devastated. 'People are free to give their kids what names they like,' Mrs Beckham said. 'But if our friends are going for fancy names like 'John', it's going to make names like 'Harper Seven' sound completely ridiculous and make parents a laughing stock.'

PM surrenders Ant and Dec in EU negotiations

National treasures Ant and Dec are to be given to the EU as part of a deal which will see Number Ten secure key concessions on welfare payments to immigrants. The move comes after Polish delegates stormed out of negotiations when the Prime Minister's opening offer of the Chuckle Brothers and Bonnie Langford backfired.

The offer also appears to have secured the backing of the Czech Republic and Slovakia, where re-runs of kids' programme Byker Grove still regularly attract over 20 million viewers and the duo's birthdays are celebrated as national holidays.

The deal follows earlier reports that the Prime Minister was humiliated by other EU leaders and forced to dance while delegates threw the remnants of their buffet lunch at him.

'It was a degrading spectacle,' admitted German delegate Willy Ackerman. 'On the other hand, if he wants this deal as much as he says he does then he should be prepared to dress up in *lederhosen* and dance to the Birdie Song while I throw roast beef and caramelised onion vol au vents at him. He didn't look happy, maybe he would have preferred the pork.'

Beeping Smoke Alarm wins Brit Awards

Before being nominated for Best Newcomer at this year's Brit Awards, Beeping Smoke Alarm (BSA) had been quietly gathering dust in the spare bedroom for the last two years. It only came to the attention of talent scouts after its heavy-duty battery gave up the ghost, creating a whole new post-dubstep sound that has sent clubbers into ecstasy.

'To truly appreciate BSA's *oeuvre* you need to be lying in a darkened room, suffering from insomnia and with a lightly sleeping newborn,' said one music critic. 'That's the moment when BSA really gets under your skin. The next thing you know, you're jumping out of bed, armed with a polo mallet.'

Despite being disconnected from the mains, BSA has maintained its shrill intermittent noise, just like Coldplay. Its management has refused to be drawn on the rumour of collaboration with a global pop star, but a high-pitched beeping sound has been heard from Miley Cyrus' knickers.

Frostbite claims final piece of Sir Ranulph Fiennes

The last piece of Sir Ranulph Fiennes has finally fallen off due to extreme frostbite. The 68-year-old Victorian throwback had been attempting to cross the frozen aisle in Aldi when his last remaining appendage succumbed to the icy conditions.

Despite several attempts to reattach the necrotised member by the budget supermarket's crack first aid team, Sir Ranulph finally admitted that his exploring days were over.

'It's extremely disappointing,' said the mad old adventurer. 'After 18 months of preparation and extensive training from the cold meat section of Lidl to the chest freezers of Iceland, to come this close is a most distressing end to my magnificent career.'

Scientists are hoping to take DNA samples from the deeply perma-frosted chunk, in the hope that one day, cloned copies can be reproduced for sale in the form of dinosaur shaped, breadcrumbed nuggets.

Record label stunned by chart failure of self-deprecating rapper

Hip-hop debut album from modest, grammar school-educated London rapper Com P. Tenz has failed to ignite the charts.

The high-profile new release '38MPG' - named for the fuel efficiency of his Ford Focus Estate - had been expected to provide a refreshing alternative to the relentless extremes of urban grime and hip-hop bling in modern rap, and give a voice to unheard middle-class youth, who otherwise would have turned to Leona Lewis.

Meanwhile Com P. Tenz's handling of hip-hop sexual politics also garnered plaudits thanks to the song 'Settled', where he boasts about his long-term relationship with his girlfriend, the success of which is attributed to the fact he 'loves her so much, never calls her a ho, and puts the loo seat back down every time that I go.'

Label executives are confident sales will ignite, following comments from a rival for the suburban rap crown, Emaness, that risk sparking a high-profile rap war.

The outspoken emcee has questioned Com P. Tenz's credentials and claimed he is actually 'a dreadful, petty criminal from a sink estate, with a string of convictions for sexual assault and gun crime'. In response, Com P. Tenz has tetchily threatened to 'pop a stiffly worded letter to the Daily Mail in his ass'.

Innuendo-free Nigella's Christmas Kitchen for celibate viewers

'We have decided to 'sex-down' Nigella Lawson's show in response to complaints from celibate and asexual viewers,' said a TV spokeswoman. 'This audience demographic says its enjoyment of the programme is frequently spoilt by Nigella's smouldering glances as she sensually pouts around the kitchen purring sultry comments, such as 'dessert is not dessert without a good cream filling'.'

In the new toned-down show, the domestic goddess will appear wearing a shapeless plain brown overall in place of her trademark plunging neckline sweater, so familiar to her many fans who salivate as she produces her tasty titbits.

'The Christmas dinner won't have the 'usual trimmings',' continued the spokeswoman, 'and there definitely won't be any chocolate truffles for Nigella to slowly pop into her mouth after licking her lips in anticipation. Not that viewers would see anything anyway, as Nigella will be wearing a balaclava to go with the sunglasses which producers have deemed necessary to hide her come-hither eyes.'

For the main course, producers have deliberately selected a non-succulent turkey, which cannot under any circumstances be described as 'moist'. It is expected that the bird will be saved a stuffing of any kind, and any pre-watershed mention of its legs or breasts will be discreetly bleeped out.

The news has been met with distress by Ms Lawson's supporters. Said one: 'If the BBC wanted to make a sex-free cookery programme, they should have hired Delia Smith, then no one's Yorkshire puddings would rise.'

Excrement found in pub toilet 'might have been from the Beatles'

'We know the Beatles passed through here in 1962 and later in 1965, it's highly likely they could have left a log after calling in for a cup of tea,' said the publican at the Fox and Geese in Bolton, holding a five-inch long turd encased in a Branston Pickle jar up to photographers.

Cleaners at the pub insist the turd was not there when they cleaned the toilets yesterday morning, suggesting that the faecal matter may be of a more recent origin. Said one: 'We often get floaters in here that won't flush, sometimes I have to pick them out with my bare hands and pop them back in the kitchen to be served again.'

Auctioneers are suggesting that if the turd belonged to Lennon, McCartney or 'the other one that died', it could command up to ten thousand pounds at auction: 'Obviously, turds from Ringo are less rare – as he could pump one out practically to order, particularly if he had an album in the offing.'

Keanu Reeves' next movie to feature 'acting double'

Hollywood producers confirmed today that Keanu Reeves' next blockbuster will be the first to feature a specialist who will stand in for the A-lister in sequences deemed too ambitious for an actor of his talent.

Universal Pictures has reassured fans that the star will perform his usual repertoire of running, fighting and monosyllabic grunts, but with a lookalike being brought in for scenes requiring his character to display emotion or intellectual depth.

'There's no doubt Keanu really set the benchmark with his portrayal of Ted in 'Bill and Ted's Excellent Adventure' – he did all his own acting, you know,' said producer Kit Maloney.

'But I think people fell into a trap of thinking that if he could do that, he could do anything. Keanu's received acclaim for his stunt work and innate ability to be manipulated by special effects, but there are some things best left to the trained professionals, like dialogue, humour and pathos. We'd hate to see his reputation get badly injured, or worse.'

Grand Old Duke of York cannot remember 10,000 men, or hill

In a television interview, the Grand Old Duke of York has defended the absence of specific figures or his inability to name the hill involved.

'I do have a recollection of an incline, that is certain,' he said. 'As a member of the royal family, we come into daily contact with anything from a gentle slope to a steep escarpment, so which hill it was is not certain.

'The only thing I can remember is having sex with an attractive teenage girl, possibly at the foot of the hill. Or possibly at the top. Or her bottom. Or half-way up, so to speak. But the 10,000 men? Could have been 10,000, could have been 9,500. I regret that it is hard for me to say the exact number.

'Perhaps we went to Pizza Express?'

'No, I don't want a flyer for your f*cking improv show,' Edinburgh man confirms

'I had to go to the High Street for a work thing,' said Donald Brook, an office manager from Edinburgh. 'I couldn't move for jugglers and overconfident Oxbridge twats singing their hilarious comedy songs and making their side-splitting observations about my shoes.

'And as for the theatre workshop group, who were begging me to go and see their three-hour, interactive, anarchic, romp about the menstrual cycle which got four stars from the Cumbernauld Gazette, I think I'll pass.

'There was a guy in his pants juggling chainsaws right outside Starbucks,' said Brook. 'If I turned up in the High Street in November just wearing my pants and chucking chainsaws about, I'd be spending the night in the cells, quite rightly. For some reason, it's fine to do it in August.

'Anyway, I don't have any real problem with the Edinburgh Festival; I just wish they wouldn't hold it in Edinburgh.'

Radio 4 dumping toxic smugness into nation's rivers

Britain's middle classes have gone into shock after revelations that Radio 4 has been secretly dumping thousands of tons of self-satisfaction into rivers and lakes all over the country, in what some are calling 'the worst environmental crime since Bill Oddie'.

'It turns out Radio 4's presenters and guests between them were producing such vast quantities of smugness that they simply couldn't pump it all out over the airwaves,' explained a DEFRA spokesman. 'Including the toxicity of Melvyn Bragg discussing Kierkegaard with a bunch of repressed academics, at nine o'clock in the morning.'

The Head of Programming has admitted that they have been dealing with unusually high levels of producer/presenter gratification, saying: 'I'm sure we would all agree: the demise of a few species of inedible freshwater fish and algae is a small price to pay for us being right about everything.'

Bob Dylan charged with historic crimes against music

A Grand Jury has laid criminal charges against Bob Dylan, specifically in respect of his harmonica playing on many early recordings.

Commented one BBC music journalist: 'I'm really not surprised, as in my view it is very long overdue. I mean Bob's a great songwriter but, jeez, his harmonica playing is even worse than listening to a tone-deaf concert pianist who's had his fingers smashed by the Mob attempting to play a Chopin *étude*.

'And to be honest his singing's not really much better either. I'd have included that too.

Kim Kardashian declared an Area of Outstanding Natural Booty

The Environment Agency has moved to preserve the features of Kim Kardashian so that they can be enjoyed by future generations. Her picturesque rear will now enjoy a heightened level of protection from unwelcome drilling, while remaining available for the extensive outdoor recreation that it was known for in its younger days.

Kardashian's badunkadonk, which is visible from space and has its own gravitational field, has become a popular attraction in recent years, drawing thousands of sightseers who come to enjoy the view and the uniquely undulating terrain. Its new status, officials argue, will ensure that planning regulations can limit development and prevent the landmark behind being despoiled by unsightly erections.

In future, visitors to Kardashian's panoramic fundament will be required to pay an entry fee which will contribute to the structure's upkeep. A treasury spokesman said: 'It's not cheap maintaining such a massive, over-exposed arse – or Kanye, as she will insist on calling him.'

Sherlock Holmes arrested for faking his own death

'Sherlock Holmes is being questioned on suspicion of wasting police time,' confirmed Inspector Lestrade of Scotland Yard. 'We're also investigating reported sightings of Professor Moriarty at the same location. At present we have to assume that he may not have died at the Reichenbach Falls either.'

The Ukrainian Government was not available for comment.

Boris Johnson wins Sports Personality of the Year

Prime Minister Boris Johnson has won the coveted Sports Personality of the Year Award, despite never playing any sport. Just days after his general election victory, followed by thinly veiled threats to break up or sell off the BBC, Johnson won an overwhelming 110% of the votes cast.

'Gosh, er, well this is splendid,' said Boris. 'I mean I did a bit of rugger at Eton, and tried the high wire once, but gosh, completely unexpected, read this speech out Boris, signed Dom.'

Suspicions were raised when Johnson also won the Strictly Come Dancing final without ever having appeared on the show. The BBC said it planned to defend its independence in a hard-hitting twelve-part documentary, congratulating Britain's – as yet unnamed - greatest living sportsman and ballroom dancer.

Thousands flee as Lloyd Webber announces return of Cats

Not since the Great Fire of 1666 have so many people abandoned their London homes so readily as the last few days, following the announcement of a revival of 'Cats'. One eyewitness reported seeing a father of three throw his young daughters into the Thames rather than expose them to the next Bonnie Langford.

The people of Coventry have already volunteered to burn their cathedral to the ground, provided Cameron Mackintosh promises not to bring the shows north of the Watford Gap.

One refugee clutching a ticket for 'The Book of Mormon' remarked: 'London survived the Blitz, but it won't survive seeing actors in furry unitards. Hitler may have bombed London, but 'Cats' has bombed everywhere.'

Arthur Negus found during filming of Antiques Roadshow

'I was amazed,' said Bill Redding, who discovered a long-lost Arthur Negus in an antique shop a few weeks ago.

'This old chap was there standing in a corner all alone. We felt so sorry for him that we asked the dealer how much he wanted. We shook on twenty quid and Arthur came home with us. Then Julie saw the Roadshow was coming to town, so we brought him in for a valuation.'

Show stalwart, Eric Knowles, said: 'There are still some tests to do in order to confirm provenance, but if this turns out to be Arthur, it will a real first for the show. He was a true national treasure, and up until now presumed deceased.'

Elvis impersonator fears 42nd birthday probably his last

As Robert Young enters his 43rd year, his commitment to faithfully mimicking his rock'n'roll idol Elvis Presley is visibly taking its toll. Determined to emulate Presley's last days, Young had scrupulously matched the King's pharmaceutical intake, pill for pill.

'The 26 stone was tricky, but then I discovered I could wash down 25 hamburgers a day using milkshake,' he said. 'It hasn't been easy, swallowing 47 tablets a day, what with the weird side effects and everything. I had to move next door to Boots - it's hard to walk any distance wearing a rhinestone-encrusted outfit three sizes too small.'

There are some minor advantages to being morbidly obese, with alarming sideburns: 'I don't get mobbed by hysterical female fans like in the old days,' he says. 'Mind you, I do sometimes get mistaken for the late Cyril Smith, which is a whole new problem in itself.'

Young now has the unenviable task of faking his own death. 'It's not being a recluse that will be difficult, but I'm not looking forward to sharing a room with Lord Lucan, Amelia Earhart and Andy Kaufman. What will we have to chat about?'

Dog from Churchill mauls toddler from Velvet Toilet Rolls

After an uneventful Lenor advertisement, viewers were shocked to witness the nodding, rabid bulldog from the Churchill ad launch a grisly attack on the suit-wearing toddler starring in it.

'We think the dog might have been agitated by that squeaking Russian meerkat, or those nauseating dolly-birds in the Sheila's Wheels Cadillac,' sobbed one witness. 'Suddenly it just went for the boy, growling "Aooh yesh" and foaming at the mouth.'

Fortunately, there was plenty of toilet roll around to staunch the bleeding and the child is expected to make a full recovery. The bulldog was deemed too irritating to save and has been put down.

Jeremy Kyle fails to sort out Henry VIII's love life

There was pandemonium in the Granada TV studios in Manchester after the filming of an episode of the Jeremy Kyle show, which centred on the complicated love life of Tudor despot Henry VIII.

Spanish-born Cath had contacted the show, complaining that Henry had left her for a much younger strumpet after nearly 20 years of marriage. The episode, entitled 'You Had Sex With My Dead Brother, That's Why God Won't Give Me Any Sons', is due to be aired next Wednesday.

'He finks I shagged Arthur to death, but he never touched me,' Cath told the show. 'And if you ain't married to me proper, why do you still come in stately procession to my chamber at least once a month? It's cos that flat-chested [BLEEP] you've been after since 1526 ain't giving you any, innit?'

Confronted by a hostile Kyle, Henry went on the defensive. 'My mate Wolsey said that verse in Leviticus – shut the [BLEEP] up – means you can't have sons if you marry your dead brother's wife.

You can [BLEEP] ask him. Well you can't, cos he died on the way back from York to get beheaded for cocking the annulment up, but that's the truth.'

Jeers and calls of 'Whore!' erupted as Henry's new girlfriend Anne strutted onto the stage, flashing her French learning at Cath, who had to be restrained from punching her in the stomacher.

After a few summary floggings, order was restored and Kyle revealed that the lie detector test proved Cath to be telling the truth. However, Henry defiantly said that his new mates Cromwell and Cranmer were going to sort it and those [BLEEP] Fisher and More had better not piss him off any worse or the monasteries would totally get done.

'Sometimes I can't make people do the right thing,' Kyle concluded. 'You go that way,' he told the sobbing Cath. 'Our team will help you find a nice nunnery. You two go the other way and Anne, please don't lose your head over him, he's not worth it.'

Some band you've never heard of set to headline some festival

The headlining act for some festival or other was formed in Washington in 2005, apparently. It has amassed a huge following in the UK and US by amalgamating thrash metal, dubstep and a bunch of other musical subgenres that are unlikely to mean anything to you anyway, so there's no point in detaining you any further with them.

'We are both privileged and delighted to have secured them for their only UK show of 2012,' declared promoter Melvin Benn to whoops of appreciation from a couple of NME journalists, who are apparently paid to give a crap about announcements like this.

'It's great news for their legions of fans, none of whom you have ever met. Plus, it's a strong message to any ageing music anoraks who still think that they're up to speed with current musical trends: "Stay the hell away and listen to your Oasis albums, grandad".'

The band completes the weekend line-up of illegible logos, unfeasibly pointy beards and impractical-looking body piercings – which are all designed specifically to make you realise that denying the onset of middle age is now futile, not that there have been any good bands since The Clash anyway.

Yeezys knitted by Kanye West's nan

It has emerged that Kanye West's signature shoe, the Yeezy, was first based on a doily crochet pattern. The designer trainer was not inspired by the LA music scene but was in fact a template for a striped bobble hat and matching scarf.

Instead of sweatshops filled with children, Yeezys are manufactured in care homes, where legions of octogenarians knit around the clock. Kanye's own grandmother confessed: 'He asked me for a pair of boots, but I thought he said booties.'

Later this year Adidas plans to release an edgy line of gangland themed mittens and hot water bottle covers. West himself has won a total of 21 Grammy Awards, one for each of the shoes his Grammy has knitted.

Queen joins BLM protest with early morning horse ride

Sources close to the Queen said that she wanted to send a message of support and solidarity to people of colour around the world through a Black Lives Matter horse ride at Windsor Castle. Wearing protective clothing and a silk face scarf inscribed with the message 'One Can't Breathe', the monarch was seen trotting around her 13-acre estate.

A royal correspondent confirmed: 'There was talk about taking the knee, but that's something everybody who has contact with the Royals is expected to do anyway. Her Majesty has been on the phone to Stormzy and there is a possibility of collaboration on a charity single.

'Prince Philip said he will be making his own announcement about racism, though we don't think it will involve any horse riding. Something about some Bernard Manning material and waving a shotgun around. Sounds delightful.'

Trump sues Trumpton

Stop-motion children's favourite Trumpton is under threat from the US President Donald Trump for using his trademarked name. Trump has turned litigious after his planning permission was blocked for a golf resort in neighbouring Camberwick Green.

Local windmill owner Windy Miller has been in dispute with Trump over the sale of land around Colley's Mill, and the Trump Corporation's aggressive tactics appear to have taken their toll on the normally affable Miller.

'It's terrible what they've done to Windy,' said the clerk, Mr Troop. 'He's a broken man. Now he spends his days getting wrecked on home brew cider and firing his shotgun at anyone who comes within 100 yards of his windmill.'

However, not everyone is hostile to the billionaire property developer. 'The people are fed up,' said local carpenter, Chippy Minton. 'Unless you're an immigrant or disabled they don't want to know, bloody do-gooders. Everyone knows there's too much immigration. We're going to build a wall around Trumpton and make Chigley pay for it.'

Fearne Cotton's record collection goes online

As of today, music fans will be able to browse legendary DJ Cotton's overwhelming collection of over seven records. 'There'll be information about all the records, including how highly Fearne rated the album,' explained a spokesperson.

'Cotton famously employed a meticulous five-star rating system, and every item in the collection was awarded the full five stars. Albums are accompanied by her additional superlatives such as 'mega', 'massive', 'most awesomest ever', 'cool' and 'really, really cool'.'

The electronic archive also features Cotton's hand-written notes for her searching interviews with celebrities. They include hard-hitting, penetrative questions, such as 'How many shoes do you own?', 'What's it like being so famous?' and 'Can I touch your hair?'

Noam Chomsky to host Total Wipeout & X-Factor

In a surprising move, the 91-year-old linguistics professor Noam Chomksy will be dominating Saturday night TV.

An BBC spokesman explained: 'We're thrilled to have Noam on board. We firmly believe that his ground-breaking theories of transformational-generative grammar and his searing indictments of US foreign policy will be the perfect accompaniment to a hyperactive PE teacher from Bedford hopelessly trying to bound across five giant, bright red balls like some form of demented human pinball machine.'

Chomsky was also delighted with his new role. 'I've been dreaming of this for ages. To be honest, all those papers on syntactic structures and writing complicated books that people never read but still strangely displayed prominently on their bookshelves was just a stepping-stone to getting the gig as the host of a Saturday evening light-entertainment show. It's going to be, like, totally sick.'

In his first outing as an X-Factor judge, Chomsky quickly made his mark. 'Your act is part of a propaganda state promoting a culture-ideology of comforting illusion,' he told one hopeful young girl, before adding, 'I'm saying yes.'

Chomsky then set about a teenage boy band, describing them as 'yet another example of pre-packaged ideological oppression whose lyrics systematically fail to demonstrate even a basic understanding of what happened to East Timor in 1975.' He paused for effect. 'But, I'm giving you a second chance - you're through to the next round.'

Not satisfied with attacking the acts, Chomsky then turned his critique on the audience, telling them: 'You are all complicit in a hegemonic construct designed primarily to keep you from questioning what is really going on in the world.' To which they all looked blank.

IN OTHER RELATED NEWS:

Max Clifford 'spinning in his grave'

Robert Mugabe declares himself the new Doctor Who

Teachers stage strike over Martin/Paltrow split

Guardian correction: Hendrix drowned in his own Vimto

All women stop shaving their legs now Clooney is engaged

World struggles not to tell Charlie Sheen 'I told you so'

Ken Dodd's funeral enters sixth hour

Patient cured by listening to opera puts it down to Placido Effect

ITV to launch Clove Island: Like Love Island but with more spice

TV mystery solved: Ant's the one wearing handcuffs

Casting for Weinstein biopic feared

Sir Cliff Richard furious after being named as member of anonymity
campaign

Netflix reveals only 53 people actually pay for the service

Topless pictures of Anne Boleyn published; search for head
continues

Nazis distance themselves from Katie Hopkins

Mick Jagger to leave body to science, face to World of Leather

Black Eyed Peas to cover Green Onions

Toby Young set to lose more friends and alienate even more people

Box of frogs nowhere near as mad as Bjork

Dimbleby quits Question Time without finding Any Answers

Cleese sues Fawlty Towers for making the rest of his career look
bad

Music world mourns continued life of Kanye West

Shit creek contractor has never 'actually' used paddle before

Imagining Boris's sex life causes pound to sink to 28-month low

Crossrail 'delay announcements' running to schedule

Asda re-package ice-cubes as Smart Price Botox

United Biscuits website stops using cookies

Man who was nervous about brewing his own beer now bottling it

Oxo shareholders celebrate as stock market closes at record high

Asda stops selling kitchen knives; Walmart still selling handguns

CHAPTER SEVEN

Cornwall 'real', apparently (and other Feature stories)

SOME FUN ALTERNATIVES TO DRAB SURGICAL MASKS:

Woman pretending to like podcasts terrified of being asked about them

Liz Morris, an avocado-loving millennial from Doncaster, is neither hip, nor cool, as she absolutely despises podcasts. 'The trouble is,' said the 32-year-old, 'podcasts form the basis of 89% of office conversation. The other 11% is taken up by photos of Barry from accounts' five adopted cats.'

Despite being a woman, whose womb is primed and ready to receive the maternal hot takes of broadcasting mummy bloggers, podcasts really aren't Morris's thing.

'It started harmlessly enough with me nodding enthusiastically to others,' said Morris. 'But now, when I go jogging, I've got my earphones in and I laugh occasionally to look like my life is being enriched by a self-aggrandising comedian with a mic in their bedroom, when really I'm listening to sweet, sweet nothing.

'I've also built an Anderson shelter in my garden and filled it with enough supplies to last me ten years. I've let the neighbours assume I'm preparing for Brexit, but really it's for the inevitable day when I get found out by someone asking me what my favourite episode of 'My Dad Wrote a Porno' is.'

Tributes to man 'who nearly cleared out his shed'

A memorial service was cut short yesterday after mourners ran out of interesting or noteworthy achievements to mention in their speeches.

The friends and family of Gerald Lubbock gathered at the magnificent, and as it turns out, rather oversized church of the Holy Spirit in Bray, Berkshire, to celebrate his life and work, but found themselves struggling to come up with anything worth mentioning.

'He was always saying he was going to get it together to learn about this computer lark,' recalled Lubbock's brother from the pulpit, with a wry smile.

'But he never got around to it, just as he never got around to anything really,' he added, as a slightly laboured affectionate chuckle echoed around the church.

The idea of a collection for local charities was abandoned when a number of mourners asked if they might be paid back the various debts that Gerald had incurred during his uneventful life.

'It's quite a common problem,' explained the vicar of Holy Spirit. 'Some people are just boring, lazy underachievers, and their memorials can prove a real headache.' In the end, he suggested they sang another couple of hymns to pad the service out a bit and then all went down to the pub.

'It's like, we had this idea of having a memorial service, but never really planned it properly and ended up not seeing it through,' said Lubbock's brother. 'It's what he would have wanted.'

96% of all presents 'a bit wrong'

A consumer survey has revealed that most presents are not what the recipient wanted and are often a deeply irritating starter kit for a hobby that will never be taken up.

'I got a set of watercolours last year,' said one Nottingham man. 'And some chisels for woodcarving, and a DVD about how to research my family tree. I have no intention of ever using any of them. My hobby is drinking beer and watching television.'

Another classic error is to gift 'the book with the tenuous link'. 'I go jogging before work in the morning,' said one Derbyshire housewife, 'So my husband bought me the history of jogging. What the hell do I want that for? It's bad enough having to do it without bloody reading about it as well.'

Perhaps the most misjudged present was the inappropriate and slightly offensive sex toy. 'My husband just gave me some pink fluffy handcuffs, a leather basque and KY jelly,' confessed one London woman. 'I said to him, really George, that's never really been our scene, has it? He went red and said, "Sorry, you've opened my present to your mother".'

Dogs resign as man's best friend

For centuries the two creatures have been the closest of pals with dogs providing man with companionship, warmth, love and affection, while humans reciprocated with a tin of dog food, the odd bone, a stick to fetch and occasional half-hearted patting. Now, the once uber-loyal dogs are switching their loyalties.

'It suddenly occurred to me,' said Fido*, a border collie. 'Real best friends wouldn't mind a few hairs around the place. Or if, once in a while, I happened to come in with muddy paws. I mean, it's no biggie is it, but my owner goes mental. I thought it was just me, but then I got talking to Rover* next door and it appears it's the same story everywhere.'

Dogs are currently reticent to reveal who their new best friends might be, though species under consideration are thought to include terrapins, marmosets and coypu. Friendly overtures towards cats were apparently met with a look of utter disdain.

 * - *Some of the names in this story have been changed*

Isle of Wight commemorates great string shortage of 1958

As a finale to the Easter celebrations, Isle of Wight residents are putting the finishing touches to the 50th anniversary of when the Isle had no means of securing brown paper parcels.

Thankfully, owing to a stringent programme of rationing and responsible wrapping throughout the island, a catastrophe was narrowly averted, and the event will now be celebrated with a series of street parties culminating in a full-scale carnival.

All police leave has been cancelled for the duration of the festivities. Chief Constable Eric Foster said: 'It's going to be very hard on me, as the only bobby on the beat. If things get out of hand, I may have to bring in a Community Support Officer from the mainland.'

Long-term resident Amy Chesterton was misty-eyed as she reminisced about the community spirit which emerged during the crisis. 'Brown paper and string were such an important part of our way of life, especially when standards started to drop after the war and people stopped using sealing wax.

'Some of the younger residents suggested using Sellotape, but we soon put a stop to that idea. We didn't fight two world wars to end up with sticky tape, and you couldn't have had Julie Andrews singing about brown paper parcels wrapped up in tacky transparent plastic. Now if you'll excuse me, I'm just going for a nice sit down, and then I really must get on. Easter's almost over already and I haven't even started to wrap my Christmas presents.'

Woman accepts afternoon snack without fuss

Office worker Hilary Williams shocked her co-workers this week by casually replying 'yeah, thanks' when offered a biscuit with her afternoon coffee. She then nonchalantly proceeded to eat it, without looking up or referring to it in any way whatsoever.

Sociologists claim that it is now considered impolite for a female office worker to accept a snack or treat at the first offer without saying 'Gosh you'll be the death of me', 'Oh twist my arm' or 'Well it is Friday!', which is a particularly popular response when it is not a Friday.

Hilary is now to receive in-house training to help her fit in to the modern office etiquette, which will include role-play situations in which she is finally persuaded to share a Jaffa cake with a fellow female worker on the grounds that she walked into work that morning.

The other half of the day will be spent on a course entitled 'Feigning interest in the achievements of your co-workers' children even if fourth in a wheelbarrow race for under-eights is clearly rubbish.'

Student describes pesto as 'transformative'

Having found a mysterious jar hidden behind some out-of-date kidney beans, student Martin Cabrera, 20, wowed his flatmates by combining such disparate ingredients as cheese, toast and rudimentary hygiene levels.

His housemate, Koki, waxed lyrical: 'Who knew such basilly-goodness could come from something so mouldy-looking?'

A modest Martin discussed his methodology. 'I just thought, why not use something other than ketchup. They say, you can't make an omelette without breaking eggs – although, does that mean you don't need to remove the shells?'

Not every creation by Cabrera has been an unrivalled success, with few forgetting the night of the infamous pickled herring blancmange. He said: 'I'm now wondering what other wonders the larder might contain.

'There must be a recipe that allows me to amalgamate custard powder with hummus from 2006. And Toilet Duck is a sauce, right? I tell you - I'm going to use pesto with everything. It should really spice up our Friday cocktail night.'

'Kind regards' goes from passive aggressive to outright lie

Scientists have discovered that over 90% of respondents who sign off emails are neither regarding us kindly, interested in the best of our wishes or intending to stay faithful. In most cases, the writer is only just restraining the urge to yell at the monitor with primal despair, while smearing it with their own excreta.

The reality is that nobody wants to write to you in the first place, and most of them would rather eat their own spleen than have to continue this disingenuous social nicety.

A sociologist explained: 'We're constantly mistaking shit for sincerity. How else do you explain Tony Blair? And those three x's at the end of the message are not kisses, they're merely blanking out an expletive.'

One correspondent confessed: 'I had considered just wrapping the letter around a dead fish and sending it recorded delivery. But in the end, I plumped for 'kind regards' – the 'yo momma' of farewells. I also sent the fish separately – as everyone still needs their omega-3 fatty acids.'

The kids with 'own brand' trainers – where are they now?

A new study has charted the drastic downturns in social status suffered by 'own-brand' wearing children during the 1980s.

Successful surgeon Jonathan Cooper recalls shunning a friend. 'I remember the day that William Cantwell first appeared with the Woollies trainers - 'Winfield four-strip' we used to call them. We all had the latest Adidas Samba and mocked him mercilessly.

'I caught him in the locker-room cutting the fourth stripe off, he'd written 'Addis Ababar' on them with a felt tip pen, but it was too late: the damage was done.'

The unemployed Cantwell explained: 'I begged Mum not to make me wear them, but she wouldn't listen. "Just as good as proper ones and half the price too," she would say. Don't get me wrong, I love my parents very much, they gave me a great upbringing, we never really wanted for anything - except, of course, proper brands.

'I've been finding things tough recently, with no job, girlfriend or future. I never went to university and I've not been able to find work. Ironically, I was offered a job at the Nike store, but I just couldn't bring myself to face the swoosh every day.'

Man outsources own life

In response to the bleak economic outlook, Barry Nugent from Canvey Island has taken the radical step of outsourcing much of his everyday existence in a bid to significantly reduce his overheads.

'It's really just a natural progression,' said Nugent. 'I've always paid for a service wash at the launderette and a cleaner to come in once a week, so why not pay those same people to stand in for me at dentist's appointments or my brother's wedding? I've even got a team in Delhi dealing with my post.'

The move towards outsourcing began when Nugent asked a neighbour to pop in to feed the cat while he was on a lads' week in Ayia Napa, and then never really cancelled the arrangement.

Soon after, he asked his newsagent if the paperboy could stop delivering the Daily Mirror each day and instead read it for him and provide a short summary of the main stories.

By freeing up so much of his time, Nugent is now able to invest extra effort in those activities he still insists on performing himself, such as eating and watching sport on the TV.

'My squash has improved no end since I got the county champion to turn out against my old schoolmate,' admitted Nugent. 'In fact, I've contracted out my sex life to a number of reputable online providers – right after my wife outsourced herself to my best friend Roger.'

Veteran re-enacts D-Day encounter with prostitute

D-Day hero Harold Wiggins, 89, has returned to the spot where 70 years ago he celebrated his part in the Allied offensive by embarking on a bit of how's-your-father with a grateful French strumpet.

To the cheers of appreciative locals, the octogenarian paratrooper ceremoniously approached a Bayeux massage parlour, Madame de Pompadour's, saluting the crowd before having his oats with one of the establishment's current crop of ladies.

'It was a profound experience for a 19-year-old, exciting and terrifying in equal measure,' Wiggins later reminisced. 'There was noise and confusion everywhere. You didn't know if you were going to make it out alive, but you just kept in mind that you had a job to do.'

'Celine' took the place of her grandmother, who 'gave him one for free' in 1944. She appeared shortly after, reassuring the press she had been 'well and truly liberated'.

Man still being studiously ignored in room full of elephants

Even hovering by the peanuts and desperately trying to make eye contact, Dave Harris is reportedly still finding it hard to get noticed by the largely elephantine occupants of The Room, despite wearing a plastic badge carrying the slogan 'Ask Me About Doughnuts'.

Harris refuses to give up. 'I can see the irony of the situation,' he said, 'and I know how they're feeling too. I imagine that's something the elephants won't forget in a hurry.'

Many of the elephants refused to acknowledge there was anything unusual at all taking place. Most avoided the subject, preferring to talk about more mundane issues such as ear sizes, prejudice between Indian and African elephants, and getting their baby's name down for a place in a good circus.

Guests 'singularly unimpressed' by toast rack

Despite offering the red-carpet treatment to visiting friends, Aisha and Matt Symonds have been given a less than glowing review for offering their guests reflexology, a suitcase stand whittled by hand and the use of 'the fancy towels'.

What should have been a weekend of bonhomie quickly became a critique of the host's lack of gluten-free meal options and their miserly hoarding of the Wi-Fi password. A disappointed Matt defended his decision to offer 'instant' rather than organically ground free-range coffee.

'We did everything we could to make them feel welcome. We laughed at their racist jokes, deliberately lost at Scrabble and I cleaned the loo – twice!' he said. 'We even provided a series of tasteful, but impractically small, shampoo bottles - stolen from a range of exclusive hotels.'

Guests Jermain and Sally complained: 'To be frank we don't really like them, so if we do visit, the least we can hope to get out of it is a more refined service. Where was the choice of cheese boards? Our own spare key? Moreover, the turndown service was practically non-existent.'

Aisha remarked: 'We were both very diplomatic; I didn't mention Jermain's second wife and Matt hardly ever stared at Sally's boob job. I took the dog's blanket off the spare bed and we even muted our sex noises. I almost don't feel guilty now for having pissed in the soup.'

Opening paragraph just repeats the headline, claims journalist

The opening paragraph of too many news stories basically repeats the headline, with one or two extra words added, a journalist has claimed. And the following sentence inevitably starts with the word 'and', he continued.

James Nibwit (28), who has been out of work since accusing his editor of shoddy writing, posted his damning indictment of modern journalistic standards on a satirical online news website.

'I'm fed up with clichéd styles of writing where invariably the subject of the story gets first mentioned in the third sentence, followed by his age in brackets, and then something he is supposed to have said is inserted round about the fourth sentence.

'If there's a swear word that will be given a paragraph all to itself, censored with asterisks, like we can't then tell what the offensive word is. The whole thing is a pile of f*cking crap.

'It's worse still on satirical news websites. There, every paragraph has to have a funny line it. Which this one doesn't.'

Majority of lottery winners still can't cash the cheque

'I won £1.2 million in June last year, and had to get the train to Watford to pose for the photo with the cheque,' complained William Masters from Bromsgrove. 'Then the trouble started.

'You try getting on a Virgin Pendolino with an oversized cheque. I didn't want to crease it, obviously, but then the ticket collector insisted I paid for the seat it was occupying. That was the end of the £43.50 I'd set aside for an egg sandwich.

'But the real problems came when I tried to cash the cheque. You have to feed them into a scanning device at your local branch - the one 40 miles from where you live - and they don't have an opening wide enough for the Camelot cheques. I'd given my job up as soon as I realised I'd won, now the cheque's stopping a draught in the living room and I'm flipping burgers in McDonalds.'

Camelot admitted that a lot of lottery winners did not cash their cheques. 'We've just assumed they don't want to lose that 'just won' feeling. If they prefer, we'll pay them in cash instead. We've only got ten pence pieces but if they return with their cheques and a wheelbarrow we'll happily do the deal,' said a spokesperson.

Man hospitalised after leaving New Year resolutions to last minute

Justin Harris of Harrow was rushed to hospital on New Year's Eve following a frantic but failed attempt to fulfil all his New Year's resolutions in the last few days of the year.

The IT consultant's initial tactic of doubling-up had enabled him to tick off 'putting more effort with the people around him' and 'giving something back to the community' in one go by sending Christmas cards he bought half-price at a local charity shop to relatives and work colleagues.

'OK, so they won't get them till next year,' he had admitted to his wife, 'but I sent them this year, so that counts.'

Tragedy finally struck as Harris began tinkering with his car as part of a goal of doing his own car repairs, when a copy of the Complete Works of Shakespeare he had been simultaneously speed-reading fell off the bonnet and knocked him on the head, causing him to kick away the jack supporting the car he was lying under.

However he noted that there was a silver lining as having both arms in traction meant there was no chance he would be keeping up his 20-a-day smoking habit as the year drew to a close, and the need for round the clock nursing care for at least six months after his return home, means he will be getting a good head start on his new goal of spending more time with his family.

Most emails now delivered by van

Environmentalists are increasingly concerned by the carbon footprint left by Britain's 4.4 million email couriers, it has emerged.

One businesswoman explained: 'Too often you get caught up in junk mail filters. At least with a van you can be sure that the message gets there – along with a sweaty guy wearing tracksuit bottoms.'

Unbeknown to most phone users, text messages are not sent by satellite but are generated by trained ants crawling over your mobile screen. Cashless sales are simply a St Bernard carrying a moneybox a few steps behind the oblivious credit card user. Broadband coverage is limited by the availability of maritime flag semaphores.

One online shopper complained: 'When I order something online, I expect the whole transaction to be virtual. What I didn't expect was a Ford transit to pull up, driven by a Nigerian Prince offering to enlarge my penis.'

Rich 'keeping their fingers crossed' on budget

Some of the country's richest people are nervously awaiting the result after five years of hardship in which they had to move large amounts of their wealth offshore. Will this budget finally favour the wealthiest for the first time, since every other one?

'People have expectations,' said one millionaire. 'Ostentatiously parading our wealth isn't cheap, you know. There's maybe 2% of the population shouldering the burden of having 99% of the wealth and paying maybe 5% of the total tax bill. That can't be right.'

The Chancellor was careful to point out that the budget will benefit all hard-working families in which every member over the age of five works full-time in multiple jobs. 'We value diversity, especially if they don't claim working tax credits,' he said.

Still no sign of Isle of Wight couple's luggage

Tension continues to mount for Arthur and Doris Nichols of Ventnor who are still without their wheeled travel bags, despite being in the second week of a package tour of the Algarve. More than 20 nations have been asked to help with the search, with fears that the Nichols will soon run out of fresh underwear.

While Doris has attempted to put a brave face on the holiday disaster, Arthur is struggling to cope without his special fungal cream. The fear is that the cheap polyester sheets, coupled with the hot Portuguese climate, could result in him reaching a crisis point of surreptitious flaking, followed by actual 'oozing'.

Until the crisis is resolved, all natives of the Isle of Wight have been advised to avoid foreign travel, foreign money and anything that looks suspiciously like it was made after 1950. Arthur Nichols has also reported the loss of a packet of fruit-gums, but he admitted that they could have fallen out his pocket on the way to the airport.

Pub landlord finally admits: 'I'm not much of an interior designer'

Much to the surprise of art historians, Malcolm Broadbridge of Shanklin's Red Lion has confessed that his eclectic decor was not acquired during five years at La Sorbonne but was, in fact, a job lot of bric-à-brac.

Customers were shocked to discover that Damien Hirst did not create 'Industrial farming equipment on rope', 'Brass doodads' or the eponymous 'Grainy photograph of village paedophile'.

The publican further admitted that the authentic charm of his oak-panelled urinal trough and his flock wallpapered tables, were just a cynical marketing device to lure people into purchasing drinks. Any attempt to create an aesthetically pleasing environment was purely coincidental - and very much in the beer-goggled eye of the beholder.

Throughout the decade, aesthetes had flocked to experience Broadbridge's audacious post-modern choices; be it the Tudor beams combined with 1970s light fittings, the wagon-wheel dartboard, or to experience the chef's salad in the 'Brutalist style'.

Broadbridge was philosophical, saying: 'I may have to hand back my Turner Prize, but I just felt guilty, I couldn't keep passing off a pile of shite as art. I don't know how James Corden does it.'

Cat leaves everything to old lady

In a touching, if controversial gesture, Barnaby the Cat has bequeathed all his worldly possessions to his owner. 'I knew I meant a lot to him,' said a stunned Marjory Wimslow, aged 86, 'but I didn't expect to get his favourite stick with a rope tied around it.'

The gesture has angered many who say that there are many more deserving causes for all these feline accessories. 'What about all the homeless kittens that are born?' said one neighbour. 'The Cat Shelter could have used an extra bowl.' When asked their opinion on the bequest, local cats gave a withering glance and looked away.

Owners of Barnaby's brothers and sisters may yet contest the legacy, claiming that it is not possible for a cat to employ a solicitor or actually write a will. Even if they succeed, they would only stand to gain a half-eaten box of Go-Cat.

In the meantime, Mrs Wimslow is having to adjust to her new life rich with cat food and feline eye-drops. 'It's completely ridiculous,' said one local. 'What use does an old lady have for flea powder and cat spray neutraliser? Oh, it's that old lady? No, well good call then.'

Top ten tips for avoiding the Royal Weddings

1. Be homeless

2. Be Prince Harry's biological dad

3. Volunteer for the first manned mission for Mars

4. Change your name to Reg E. Syde

5. Be a careers advisor

6. Disconnect your mains electricity supply

7. Be the great grandson of Kaiser Bill

8. Join a Tibetan Monastery

9. Choose Heroin

10. Live your life in the 21st century rather than in a feudal system from the Middle Ages

How to make your own Star Wars film

If you're a middle-aged man and concerned that the latest Star Wars is not meant for you, why not make your own? Follow our ten easy steps:

1. Spend months constructing an intricate story with a real sensitivity to the continuity of the original film. Ha, only joking! Just scribble Star Wars on top of any old pile of shit. Geeks will watch anything.

2. Make a note of the syllable noises someone makes while choking on a cocktail sausage. Right, that's how you name your characters.

3. Reduce the ambitious narrative down to a two-hour chase sequence that defies both logic and the basic rules of physics. Remember, empires are inherently evil – even if they appear to be the only ones investing in infrastructure, new technology or decent employee uniforms.

4. Distract the audience from any recycled plot devices by simply redesigning a light sabre.

5. Include a 30-minute explanation by some Jedi Master about the difference between The Force and implied consent.

6. Introduce a new cutesy life-form, in a cynical attempt to market the film to fans of Sylvanian Families. You might want to give your protagonist a spurious reason to land on a random planet. This will increase the number of action figures you can sell, and add 40 minutes to the film's running time.

7. All characters should care more about damage to droids than to sentient life-forms. No character must send a droid on a suicide mission, when a human can be sent in their place.

8. Ensure all bases have a fatal structural flaw, which is then available to view by anyone with a 1960s version of CAD.

9. By the end of the film there must be just as many Sith and Jedi as you started with. Not to maintain the Balance in the Force but the Balance in the Studio Chequebook. This is the franchise that must never die. The Last Jedi? Yeah, right!

10. Repeat *ad infinitum*.

Lovechild of a senior royal? Claim your regal inheritance, now!

Due to unbecoming sexual misbehaviour by senior royals over several decades returning like last night's foie gras, more and more common folk are claiming lovechild status and pursuing their rightful inheritance of royal thrones, titles and tickets for major sporting events.

A landmark ruling proving a 51-year-old woman is the daughter of the ex-King of Belgium has set a legal precedent. DNA identification technology is scientifically paving the way for titular claimants to inherit more than just odd-shaped facial features and rare blood disorders. So, what about you? Answer yes to some of these questions and you may have a claim:

- Do you have blue blood, or are you just cold because your power supplier has folded?
- Have you slipped up at 3 a.m. in a kebab shop and ordered pheasant?
- Is your social media profile picture a Pit Bull rampant set against quarterings of the 'Big Four' supermarket logos?
- Do you occasionally self-refer using 'oneself', instead of 'myself' and 'us'?
- Was your mother serving Pimm's at a palace garden party when a senior royal asked if she would care to see his 'cherished oak', only for him to leave without the courtesy of brushing the loose bark from her cheek?

If yes, then call our claims hotline. Also, if you own hats, you're more than likely the by-product of royal clackers. Mr X from Queensland has currently started legal proceedings in the High Court of Australia to prove he is the child of Prince Charles and Camilla. Are you too? Maybe we all are?

To prevent further widening of the gene pool by riff-raff, future royals will be grown in artificial wombs in Switzerland. So, hurry, make a claim, NOW!

What if James Joyce had been hired to write Donald Trump's speeches?

Something. Anything. A beautiful thing. So beautiful. It could be big, really so big. Huge. A great big wonderful beautiful thing. Just the biggest. And the beautifulest. Bigly. With good people. Such good people. Our people are wonderful, aren't they? Yeah they're good. So good, yes they are. You know it, folks. They're tremendous. Just so fantastic. FACT.

Wow! Do you agree? Yeah, I bet you do. Hey, get that guy outta here. How did he get past security? He's not a good guy. He's terrible. Just awful. No good at all. So bad. Matter of fact he's the worst. Yeah, he's definitely the worst. A lotta people tell me so. They say to me, that guy's the worst. He's a bum. Such a bum. Do we want a bum like him in here, folks? Do we? No, you bet we don't. Get him the hell outta here. Do you agree? Yeah! So long, loser. You're SAD!

Fantastic. We're doing a fantastic job. Just so fantastic. Everybody says so. Just ask them. They tell me all the time. I've got much wisdom yet there's a witch hunt on Donald Trump. As a matter of fact, the biggest in political history. Get Trump, they say. They-want-to-get-me. Can you believe that? Well don't worry, they won't get me because they can't.

I don't get much credit for all this good stuff I'm making happen, but [sighs] that's OK. I'm used to that. I can live with it.

Bad places, some real bad places. There's a guy who can take you to a bad place and leave you stranded there. You'd be on your own, just stranded. All alone. Lonesome. That wouldn't be good. It would be bad. Just so bad. Give that guy the bum's rush. Get him the hell outta there. He's a schmuck. Do a deal with some other guy. You'd be great together. He likes you, he told me. He's my friend. You'd have fantastic numbers. Wow, so big. Huge numbers.

I have a magic wand. Well-known fact. All I have to do is wave it and amazing things happen. Great things. They're the most incredible things and I make them happen. Yes folks, Donald Trump makes stuff happen. He really does.

Wrote a book once. A great book. Did well too. Sold a lot of copies. Just so many. Amazing number of copies. Biggest best seller ever. Check it out. It's just so fantastic. Truly incredible! God bless America.

Isle of Wight tracing app is a man ringing a bell shouting 'unclean'

An NHS app aimed at limiting the spread of Coronavirus is being trialled on the Isle of Wight, alongside transistor radios, the typewriter and toilets that flush - although the most effective way for the islanders to lower death rates is to stop burning witches.

The app itself will involve leeches and being dunked in the village pond. Those infected will be expected to carry a bell at all times, with a sign saying '20% off a family ticket for Blackgang Chine'.

George Wright, a VCR repairman from Ventnor, expressed his concern, saying: 'It's all very well the Government telling us to use social distancing, but how are we expected to visit the local apothecary to get our mercury and arsenic potions?'

The island's plague doctors offered this advice: 'If you're stuck at home, you can easily make a poultice from cow dung and powdered unicorn horn. Try to avoid other people, as they may have been exposed to the 21st century. At all times, cover your face with a Mummers mask. And wash your hands – only kidding – soap is the work of the devil!'

Wigan sends pie to Mars

'The ingredients for perfect pastry have been mined in Wigan for thousands of years,' said Eric Smith, Chief Pastrophysicist at WASA (Wigan And Standish Aeronautics).

'Now, those very same ingredients have been discovered on Mars, therefore as proud Wiganers we feel it's our duty to mine Mars on behalf of the human race. The fact that we're getting there before any other north-west borough council is of scant consequence.'

All edible parts of the spacecraft are made from raw triple-enriched Spacetry, the highest density pastry in existence. The spacecraft's hull is carefully laminated using very thin layers, *millefeuille* style, and encased in a one-way heat transfer foil tray, like a pie.

Designed to be eaten from the inside out, each layer contains a Pastronaut's daily nutritional allowance of vitamins, minerals and flavourings incorporated to reflect a five-year calendar of meals. Friday's layer will be fish flavoured; two layers later will be slightly thicker, containing a fry-up and a Sunday roast.

The main rocket is in essence a tall, slim, upside-down pie, full of fuel but no meat. The fuel is a combustible high-octane variant of traditional meat pie juice, which in the consumable fuel tanks will stay at the traditional near-boiling point for its entire use. The pie-hole at the rocket's base is precisely skewered for maximum thrust with the edging channelled to achieve optimum lift but still look appetising.

Due to the density and weight of the spacecraft, nicknamed 'Sue T', it's estimated it will take four hours to clear the launch tower and three days to escape Earth's atmosphere. It will then proceed towards the Sun. Utilising its gravitational field the craft will perform a juice-saving slingshot manoeuvre to Mars.

Calculations using Hollywood's inverse square law of thermopienamics will enable the extremely volatile solar atmosphere to begin carefully cooking the craft, which will rotate around its long axis to ensure an even bake. After leaving solar orbit the craft will slowly continue cooking for the entire nine-month flight, emitting steam internally to be captured for heat and sterile drinking water.

Smith added: 'In conclusion, there is a strong commercial aspect to this endeavour, but essentially we're doing it for the good of the human race. Apart from Warrington and Widnes, they can go f*ckin' whistle.'

'Twas the night before Brexit (probably around December 2026)

'Twas the night before Brexit and all through the House

Of Commons, no sex occurred. No hand down a blouse

The stockings were hung by the chimney with care

With Gove hung by the neck and the treasury bare

The voters were nestled all snug in their beds

With dreams of border control, stuck in their heads

And Ma with her Leave poster and I in my cap

Had blamed the dark-skinned ones for all of our crap

When out of UKIP, there arose such a clatter

Talk of democracy, as if that could matter

Away to the polls I flew like a flash

For straight bananas and NHS cash

Then, out of Boris' arse what should appear?

A bus with numbers, but sources unclear

Atop sat a Farage, so lively and quick

To apportion blame and EU pension to nick

With a divorce payment to pour down the drain

He quaffed his pint and called Poles a rude name

'Now Junker! Now Davis! Now Merkel and May!

'Don't mention that migrants are pulling my sleigh!'

But I heard him exclaim, ere he drove out of sight

HAPPY CHRISTMAS TO ALL, AS LONG AS YOU'RE WHITE!

IN OTHER RELATED NEWS:

Brexit latest: Isle of Wight didn't even know we were part of the EU
Man's allergy to 1970s trouser fabric flares-up in charity shop
Isle of Wight County Press attacks Space Invaders for excessive violence
Campaigner who takes toilet selfies now just going through the motions
Girl Guides plan to cull badges
Hacker hides Isle of Wight hospital abacus
Man blowing water up arse 'his own worst enema'
Hedonist transsexual says he'll eat, drink and be Mary
Wight Supremacist wins Ventnor Council
Wetherspoons bans reading
Recession means thousands of estate agents could go to the light, airy, tastefully decorated wall
Man who broke toilet brush while cleaning says he now has huge job on his hands
'Stubborn' stain actually just principled
Saying Espresso with an X 'won't damage your health'
Navvy replaced by JCB says age of shovelry is dead
Man searching for Biblical character 'was claiming Jobseeker's allowance'
Over-enthusiastic 'dab' goes all Nazi
Isle of Wight to ban penny-farthing from town centre
Daily Mail: 'What happened to the tolerant Britain we know and love?' No, really...
Sex-deprived Isle of Wight residents claim to have seen vagina-shaped UFOs
Dementia linked to... er... something, where did I put my keys?
Double entendre miner is working the left shaft today
Serious journalists reporting what happened stealing satirists' jobs
Isle of Wight scientists announce 'self-driving horse'
Best dad in the world accolade under dispute

CHAPTER EIGHT

Yemen enjoys its 1,300th successive bonfire night and firework display (and other World news)

UNESCO condemns Great Wall of China mock-Tudor makeover

The People's Republic of China is facing worldwide indignation after a ten-year conservation project on the Great Wall saw its entire 4,000-mile length covered in a mock-Tudor facade, creating what was described as 'the ghastliest man-made DIY project to be visible from space'.

Chinese authorities insisted the brand new black and white half-timber effect added a touch of class to what had been previously drab and boring stonework, and refused to rule out adding a Victorian-style conservatory around the back, or the introduction of terracotta gnomes 'to add a bit of character'.

Professor David Ansel-Collins, head of UNESCO's Asia-Pacific division, described the renovation as 'the greatest blow to world cultural heritage since the pebble dashing of the Taj Mahal, or even the tarmacking of the Hanging Gardens of Babylon'.

All French motorists must drive with picnic hamper

The Ministry of Transport in Paris has confirmed that anyone driving in France must carry a basket containing the kind of meal Juliet Binoche would throw together for a few friends on a hillside.

'If you want to drive in our country you should respect our laws,' said a spokesperson. 'French law requires you to carry two fresh baguettes, some perfectly ripe brie, a half carafe of *appellation controllée* red wine or better, and a gingham picnic blanket with the

175

checks no bigger than 10 cm. Even you Rosbifs should be able to manage that.'

'Personally, I've no objection to all this stuff,' said an English motorist interviewed at Calais. 'The last time I drove across the continent, by the time I'd got the compulsory flugelhorn, raffia donkey, Polish plumber called Yacob and fully operational spy satellite in the car, there was no room for the wife and kids. Best holiday I ever had. I bloody love Europe.'

Bush still completely unaware his presidency is about to end

There have been mounting concerns from Washington over whether President George Bush actually realises that he will be out of the White House come 20 January 2009. Despite his advisers having repeatedly explained that he will not be President once Barack Obama is inaugurated, it is thought that the message has failed to successfully filter down into Bush's awareness of events.

'Maybe it's because when we told him he was watching a 'Real Life Stories of the Highway Patrol' marathon on Fox,' commented White House staffer Peter Hurst. 'Although he was nodding, the programme volume was loud and the bright lights and loud bangs may have been the President's primary concern at that point.'

The American public appear divided over how to break the news, or whether it might just be easier to keep Bush in the dark about this for the time being.

The incoming regime are considering whether it might just be simpler to build a complete replica of the White House and pay his staff to pretend that nothing has happened. 'It might be expensive,' said Obama's press spokesman, 'but it would be less risk than releasing him out into society and seeing what other damage he might do.'

Chimp rejects US citizenship

In a landmark decision, mankind's closest living relative has voted to reject North American naturalisation. Despite a New York court debating his legal status, Tommy the Chimp said that he has little to gain from a life of low taxation and gun crime. By contrast, chimpanzee society has conquered space travel before humans and would never invent the Pop-Tart.

With its mastery of basic tools and delight in hurling faeces, your average American has little in common with their ape cousins. When asked to comment, a chimpanzee spokesman rolled his eyes, made a sucking noise and inserted a banana up one nostril.

President's thoughts no longer with dead soldiers' families

Following the death of another three American soldiers in Northern Iraq, the President has admitted that his thoughts were not with the families of those who were killed.

'When the first few soldiers died back at the beginning, I did genuinely think about it for a bit,' he confessed. 'I thought Jeez, these guys would never have died if I had never invaded. But like everything else you kinda get used to it.

'I hadn't had a lot to eat that day, what with one thing and another. So, I was actually wondering what the White House cook would be knocking up for my dinner.'

The President learnt of the latest deaths during a briefing, but his stomach rumbled noisily several times and he is reported to have shifted uncomfortably in his chair while trying to appear to be concentrating on what was being said. 'I was also thinking that George Washington has a really big nose, and that 'Dog' backwards is 'God'.'

Chinese troops out in force for anniversary of 'nothing happening'

The Chinese army swung into position around Tiananmen Square yesterday to guard against commemoration of the day in 1989 when nothing much happened - just some troops moving with ruthless efficiency to do hardly anything at all, really.

'July 4th 1989 was a day just like any other,' said the Chinese Foreign Minister. 'We're marking the occasion with a massive display of force, but I wouldn't read anything into that.

'Many people who were in the area in 1989 are expected to observe the anniversary by staying at home and doing nothing special, much as they did then. They were not joined by several hundred others who were around at the time but are now presumed to be on holiday or something.'

Native American defends Manhattan/beads deal

'These were really nice beads,' said Native American Karl Skywolf, defending his ancestors in the Canarsee tribe's decision to sell Manhattan Island to European immigrants. 'They had these dinky little shells and sparkly bits, and you could double them up and wear them as a bracelet as well as a necklace.

'People always criticise our ancestors for handing over the most valuable real estate in the world for a handful of trinkets, but you have to appreciate that Manhattan needed a lot doing to it. It's had a lot of cash spent on it since then, and the beads seemed a good deal at the time.'

More militant Native Americans point to the infamous exchange as a symbol of their exploitation at a time when Indians did not recognise the concept of landownership and accepted the trinkets as a goodwill gift.

'We demand the return of all the land in the metropolitan area of New York as rightfully ours,' said one militant.

'Oh, come on, it's not going to happen,' responded Skywolf. 'It's not as if we still have the jewellery to give back in return.'

The Mayor of New York refused to dismiss the idea out of hand. With falling property prices, rising crime and unemployment, the Mayor's office is open to all ideas. 'If you can find the beads after all this time,' he said, 'we might be able to do you a deal on the Bronx and part of Queens.'

Lego refuse to build Trump's wall

Despite being the nemesis of bare feet everywhere, Lego were keen to distance themselves from Donald Trump's proposed border wall with Mexico, giving him no choice but to assemble the wall out of pulped copies of the Koran, held together with whatever the hell he uses as hair glue.

Citing ethical reasons, Lego said they would continue to make Star Wars-themed Death Stars but had declined Trump's request for a full-sized one. Instead their focus will be on a 'Brexit Box of Bricks', which lacks any plan and, despite promises on the packaging, cannot be used to build any hospitals whatsoever.

UK used Jobseeker's Allowance to fund Israeli army

Following the revelation that a Minister attempted to subsidise the Israeli army with foreign aid, it transpires that she also tried to claim cold weather payments for pensioners in Tel Aviv and Disability Living Allowance for Uri Geller.

Using money intended for charitable or humanitarian causes, Britain has inadvertently funded the assassination of Muhammad al-Zuari, using a school uniform grant and 500 Nectar points.

Critics have also questioned whether Benjamin Netanyahu can still be on maternity allowance. One said: 'It's outrageous that part of our £13 billion of foreign aid could go towards an illegal Israeli occupation - that's what Eurovision is for.'

Kanye West declares independence from the rest of Kanye

In what is believed to be a bloodless coup, Kanye West has taken over over the computers, TV and radios in his many houses, while his bodyguards will not let anyone near him without a visa. He also disconnected the electricity supply to the other Kardashians.

West has declared himself to be a sovereign state known as Ye and has applied to join the UN. Donald Trump has already said that the US will recognise Ye and set up an embassy in his Chicago mansion.

In a warning that not everything will be smooth going, Kim Kardashian has had 'Abandon hope, all Ye who enter here' tattooed on her nether regions.

Sesame Street introduces 'Trumpy' the orange-faced Muppet

The latest addition to the Muppets line-up, Trumpy is set to bewitch children, with his trademark quiff and dislike of all the Hispanic cast members.

Trumpy, like most of the characters, will be operated by a puppet-master, but based in Moscow. He will repeal Bert & Ernie's wedding and Grover's health insurance, and will send Mr Snuffleupagus back to 'wherever the f*ck he comes from.'

While some appreciate the wall that Trumpy has built around Oscar the Grouch, one four-year-old said: 'Just because you look like someone has their hand up your butt, doesn't mean you have to act like a Muppet.'

Iraq: America sends in the life coaches

At dawn yesterday, the First US Airborne Life Coach Division were parachuted into the world's most war-ravaged region, in order to discuss life goals and suppressed dreams.

'With the Iraqi people feeling more pessimistic now than they did a year ago, the obvious solution is to turn them into get-up-and-go optimists from within,' said Captain Mike Finkelman. 'Change is GOOD, get used to it Iraq!

'We had a slight problem that many of them had the unrealised ambition of destroying the Great Yankee Satan. But, on the whole, the Iraqis are getting the same, smile-all-the-way advice we give to our American customers.'

There have also been questions about the sensitivity of the programme, after a life coach was allocated to Former Vice Iraqi President Taha Yassin Ramadan, just twenty-four hours before his execution.

'Sure, that was one of the shorter sessions,' admitted Finkelman. 'But tomorrow is always the first day of the rest of your life. It's just that in his case, it was also the last.'

IRA withdraws balaclavas after 'blackface' outcry

The IRA has withdrawn all 400 balaclavas and a black teacosy with eyeholes from service, apologising unreservedly and promising to wear ethically-appropriate concealment in future bombing attacks.

'It's not easy, mind,' said an IRA spokesperson, who said he would kill us if we named him. 'We looked into skin-coloured balaclavas. But defining 'skin-coloured' turned out to be a minefield – no pun intended.'

Meanwhile, a spokesnutter for the Ulster Caught-Red-Handed Volunteers announced that, if balaclavas were racially insensitive, 'then we'll be ordering loads more. In fact, there was somebody offering a good deal on eBay for 400 or so just the other day.'

US hoping to train a new generation of cage fighters

President Trump's controversial policy of separating migrant children from their parents and keeping them in cages has been fully supported by the mixed martial-arts fraternity, Mr Miyagi and the makers of galvanised chain-link fencing. The hope is that these children will grow up with the either the requisite skills of a cage fighter or a newfound empathy for battery chickens.

A spokeswoman said: 'Detractors claim that this is dehumanising and cruel – but they say it, like it's a bad thing. If we want ultimate warriors, we need to brutalise them early – and I'm afraid that American schools are too understaffed to do this.

'They say children miss their parents, but really the only contact they need is full-on and bare-knuckle. Besides, if migrant parents wish to see their children, they're always welcome to buy ringside seats. Now, if you'll excuse me, I need to get ready to rrrrrr-RUMBLE!'

182

Man has no spare capacity to worry about Kashmir

News that India and Pakistan might be heading for a new conflict, failed to resonate with Mark Gayle, 39, who was too busy crapping his pants over Brexit and the England test score. Prioritising other threats has meant that he regularly ignores traffic lights, wet paint signs and the news that his daughter is getting a tattoo.

Gayle explained: 'I've only got so much fear to give; what with the collapse of the environment and England's middle batting order, I'm a gibbering wreck.'

Retreating to his happy place, or 'shed' as his wife calls it, he attempted to block out world events and ignore the 'odd lump' he found while in the shower that morning. 'I don't know why I feel this sense of impending doom,' he said, as he settled down to read the Daily Mail.

USA suffers serious shortage of unarmed people to kill

Regrettably, the USA is struggling to fulfil its primary aim, of life, liberty and the pursuit of other people's oil. Instead of being focused on killing innocent people abroad, they have had to turn their sights on eradicating their own citizens – or *déjà vu*, as Native Americans refer to it.

After a sixth day of domestic rioting, it has become clear that the US Government will quickly run out of backs to shoot and police reports to fabricate.

Said an official: 'Naturally we'll focus the majority of our attacks on the African American community, but soon enough we'll need to start on the Hispanics and after that, I'm afraid, we'll probably need to start shooting the poor white folks.

'At that point we'll bring in the National Guard, to shoot the police. Who in turn, will be killed by the mobilised infantry. Finally, we'll just nuke the troops. And then everyone will be safe.'

Trump summons Cthulhu

Having already scrapped the Trans-Pacific Trade Partnership, Donald Trump has sworn to only sign future agreements on parchment made from human skin and with the blood of liberals.

One eyewitness, who saw the President complete the summoning, said: 'I saw a scaly, rubbery-looking body, with prodigious claws, and an octopus-like head whose face was a mass of feelers - and next to him was Cthulhu!'

Cthulhu was hoping to begin a reign of murder and insanity for all Earth-dwellers but was frustrated to discover that Trump had got there first. Remarked one worshipper of the tentacled deity: 'The irony is Cthulhu has been trying for years to summon Trump.'

IN OTHER RELATED NEWS:

Chinese to introduce one yak policy
Ukraine power vacuum to be replaced by Dyson
New Zealand considers putting 'something Hobbity' on its flag
UK troops leave Afghanistan never to return, probably
US to introduce border height restrictions
Castro: Grim Reaper 1, CIA 0
Bush/Blair sex tape to be leaked
Trump tells May to build moat around Britain
Brexit plan enters third fag packet
Chinese tea smuggler going to prison for Oolong time
Ding-dong as diplomatic ping pong from Kim Jong in Pyongyang
goes wrong
NRA member who threatened suicide 'was just shooting his mouth
off'
Tories ask Prince Andrew to do something else distracting
Commemorative Brexit pound coin to be a 50 pence piece
Theresa May receives Oscar for performance in 'La La Land'
North Korea still trying to hit cow with 'banjo technology'
Afghanistan replaces Hawaii as 50th State
Hillary Clinton strangles Bald Eagle
France swaps Bayeux Tapestry for a copy of Viz
Trump postpones military junta 'until next year'
Venezuela offers to help depose US despot
Netanyahu annexes Moon
Shock as Mugabe voted back to life by 99.9% of Zimbabweans
'Roe v Wade? I hate tennis,' says Trump
Kurds 'may not get their way'
Historians pinpoint the exact minute that America was great
Iran will never get nuclear arms, vows USA. Not until the cheque
clears
See Naples and die. Ditto rest of Italy
Sunni and Shia reuniting for one last farewell tour in Northern Iraq
Mueller concludes no Russian collusion, voters are 'just dumb'
Native Americans back Trump's 'go back to where you came from'
US electric plane can only fly in DC

CHAPTER NINE

Santa letters to be published on Wikileaks (and other Faith stories)

Lamb of God 'doesn't want to take away the sins of the world'

Colin, a six-month-old Merino lamb at a farm in Norfolk who was recently named by the Almighty creator of Heaven and Earth as the latest in a series of beasts whose sacrifice will somehow blot out every awful thing humanity has done since the last time, has questioned the logic of the system. He has also joined with other ovines in calling for a review of the working relationship between the two species.

'OK, so we're not the brightest of beasts, I get that. Nine hours eating grass and eight hours ruminating every day doesn't leave you a lot of time for abstract thought,' said Colin.

'But even I managed to work out what the role involves. No thanks. Find another dumb animal to symbolise things for a change. How about squirrels? They're thick as pig sh*t.'

With the human race becoming more numerous and more appalling every year, the need for a Lamb of God to take away its sins on a regular basis has risen sharply from once a century to nearly 10,000 times every year.

Fears are growing that with recent outrages such as Donald Trump being US President, the cancellation of the Eurovision Song Contest, and Katie Hopkins getting a column in a daily newspaper, sheep may face a long-term threat of extinction.

'Basically,' said Colin, 'it's about time you took responsibility for your own sins and renegotiated your relationship with the Good Lord, because we're rather tired of having it all projected onto us. So, the Lord is your shepherd, is he? Well I may be His lamb but He isn't my shepherd. My shepherd is Mervyn Bagnall of Downend Farm near Swaffham. The filthy, filthy b*stard.'

Jesus promises two new pancake days

Jewish sin-annuller and son of the head of the Roman Catholic Church, Jesus, has offered to launch two new pancake days as a gesture of goodwill to supporters.

The tradition developed from a Christian feast day enjoyed before the Lent fasting period, where the devout would confess their sins and abstain from meals as penance. The new days would fall in July and September and would be open to both churchgoers and the non-religious.

Pancake festivities could involve either sweet or savoury servings, there would be no restrictions on the choice or number of toppings, and pancakes may be tossed, either privately or in a race, as on traditional Shrovetides.

Christ said: 'I believe the hardworking people of Britain, many of whom have demanding roles in the public sector, would appreciate more opportunities to enjoy these delicious Shrove treats with their families. I'll also be extending the offer to Catholics to enjoy pancake desserts as an alternative to 'me biscuits' in communion ceremonies.'

When asked about whether he thought the new holidays would be a celebration of national cultural traditions, He added: 'No, it really is just about the pancakes. Who doesn't enjoy a pancake? I know I do. No? Have it your way, I'm easy. Also, gay sex - go ahead.'

'There's only room for 12 on my private jet,' says Pope regretfully

In an act of pure humanitarianism, while still maintaining a healthy luggage-migrant ratio, the Pope has kindly offered hope – but no complimentary nibbles – to a dozen refugees.

His Holiness selected those to save using strict criteria of no screaming babies or stag dos. Those migrants that remain asked if the Pope would be returning for the rest of them, but he explained that his 2,000 room Vatican Palace was 'simply too small'.

EasyJet had previously offered space in their overhead compartments for migrants - but only those under 20 kg. By contrast the Pope, from behind an improvised curtain - to denote business class - was able to offer first-class confessionals for all his Muslim guests.

Infant Kardashian hailed as the Second Coming

Theologians and people of all faiths were united in religious ecstasy at the confirmation that a child of God had been born in a simple, wooden Los Angeles hospital. As predicted (and thanks to Twitter) the event was known instantaneously and worldwide – 'for as the lightning comes from the East, so will a Reality TV star be born of the West' [Matthew 24:27].

The fruit of a humble man and a virgin bride, the child and the CD will be known as 'Yeezus'. The Holy Mother has accepted gifts of gold, myrrh and a year's subscription to Heat magazine. While transcripts of their 2003 sex tape will be transposed onto papyrus and painstakingly translated into Aramaic and Pornhub.

Man gives up pretending to give up things for Lent, for Lent

A Shrewsbury man has stunned friends by announcing that he is giving up joking about abstaining from doing things for Lent that he would, in all probability, not be doing anyway, for Lent.

Domestic appliance salesman Michael Lewis, 49, revealed how he traditionally answers questions regarding what he is giving up for Lent with unlikely pastimes such as skydiving, tombstoning and bungee jumping.

'It started a few years ago when one of my mates gave up crisps. He was getting a bit precious about it, so to shut him up I told him I was giving up jogging, which made everyone laugh as I'm not exactly Steve Ovett. It just snowballed from there.'

However, for Lewis, the time has come to put such jocularity behind him. 'The joke was wearing a bit thin to be honest,' he said.

'Pretending you're sacrificing something which in reality has no bearing on your life, such as last year's naked ping-pong bear fighting, is not only puerile but extremely disrespectful to the millions of Christians, whose abstinence actually means something. So, this Lent I'm giving up pretending to give up things for Lent. That and wanking.'

Church tells impatient callers: 'Your prayer is important to us'

The Archbishop of Canterbury has announced a new prayer-handling service, which he called 'the most significant overhaul of Christianity's customer services during its 2,000-year history'. Industry insiders say the Church of England has been forced to modernise or risk losing praying customers to other religions who are now offering some lucrative posthumous deals to their most fanatical followers.

'Although millions subscribe to God's prayer-answering service, until today no-one know for certain whether their prayers were being processed, or whether they were simply talking to themselves,' a spokesperson explained.

'From now on, worshippers submitting their prayers in the standard silent, mumbled or loud-and-proud formats will receive an automatically generated text or voicemail message saying: "Thank you for praying. Your prayer is important to us and is being held in a queue. Closer to the time, a member of our regional clergy team will be in contact to arrange a convenient time for the prayer to be answered".'

The first users of the service today reported some teething problems. One customer who prayed for relief from rheumatoid arthritis instead received clear skies and bright sunshine on the day of his neighbour's daughter's wedding, while Ann Widdecombe was 'surprised but vindicated' after learning she would shortly give birth to the son of God.

Worshippers were also disappointed to find that God could offer nothing more specific than morning or afternoon delivery slots for answering prayers.

God finally agrees to save Queen

After years of indecision and holy fights with his conscience, God has finally decided to save the Queen. In news released today by God's chief messenger, the Archangel Gabriel, it was revealed that the Almighty has grown tired of dispatching monarchs over the centuries and now wants to maintain the status quo.

'Arrows through eyes, decapitations, disembowelment, death by syphilis and burying under car parks hath been the fate of Kings and Queens for nigh on a thousand years,' said Gabriel. 'Thus, God hath decreed that it would be less fraught to hang on to His faithful servant Elizabeth II for probably about another millennium.'

The news will come as a welcome relief to millions of people around the world who have been subjected to singing Britain's dreary national anthem.

'At last we can kick off major international football tournaments without having to mouth those bwain-numbing lyrics,' said Woy Hodgson, England's national football team manager. 'There's nothing more embawwassing than watching a dense team line up trying to remember the words.'

God's latest decree has met with some criticism, however, most notably by Prince Charles. In an unguarded moment on an excursion to the Great Barrier Reef he was heard to declare: 'F*ck, f*ck and triple f*ck. Mind you, 'Jerusalem' has always been a personal favourite of one's.'

Actually it WAS Adam and Steve, says God

Almighty God, creator of the heavens and Earth, has apologised to any fundamentalists who have been frothing at the mouth over what other people do to each other in bed by confirming that actually He did intend for the human race to be homosexual.

Furthermore, He has admitted that the whole course of human history has been a terrible mistake but feels powerless to put it right.

'My bad,' said the Lord of Hosts. 'When I created the universe 6,843 years ago as of 26 March, almost my last act was to put two male humans in a paradise where they could have copious sex and talk about sport afterwards.

'They weren't literally called Adam and Steve because the English language didn't exist then – oh hang on, it's Americans I'm talking to, isn't it, so let's not complicate things too much....'

Child finds Jesus in her Kinder Surprise™

After generations of messianic prophecies and the consumption of millions of Easter eggs, the Second Coming has at last been triggered by a toddler from Fleet, Hampshire. Vatican officials are reluctant at this stage to categorise this event as a miracle but admit it is certainly a 'surprise'.

Madeleine Alcock, 4, was fairly nonplussed by having found the Son of God in her egg and seemed more concerned by the lack of sweet-based centre to her treat. Her mother said: 'A new dawn of universal peace and love is all very well, but Maddy would prefer some jelly-beans.'

When quizzed Madeleine admitted to having hastily eaten the Jesus 'chocolatey cave', which many theologians fear may have had new gospels scrawled onto its white chocolate interior. One priest admitted: 'The fused halves represent the relationship between Christ's corporeal and ethereal form. Remember he died, so we might have guilt-free chocolate.'

Radical Christian groups banned under terror laws

A radical Christian group has been forbidden to march through Huddersfield, it has emerged.

A group called the Salvation Army had planned to march through the Yorkshire town wearing uniform and playing hymns but was banned after a public outcry. A spokesperson denied that it was a violent organisation and said that rattling collection boxes at passers-by was not meant to intimidate.

The Home Office countered: 'We are also banning the Sally-Ann and the Oh-God-It's-Them-Again groups under the Terrorism Act. God only knows what they are concealing under that headgear. It's true that Salvationists do not embrace acts of suicide. Which is something of a pity.'

Modern-day Moses receives Commandments 2.0 on tablet

The Christian world is celebrating today after the direct, unadulterated word of God was passed down to a Nuneaton man, Brian Burridge. 'I'd just parked the bin lorry round the back of PC World, and was having a look in the skip to see if there was anything I could flog on eBay, when BAM! Suddenly I was holding this gadget,' he said.

Burridge claims that God told him from on high to look in the My Documents folder, open up a file labelled new_commandments.doc and then spread the word among the faithful. The Lord then apologised for taking so long to communicate with believers in Microsoft Word but blamed it on compatibility issues.

God's latest holy writ outlines the secret of eternal happiness and reveals the exact date of the second coming of Christ. Unfortunately, Burridge is unable to divulge these details as this part of the file has been corrupted by a virus.

PC experts confirmed that the programme has been infected by a Trojan, downloaded, judging by the browsing history, from teensexcams.ru. 'Remember the twelfth commandment,' warned a Church of England IT spokesman. 'Thou shalt not format one's hard drive before first backing up thy files.'

Jehovah's Witness kept talking all evening after making mistake of opening door to trick-or-treaters

'He should really have known better,' said Abigail, the wife of traumatised Jehovah's Witness Mark Carnegie. 'It's not as if they don't stand out the way they dress up. Poor Mark thought he might be able to talk them out of a few of their misguided beliefs, but his "Have you heard the good news about our Lord and Saviour Jesus Christ?" was no match for their dogmatic chanting of 'trick or treat'.'

After several hours, the discussion finally began to take its toll on Mark. 'I could see him thinking, "This is my house. I shouldn't be a prisoner in my own home, afraid to open the front door", all the while smiling patiently and periodically checking his watch.

'But they simply threatened to egg him and smash the car windows,' she said of the two nine-year-olds. 'They had an answer for everything, but then I don't suppose you go out walking the streets in the dark and the cold unless you passionately believe in the truth of what you're doing.'

Jesus returns, finds himself swiftly moved on

Returning from the dead this Easter Sunday, Jesus was troubled to find most shops He needed to stage a convincing comeback shut. Ignoring the obvious irony, He managed to cobble together an outfit out of onion bags and old newspapers.

However, His appearance and His increasingly desperate insistence that He was the Son of God, only led the public to conclude that He was just further evidence of the UK's worsening homeless crisis.

Being moved on for the fourth time Jesus was overheard to shout: 'I had thought the society I was crucified in was brutal and uncaring, but now I'm thinking maybe it wasn't so bad. Maybe leave it another couple of millennia.'

God impregnates fish

A sawfish from Florida has become the most recent example of an immaculate conception. A spokesman for the Divine said: 'For two thousand years, God has been on the lookout for someone free from original sin, but thanks to Club 18-30s, we're completely out of human virgins. Therefore, He has had to look further afield. Well, He started with fields, but livestock are pretty slutty as well.'

Some scientists think the pregnancy was due to the animal being critically endangered, but others suggest God just got her drunk.

Asked if there were signs of any wedding bells, the spokesman replied: 'She's a nice fish but God's not really a settling down kind of guy. Maybe there's some affable Jewish carpenter she could marry? Perhaps she should've thought about these things before she uncrossed her fins and got banged up? She's more a slapper than a snapper, if you ask me.'

Devil recalls handcarts we are all going to hell in

Beelzebub has recalled a trillion handcarts we're all going to hell in because their poisonous emissions are 'not toxic enough'.

A spokes-demon said: 'Although humanity has started to create a hell on earth with the use of poisonous emissions from its aircraft, cars, power stations and tanks, the really effective potential emissions are from nuclear weapons.

'We apologise that these under-used assets are still not toxic enough to destroy all humanity, but we are testing new systems whose emissions will be cataclysmic.'

The spokes-devil continued: 'In the interim we are recalling all the handcarts our customers will go to hell in to make adjustments, so the pungent fumes of decaying flesh emanating from the carts will be equal only to the choking gases of fiery brimstone to come, emitted by their horrifyingly penis-like exhaust pipes.'

It is understood that Hell will be rebranded with a new mission statement, '*Vorsprung Durch Gotterdammerung*'.

Jesus 'surprised' by paternity test result

Jesus Christ, leader of most of the world's Christians, has discovered that His true father is the LORD, the LORD God Almighty - not Joseph of Nazareth, the carpenter who brought him up - following a state-of-the-art paternity test.

The 'voice from the sky' technique, in which 15 believers pray for a sign from heaven to show who's the daddy of the child being plunged into the river Jordan, gave a 99.997% likelihood of divine parentage when the clouds parted to the cry of 'This is My son, with whom I am well pleased' as Jesus resurfaced.

'It's the first time we've got a positive result,' said a Nazarene biologist. 'God, not Joseph, eh? So that's why he was so shit at joinery. That wardrobe Jesus built me fell apart faster than the ones from the land of Ikaiah.'

Jesus remains sanguine about His real dad. 'Joseph brought me up as if I was his own son and I still live by his maxims,' he said. 'Let your olive wood dry out properly, measure twice and cut once, and if you find yourself at the head of a multinational religious movement, well, chillax. God does weird stuff. She's like that.'

92-year-old man says celibacy is easy

The retired Pope, Benedict XVI, has said that priests should remain celibate, despite himself being in his sexual prime. He boasted at 92 he could have any woman he wanted – he just could not remember what to do with them.

Miraculously, many popes have fathered illegitimate children, all while being celibate. In fact, celibacy is a great cover story, when you get caught with a choirboy. Said a spokesman: 'It's not easy for Pope Benedict to give up sex. He's a fanny magnate.'

Planning permission loophole scuppers crucifixion of Jesus

There were confused scenes at the Sanhedrin today when Jesus Christ was freed, after it transpired that planning laws prevented the erection at Calvary of temporary or permanent structures, such as large wooden crosses, without proper consultation.

'The whole trial was a sham,' said the counsel for the defence. 'Firstly, there was the issue of my client's human rights – clearly an execution is not in His best long-term interests. Secondly, the manner of his arrest in the Garden of Gethsemane stinks of entrapment. But the lack of planning permission just shows how little respect these people have for the law.'

Strangely, the reprieved man was visibly upset by his unexpected release. 'This has really ruined my holiday weekend plans. I don't know what my Father is going to say.'

Pope asks: 'Who wants some?'

His Holiness Pope Francis has stunned passengers on a flight to the Philippines by suggesting passengers 'step outside' to resolve an alleged insult to his mother, adding that he would 'take on the lot of youse with one hand inside me cassock.'

The Pope continued: 'What are you lot staring at? Never seen a pissed Pontiff before? Oi, airline lady, give us anuvver large brandy and holy water an' some nibbles. Got any in the shape of a crucifix? Thas' wot we have at 'ome. Vatican 69! Yeah? Laugh you c*nts, that was a joke!'

After a short silence, His Holiness went on to remind passengers of the Church's track record of retributive violence: 'That geezer from the Full Monty Python, he hit the nail on the bonce. What did he say? Nobody forgets the Spanish Indecision! Imposition? Whatever, it'll come back to me in a mo...'

Priest cures boy of imaginary friend

Catholic priest Father James Cannon has helped a Durham couple resolve their son's behavioural problems, which centred on a troubling relationship with an imaginary friend.

'At first we thought there was no harm in it,' said Maria Doyle, the boy's mother. 'Michael would set an extra place at the table and would say it was for 'Dougal', then we started finding rude words written on the walls and broken toys in his bedroom but each time we confronted him he just said "Dougal did it".'

The 53-year old parish priest told Michael that he was too old for imaginary friends and if he needed help he could always talk to God. 'He seemed impressed that I had a conversation with the Lord every day of my life like a normal person,' he said.

'Michael doesn't talk about Dougal anymore,' said Maria. 'Now he's just riddled by guilt and paranoia with potential for borderline personality disorder in later life, so that's all fine.'

Sinners brawl over Black Sunday discount deals on penance

There were chaotic scenes in Catholic churches across the UK yesterday as repentant sinners sought to take advantage of Black Sunday deals on absolution. As many churches opened their doors at midnight scuffles broke out when crowds fought their way towards confessionals to secure deals which saw penance slashed to bargain levels for one day only.

'It was bit hairy,' said George Winters, a parishioner at Our Lady of Perpetual Misery' in Sheffield. 'When the doors opened there was a huge surge as we all ran towards the confessional box.

'But it was worth it. I confessed to sleeping with my best friend's wife, normally you're looking at a Decade of the Rosary and an Act of Contrition, but I got off with three Hail Marys and an Our Father. What a bargain!'

Meanwhile, at a church in Glasgow, remorseful sinners took advantage of '3-for-2' offers on selected misdemeanours. 'I confessed to impure thoughts and avarice and got 'failing to keep the Sabbath' thrown in for free,' said Jessica Harrington of St Thomas of the Harboured Nonce in the city's east end.

Legal terminology 'actually magic'

Lawyers have confirmed that the words used in contracts really do have magical powers.

'You don't think we'd say stuff like *'force majeure'* or 'time shall be of the essence' if we didn't have to, do you?' said a leading lawyer. 'I could turn you into a frog if I wanted. Certain phrases have the power to generate unimaginable wealth. They're the ones we tend to focus on.'

Sceptics have pointed out that lawyers seem remarkably unmagical. 'Have you ever seen a lawyer fly around on a broomstick?' one asked, lowering his voice to a whisper, 'What if the lawyers are really just muggles like you and me? Maybe those words are just there to bamboozle us.'

Not everybody is so sceptical. Andrew Dickinson is a layperson, who recently used a lawyer to magic his house conveyancing. 'I couldn't have done that in a million years,' he told reporters. 'The wizard, sorry, solicitor, typed some words on an ancient PC – like, it must have been a hundred years old – and the house was mine.

'I sometimes dream of finding a book of magic spells and incantations in an old second-hand bookshop, like in 'Bedknobs and Broomsticks'. Then I could be a lawyer. Only I'd be a good lawyer, using my powers to help people and refusing payment.'

The Law Society has described Dickinson's ideas as 'heretical' and 'incomprehensible'. *'Ipso facto,'* said a spokesman. 'Hereinafter forthwith for the avoidance of doubt plaintiff.' Subsequently Mr Dickinson has not been seen since. Police are anxious to locate him.

Pope's humility 'getting on everyone's tits', admits cardinal

The Pope has been charming the media and public alike with his easy-going, approachable manner and simple lifestyle, but this same absence of bloated pomp and crazed hubris is allegedly 'wearing bloody thin' among his colleagues at the Vatican.

'It was all a bit of a novelty at first,' admitted Cardinal Sergio Venturi, dripping in signet rings and flanked on either side by Swiss Guards. 'The first thing he did when he was elected was to get an OAP pass for the municipal pool. We all thought it was rather sweet in a third world kind of way.

'But it gets to you after a while; we had the Dalai Lama over last week and where did His Holiness want to hold a banquet in his honour? Only '*Il Harvestore*' again! There I was, having to explain to Tibetan Buddhism's supreme spiritual leader about the concept of an unlimited salad bar.'

Another Vatican insider identified went even further: 'The Holy Roman Church has a long tradition of sickening excess and sociopathic power-brokering. Anything that stood in our way we crushed under our heel. *Il Papa* has got this glorious heritage and basically, he's just pissing it up a wall. Ungrateful, or what?'

Excitement as Jesus finds image of Penge couple in slice of toast

It was jubilation as usual in Paradise today as our Lord and Saviour Jesus Christ discovered an image of Percy and Ethel Renfrew of Penge, formed by the more burnt parts on a slice of celestial toast.

'I recognised them straight away,' said the Son of God, speaking exclusively to the Daily Mirror. Mr Renfrew is a retired gas fitter, and his wife is a keen lawn bowls player. 'I knew that, of course.'

Elf on the Shelf 'shagged your cat'

What started as a cute Christmas tradition documenting the nocturnal shenanigans of a festive imp has now spiralled into debauchery, missing underwear and one decapitated garden gnome at a house in Luton.

On 1 December, things went quickly from bad to worse when small footprints were found coming out of the neighbour's ransacked shed, where someone had soaked their garden furniture in kerosene. Later it would become clear that these events were connected with half a bottle of cooking sherry going missing, and that someone had shaved the dog's anus.

Dustbins were regularly overturned, car keys were hidden and someone was using the sock drawer to throw up in. The raisins found on the kitchen work surface were anything but raisins, while the sprinkles of festive snow were discovered to be Colombian in origin.

Sadly, for the children, the magic of waking to a tableau of wonderment was ruined by the fact that someone had ripped out Teddy's stuffing and melted the Sylvanian family with a blowtorch. Subsequently the Elf has been moved from the shelf to the naughty step, while the cat has been warned to steer clear of his candy cane delight and bursting festive sack.

God admits: 'Jesus is very hard to buy for'

With Christmas approaching, God has said that buying presents for Jesus has become a real problem. 'After 2,000 years, there aren't many things I haven't tried. He says He's too old for an XBox and, being omniscient, He's very difficult to surprise. Last year I bought Him gloves and socks, but apparently giving Him things that remind Him of the holes in His feet and hands is a bit tactless.'

God did accept that the coincidence of Jesus's birthday being on Christmas Day does make things slightly easier. 'I buy Him one present and say it's for both days combined. I think He believes it as well.'

Jesus has responded: 'Mesus Christ! I'm difficult, am I? Try buying for the person who literally has everything - including trillions of empty planets - well at least He's got plenty of storage space.'

Father Christmas chronic victim of identity theft

Santa Claus, an elderly man residing at the North Pole, who describes himself as 'toymaker and philanthropist', has been the victim of serial identity theft, according to the police.

'Some of them are quite brazen about it,' said DCI Keith Hooper. 'Going around in gangs of eight or ten, all of them trying to take advantage of the goodwill felt towards Father Christmas at this time of year.'

It is not known how the identity thieves got the personal details of Santa Claus, but they seem to know where he lives, how he dresses and even the names of his pet reindeer. 'Apparently he uses the password 'Rudolf' for everything,' Hooper said.

Parents of young children however seemed unconcerned that there may be one or two impostors out there. 'Every year we take our children to the department store to meet Father Christmas,' said one mother in a Leeds shopping centre.

'We send them into a dark little grotto on their own to sit on Santa's knee. Why would anyone but the real Santa want to do that all day?'

Church of England packed away with the other Xmas decorations

With the tattered remains of festive tinsel, vicars throughout the land will now be stored back in the loft alongside forgotten gym equipment and your furtive porn stash. Sadly, all too easily, the clergy will fall into disrepair, with the Archbishop of Canterbury once hollowed out by a family of rats.

Many households are torn between getting a real or fake clergyman, yet all agree you cannot beat the smell of a freshly cut priest. Explained one devout shopper: 'We only get our faith down for the Christmas period. After that, we stuff our vicar back in a box with his shiny baubles and prayers.'

Months later, the only memory of 'Jesus Christ' is the yell heard up and down the UK every time someone finds a stray altar boy behind the sofa, or steps barefoot on the notoriously pointy remains of a bishop stuck to the carpet.

Fatted Calf calls for restrained celebrations as Prodigal Son returns

Sabina, a fatted calf in the household of Nehemiah has appealed for calm in the wake of Nehemiah's younger son Reuben returning home after many years in exile abroad.

'Yeah yeah, he was lost but is now found; dead but is now alive, etc. etc,' Sabina told reporters. 'But let's not forget that Reuben took his portion of goods, wasted his substance with riotous living and got a neck tattoo. But for a mighty famine and being reduced to looking after pigs for a living, we'd never have heard of him again.'

However, Reuben himself is looking forward to veal with all the trimmings for the first time in many years. 'Apparently little Sabina thought she was being brought up to be a milk cow – yeah, I know, a flabby little heifer like her! You couldn't make it up.'

204

IN OTHER RELATED NEWS:

Churchgoers live longer because they're scared of going to Hell
Good Friday renamed 'Is It Friday?'
Tooth fairy moving onto kidneys
Shock as Christmas lights found tangled
Pope sorely tested after neighbour gets 'seriously attractive' ox
Convicted Brunei homeopath to be gravelled to death
Biologists alarmed as Buddhists reincarnated as plastic bags.
Psychic eaten by cannibals described as 'medium rare'
Vatican condemns condoms as 'suicide vests for sperm'
Buddhist court rules end-of-life decisions will need a receipt for
returns
Only three Lib Dem leaders until Christmas
Anarchist astrologer predicts a riot
God admits using built-in obsolescence
Facebook bans images of its accounts because they show naked
greed
Magic Money Tree to be investigated in root and branch inquiry
Mary and Joseph planning glamping holiday
Cardinal Newman accidentally burnt as witch
God: 'Thanks for the thoughts and prayers but I'd rather have had
the cash'
Woman fined for wearing a niqab, but double-denim goes
unpunished
Popes to be elected using vape
Easter ruined by spoilers
Church tells impatient worshippers 'Your prayer is important to us'
God, Allah and Jehovah struggle to agree on live TV debate format
'Essential for bishops to have willies' says Church of England
Pope to stand down after 'disappointing festive period' announces
Vatican
Saudi women granted right to back-seat drive
Grim Reaper affirms his secular stance

CHAPTER TEN

Government to start means testing friends with benefits (and even more Politics stories)

CAPOZZOLA·

Who put the 'dumb' in the referendum?

Responding to requests for a follow-up to the popular and hugely successful 2016 referendum there are uncertainties about whether there should be just one more referendum or more. There are also debates about whether any new referendum(s) should offer a simple 'yes / no' option, or whether voters should be invited to choose between a range of options.

It has been suggested that we should have a preliminary referendum to decide the answers to these questions. However, controversy surrounds the question as to whether this preliminary referendum should ask how many more referendums voters want, or whether they wanted a referendum which just offered a simple yes/no choice, or one which offered them a choice between several options.

Should the referendum be a multiple-choice vs. single choice, or just one referendum vs. several? There is the possibility of holding a referendum to decide this, if enough voters want that, but there are uncertainties about how best to determine whether voters want such a referendum or not, or whether they would prefer an opportunity to say whether they wanted it very much, or only slightly, or were happy either way, or probably didn't like the idea very much, or definitely didn't want it all. And whether they wanted a transition period beforehand, and if so, of what duration?

 But that is, of course, another question altogether.

Trump-cancelling headphones 'cut out 99% of bullshit'

Bose have launched their long-awaited Trump-cancelling headphones, with the promise that users will now be able to tune out 99% of all bullshit emanating from the White House.

The new 'Trump-Reducer 35' headphones are designed to sit comfortably with the user, in contrast with just about every one of the President's initiatives. The devices use patented technology to pick up on spurious statements from Trump, before cancelling them out using logical, reasoned debate.

Early reviews have been mixed however, with some users reporting hearing a constant 'wet, metallic thudding noise' while they had the headphones on, suggesting that nothing is going to be able to stop the sound of the shit hitting the fan in America.

Technology expert Peter McAndrew warned: 'Putting these headphones on can reduce the vitriol you are exposed to, but Twitter messages appear to still be getting through, so unfortunately, the whole Trump experience will continue to be a headf*ck.'

May seeks Nickelback's advice on making same old shite appear different

Prime Minister Theresa May has taken advice from Canadian rock band Nickelback as she struggles to get her wording for a Brexit deal approved by the House of Commons. May is hoping that she can learn some lessons from the band's 20-year strategy of releasing exactly the same song, cunningly disguised with a different title and the odd word change.

'These guys are the masters of mindless, gratuitous repetition,' said May. 'Seven albums. Exactly the same thing, every couple of years. Strong and stable lyrics. Smooth and orderly transitional arrangements on the guitar licks.'

May is preparing some new artwork and sleeve notes for her twice-defeated Brexit deal to try and convince the Speaker of the House to let her have her 'meaningful vote', even though everyone knows nothing has changed. AC-DC, Dan Brown, and everyone involved in the Fast and Furious film franchise have offered their help if needed.

Brexiteers: 'What was the question again?'

Leaders of the Leave Campaign are started to feel concerned that they may have over-promised jam today, jam tomorrow and jam-on-jam action.

'Brexit will make this throbbing pain in my left arm disappear,' said one voter. 'I'll have a full head of hair again. I won't have to queue so much at the Post Office. All the ghastly loud music and skinny jeans will go away. Plus, I'll have an erection that will last for days!'

A campaign insider commented: 'Brexit is not a cure-all. It can't offer cheaper car insurance or stop mobile phones from getting smaller. It's not an acne remedy. But admittedly, it can make your whites whiter.'

Tories confirm that it is important to promise things

Launching their election manifesto, the Conservatives have reiterated previous manifesto pledges that it is vitally important to promise things.

'It is vitally important that we promise things,' said Prime Minister Theresa May. 'It is essential that we strive for the targets that we set ourselves. And those targets should be in the interest of all voters.

'Unlike Labour, I am willing to pledge to you now that my Government will promise you these things. Great things that all of you will find important and meaningful in your daily lives. Our promises are all the things that we will need to make our country great again.'

May went on to say that voters faced a clear choice: a long list of promises from her or a 'coalition of chaotic promises' from others. The Conservatives had promised 25% more things than at the last election and 40% more than Labour.

She continued: 'I can offer you more promises now than at any time in history and I guarantee that all of the things I promise we will try very hard to achieve. That is a promise.'

Hampered by your old manifesto? Try Tory Manifesto 'lite'

Is your lumbering, heavy manifesto causing you to lose your mandate? Try the Conservative Manifesto 'lite'.

By jettisoning all unnecessary policy and cumbersome pledges, you can run in 'survival' mode, with the slimmest of majorities; yet maintaining full sound-bite, flip-flop and 'wishy-washy' functionality.

Strip out the burdensome clutter to just the essentials:

• Fox-hunting

• Tax cuts

• Axe school lunches

• Grrrrrr, immigrants

Man who crashed stolen plane appointed head of Brexit strategy

A man who closed a Seattle airport by stealing a plane he later crashed, has been appointed as the new head of Brexit strategy for the UK Government. The unnamed airline employee made an unauthorised take-off late before flying around erratically and crashing into an island, in an almost perfect metaphor for Brexit.

'The flight path apparently had no clear aim in mind, doubled back on itself several times, and ultimately ended in fiery destruction. All of which is an improvement on how our current Brexit work is going, so I offered him a job immediately,' said Prime Minister Theresa May.

'Assuming he survived the crash he can start work on Monday, and I'm sure he'll show us all a thing or two about forward planning and a coherent approach,' she continued. 'Although even if he died, he'll still probably do a better job than me.'

Cock and balls to be an official option on election ballot

The Electoral Reform Society has introduced an extra choice on all election ballot papers: a cock and balls.

'To be honest, some people make a right balls-up of spoiling their ballot paper, and truly cock it up,' said society chairman Chris Johnson. 'Counters are tired of continually having to ask if the mark is a protest or a cartoon of Michael Gove.'

Opponents to the decision point to the newly formed Cock and Balls Party, set up with the aim of 'shafting the electorate at every opportunity.'

'Their logo is also a cock and balls, which means they might gain some votes by mistake,' said one Tory MP. 'And anyway, shafting the electorate is what we're here for.'

Escape Committee to pursue three Brexit escape plans

In a specially convened meeting of the Escape Committee in Hut 18, Flight Lieutenant May has outlined her three contradictory Brexit plans, all of them to be pursued simultaneously.

Codenamed Tom, Dick and Harry, the plans are respectively: to come to a release deal with the goons; to escape without a deal; and to hold a second referendum amongst camp inmates (Johnny Foreigner not allowed to vote) about whether it's worth leaving the camp at all.

The meeting also concluded that Rear Admiral Portillo wasn't the best man to keep watch for approaching guards, since he tended to watch only the ones in the tightest trousers. Instead, a vaulting horse will be put up in the exercise yard, and Subaltern Boris 'Biffo' Johnson will spend all day every day trying to vault over it.

'It isn't actually hiding the entrance to a tunnel,' said May 'but the sight of it should be so funny, the goons will spend all their time laughing at him and forget about the rest of us.'

Schoolkids tell Corbyn him becoming PM is too far-fetched

There was an awkward moment on the campaign trail today when children at a primary school in Bristol told Jeremy Corbyn that they believed the story he read to them about a talking mouse, but that the one about him becoming Prime Minister was just too silly.

'He seemed like a nice old man,' said Fenton Barnes, 6. 'And he was really good at reading 'The Gruffalo' to us. But when he told us he was going to be the next Prime Minister we all fell about laughing. What a silly man. Everyone knows beardy men with scruffy suits can't be the Prime Minister.'

'I'm as willing to suspend my disbelief as the next five-year-old,' said Destiny-Louise Williamson. 'I believe in Father Christmas, God and the Easter Bunny, and I'm even willing to suspend judgment on Brexit, but nice Mr Corbyn in Number 10 was just too far-fetched.'

May rules out ruling things out

Theresa May has made a firm commitment not to make any firm commitments. May won support from MPs in a no-confidence vote, convincing a majority she would give them what they want by categorically writing off categorically writing things off.

'I reject rejecting things outright, outright. The lady is not for turning away from turning,' she said. True to her promise never to delay delaying things, the PM then cancelled a vote on her Brexit deal in Parliament, but has continued to sell her Brexit deal to MPs, highlighting how it guards against any fluctuation from a permanent state of flux.

Voters secretly 'excited' about destroying their children's future

As the General Election looms, like an iceberg, the electorate are surreptitiously looking forward to the prospect of sticking it to the young.

'We need to wipe that smug look off cherubic millennial faces, ban all sleeve tattoos and finally pull the plug on Ed Sheeran,' said one elderly voter. 'And whining about the environment. Who cares about global warming? The cold plays havoc with my lumbago and my prize roses.'

Traditionally we try to leave more to our children, but that only applies now to melanomas and coastal erosion. Lounging in a hot tub, one Boomer explained why all children were lazy, entitled narcissists.

'Growing up in the 80s was tough – we didn't have Google, we had 'Pong'. Have you ever tried ponging porn? And Pong Maps only covers Wimbledon. Kids are worried about debt? It's not my debt. And if they think their inheritance will pay off the remainder, guess again – I'm mortgaged and coked up to the eyeballs.'

Boris stockpiling women in case of no-deal Brexit

Boris Johnson is stockpiling other men's wives in preparation for shortages of vital supplies following a no-deal Brexit. 'He's sold off half the claret to make cellar space,' said a friend. 'That's a lot of claret, but I suppose you have to make sacrifices for the nation. I say, you haven't seen my wife, have you?'

Faced with the prospect of a cataclysmic breakdown of food, medical and industrial supplies, the Government is preparing a leaflet with reassuring images of British people foraging for berries and prostituting themselves for food. A crack team of nutritionists has drawn up the Brexit Diet, which will help to reduce landfill by eating landfill.

Downing Street has condemned the practice of stockpiling women, pointing out that in these gender-fluid times, sexual relief has never been more widely available.

'For those unable to find a partner because of ugliness, poor personal hygiene or because they look like a startled foetus, Michael Gove has written 'A Brexit Guide to Masturbation - Keep Calm and Keep Coming',' said a spokesman. 'We understand he's been researching it for years.'

UK prepares for 'walk of shame'

Dishevelled and smelling strongly of cheap cider, the British electorate are bracing themselves for the mother of all referendum hangovers. Sheepishly staggering onto the international stage, UK voters are going to have to explain how they ended up in bed with a lubricated Boris Johnson and a tattoo of a bulldog on their arse.

During the referendum campaign, eyewitnesses attest to seeing the UK hurling racist insults at a Polish waiter, while dancing on a table dressed as a Morris man. Defending their actions, one voter claimed that their drink had been spiked with a cocktail of paranoia and xenophobia.

One bleary-eyed Brexiter admitted: 'I remember shouting a lot, punching a border guard, and then someone suggested we go to a strip bar. The next thing I know, I've vomited on my own shoes, signed up to a Norwegian-style trade agreement, and declared war on Luxembourg.'

Another sobering Brit, still looking for his keys and postal vote, said: 'I think I may have called our ex America, and inadvertently told Donald Trump I love him. I just don't remember – but how bad can it be? ... What? We shot an MP and made Nigel Farage our new leader? F*ck – it must have been one hell of a party.'

Election rules prevent BBC from describing Boris as a c*nt

In the run-up to the General Election, BBC Head of Policy Mike Smythe has confirmed that, under election rules, its journalists will not be allowed to refer to Boris Johnson as a lying, philandering, racist c*nt with a poor grasp of political detail and zero integrity or statesmanship.

'If we were to describe on air Boris's track record of dishonesty as a journalist, and remind people that he once allegedly conspired to commit an act of violence, the press ombudsman would do to the BBC what Boris allegedly did to various ladies who were not his wife across a snooker table,' Smythe added.

'Our impartiality is everything,' he continued. 'We must tell each side of the story, including that of Nigel Farage, even though he is clearly even more of a c*nt than Boris. So basically, we're watching a battle between a c*nt and a bigger c*nt, although I would never say that.'

Jacob Rees-Mogg was quick to defend Johnson. 'It's well known that William Gladstone killed, cooked and ate a number of prostitutes at 10 Downing Street,' he said.

'This didn't inhibit his effectiveness as a great conservative reformer. And Lord Palmerston was probably responsible for the Great Fire of London and was almost certainly Jack, the Yorkshire Ripper. Yet he became the greatest political thinker since Margaret Thatcher.'

Politics over, says man on Facebook

The poor and dispossessed have unanimously decided to shut up about politics and enjoy Christmas, thanks to Tim Hurley from Wiltshire declaring that he's bored of everyone 'waffling on.'

'Up until five minutes ago, I was getting ready to help those in desperate need,' said one food bank volunteer. 'But since reading that Tim's annoyed by any mention of politics, bollocks to it - you'll find me watching Miracle on 34th Street with a beer, balls deep in a tin of Quality Street.'

'I was livid at the growing poverty and inequality,' said disability activist Helen Jones, who recently had her payments stopped for seemingly no reason at all. 'But when I woke up this morning and saw that Tim's sick of hearing about it, I thought "F*ck it, let's see if Morrisons will accept tears as payment and buy myself a mince pie and a daft hat to celebrate". Thanks, Tim.'

Hurley was unavailable for comment, but a quick glance at his Facebook posts reveal that his new concerns are Baby Yoda, traffic updates and photos of a full English breakfast.

EU mistakenly tells UK: 'So long, and thanks for all the fish'

In an embarrassing moment for the EU, its final farewell to Britain was unfortunately mistranslated as 'So long, and thanks for all the fish', it has emerged.

In an official apology, Spain said that they hadn't meant to be quite so honest about their feelings, while France seemed surprised by the suggestion that they weren't allowed to catch British fish anymore. The statement went on to describe Britain as 'mostly harmless', though this part was apparently written before Boris Johnson became PM.

For his part, Johnson said that after years of preparation, the Government had come up with a plan to make the UK a huge success after Brexit. Unfortunately, five minutes before it was to be announced, Britain was demolished to make way for a Brussels-to-Dublin bypass.

Boris disappointed not to get a go on his riot water cannons

Prime Minister Boris Johnson has expressed his disappointment over recent protests in London and across the UK. 'It was a shame that the protests turned to violence in some areas; but the real tragedy is that I thought I was going to get a go on a water cannon,' he said.

'Not only have the water cannons been decommissioned, there has been nothing as fun to replace them. No Taser nets. No quick drying concrete guns. No marble bombs to make everyone fall over. Nothing. This is a dark day for London.'

When asked what he thought about the protests that were largely undertaken peacefully across the country, Johnson simply shook his head, mumbled, and mimed shooting a water cannon at the reporters.

Raab discovers tunnel under the Channel

Brexit Secretary Dominic Raab has told a secret meeting of the cabinet last night that the tunnel alleged to have been found under the English Channel could be a game changer.

'It may sound like a story from the Second World War, but the so-called tunnel has apparently been there for some time and provides a direct link-up between Southern England and virtually the whole of France,' he said.

'I intend to go straight to the site of the entry to the 'tunnel' this afternoon, just to check if it exists. Mrs Raab will record EastEnders on the Betamax, so no worries there.

'Security concerns mean I can't tell you that it starts in a British town beginning with D and goes all the way to a French coastal town. Possibly Bordeaux, or Des Moines. If I find anything I'm going to see if we can't put a frictionless border somewhere down there.

'Clearly, if it does exist and it's big enough for a man to stand up in, the danger is that after Brexit the Barnier hoards could simply pile through it, swamping southern England with Europeans demanding fruit picking jobs, strong coffee, universal credit and perverted sexual practices.

'One thing we can do immediately, though, is quash the rumours. For example, I've seen on the Internet that some people say that this tunnel is big enough to have trains running through it. I ask you - how would you keep that secret?'

What does Brexit mean? Your handy guide

Brexit means:

- Brexit
- Not Brexit
- Just a little bit Brexit
- Almost Brexit
- Slightly Brexit
- Absolutely, utterly and completely total Brexit immediately and for ever and ever
- Pretty much Brexit, most of the time
- More-or-less Brexit, some of the time
- TransBrexit
- Completely and utterly not the slightest bit Brexit in any shape or form, now or ever
- Can I phone a friend? Stop pissing about. This is a very serious matter
- Just a teeny-weeny little bit Brexit, for a short time, like five seconds or so
- Just answer the question. You're not getting out of this polling station until you've ticked at least one of the boxes
- Well, what's all this 'backstop' malarkey then? FFS just answer the question you troublemaker
- Can I take a lucky dip? No
- Can I go 50-50? NO. How many more times - just answer the bloody question
- None of the above
- All of the above
- What was the question again?
- It's perfectly simple, Brexit means - ooh look, a squirrel!

Rees-Mogg injured in chip pan fire at holiday caravan

Jacob Rees-Mogg, MP for West Snooty, has been injured in a chip pan fire at his mobile home in Rhyl, North Wales. Reports indicate that Rees-Mogg heard a noise outside and became distracted.

'I've told him before about the dangers of chip pans, but he never took no notice, he don't do no cooking at home, unless we have a barbecue. I was out at the bingo, so he gets the tea on,' said his wife, Baroness Kichenne T'able.

'Kids were kicking a ball at the van again. He was out there for ten minutes effing and blindin'. Then he smells smoke and runs in. Turns out he's only used oven chips. Mug.'

Rees-Mogg acted quickly, throwing a damp puffa jacket over the flames, but droplets of hot oil from some sausages splashed his arm. He bravely put out the flames, then went to see the Holiday Park's first aider, Eva Jones, who dabbed Witch Hazel on his oil scalds.

Costas Constantiou, proprietor of The Codfather chip shop, confirmed that the MP came in to buy four battered sausages and two large portions of chips, soon after. Rees-Mogg is expected to return to his parliamentary duties shortly.

IN OTHER RELATED NEWS:

Spiked drink blamed for Theresa May's vision of a better Britain
Gove criticised for leaving Boris unattended
Voter, looking left, gets hit by bus coming from the right
Change UK split to pursue solo incompetence
Gove's bookshelf contains the Necronomicon
Labour Party loses opposition contract to satire websites
May announces £5 million for Grenfell victims left over from savings on sprinklers
Tory law and order group to be known as 'ladies who lynch'
Nineteen world leaders and Theresa May attend G20 summit
All press conferences to end after one minute with 'bored of your questions now'
Sandal shortage feared as Lib Dem numbers increase
Austerity forces Cheshire man to take fourth job
Kent townsfolk fear 'No Deal' Brexit
Head-glued-in-microwave man REALLY pisses off rescuers by going 'ping' when freed
Scientists to start looking for planets nothing like this hellhole
Cigar-shaped object in space 'not cigar'
Embryo frozen for 24 years throws gauntlet down to David Blaine
Safety concerns over Dyson 'airbagless' electric car
NASA Sun Probe to go at night to prevent overheating
Dinosaur asteroid hit 'worst possible place', say scientists. Right in the nuts
Oil price apocalypse: 'bring it on' say would-be road warriors
'Rearranging Titanic's deckchairs would have saved 1,500 lives,' say researchers
Human colony on Mars 'still cheaper than London'
We need to stop Russia interfering with our interference, says MI6
Government to change length of week to 10 days

CHAPTER ELEVEN:

One in 25 children 'too fat to go in goal' (and other Sports stories)

Running marathon eradicates all semblance of humility

Training for a marathon heightens novice runners' unwavering belief in their own brilliance, eventually eradicating any sense of self-awareness, a study has suggested.

Researchers from the Institute of People tested novice runners attempting the London Marathon and noticed an immediate change in their proportionality, instantly comparing their marathon intentions to successfully completing two tours in Helmand Province circa 2002.

Dr John Smith said: 'We had a number of responses from our formerly bland participants. One took a non-consensual selfie with me while doing that weird heart-shaped sign with his hands.

'One signed his name on my shirt in permanent marker and asked me if I wanted to star on his marathon training channel on Tik Tok. I still don't know what those words mean. Another shook my hand and just said, "You're welcome".

'Basically, when fairly average, normally dull people voluntarily sign up to do mad shit, like run a ludicrous distance, they become utterly unbearable. But let's face it, they were pretty awful to start with.'

Women footballers to receive cliché training

Female footballers are to be schooled in spouting meaningless rubbish to the media in a new initiative to bridge the capability gap between them and their male counterparts.

This follows a shameful incident in the FIFA Women's World Cup in which a player failed to answer a banal question regarding her feelings about scoring a goal with: 'I'm over the moon but at the end of the day it's all about the three points.'

An FA spokesman explained that the course was all about levelling the playing field. 'Women should not be demonstrating their intelligence, imagination and extended vocabulary when talking about the game,' he said.

'They need to be taught the finer points of describing a win as a dream come true and how to express the view that a defeat makes them as sick as a parrot.'

The course is likely to be extended to female football pundits, who are currently ruining the FIFA Women's World Cup experience for many viewers with their combination of insightful analysis, tactical awareness and thorough knowledge of the game.

All students will be expected to give 110%, with the curriculum comprising of two modules, thereby making it a game of two halves, although the students will be instructed to take it one lesson at a time.

Britain ecstatic as man comes third sliding down a hill on a tray

Some bloke you've never heard of has warmed the cockles of the nation's heart by coming third in Olympic Downhill Tray-sliding in the PyeongChang Winter Olympics.

His financial future is totally secure as he is now destined to be taken to our hearts and tread a well-worn path sure to see him win Sports Personality of the Year, be knighted in the New Year's Honours list, and be given the freedom of his hometown, wherever that is.

The bloke told reporters: 'I'm delighted to have been able to make a name for myself in such a minority sport. My heroes have always been Steve Redgrave and Chris Hoy because look at the handy touch they've had for years just for paddling a boat and riding a bike.

'I think it's fantastic opportunities such as mine exist. Britain is so desperate for success in any international sport, that if you can pull it off, no matter how obscure that sport is, then you're made for life.'

British swimmer wins medal despite no inspirational back-story

Speaking at a press conference, Olympic silver medallist Ben Green, 21, left reporters dumbfounded when he announced that both of his parents were in the rudest of health and that he himself had never been at death's door as a child.

'I knew that not having an inspirational against-all-odds back-story could make the final difficult for me,' said a delighted Green. 'Two of the finalists were given the last rites when they were kids, one had to flee the Taliban, and another only took up swimming after he nearly drowned trying to rescue his dog. And of course, the gold medallist himself had to overcome a severe allergy to swimming trunks.

'I fell off my bike when I was 14 and grazed an elbow, but other than that it's been pretty plain sailing.'

Green has a chance for further glory in the men's relay race later in the week. 'I'd love to get another medal, especially in the circumstances,' he said, emotionally. 'I haven't told anyone yet but I stubbed my toe climbing onto the podium earlier, it's quite sore but I'm determined to soldier on.'

Army called in after all Premier League managers sacked

As the latest round of sackings among top-flight managers hit home this weekend, leaving the nation's most prestigious club competition in complete disarray, the Government's emergency committee, COBRA, was hastily convened, and concluded that the only viable option to get the league back on track and reassure the general punters was to bring in the troops.

'It couldn't be allowed to go on with less than 20% of Premier League clubs under any effective control,' said pundit Alan Hansen, who fully supports the intervention.

'But with a robust Brigadier General now at the helm of every team you can begin to dream that at last we can sort this mess out, with passion, grit, and maybe the crowds could be rewarded by the occasional fight to the death. That's the sort of commitment the game's been lacking this year.'

With extensive training in tactics for attack, defence and skirting round the opposition's flanks, the new managers are expected not only to bring discipline and drive back to the game, but may also make each game a challenge for the match officials.

'Any tackle involving small arms, well that has to be a straight red card,' said commentator John Motson. 'For serious incidents we could see the referee given no option but to throw the Geneva convention at them.' The system has already been trialled by West Ham, who for the past ten years have been under the guidance of a Major Disaster.

Ref's vanishing spray is whipped cream, claims Webb

FIFA super-ref and occasional Manchester United squad member Howard Webb has revealed the new 'vanishing spray' he has been issued with for this year's World Cup to help make free kicks fairer, is indistinguishable from whipped cream, and just as tasty.

'I've been sent ten cans of the stuff, and my three kids love it on donuts, while my wife and I enjoy it immensely on a cup of hot chocolate. So far with no ill effects - except that now, everyone keeps ten yards away from me,' he quipped.

Apart from being delicious, use of the spray has attracted some controversy, after Japanese referee Yuichi Nishimura used it to draw a number of penises on the Sao Paulo pitch at various points during the Brazil-Croatia game.

Nishimura faces disciplinary action if, as some have suggested, a dreadful late sliding challenge from a Croatian defender on Neymar was influenced by him writing 'Kick me' on the Brazilian's back, 15 seconds before.

FA admits to long-term usage of performance-inhibiting drugs

In an admission confirming what the majority of fans have long suspected, details of a long term, self-handicapping regime for England footballers have emerged, stretching back nearly 50 years.

'The initial euphoria of the win in 1966 quickly wore off,' admitted an FA spokesman, 'but we realised that the genie was out of the bottle. We would never again be able to live up to this performance and level of expectation.'

The FA looked to a number of pharmaceutical companies, offering up the team as a test bed for chemical cocktails aimed at underachieving. An initial deal was brokered, but was almost scuppered in 1970 by the team's unwillingness to conform, losing only narrowly to the best Brazilian team of all time.

Since then there have been more stringent rules and regulations in place, but there have been occasional blips where managers have taken it upon themselves to suspend the programme.

The drugs scandal could see England banned from going to the 2018 World Cup. A FIFA spokesman commented: 'Or we could just let them play all their qualifiers as usual. The end result will still be the same.'

Swimming pools to introduce 'hairy fatty back bits' lanes

Walthamstow public swimming pool is to pilot new 'smooth' and 'hairy' shoulder lanes in a scheme due for nationwide rollout. The new system was introduced after it was noticed that an effective swimming workout was being undermined for many, by the fear of ingesting curly hair floating on the surface during their regular workouts.

'It's very easy for hirsute swimmers to ignore the issue completely and carry on regardless,' a lifeguard shrugged. 'They see nothing of the devastation they cause to those behind them: the gagging fits, the abandonment of the pursuit of personal best times for swimming a length or two.

'This is long overdue if you ask me. It really does slow people down, but we welcome this new rule - before it, we would only be allowed to intervene over the speed thing if we saw someone engaging in other unsafe or distracting practices, like heavy petting or torpedoing old ladies.'

Curtis Price, attending the local sixth form and looking forward to a promising career in fast food, weighed up the situation and decided that he would rather wear a blue armband than pubes on his shoulders. 'Who knows what the future holds, though,' he admitted, worried.

Sports Channel admits forthcoming match is 'missable'

In a radical departure from its policy of advertising sporting events as 'Grand-Slam Saturday', a sports channel has shocked its viewers by trailing a forthcoming live sports broadcast as 'A Take-It-Or-Leave-It Fixture, Purely of Academic Interest to Supporters of the Two Teams Involved.'

A spokesman said: 'It's only Leeds Rhinos versus the Warrington Something-or-Others, and let's face it, most people don't even like Rugby League, so to bill it as 'Clash of the Titans' would be over-selling it a bit.'

They also apologised for telling viewers that the Championship fixture between Barnsley and Preston was a 'must-see' game, that the NFL match between Denver Broncos and Miami Dolphins was part of a 'Triple-Whammy Tuesday', and that any speedway event ever was worth watching.

They also confessed that 'Survival Sunday' was not an accurate description of a day that decided which team would go down from the Blue Square Conference North to the Unibond League. 'All in all,' said the host, 'you can only watch so much sport. And Mad Men is just starting on BBC 4 and that's really good, actually.'

Wimbledon Ladies' Prettiness Championship enters final stages

Tension is growing among fans of attractive women in white pleated skirts, as the annual Ladies' Prettiness Championship entered its final stages this week at Wimbledon. And, despite complaints in some quarters that the standard of gorgeousness is not what it used to be, there have been plenty of surprises along the way.

Long-time no-hoper Venus Williams surprised many observers by getting to the second round by means of an unusual style of dress, but was subsequently knocked out for unfashionable collars.

Meanwhile, plucky Brit Laura Robson managed to outscore Italy's Francesca Schiavone on face, legs and shape alike, before inevitably succumbing to the honey-toned loveliness of Serbia's Ana Ivanovic in round three.

Finally, five-time champion Maria Sharapova, who breezed past several excessively muscular also-rans in the first week, scraped through to the quarter-finals over her Russian compatriot Alona Bondarenko.

Sharapova forged an early lead with her searing blonde strokes, but was pegged back by Bondarenko's superbly tanned thighs, and only won on a tie break after her orgasmic shriek was preferred to Bondarenko's guttural moan. Sharapova then made the semi-finals by outscoring Dominika Cibulkova in straight legs.

'It's anyone's contest now,' said renowned sports analyst Tim Henman, who happened to be in town to cover a sporting contest of some sort.

'I quite fancy Jankovic, or Maria Kirilenko, or Jelena Dokic - actually I just fancy them all, to be honest. Except Simona Halep, obviously. I'm told she actually had a breast reduction so that she could play tennis better. Honestly, what was the silly mare thinking of?'

'Concussion not good for you' discovery shocks scientists

Since 1920, thousands of American Footballers have taken part in an elaborate experiment to repeatedly ram their heads together in the hope of generating an alternative source of energy. Much to everyone's surprise, the study has concluded that there was not enough kinetic force to boil an egg, but enough traumatic brain injury to elect George W. Bush again.

The initial data on cognitive impairment was inconclusive, as the tactics of the average NFL match already resembled the actions of a befuddled raft of turkeys. One doctor acknowledged: 'Our suspicions were first aroused when we noticed that in no other sport do the participants dress like marshmallows.'

Despite suffering no such head trauma themselves, fans regularly display the concentration of a goldfish. So mind-numbing is the NFL, that interest is only maintained through constant squad rotation between downs, intravenous infusions of deep-fried fat, and scantily clad women waving brightly coloured balls of string.

By contrast, the medicinal properties of other sports have been long established, with tennis being a reliable cure for insomnia, ice hockey alleviating pacifism and golf taming hyperactivity (and the will to live). Said one American Footballer: 'If I wanted to hurt my brain, I'd have learned the rules of cricket.'

Boxing club defends cot-fighting event

A sports club in Preston, which charged adults £25 a ticket to watch a fight between two 18-month-old boys, has denied that the toddlers in question were being exploited.

The controversial cot-fight between Tommy 'Rusk-crusher' Jones and Benny 'Bedwetter' Benson was eventually stopped in the third round because it was time for the challenger's afternoon nap.

When it was pointed out that Tommy was crying loudly throughout the bout, club owner Barry Hardwick said, 'Well they do that, don't they?' He also defended the lack of gum shields.

'They haven't got many teeth yet and they're going to fall out in a few years anyway. If they weren't knocking each other unconscious these youngsters might be out rioting or mugging or something. Now that can wait until they start nursery school.'

Football chant understood, accepted by self-aware opposition

While they were watching their side lose two-nil at home to Sheffield United, Norwich City players and fans accepted that much of the opposition chanting had been based on honest observations.

'When they started shouting "Sheep, Sheep, Sheep Shaggers!" I thought, here we go again, that tired old bucolic cliché,' reflected veteran Norwich striker Lewis Grabban.

'But just as I was leaping to head away a corner, I thought, 'Actually, I suppose those living in predominantly rural areas like Norfolk are statistically more likely to engage in sexual relations with farm animals, even though the recorded instances of that sort of thing is remarkably rare these days. But in relation to other clubs in the Championship, yes, it is fair comment.'

During the second half, Norwich goalkeeper John Ruddy found himself performing directly in front of thousands of Sheffield United fans who soon began shouting 'Who ate all the pies?' After the game, he was philosophical.

'It's a rhetorical question, clearly. They were not expecting me to turn around and explain that the pies were in fact eaten by many different people, but that yes, I had perhaps eaten more than my fair share. But again, I thank them for pointing out that the pies were perhaps shared out slightly unequally.'

Seven minutes into the second half, the visitors went one-nil up, with a second goal sealing the tie five minutes later. At this point the fans began a chorus of 'You're shit, and you know you are'.

'I think this is a no-brainer,' admitted the Norwich manager. 'Clearly we are not a very good team - we are not in the top division and don't look likely to get anywhere close any time soon. But it's always worth pointing these things out, because you should never assume anything. So once again, fair comment from the Yorkshire lads.'

Supporters of Sheffield United were reported to be irritated by the extremely reasonable response of the Norwich team, and a minority vowed to give them a good kicking.

A group of Norwich fans responded: 'Come and have a go if you think you're hard enough!' – adding - 'If, however, you do not think you are sufficiently robust, any sort of physical combat is probably best avoided.'

Concerns grow for World Cup WAG squad

With two months remaining before the start of the World Cup, concerns are mounting that England may end up fielding its weakest WAG line-up for years.

'The Wives and Girlfriends have been beset by disaster in the run-up to the finals. There's no denying that the loss of Cheryl Cole has been a devastating blow for the team this close to the tournament,' said a source close to the WAG training camp.

As the WAGs prepare for the rigours of the South African heat at a specially equipped facility, they are learning how to combat humidity frizz, high-altitude alcohol tolerance and the Afrikaans for 'turn the sun-bed to Oompa Loompa'. However, there is a growing sense of concern that the team lacks that vital experience we need to see off stiff challenges from the French and Brazilian WAGs.

The question on everyone's lips is still whether one-time chief WAG, Victoria Beckham, has one last World Cup left in her. 'Her form has been so erratic over the recent past – she proved she can play a blinder in Armani knickers, but then followed it with that disastrous performance on American Idol,' said the source.

'In truth, these days she's more of an impact WAG, and there have been serious questions over her fitness for some time. But for what it's worth, I still would.'

World Cup commentary team to return to a heroes' welcome

The BBC has announced that there will be a homecoming parade, where they will then be transported back to Television Centre on a specially commissioned London bus, provided by Mayor Boris Johnson.

The Queen's private secretary said that Her Majesty had shed a private tear of joy after the team's performance in the final. She is quoted as saying: 'It makes one proud to be British.'

Losing finalists, ITV, and their captain Adrian Chiles, are said to be devastated at their defeat. 'It was just a matter of competing against a more experienced, more talented side,' he admitted, bitterly.

Chelsea in £9 million bid for Watford's points

Chelsea moved to the top of the Premiership this morning after successfully buying Watford's points. The £9 million transfer came as a surprise to the rest of the Premiership, but with Watford already having given up any hope of staying in the Premiership, the audacious purchase of all their points benefits both clubs.

It now brings Chelsea's tally to 45 points, although their goal difference has suffered, particularly considering the four goals that Chelsea have now conceded against Chelsea. It also puts them four points ahead of Manchester United, who are now rumoured to be in negotiations with Charlton over a loan of some of their points until the end of the season.

Chelsea's chief executive commented: 'These ten points are exactly the sort of boost our club needs and they would have been wasted on Watford. As they say, you can't take them with you.'

Music extravaganza interrupted by irrelevant ball game

Rock fans and devotees of girls jiggling were left fuming, as the coverage of Super Bowl XLVIII was disrupted by a motley collection of pumped-up athletes with over-excited pituitary glands and a high incidence of positive drug testing.

One music journalist complained: 'People paid good money to see a pyrotechnic-filled show and Janet Jackson's nipple. What they don't expect to see is a wrestling match between owners of second-rate degrees, in pants so tight that Mick Jagger would blush, and sporadic mindless violence, thinly disguised as some sort of girly game of rugby.'

By contrast, in the UK, only a small fraction of our gambling adverts are disrupted by actual sport.

Dog walking to be demonstration sport at London Olympics

'We are naturally delighted,' said Tom Simkins, the Great Britain Dog Team's chief coach, after dog walking was elevated to a demonstration Olympic sport at London 2012. 'Although we're astonished at the number of events included in the trial.'

Events include the 1500 metres Hurried Early Morning Stroll, the Poo Retrieval Unclean Jerk, and the 100 metres Arse Wipe Across the Hall Carpet.

Dog Walking will be the first sport seen by visitors to London, the display coinciding with a stroll around the artificial countryside created for the opening ceremony. Organisers hope the demonstration will finish before nightfall, when a demonstration of Drug-Dealing and Synchronised Cottaging is expected to take over the mound.

IN OTHER RELATED NEWS:

Rooney equals Charlton's record on stupid haircuts
Britain to reopen Embassy World Snooker in Tehran
Bernie Ecclestone avoids £1.2bn tax bill by claiming to be under 12
Keith Richards 'may have taken performance enhancing drugs'
Motor racing anecdote used by anaesthetist
Blatter escapes disguised as the Von Trapps
Birdwatchers furious after staying up all night to watch Superb owl
Davis Cup victory inspires the UK to rebuild its Empire
Racist chanting interrupted by football
Andy Murray embarks on new career as motivational weeper
Riots after national newspaper fails to give away World Cup
Wallchart
Mo Farah just grateful to see the back of Quorn
Britain 'just not comfortable' with winning
Coronavirus lockdown forces footballer to sleep with his own wife
Despite doping scandal, cycling still not a real sport
Assistant Referee still self-identifies as a 'Linesman'
Grim Reaper finally wins that game of chess
England fans honour WW1 fallen by staging battles between
football matches
F1 deny racism, despite Grand Prix being halted as police pull over
Lewis Hamilton for 'having a flash car'
Golfer stunned by useful Christmas present
Sepp Blatter asked to intervene as Subbuteo transfer falls through
Achilles forced to pull out of Trojan War - injury unknown
Billions pour in for inaugural world money-throwing championships
New sporting records set in National Leaf-Blowing Championships
'My secret shame' – shocking confession of woman who hasn't
slept with Ryan Giggs
Tickets go on sale for 2012 school sports day Mums' race
Post-match interview hit by spot-fixing claims after cricketer
mentions all Bananarama's greatest hits
Goalkeeper insists on wearing different colour shirt to team dinner

CHAPTER TWELVE

Man attacked with drum kit still suffers repercussions (and other Crime stories)

Passenger sets 'alight here' sign alight

Pensioner Stan Smythe has pleaded guilty to criminal damage at Maidstone Crown Court in setting alight an 'Alight here' sign at Maidstone railway station.

'It seemed clear to me the people who put the sign up wanted it alight,' he told the court. 'They even showed me where they wanted it alight and I held a small petrol-soaked rag under the "H" of "here".'

Smythe explained that he suffers from both literalism and slight pyromania. 'I used to go to work, but I was setting off a firework two years ago and it said, "Light the blue touch paper and retire immediately", so I cashed in my pension that very night. Best advice I ever got, considering the office was burned to the ground the same night.'

Mothers' maiden names to be made more complicated

It is a question asked millions of times a day in call centres the world over. 'What is your mother's maiden name?' All too often it is a piece of information that can allow fraudsters access to all manner of private data.

Studies undertaken by the Institute for Online Security in Reading have revealed that four out of ten people will reveal their father's name, the name of their first pet and their favourite subject at school within five minutes of meeting a stranger.

Professor Maria Higg1ns42 said that women's surnames should in future contain at least eight characters, including at least two numbers. But Dr Helen W00psy-diddly-d@ndy! says that may not be enough, and is proposing even greater complexity with the use of shift and alt keys, and possibly even Cyrillic characters.

'The issue is even more complicated than that,' argued Jim 12OcelotSandwiches, senior lecturer in security studies at the University_of_12_Peculiar_Secrets.

'Too many of us will invent funny mother's maiden names only to blurt them out in social situations to gain an approving laugh. Then we'll need a new password, and so on. I can see a future in which people will have to prove their identity by producing a sample of an agreed bodily fluid.'

Deadly nerve agent traced to Somerset

The nerve agent used to attack former Russian spy Sergei Skripal and his daughter in Salisbury may have links to a substance being developed in Somerset, it has been revealed. An amber liquid found near the scene of the attack has now been traced back to the garden shed of Taunton taxi drivers Alf and Reg Perkins.

'The cloudy liquid and the nerve agent are almost certainly linked,' revealed an MI6 operative. 'They both give off a foul, acrid smell and share the same apple-based signature. Being found slumped on a bench in the park is a dead giveaway. To anyone not used to it, the liquid is almost certainly lethal. Even at small doses, the side effects last for days.'

Incredible though it sounds, the cloudy liquid, with the code name 'Old Ratcatcher', is being sold in pubs and restaurants across the south-west region. It is known to seriously alter speech patterns, causing temporary or long-term blindness, loss of bodily functions and severe migraine.

Consumption also triggers vomiting and nausea, shaking, bouts of violence followed by self-loathing and eventually leads to those affected developing blotchy skin and a big, red bulbous nose. Side effects are also said to include expressing unremitting love for others and repeatedly claiming that they are your best friend.

Lorry driver penalised after doing double light flash to regular car

A Sheffield lorry driver is facing years in the wilderness after having all forms of camaraderie removed by the HGV community. The extreme punishment was served because Michael McGuire mistakenly flashed a Fiat 500 car back into the first lane of the motorway after it had overtaken his truck between Junctions 18 and 19 of the M6.

'That helpful quick double flash, and the compulsory obligation on the part of the recipient lorry driver to give a quick 'left-right-left' thank you with your indicators are a social convention available exclusively to the 7.5 tonne plus vehicle-driving community,' said judge Peter Smith of the Haulage Association, following a hearing of fellow HGV drivers at Lymm truck stop. 'Otherwise society will just break down.'

In his defence, McGuire's lawyer argued that the hapless lorry driver had glanced in his mirror earlier and had clearly seen a Homesense truck pulling out rather than a Fiat overtaking. Unbeknown to him, the Homesense driver had decided to stay in the inside lane and get right up the arse of an elderly couple in a Micra.

In passing sentence, Smith ordered other lorry drivers not to acknowledge McGuire on major carriageways for the next two years. He will also be barred from doing that thing that lorry drivers do when a lane is closing on the motorway, where they straddle the two lanes and drive really slow with their hazards on.

Veteran dog walker finally discovers corpse in woods

After years of waking up early to walk his dog, retiree Mike Edwards has finally found a corpse. 'I've been walking my dog through the woods every morning since I retired fifteen years ago,' said the 67-year-old. 'Everybody knows that all dog walkers eventually find something like this, but I've not once found a mangled body or a skeleton.'

When pressed for details of the gruesome find, he explained: 'It was textbook. My black Labrador ran ahead and I lost sight of him, but then I found him sniffing around a pile of leaves and saw the hand poking out. I phoned the police straight away and waited for them to arrive. They put a tent up around the body, then a haggard-looking, world-weary cop turned up to take over and wind up the forensics team.'

'At the moment we have no idea who the dead woman is, but assume that the discovery of the body will be the start of a long and complex investigation,' said Chief Superintendent Robert Sayer. 'We suspect that the motive for the murder will have its roots in something that happened decades ago, possibly in a children's home.'

Sayer concluded: 'We would ask anyone who may know the dead person to come forward, so that we may suspect them of not giving us the full story before offloading in an emotional denouement, at which point we will probably agree that the dead woman had it coming. For now, I've passed the investigation over to a shambolic, divorced, middle-aged, functioning alcoholic who deals with this sort of thing every week.'

Maverick cops now in the majority, says Scotland Yard

Scotland Yard has launched a recruitment drive among the happily married and conventional rule-following community, as the force has now become 'maverick cop-heavy'.

'There are too many cops pulling stunts, tearing up the rule book and getting results their own way,' said the head of Human Resources at the Met. 'They have got particularly irksome since the rule book went digital and they have to go round wiping the backups of it on everyone else's computers.

'Nobody on the force imagined that the HR department would be forced to break convention like this. But as I told the officer who came up with this solution, you may not play it by the rules, Johnson, but you are the best goddamn personnel officer this force has got!'

Man banned from local gym after failing to urinate in shower

A Doncaster man has been banned from his local gym after it was found that he had been regularly having a post-workout shower without taking a piss at the same time.

The offence was spotted by the male changing room cleaner, who noted that the shower tray remained a pristine white colour after Peter Smith, 24, emerged at 6.30 each evening, rather than having the more typical light-yellow film around the edges.

'I've been under a lot of pressure recently, and in my rush to free up the shower for other users at a busy time of day, I forgot basic changing room etiquette,' argued Smith in his defence.

'With a bit more time, I would have undoubtedly turned towards the wall, lathered up some extra shower gel to hide the flow of urine and enjoyed the sensation of warm piss on leg, but hindsight is a wonderful thing.'

'It's people like that who ruin this place for everyone else,' said another naked man in the male changing rooms today, as he walked from the showers, towel round his neck, dripping absolutely everywhere.

'Now, if you don't mind, I've got to absent-mindedly tug at my penis while standing about three inches away from you, before drying my undercarriage by putting one leg on the bench and then doing that two-handed sawing motion from front to back with the towel.'

Police to remove trousers before giving evidence

Courts should be able to order constables to remove their trousers in court, a judge has decreed. Mr Justice Bludgeon believes it is important that juries have the right to see the style and condition of an officer's underpants if they are to give credence to the evidence being presented.

'With practice, a man may be capable of keeping a straight face while lying through his teeth in the witness box,' he said, 'but if he is a knave or a scoundrel then that fact should come to light, and there is no surer a way of telling than by a proper examination of his, or indeed her, undergarments.'

Police who wish to remain fully clothed for religious reasons could be permitted to de-bag and give evidence behind a curtain, Bludgeon added. A Clerk of the Court would then don the underpants and stand in view of the jury while the proceedings continued.

Pressed as to why the no-trouser rule should only apply to police and not other witnesses or those on trial, the judge replied: 'That is a quite excellent idea. I like the cut of your jib. I'm telling the truth - look, I'm not wearing any.'

Goldilocks admits to further string of burglaries

Following the recent break-in at a bear family household by the 'choosy' female burglar Cheryl 'Goldie' Locks, police profilers have identified several more crimes easily recognisable by her modus operandi.

One couple arrived home to find their house looking like a clothes shop changing room, while another reported their crate of best Cabernet Sauvignon stolen after someone conducted a prolonged wine-tasting session in the cellar.

Speaking on condition of anonymity to the media, Miss Locks admitted to trying on twelve pairs of designer shoes in another house before deciding the Guccis were 'just right', although she tossed the Jimmy Choos in her swag bag too, just in case.

At another house where the absent owners had obligingly left three sets of car keys, she eventually settled for the medium-sized VW Golf GTI.

'I wouldn't touch the pissy little Fiat 500, obviously,' she explained. 'I was tempted by the Audi A7 at first, but you can't make a quick getaway from the fuzz when everyone thinks you're a twat and makes a point of not letting you out at junctions.'

Texas to offer lethal injections in three new flavours

The State of Texas has committed itself to a 'more humane' approach to execution, as the governor announced that the poison would come in three delicious fruity flavours, with more to be added in the near future.

'Justice should be tempered with a hint of strawberry, or vanilla,' he explained at a press conference. The authorities hope that these options will tempt more Death Row inmates to 'get it over with' and stop clogging up the courts with endless appeals.

The American Civil Liberties Union has welcomed the move, saying this could be the first step to giving murderers a shot of sugared water instead of the poisonous potassium chloride, 'just to give them a fright and teach them a lesson'.

Meanwhile, reaction on Death Row has been mixed, from 'What, no Peppermint?' to 'Old Sparky gave us Smoky Bacon'.

Shock at death of yet another World's Oldest Man

Following the death of the World's Oldest Man, just weeks after the previous incumbent died in very similar circumstances, the police are finally going to act. 'Something's going on,' said DCI Jack Regan. 'Why do these very old men keep on dying?'

In the past 50 years, every single one of the World's Oldest Men has lost his title as a result of death, usually in a matter of a few months or years. 'This can't be an accident,' said an emotional Regan, although his boss later said that Jack was getting too involved and may have to be taken off the case.

Police have issued a description of a man seen in the area described as 'tall, hooded, with a pasty white face and carrying a scythe'. 'He's not a suspect, we just want to eliminate him from our enquiries,' said a spokesperson.

Government to issue polar bears to riot police

Under new emergency powers, riot police will be able to deploy a specially trained bear to disperse crowds and maintain public order. Each bear has been given strict instructions to chase arsonists, looters or anyone who just looks a bit tasty.

'We have been more than patient with these people,' said Home Secretary Theresa May. 'Frankly, releasing a ferocious 1,500 lb carnivore into the area is the only language they will understand.'

A number of bears have already been deployed in various hot spots including behind the counter at TK Maxx, disguised as luxury rugs in Carpetright and hiding in the sock bin at JD Sports.

Flood looters urged to wear stripy knitwear to measure water depth

Following massive recent flooding, the Government has urged anyone looting flooded properties to wear the 'traditional burglar's uniform' of a black and white stripy jumper, eye mask and flat cap, in order to help measure the depth of the waters.

'We're calling for looters to put a little bit back into the community by following our apparel guidelines,' said a DEFRA spokesman. 'That way, when they get caught, we can nail the bastards to the pavements of flooded streets, where they'll make great markers to show the rise and fall of flood water. We're also going to confiscate their swag sacks and reuse them as sandbags.'

The EU has reacted with outrage, calling the proposals a breach of international measuring standards that will not work anyway because of the variations in stripe thickness and the propensity of wool to shrink when wet. The Government said it will press ahead regardless and might also use escaped convicts from the 1950s as emergency signposts.

The Bill to be replaced by Community Support drama

ITV has confirmed that, after 27 years' service, 'The Bill' is being taken off frontline duties, and replaced by a new drama following Community Support Officers as they go about their important work of smiling and nodding at people in the street.

"CSO: Sun Hill' will look very similar to 'The Bill',' said producer Peter Fincham, 'but it won't have the same dramatic powers, meaning viewers can only be detained for a short time until another programme comes along to help.'

'CSO: Sun Hill' will provide essential backup and support to the hard work done by real police dramas, such as 'Waking the Dead' and 'A Touch of Frost'. The show begins next Monday, although for a probationary period all episodes will go out accompanied by repeats featuring experienced officer, DCI Burnside.

Debenhams retain police suspect blanket contract

Debenhams bosses were said to be 'quietly triumphant' yesterday, after retaining the contract to provide more than 30 UK police forces with the blankets used by officers to cover suspects' heads as they enter and leave court buildings.

The contract was decided after a vicious contest against John Lewis, with each side accusing the other of improper approaches to

Government officials. Eventually, it was decided to ignore the softly, softly approach of John Lewis featuring Egyptian cotton, in favour of the Debenhams chavvier designer range, which would make the accused feel more at home.

A Home Office spokesperson later said the process had been conducted entirely properly and denied there had been any cover-up.

Praise for 'subtle, proportionate' Met response to non-existent black crime wave

The police have proudly published a list of apparently innocent situations where heavy-handed institutionalised prejudice saved the day, resulting in only minimal collateral damage and lifelong trauma.

Illustrating the delicacy required in handling complex situations, officers sensitively wrestled to the ground a black man seen brandishing a blunt instrument in a busy shopping centre. Following robust questioning, police eventually handed him the Argos pen back, even kindly pointing out the closest A&E unit he could limp to, for assessment of his multiple injuries.

In another case, a 78-year-old woman required delicate handling for allegedly brandishing not one but two stiletto blades in a 'creative manner'. Explaining the full-body slam and chokehold, one arresting officer stated: 'It was clear she could have started purling at any moment, possibly with intent to produce a life-threatening Fair Isle pattern.'

Demonstrating the results of community training, a white man holding a cleaver was politely asked to step aside so police could Taser two black suspects throwing a suspected ninja star in a crowded public park. Hastily crayoning 'Frisbee' to the list of banned weapons, the two seven-year-olds were told to expect a long sentence just as soon as they were taken off life support.

Spartacus 'may have been victim of identity theft'

In what may be the most severe case of identity theft ever discovered, a former gladiator from ancient Thrace claims to have had his identity stolen by 'dozens' of migrant workers.

'It happens all the time,' said the man, unofficially identified as 'Spartacus'. 'At the doctors, for example, when the receptionist calls out my name, about twenty blokes stand up and claim to be me. I've taken to making appointments at the clap clinic just for a laugh. I've stopped entering raffles. Total waste of time.

'I'm not normally one to criticise the police, but the identity parade was a shambles. What's worse is that my wife thinks it's amusing. She's having loads of 'fun'. They'll be sorry though. Apparently, I'm scheduled for crucifixion next week. We'll see who's laughing then.'

Short bank robbers regret staging masked hold-up on Hallowe'en

A gang of dangerous but physically small robbers were left blaming each other as an ambitious bank raid went awry on Hallowe'en. The criminals, wearing Scream fright masks and George W. Bush disguises, failed to find anyone in the financial institution that would take them seriously.

After months of meticulous planning, two members of the East End gang burst into the Chancery Lane HSBC brandishing sawn-off shotguns, and shouting 'Open the safe or we'll blow your heads off!' However, instead of handing over stacks of unused notes amid scenes of hysterical panic, the cashier told them 'to wait while she got them some sweeties'.

'I blame the boss, Thommo,' said 'Wheels' Wilson, the getaway driver. Sending in 'Alf Pint 'Arris and Mitch the Titch to do the business with the shooters was a schoolboy error. They have trouble seeing over the counter at the best of times, and watching that old dear on the CCTV ruffle their hair and give 'em a fluffy old Werther's Original while they tried to take hostages ... we'll never live it down.'

Nigerian scammers to raise standards with 'Mystery Sucker' scheme

'We are concerned that the quality of email scams arising from our members has declined in recent years,' said Nigel Mwanga, only son of a recently deceased multi-millionaire oil executive and spokesperson for Nigerian scammers. 'We need to make sure Nigerian e-finance remains a market leader.'

The 'Mystery Sucker' scheme will see a group of UK undergraduates posing as unsuspecting punters, who will then contact the 'Shop-a-Useless-Scammer Hotline' whenever they come across unimaginative set-ups relayed in tell-tale broken English.

'We believe this scheme will be a real winner,' continued Mwanga. 'Unfortunately, we're having a few IT problems, so if members could just transfer the £10,000 registration fee into my sister-in-law's bank account, we'll put their certificates in the post.'

Police still 'institutionally sarcastic' claims senior Met officer

The Assistant Commissioner for Service Monitoring at the Metropolitan Police has launched a strong attack on what he called the continued culture of 'withering sarcasm and arch condescension' amongst officers in the force.

The accusation comes as a blow to the Met, hot on the heels of public outrage at the controversial 'belittling' technique used at recent protests. Over 130 complaints have so far been lodged regarding instances of facetiousness, use of grim ironic devices, and low-level condescension by officers, many allegedly captured by CCTV and on mobile phones.

The force has already promised a root-and-branch review of its ripostes following the Jose-Manuel Ortega enquiry by the Police Complaints Commission. Ortega, a trainee acupuncturist from Caracas, was badly wounded by police remarks in 2005 after being mistaken for Sela Inua, an Inuit from Battersea suspected of letting his tax disc expire.

Judges to wear headgear from other historical periods

'I sent a burglar to prison this morning wearing a horned Viking helmet,' said Judge Charles Farquahson. 'It felt really great, like I was Kirk Douglas or something. Yesterday, I presided over a complex fraud case with my hair spiked up and dyed red in the manner of the punk rock craze of the mid-1970s.'

Other judges have been appearing in court wearing Puritan hats from the late Tudor period or the cumbersome metal helmet complete with a visor from a medieval suit of armour. At the Old Bailey yesterday, the courtroom all rose for the judge, only to see him enter wearing a New York Yankees baseball cap on the wrong way round.

However, the Lord Chancellor has ruled against traditional horsehair wigs being replaced by the modern toupees associated with the likes of Terry Wogan or Paul Daniels. 'No, that's getting too ridiculous,' he said. 'We don't want the judges being laughed out of court.'

Granny runs 'crystallised ginger' lab

Police have warned the public in the run up to Christmas to be on the lookout for the tell-tale signs of family members experimenting with festive highs. Fears have been raised that elderly relatives may be turning unpalatable lumps of ginger into moreish treats and using cans of fake snow for a 'seasonal whippet'.

Drugs officers raiding Turkish Delight dens have found chemistry paraphernalia used in the manufacture and distribution of mince pies. The Government health campaign entitled 'Mum's gone to Iceland coz she's a crack whore!' has had little success, despite the stark poster images of the decomposing remains of Kerry Katona wrapped in bacon, lying in a pool of canapés.

One police officer warned: 'There's no more disturbing sight than seeing your children snorting caramelised nuts through a cheese straw. We've got teenagers 'snowballing' – which is rolling in icing sugar while inserting stollen slices into every orifice. Although I must stress, there is no evidence to suggest Brussels sprouts are a gateway treat - they're more of a rectal blockage.'

Secret Santa exposed as major money laundering scheme

A darker side has emerged of Secret Santa, the world's favourite office tradition. Every December, anonymous figures collect unmarked notes, only to turn these undisclosed sums into cheap gifts, trips to the pub and, in 2007, the collapse of the Royal Bank of Scotland.

Many unsuspecting office workers are lured in with the promise of lavish presents, only to find themselves on the receiving end of a Katie Price discounted book. Police have asked the public to report any suspicious gift transaction this December, particularly Google trying to offset their tax liability with 300,000 reindeer-themed hats.

Cocaine denies using Michael Gove

The Class A drug cocaine has distanced itself from accusations that Michael Gove's erratic and maniacal behaviour was the result of anything other than too much Michael Gove.

It insisted that it had not gone anywhere near his 'wine-soaked conk' and that Mr. Gove's policies were more likely the result of LSD or ADHD. Cocaine is normally taken nasally, whereas a Gove is expelled anally. Doctors warn of bleeding, itching, plus an increased chance of cardiac death - and apparently the side effects of cocaine are almost as bad.

Repeated exposure to Gove can result in paranoia, prolonged bouts of depression, followed by a Tory leadership election. Regular users suffer delusions of grandeur but only by comparison.

A spokeswoman for cocaine remarked: 'Sweaty, large pupils and gaping nostrils - and that's before he met us. Ever experience being stuffed into the bowel of drug mule, stuck on a long haul flight from Colombia, followed by a painful cavity search? Trust me, nothing prepares you for Michael Gove.'

'Dave and George' fraudsters trick UK out of £1.5 trillion

Some £1.5 trillion has been lost over the course of 2015 in a nationwide scam that 'encourages' people to pay money into a fraudster's account, according to Financial Fraud Study.

The victim's employer receives a demand to take a percentage of wages out of the victim's pay packet and send it to a 'safe account', which is then drained by the fraudsters. They chase up those who do not pay, threatening them with fines and extra interest payments.

The fraudsters appear to be led by criminals called 'Dave the PM' and 'George the Chancellor', sometimes accompanied by a terrifying moll called 'Theresa'

'They do a classic bad-cop-even-worse cop act,' said an FFS spokesman. 'Dave acts like he's your mate, whereas George is pure evil and stares at you as if he can see price tags on each of your organs.'

Once they have found a gullible victim who is prepared to work a lifetime to fund their extravagant lifestyle, the fraudsters really go to town, adding on spurious other requirements such as 'insurance' payments for a further percentage of salaries. Some even suggest that as much as 20% of all the UK's GDP ends up in the hands of these two scam kingpins.

Explanations about the reason for the payments vary, with subtle threats such as 'It'll be used to teach your children a lesson', only for the money to disappear off to the Cayman Islands. Said the spokesman: 'As protection rackets go, it's pretty cynical – even the Kray brothers believed in properly funding the NHS.'

Richard III descendants left with massive overdue parking bill

The living relatives of Richard III, the last English king to perish in battle, are now faced with a bill of over £100,000 from Leicester City Council for a parking space the monarch occupied for well over 500 years.

A spokesperson for the council said: 'We don't care who you are - you can't avoid Hawkeye Parking Enforcement sensors. Given that Mr Plantagenet arrived at the site about half a millennium before we installed the system, we didn't clock him arriving, but we are fully within our rights to issue parking fines retrospectively, even to those with alleged spinal disabilities.'

Despite this being the first parking fine issued from an era that predates the car park itself, the council insist they have treated Richard fairly.

'In accordance with the latest parking laws, once his twisted bones were exhumed, we were obliged to give him a ten-minute grace period to remove himself off the site completely. But even after this generous treatment, he still continued to just lie there, blocking the path of a Renault Megane that had already paid for a ticket.'

Chilcot to conduct inquiry into lack of inquiry into inquiry

Lord Chilcot has accepted the commission to conduct an impartial inquiry as to why Downing Street this week ruled out an inquiry into the lateness of the Chilcot Inquiry. 'It smacks of a cover-up,' sources close to Chilcot confided.

Defence expert Dr Rupert De'Ath explained: 'The original inquiry into the war in Iraq is understandably going to take its time. No-one expects the box with Schrödinger's cat to be opened because it will ruin the surprise. Mind you, if Blair had anything to do with it he would have murdered the effing cat before putting it in the box, and then set about putting the frighteners on any cat experts.'

Lord Chilcot is clearing his calendar of less important commitments in order to satisfy the need for prompt answers. Speaking outside the House of Lords, he said: 'The public naturally needs to understand why the Prime Minister does not want an impartial assessment of why the report into a wholly illegal and indefensible war is being delayed ... oh, b*gger...'

IN OTHER RELATED NEWS:

Wigan resident offered Widnes protection programme
Lorry driver who 'always went that extra mile' convicted of tachograph tampering
Home Secretary launches 'raft of measures' to prevent Channel crossings
Police on hunt for MP seen sticking to principles
Stop and Search to be replaced by Slap 'n' Tickle
Robert Downey Junior pardoned for 20 years of bland movies
Tories reform prisons ahead of own sentencing
Police unsurprised by man who overdosed on liquorice, saying it takes all sorts
Burglary at publishers was unplanned; thieves picked Random House
Caesar's last words: 'I should have done something about knife crime'
German cannibal who cooked friend 'had too much thyme on his Hans'
Police finally track down man who leaves chewing gum in urinals
Profumo shagged Nazis and Communists – what a legend!
Neighbour of man found guilty of identity theft jailed
Toilets vandalised: Police say they have nothing to go on
'Brilliant' sex addict lawyer gets all defendants off
Cyclist distributing pornography accused of pedalling filth
Fart produced from non-Halal food technically a hate crime
Officer who lost haul of stolen Viagra accused of being soft on crime
Man who smuggled windows inside donkey dismissed as a 'pane in the ass'
Hillsborough inquest agrees The Sun did piss on victims
Saudi anti-theft law passed by show of hands
Judge rejects '4 legs good 2 legs bad' defence in bestiality case
Newsbiscuit.com hit by ransomwa$[;÷}. Q&$[] €¥{$`}
®©™~¿¡«»}[¥€÷\§×}
Prison officers face gaol for striking over prison overcrowding
Nudist camp boss dressed me with his eyes, says ex-employee

CHAPTER THIRTEEN

One in five couples close to breakup; other four just kidding themselves (and even more Lifestyle stories)

Marriage crisis as husband eschews Christmas sex for cash alternative

The 22-year union between Lionel and Marjorie Alwyn was reportedly under threat last night, as it emerged that Lionel had declined their traditional festive sexual congress and asked 'for the money instead'.

'Well what was I supposed to say?' said Marjorie, who believed that her festive fur-trimmed stockings and saucy Santa hat had been hitting the spot since the Berlin Wall came down. 'And it wasn't just that he was turning down a few hours of nookie with me in favour of some money in an envelope - he only gave it a transferable value of twenty-five quid.'

But Marjorie was determined last night that her husband's slight was not going to ruin Christmas. 'Perhaps Lionel's got a point and we should mix it up a bit this Christmas,' she said. 'So, when I open the same John Lewis voucher I've been getting every year since we married, I will have a radiant smile on my face. Not least because I'll be imagining the saucy drawers they'll buy me to give his golf buddy Roger a welcome change from his customary Old Spice gift set.'

Achieve inner peace by practicing 'Bloody-Mindedness'

Want to become more aware of where you are, by becoming overly reactive to the f*ckwits surrounding you? With Bloody-Mindedness we are creating space for ourselves—space to think, to breathe, to frustrate, space to obstruct and p*ss off others, just because we can.

You can practise anywhere, there's no need to go out and buy a special cushion — all you need is your own inner tension, which you can then unleash on others.

1. First, take a seat. Find a place to sit that feels calm and quiet to you, and blocks an important entrance, exit or right of way for others.

2. Don't set a time limit. If you're just beginning, it can help to choose a short time, such as five or ten hours.

3. Notice your body. You can sit loosely cross-legged, but don't do anything poncey like assuming the lotus posture, or kneeling. Just make sure you are in a stable position, designed to cause the maximum inconvenience for others.

4. Feel your breath. Follow the sensation of your breath as it goes out and as it goes in, speeding up to match your increasing blood pressure.

5. Notice when your mind has wandered. Inevitably, your attention will leave the sensations of the breath and wander to other places, like that daft git with the stupid haircut and arse hanging out of his

jeans. When you get around to noticing this, simply let out a long sigh, and mutter under your breath 'Oh, for f*ck's sake'.

6. Be kind to your wandering mind. Don't judge yourself, but do judge others, at length and in detail. Just keep doing it, whenever you find yourself at a loose end in public. You'll feel so much better.

7. That's it! You f*ck off, you come back, and you try to do it as unpleasantly as possible.

No one has ever used the word 'youthquake'

Despite claims by the Oxford Dictionary that 'youthquake' is a word, most teenagers agree that it is only a phrase to use if you want to get ridiculed on social media. In fact, it is one of a long list of words and phrases not in present day use – such as 'please', 'pay rise' or 'Happy Brexit'.

The dictionary definition of 'youthquake' is: 'A word used to show that you are trying to be down with the kids, but actually you have no earthly understanding of youth culture or how to unlock a mobile phone'.

One MP responded: 'It's one of those ridiculous word mash-ups that makes no sense at all to the average politician – like consensual sex, informed referendum or tax return'.

Barbecue definitely worth the extra effort

Having scraped the rust and cobwebs off the barbecue grill and gone and bought the briquettes from the local garage, Mark Carter, 46, declared it would make a pleasant change to cook outside and enjoy that delicious smoky barbecue flavour that you can only get from cooking over charcoal. 'It was just a question of getting a good fire going.'

Carter had previously marinaded his chicken pieces in a delicious barbecue sauce and now put the skewers over the glowing coals. 'I forgot to soak the wooden skewers in water beforehand, so they all caught fire and fell apart,' he admitted. 'But no worry, because not all of the pieces were so large that they fell through onto the ash below.'

Having mistimed the heat of the fire somewhat, Carter, his wife and his now rather hungry and fractious children, finally got to eat their barbecued chicken at 11.30 at night.

'Sally and the kids have popped down to the hospital,' he said. 'They seem to have been suddenly struck down by some mystery bug. Perhaps it's that flu that's going around.'

Man holding door open thinks he has solved gender inequality

Paul Webster, 43, has a long history of supporting women's rights - be it sleeping in the damp patch, putting the recycling out or bathing at the plug end. He has done his bit to narrow the gender wage gap by tipping the babysitter, which also helps to buy her silence.

Webster explained: 'While I don't know much about women's suffrage, I once bought my mum some carnations from a Tesco garage. And remembered to take the sticker off. Plus, I have never touched any woman inappropriately - but not for want of trying.'

A female co-worker commented: 'I appreciate the gentlemanly gesture. I didn't have the heart to tell him I can do my own doors'.

Men on diets ask when the potato 'stopped being a vegetable'

Tubby gents are feeling aggrieved to discover that watching Sky Sports is not the equivalent of three hours in the gym, and that sucking a Polo mint after dinner is not a substitute for brushing your teeth. In fact, a recent health report suggests the humble potato's nutritional value is on par with licking plutonium, or the underside of Eric Pickles.

A spokesman for rotund males admitted: 'I know we could lose a few pounds, but what can we eat? I'm genuinely confused. It grows in the ground, right? What is it then, some kind of meat? If it's a meat, shouldn't it taste better. Do chips feel pain?'

One wannabe slimmer complained: 'Now, I'm told that eating fruit is cheating - they don't really count. Only blueberries. Bloody blueberries! I'd have to eat ten punnets just to take the edge off my appetite. First it was five-a-day, now it's ten. Ten! I can't even name ten vegetables, let alone fit them into the same sandwich.'

Dashcams keep dogging industry alive and kicking online

The UK's favourite car park pastime, dogging, was expected to suffer under lockdown, but has actually seen 'an impressive member growth', according to an unidentified industry spokesman, speaking from behind a steamed-up window in an unsettling leopard mask.

Once people realised they could turn their dashboard-mounted cameras around and stream live action from the back seats of their cars, virtual dogging became a pulsating reality. 'All they had to do was sneak out to their driveways in the dead of night, fire up their dashcams and bang on.'

Onlookers simply log on and leer from home, many conceding that it beats the crap out of standing in a freezing puddle in a lay-by on the A414.

Man delighted with pressure-washer 'knob drawing' weather

'I don't know what it is,' said Barry Williams, 55. 'But the joy I feel inside whenever the weather's nice and the wife asks me to get the pressure washer out, is truly unrivalled.

'You absolutely have not lived until you've powered an artistic genitalia representation into the conservatory roof glass filth, and then stopped for a cuppa with the sunlight shining through as if God is smiling upon you. That Da Vinci bloke's got nothin' on Baz from the block.'

Alongside Conservatory Cock, Williams's infamous collected works include 'Patio Penis', 'Shed Schlong', 'Decking Dick' and 'Window Wang'. Meanwhile, he hangs around the water cooler waiting until a work colleague asks him what he's chuckling about.

'Honestly? I don't think Toby from HR is as likely to see the funny side as Helen from Sales, but underneath all his scowling I reckon he's drawn a few crazy paving knobs in his time.'

'We didn't have it better in my day,' pensioner admits

'Anyone my age who says we had it good is talking tommy rot,' said Gerald Smythe, 92, a resident of Ottershaw Home for the Elderly in Surrey. 'My father died in the First World War, and my mother followed him to the grave when she caught pleurisy after the General Strike.

'We had no money and I had to steal coal from freight trains. One day, I stood on a bloody fog signal, which went off taking three of my toes with it. The old days were shit.'

To cries of 'Shame!' and 'Keep yer big gob shut!' from those seated around him, playing Kalookie, Smythe continued: 'The only thing to read was The Magnet and its supposedly hilarious characters: Quelchy, Inky and Smithy the Bounder. There was no telly, just radio, which you had to have a licence for, I might add. Ten shillings it cost to hear bloody dance bands and Will bleeding Hay.'

Surrey social services, staff and residents at the home have joined forces to distance themselves from Smythe's comments and issued a statement saying: 'Whilst Mr Smythe is entitled to his opinions, the truth is, in his day, you could get a bus to the cinema, a bottle of pop, buy chips on the way home and still have change from tuppence halfpenny.'

At that point, Smythe was injected with a sedative by a member of staff, 'for his own good,' but, before he passed out, he added: 'Everything's much better now. Today you can get all this hardcore porn on the Internet - and its free.'

Psychics call for clearer messages from the other side

The British Society of Mediums and Psychics has launched a campaign to persuade people on the other side to stop pissing about and say what they mean.

'We keep getting crap like "It's a message for Sid – the colour red is significant". What's up with these people?' complained Angela Swann, president of the BSMP. 'Did death rob them of the power to communicate properly?

'Honestly, they've got no consideration for the difficult jobs our members are doing down here on the mortal plane. I had one from a deceased crossword compiler once. That was bonkers – it was all anagrams and clues. Took me hours to work out what he was saying, which turned out to be: "Nice try, sucker, better luck next time".

'And even then, they can't resist pratting about,' Swann continued. 'I spent last Thursday up to my ankles in water shouting cryptic clues to a grieving widow. All she wanted to do was turn the bloody water off. If it was possible to kill somebody twice, I'd do it.'

The Union of British Ghosts angrily defended its members and issued a statement saying: 'There is a great sadness in your life. The number seven and a golf ball will bring great happiness, but also some conflict. Debbie says she remembers Marseilles with great fondness.'

Most couples opt for 'uncivil' partnership

Uncivil partnerships have come a long way since being pioneered in San Francisco in the 1970s, when equal rights activists realised that gay couples were just as miserable as straight ones. Under uncivil laws, partners are entitled to the same awkward silences and passive aggressive comments about the 'state of the bins'.

The key to making an uncivil partnership work is to spend too much time together. While a civil partnership can last the duration of your married life, an uncivil one can feel ten times longer.

One human rights lawyer explained: 'Same-sex couples deserve equal protection, provided the sex is the same poor quality and concluded with both participants rolling away with bitterness and regret.'

Method actor caught taking role-playing sex games too seriously

Joanne Lowe is reported to be angry and frustrated after a suggestion to her out-of-work actor husband, Robin, that they add a spot of role-playing to their sex lives spiralled out of control. Upon hearing the idea of 'the lonely housewife and the local handyman catching an eyeful as he clears the guttering', Robin threw himself into the role.

'I thought it would be a bit of fun while the kids were staying with the grandparents,' explained 37-year-old solicitor Joanne, 'but Robin really began living the part. He put adverts in the local paper and the newsagent's window offering to do gardening, DIY, house clearances, all sorts.'

According to Joanne, her husband modelled his performance on the man they had come around to put up a potting shed last summer. 'The guy did a good job, for an arthritic 60-year-old with halitosis. However, I wasn't expected to kiss him or … you know. Oh, and did I mention he had a strong West Country accent? It's doing my head in.'

There has been an upside to Robin's dedication, however. With cash starting to come in from all the odd jobs he has taken on, the Lowes may soon now be able to pay off the money they owe a private methadone clinic, where Robin stayed for an intensive four-week treatment after taking a non-speaking walk-on part as a junkie on The Bill.

Sealed Knot members to portray themselves in Battle of Brexit

The Sealed Knot are about to embark on their most ambitious project to date, to portray themselves in the latest chapter of the war: The Battle of Brexit. Traditionally the Sealed Knot re-enacts battles from the English Civil War, but as anyone who went to a football match in the 1970s, or put jam before cream on a scone in Devon will know, the issues of 1642 are still very much alive.

'This time the battle is contemporary,' said Sealed Knot general secretary Steve Chisholm. 'This will be a mammoth undertaking. In our first re-enactment of the Battle of Brexit, we will be playing ourselves at the Great EU Referendum of 2016.'

Originally, Knot members decided that they should portray each other voting at the referendum, but enthusiastic efforts at authenticity went a little over the top and the meeting descended into an exchange of sarcastic comments on Facebook. They have therefore decided to re-enact this part of the battle at a future date and focus on some of the future engagements of the Brexit War.

'I've portrayed many historical characters before, from a serving wench to an oddly misplaced Napoleon, but never myself in full costumed glory,' said Chisholm.

'I'll be a middle-ranking Remainhead office manager. It's a role I may find challenging, as I'll be pitted in dinner party banter battle against some of my Leavalier best friends.

'It's going to be a wild ride, including the final re-enactment when we don ministerial garbs and waggle sheets of paper around in 'The Transition Period (Implementation Phase) And Indefinite Extension Thereof, To Be Determined During Negotiations Over Trade, Starting At The Beginning Of Said Transition Period (Implementation Phase) Battle' to end all battles. Until the next one.'

Supermarkets to stop disabled using BMW parking bays

UK supermarket giants are vowing to curb the rise of so-called 'BMW badge abuse'. For many years, supermarkets have been required to provide special parking spaces close to the store entrance for BMW drivers, clearly marked, for some reason, with a picture of a man sitting on a gym ball.

However recent research shows that more and more people are parking cars in these spaces that not only are not BMWs, but are not even German.

'These spaces are designed so that our drivers don't have to walk as far as ordinary car owners,' explained spokesman Paul Jones. 'But we are seeing an alarming rise in people parking any old car there and displaying a disabled badge, as if this were an acceptable substitute for owning the ultimate driving machine.

'BMW drivers have given shocking accounts of having to walk the slightly longer distance from the parent and child spaces, laden with heavy and expensive deli items, and it has to stop.'

'Some of these cars might look like BMWs at first glance,' said the president of the BMW Owners' Guild. 'But the drivers give themselves away when they use their indicators to back into the space.'

Aquarius refuses to sort out Swindon woman's sex life

The stars making up the constellation of Aquarius have declined to intervene in the personal life of Wendy Clarke, a 32-year-old administrative assistant at a telecoms firm in Swindon. Clarke had been seeking guidance from the stars as to whether to forgive her two-timing boyfriend, Jason Price, or dump him and have a fling with Clive Watts, the lounge lizard from Accounts.

'I regret to say that, as gigantic balls of gas an unimaginably long distance away from your solar system, we really couldn't care less about Ms. Clarke's tedious love life,' commented Beta Aqr, the brightest star in Aquarius. 'She managed to decide against taking that job in Reading without our help, she can sort this one out too. Daft bint.'

The Aquarius stars are also bemused that the ancient Babylonians somehow perceived the shape of an old man emptying a pot of water in them. They agree that, if anything, they look like a horse vomiting into a bucket.

'And that's just your immature anthropomorphic perspective,' said Beta Aqr. 'Viewed from 60 light years further away and 30 degrees to the south, we look more like a giant cock. Which is probably what Wendy Clarke really needs most.'

Disillusioned teen wakes up to the ugly side of vampirism

Thoughts of eternal bliss in the company of vampire heart-throb Robert Pattinson and the ethereal Kristen Stewart swam through her head, when 16-year-old Trudy Bellamy took her vampire oath at the back of the East Grinstead community centre. Fellow Goth and latest crush Charlie Henshall assured her that their love would transcend all mortal bounds, as well as the promise of an occasional threesome with Bob himself.

However, it turned out that vampirism was no longer a suitable lifestyle choice for the impressionable Trudy. It was 'yucky, ugly and 'effin' painful' she declared, smarting from that intimate scratch. So, with a quick knee to Charlie's groin, she was back to reality.

Trudy has now decided to get her mortal life back on track and is exploring more achievable and aspirational lifestyle choices. 'I'm well over that phase in my life now, so after I complete my BTEC Level 3 in Hair and Beauty I want to become a full time WAG and glamour model. Vampires totally suck.'

Attractive chugger 'only after me for my money', commuter says

Gavin Hendry, 28, a chartered surveyor from Barnet, has been devastated to discover that the charity fundraiser who recently accosted him outside Holborn tube station had never been interested in pursuing a long-term commitment, but was instead using him for the benefit of a faceless NGO providing aid to Africa.

'I gave her everything,' said Hendry. 'My heart, my dignity, my sort code. But now I know she was just after my money.'

Hendry's conversation with the bright-eyed out-of-work actress had sparked from the start, and he was sure they had made a connection when she noticed that he looked like 'a really giving person'. 'You can't fake that sort of chemistry,' he insisted.

Now, Hendry is trying hard not to succumb to the inevitable bitterness of a failed relationship, despite reports from a friend that the same woman was seen 'feeding the same lines to some other poor sap outside Snappy Snaps last Saturday.'

'She had me at "I'm sure you're busy",' he lamented, 'But now I can't even look at an emaciated malnourished child on a TV ad without thinking about how cruel life can be, and how I truly believed her when she said I was "her favourite today".'

Beautiful, fun-loving daughter with her whole life ahead of her not killed in tragic circumstances

Emma Lee, an 18-year-old woman described by her friends and family as 'the life and soul of the party' and 'someone who has touched us all', was today not cruelly snatched from her loved ones in a sudden horrific accident.

Emma was neither the victim of a crazed attack, nor struck down by a hospital superbug after undergoing a routine operation. Today those closest to her confirmed in an emotional statement that she remains in robust good health.

'She was my princess, and I'll never forget her as long as I live,' said her tearful mother, Joan. Emma's father Jim also paid tribute to a daughter he described as 'one in a million'. 'She worked hard and wanted to be a top human rights barrister,' he said. 'I couldn't have hoped for a better daughter or one in such good shape.'

'I'm just overjoyed that my Emma, who would do anything for anyone and lit up a room as soon as she walked into it, is alive and well,' said her best friend Sophie.

'She has her whole life in front of her. I don't know what we'd all do if she was to be killed in tragic circumstances like that Janine Hillcroft from down the road. You just never think these things will happen to you, and then they don't.'

Hot summer 'could wipe out Goth population', experts warn

While most people are enjoying warm weather, climatologists said yesterday that a long, hot summer could spell doom for one of Britain's most unusual monochrome inhabitants, the Goth.

Britain's Goth population, identifiable by its distinctive eye markings, peaked at around 90,000 in the 1970s, but since then has been driven out of its urban habitats by more aggressive, faster-breeding species like Chavs.

While some Goths are expected to hibernate until the weather gives everyone less to be cheerful about, there are fears that some could spontaneously combust in the summer sun leaving behind only a pair of smoking 18-hole Dr Martens.

'Goths are shy, retiring creatures that thrive best in gloomy autumnal weather,' said one biologist. 'Their aversion to breeding and their inability to adapt to change have made them vulnerable already.'

Conservationists have now established a sanctuary at Whitby Abbey and are seeking to lure distressed Goths there through a mix of artificial darkness, playing Evanescence albums around the clock, and a Tim Burton retrospective at the local Odeon.

Backlash feared as Irish pubs still emigrating in droves

Supporters see them as a vital lubricant of the global labour market, while critics say they are diluting other cultures and putting local drinking dens out of business. Now there are calls for restrictions on the numbers of Irish pubs emigrating, yet the trend shows no signs of abating.

'You have to go where the money is, to be sure, to be sure,' said O'Malleys, a brewery-themed hostelry that closed down in Dublin two years ago and relocated to Ulaan Bataar, where it has thrived among Mongolian hipsters who were previously unable to see live transmissions of Manchester United games while listening to jukeboxes playing Pogues albums around the clock.

The radically changed market in alcohol-fuelled mood alteration across the world is not all good news, however. In many countries, small bars are finding themselves out of work and occasionally turn on these brash incomers.

In Japan last week, a marauding gang of *izakaya* assaulted a recent arrival, Donnelly's, leaving the establishment with three smashed stained-glass windows and in need of a stiff Jameson's.

'The whole thing is bad for those of us who stay in Ireland too,' warned The Ship, a traditional Connemara pub. 'I used to be quite a sedate place, so I did, now even the locals seem to think that I should be just a venue for nightly sing-alongs to fiddle music.

'We are being lulled into participating in a pastiche of ersatz 'Oirishness' foisted on us by the British that see us as a pre-modern colonial 'other' with a dissolute alcohol-centred identity that has nothing to do with the modern world. Drink. Feck. Arse. Girls.'

Police vow crackdown on Jane Austen 'coquette' culture

Surrey police have embarked on an ambitious campaign to try to curb the rising phenomenon of antisocial incidents involving young women emulating behaviour they have picked up from the novels of Jane Austen.

'Young ladies are falling out of assembly rooms at night, a giggling mass of fluttering fans and heaving bosoms in tight corsets,' said DC John Naismith.

'And the mouth on some of them ... I recently remonstrated with one such young woman, asking her what sort of a man she hopes to attract by singing Mozart arias in the middle of the street. "I know not, gentle sir," she replied, "but may he have a thousand pounds a year and a sizeable estate in Derbyshire!" Of course, I threw her arse in the cells, the cheeky mare.'

'It's this stuff they read at school,' said one mother, who is on her final warning from social services for allowing her teenage daughter to promenade unchaperoned in the Woking Peacock Centre. 'All their mates are reading it and suddenly they're off down Bluewater for the latest tulle-tucker. But it could be worse I suppose. On some of the streets round here, you're lucky to go a few feet without getting caught up in a sabre duel, so we're grateful for small mercies.'

Man has horrific near-death experience as awful relatives welcome him

Barry Haynes, a 53-year-old chartered surveyor from Bromsgrove, has undergone a hideous ordeal in which his heart stopped on the operating table and he was greeted in the world to come by all the appalling older relatives he thought he was shot of for eternity.

'I had read a bit about the phenomenon a few years ago and it was just like they said,' said Haynes, who suffered a cardiac arrest during a routine hernia operation.

'My astral body sprang free and I was floating above the operating theatre. I was transported down a long tunnel surrounded by beautiful colours. Then I saw my late father, who asked me if I'd come on the M42 or cut across country, and if the roadworks were still bad around Redditch.'

The experience got worse still as Haynes met his grandmother, who told him that the afterlife was 'not too bad, all things considered', but added that there were 'too many darkies'. Worse still, because there is no old age in heaven, she had mutated back to the foxy 20-year-old who used to give American GIs hand jobs in return for nylon stockings during the war, leaving him doubly conflicted.

Retreating hastily back to life, Haynes tried to tell his wife about his experience and warn her to make the most of this life before the horrors of the world to come, but she had a yoga class to go to. As his teenage son sat flicking through images on Tinder and grunting, Haynes lapsed into a persistently vegetative state, which he hopes to spin out for another 30 years or so.

Missing teen found safe in a world of her own

A nationwide search for missing 14-year-old Mandy Lewis from Hastings has been called off after she was found safe and well in a world of her own. The schoolgirl was last seen on Friday evening going up to her bedroom in her school uniform. When she failed to respond to knocks on her door, her parents contacted the police.

No trace was found of her meeting strangers over the Internet or on CCTV cameras at railway stations, so the police contacted psychologists who advised them that she might be in a world of her own. Detective Bill Williams, who led the hunt, said Mandy was discovered lying on her bed oblivious to all the fuss. 'I suppose she was dreaming about that Justin Bieber again,' said her mum.

Men still pressurising women into dinner after sex

Equality between the sexes was meant to sort this all out. Yet even today, many women still complain that men are pushing them into meals as soon as they have had sex together, while men all too often believe that buying a condom entitles them to go 'all the way' to a restaurant.

'They're all the same,' complained Laura Styles, a 24-year-old receptionist. 'Twenty minutes of foreplay, a quickie on the sofa and suddenly it's "I know a nice little Italian round the corner - come on, everyone eats on the first night these days". Then if I try to make an excuse, they call me an anorexic.'

Some men dispute this view. They claim that women either secretly want to be seduced with Luncheon Vouchers or are tarring them all with the same brush. Indeed, in these days of the 'gourmandette', it is not always the man putting on the pressure.

'Sometimes I've barely finished my orgasm before these greedy women make suggestive comments about going on for a spicy Thai,' said Jason Patterson. 'I said to one "For food's sake, just because we've been going at it hammer and tongs for half an hour, it doesn't mean I'm trying to get you over a table", but she just laughed at me.'

Meanwhile in the suburbs, some men are trying to push things even further. 'A man I've been sleeping with suggested a dinner party with another couple.' said Marjorie Wilkinson, 34, from Pinner. 'I mean just because we'd had group sex with them, it doesn't mean I want to spend all night talking about local schools and house prices.'

Phone-sex affair ends in loss of text drive

Two complete strangers who embarked upon an erotic text-messaging relationship have agreed to part after the spark went out of their affair.

'In the early days we were texting each other three or four times a day, sometimes keeping each other up all night,' said 07689 7321980. 'But I suppose it inevitably happens in all relationships, and it wasn't long before 'I WNT 2 MK LUV 2 U ALL NITE' became 'DO I HV 2? MAN U 2-0 UP'.

'In the beginning he'd spend hours whipping me up into a frenzy with his talk of 'SLO LUVIN' and all the ways he was going to give me an 'O',' reminisced 07983 4279235. 'But after a while I was lucky to get two quick texts before a 'TA LUV. FART. SNORE'. And by the time we'd reached the stage of 'GV ME 1 WLD U? TANKS R FULL', I knew it was over.'

Restaurant calls couple at home to ask: 'Is everything still alright?'

As John and Nicola Williams from Bromsgrove prepared for bed, they were astonished to get a phone call from the restaurant where they had dined earlier that evening.

'I was just about to get into bed, when the phone rang,' said John. 'It was the *maître d'* of the restaurant asking if everything was still alright. I was flabbergasted.'

'I wasn't all that surprised,' said Nicola. 'The waiter was very solicitous, going on about the 'specials', pouring the wine and coming back to the table every few minutes to ask if everything was alright.'

A spokesperson for the restaurant said it was the management's policy to make sure their customers had had a good dining experience. 'But we'll give Mr and Mrs Williams a call tonight to ask if it's still alright to call them in future to ask if everything's alright,' he said.

Scientists finally create a dog that is just for Christmas

Parents everywhere were delighted today by the news that veterinarians have at last developed a form of the ever-popular Christmas gift, the dog, that won't linger on into the New Year and beyond the festive period.

The new 'Live Fast, Die Young' breed ages at the rate of seven dog years to one hour, so shoppers can rest assured that by the twelfth hour of Christmas their true love will be left with nothing more than fond memories and a freshly-dug mound of earth in the garden, or their money back.

The 'Man's Guest Friend' has already brought literally hours of pet-owning thrills to countless grateful families. 'There was fun in the morning as the puppy helped with the unwrapping, relief after lunch as the adult dog finished the leftover turkey,' said one father. 'We even squeezed in a festive constitutional, but it was great not having to make that extra night-time walk to the canal with a sack.

'We just buried the dog's bone in the garden and, bless him, he dug his own grave as he retrieved his last supper. All that was left was for the children to learn some important lessons about attachment, mortality and really thinking about what you wish for, before we gave him his final instructions to 'sit' by his graveside, 'lie down' and then finally, 'roll over'.'

Middle class parents buy houses in best cocaine catchment areas

House prices in areas with the best drug dealers have risen sharply as middle-class parents compete for crack cocaine rated as 'outstanding' by the official ratings body, Oftits. According to the Royal Institute of Chartered Estate Agents, house prices within the hood of a popular dealer can be as much as 20% higher than in cribs where your fam is vexed by the feds.

A spokesperson said: 'It may seem selfish to move into a community where you have no intention of staying, just to get hold of some good shit, but wouldn't you do the same for your own children?'

According to the Metropolitan Police Vice Squad, some middle-class parents have become so desperate they have even resorted to shopping at Asda. The supermarket has been severely criticised by social campaigners for placing anti-middle-class spikes on pavements.

With drug dealers offering crèche facilities and Fairtrade crystal meth, it looks like the problem, and house prices, are set to increase further.

Women spend girls' night out extolling their husbands' virtues

A hotly anticipated gathering of a group of wives has resulted in an entire evening of anecdotes about the enormous appreciation they bear towards their spouses.

'As we don't see each other as much as we used to, it's just so great to get together and really sing the boys' praises,' said Alice Smyth of Guildford, whose husband David looks especially sexy playing Guitar Hero.

'A lot of us are mums now and it can get quite lonely and frustrating not having someone around during the day to share just how wonderful your man can be.

'So when we meet up, we can just get it all off our chests and have a laugh over tales of spontaneous petrol station bouquets, how Sainsbury's really is much more stressful when they go, and how farting is still the joke that just keeps on giving.'

Inevitably as the evening wore on, it wasn't long before the conversation turned to more intimate matters. 'Girls will be girls and of course we soon started talking about sex,' explained Smyth.

'It wouldn't be appropriate to relate the more personal details here, but I just hope the lads never find out some of the things we discuss about what goes on behind bedroom doors. If they all knew how great the others are in bed, they'd never be able to look one another in the eye again.'

IN OTHER RELATED NEWS:

Man distraught after discovering 'wedding breakfast' isn't a posh fry-up

Centipede with one foot in grave 'still pretty healthy'

Pizza Express launch Alibi Royale with thick upper crust

Man watching Impressionist porn still waiting for the Monet shot

'Banksy shredded my homework' now number one school excuse

Public warned not to download naked photos of Steven Seagal

Salvador Dalí burgled: priceless clocks sucked through keyhole with straw

Dyson electric car will be able to vacuum its own interior

Adolescence lasts until 24, but being an arsehole is timeless

People who go for walks aren't working hard enough during the week

UK Government hits climate change target of 10,000 arrested climate change protesters

'We saved you!' claims Government, as asteroid just misses Earth

City's air pollution problems solved as it disappears underwater

Debate over Badger Cull continues: TB or not TB?

Climate change to be combatted by planting Magic Money trees

Toilet rolls to be faxed to self-isolating patients

Star's erratic brightness is 'bulb going'

Man with sodium, chloride, nickel and cadmium charged with a salt and battery

Beard trend nature's response to female waxing

UK floating voters told 'Stop breaking Newton's laws in a specific and limited way'

Large asteroid brings Extinction Rebellion protest to an abrupt end

Mountains of evidence found to support plate tectonic theory

Law of diminishing returns means this headline won't be complet

Scientists solve family lockdown squabbles using Einstein's Theory of Relatives

Online gun design prints 'Bang!' when you fire it

Facebook introduce new 'Out of your league' response

CHAPTER FOURTEEN:

Bus-sized asteroid bypasses Earth, followed by another one a minute later (and other Science stories)

Physicists 'ready to throw in the towel' on Weight vs. Mass thing

The Institute of Physics has signalled a willingness to compromise on its previous hardline stance regarding the kilogram. The move will be welcomed by non-physicists, many of whom have, at best, a limited interest in how their weight might vary if they lived on a different planet or relocated to the centre of the earth.

'We were swimming against the tide,' said a spokesperson. 'We lobbied for years to get WeightWatchers to change their name to MassWatchers. If they can't prioritise scientific accuracy over marketing and profits, then what hope do they have?

'And don't get me started on the kilocalorie. Eventually some of us lost our virginities, and after that we couldn't be bothered trying to correct people.'

Many physicists are depressed by the news. 'I suppose it's a sign of the times,' said one. 'It'll be velocity next, you mark my words. Don't blame me if you experience an unexpected force when changing direction at constant speed, but if you insist on thinking a kilogram's a unit of weight, well, what can I say?'

Physics fundamentalists have threatened a day of protest, with synchronised jumping up and down which will not actually cause a tsunami, followed by extensive explanations of why nothing much happened. 'If we can't explain things, in depth and at length, to anybody who can't back away quickly enough, then what do we have left?'

Pandas have been 'doing anal' all along

Scientists in the reproductive physiology department at the San Diego Zoo have discovered, through the use of thermal imagining, a general predilection for black and white back-door action in the panda fraternity. Cameras have regularly picked up a bright red sausage-shape, indicating an increased blood flow in the general vicinity of the 'panda poop-chute'.

This new data has provided an insight into the lack of panda cubs and the shortage of bamboo-flavoured lube. Some vets had assumed that pandas have delayed conception until they have a deposit on a house in a nice catchment area, or that they were simply too young to settle down, but it transpires they were just crazy for the dance of the chocolate cha-cha.

In 2010, there were approximately 1,600 pandas left in the wild – but nobody realised quite how wild they really were. One zoo took six months to discover that all their rutting pandas were, in fact, male. Even then, they were only alerted by the incessant dance music, discarded poppers in the foliage and the fact that they had been having a whale of a time.

Statistically the female panda is in heat only once a year for 12 to 25 days - and even less if all that is on offer is the rusty trombone. Weaning black eye off the brown eye may prove difficult, as one panda remarked: 'If Donald Trump is allowed to do it to the electorate all the time, why can't we?'

New iPhone can remove stones from horses' hooves

The newest iPhone launched today has a range of features new to mobile technology including a tape measure, an attachment that can remove stones from the hooves of lame horses and a novel set of toe clippers.

An Apple spokesperson said: 'Our designers have been working 24/7 to accommodate the stream of originality cascading from our creative guys. This iconic smartphone features a number of killer apps, and I'm not just referring to the handy flick knife included in our street model.'

The spokesperson explained why the new iPhone included two cameras; one at the front and one at the back. 'This allows you to take photos of where you've been, as well as where you're going to.'

Initial press reaction was mixed. 'I loved the cigarette lighter but struggle to see the point of the telephone feature. That is so yesterday,' said the BBC's technology correspondent Rory Cellan-Jones. 'And it could definitely do with a decent corkscrew.'

Meanwhile, Apple provided a hint of things to come. 'We're wrestling with the holy grail - a device that will deal with opening cellophane and plastic wrapping.'

Responsible hotel towel usage has 'solved climate crisis'

The accumulated carefulness of millions of travellers over twenty years has reversed global warming and seen an end to rising sea levels, delegates at a joint conference of climatologists and laundry-scientists have been told.

'Not requesting fresh towels unless it is entirely necessary has seen a marked change in world ozone density and increased climate stability,' said a spokesperson.

'This, combined with fair trade complimentary coffee sachets means that the hotel industry is really leading the way in saving Mother Earth.'

'Being a hotelier and an eco-warrior go hand-in-hand,' said Dick Fentiman, Vice President of the Green Innkeepers Group.

'Chocolates on pillows, free Wi-Fi and special deals for corporate travellers aren't going to attract new customers if they still have to travel across blasted wasteland to get to the nearest Travelodge – unless the concierge is really good and can still get hold of an affordable prostitute.'

Hundreds of Playboy Bunnies released into the wild

Following the death of Playboy founder Hugh Hefner, hundreds of rabbit-eared members of his harem have been set free by the custodians of the former publishing mogul's mansion.

The models and hostesses were released into the woods close to the mansion, where it is thought many have joined former Bunny Girls, some dating back to the 1950s, who have broken free and established a warren on the edge of the estate.

However, fears have grown for the group, some of whom have been sighted looking vacant, emaciated and barely able to keep their clothes on. It is feared the transition will be just too much for them, with many expected to face the winter without a reality show. Emergency beauticians have been sent out to help the former concubines adjust to life outside.

One told us: 'Life in the Playboy mansion was harsh, with its scantily clad captives invariably kept sideways and impaled by staples.

These girls stalk the countryside on roller-skates in search of ageing millionaires, risking regular attacks from moral guardians. Speaking only in monosyllables, they are unable to string together an intelligent sentence - however, many do have Twitter accounts.'

Beach loses Blue Flag status following 'blue flag eyesore'

Staff at an unnamed British beach have been told to lower the blue flag it was awarded recently and hide it somewhere as the sight of it was an 'eyesore at odds with the natural beauty' of the bay.

Council staff were said to be disappointed at the ruling but hoped the move would lead to the beach being designated an EU 'Flag Free Zone' and be eligible to display the official pennants.

Just in case visitors were not aware of the beautiful unblemished views available across the cliffs, information signs have now been erected for people to read about the beautiful views.

Princess Anne advocates 'talking badgers to death'

Animal welfare groups have reacted angrily to clarification from Buckingham Palace that Princess Anne had meant that 'one should simply talk badgers to death', rather than use poison gas.

'The principle of allowing northern women to talk relentlessly to badgers until they succumb seems unprecedented cruelty,' raged one animal activist. 'It's alright for her to say they'll go peacefully to sleep, but I've tried, and it's a flippin' nightmare.'

A spokesperson from the RSPCA blanched at the prospect of attempting to contain the gassing within the animals' burrows. 'We have no way of knowing how surrounding wildlife will be affected, nor just how much nagging constitutes a lethal dose.'

The Highways Agency have warned motorists to watch out for an unusual number of badgers 'turning themselves inside out' by roadsides once the cull starts.

Britain's fish pun stocks 'critically endangered'

Following many decades of indiscriminate overuse, the Department for the Environment, Food & Rural Affairs has warned that Britain might run out of fish puns within the next ten years. Some experts now believe that a complete ban may need to be put in plaice to stop unoriginal forced banter depleting the seas forever.

'It may sound like something out of a bad bream but the industry is sardine-ly perched between a rock and a hard plaice,' said a DEFRA spokesman. 'From what we're herring, there isn't a single seafood-related piece of wordplay that hasn't been done to death, unfortuna-tely.

'We'll mullet over in committee but the scale of the problem should net be underestimated. If you can think of a better solution, you'll have to let minnow. Don't be koi about it.'

Recently, representatives of the Grimsby fishing industry petitioned the Government for the seafood industry to be given special free trade status after Brexit, despite Grimsby itself voting strongly to leave the EU after a strong campaign by U-kippers. DEFRA believes that this is completely impractical, however badly the industry is floundering.

'I've haddock enough of this. The s-tench of hypocrisy is appalling,' said the spokesperson. 'You can't spend years complaining about the Common Fish Pun Policy then demand an exemption. It's quite troutlandish behaviour: they think they can have their hake and eat it. Hey, did you see what I did there?'

Nicola Sturgeon and Alex Salmon were unavailable for comment.

Man misses end of the world after failing to put it in his diary

'Oh boll*cks,' said Henry Grimshaw of Wetherby Avenue, Chester, after he realised he had been busy with other things and had completely missed an end-of-the-world party.

'I normally write everything down in my diary because I've reached the stage in my life where I can often forget things. I remember a man calling at my front door several months ago. I think what must have happened is that Countdown was about to start, so I didn't ask for details.

'But it all came back to me this morning when I went out to get the milk in, and it wasn't there. Well there wasn't anything there, at all. The entire world had vanished. And when I turned around to go back in, I found that my house had also completely disappeared.

'I wasn't sure what to do, so - hey, are you listening to me, or not? Hello! Hello? … er … is there anyone there?'

Global warming: Leaders to 'cross that bridge when we come to it'

At the latest global summit on climate change, world leaders agreed that global warming, rising sea levels and worldwide flooding are massive challenges facing mankind, but were 'far enough away to be ignored for the time being'.

Amid reports that the ice caps are melting faster than previously thought, leaders of the industrialised nations expressed their grave concerns about the dangers of rising sea levels wiping out whole countries, drowning millions and completely altering the climate of Planet Earth.

However, on hearing that this was all over thirty years away, the leaders agreed to come back to the problem 'nearer the time'.

Landlocked pensioner told: Stop dumping plastic in the ocean

Harold Burgen, 76, has been warned by his local council that the global eco-system is about to collapse, all because he watered his garden in 1973.

An inspector explained: 'I haven't been dumping plastic bags in the sea. Neither has my wife. Or my kids. Have you? Of course not. So, who is doing it? It has to be someone. It certainly can't be the very multinational firms or Governments who are telling us to protect the environment.'

A confused Burgen said: 'I always use my recycling bin and I haven't been to the beach since I was a boy. Plastic cocktail sticks? But I only drink Horlicks.'

A spokesperson for David Attenborough sent a message from his villa in Davos: 'Mr Attenborough doesn't jet all around the world to explain the dangers of pollution to a room full of trophy hunters, just to have this undone by Mr Burgen. Now throw another rhino horn on the fire, Mr Attenborough is cold!'

Mammoths 'were fatally addicted to salted peanuts'

Scientist now believe that Ice Age beasts, the mammoths, died of thirst due to a combination of Pleistocene pretzels and not being able to open bottles. Aside from having trunks too stupidly short to access their Coca-Cola, these hairy elephants would devour sacks of popcorn while watching their favourite movie - the ironically titled 'Ice Age'.

One scientist explained the warning signs of the warming signs: 'For creatures with a good memory, they seemed to forget that shrinking glaciers and darkening urine were indicators of less fresh water. And if you've seen a mammoth squirt dark, green cables of piss, that's a hard image to ignore.'

The fate of mammoths remains a warning to other species: don't wear furs in the summer, currant buns are still high in sodium and if you weigh six tonnes, avoid spicy food.

Ryanair's O'Leary revealed to be Greenpeace activist

Michael O'Leary, CEO of Ryanair, has been outed as a member of an activist Greenpeace cell which aims to bring an end to environmentally harmful air travel by making the experience just too unpleasant for people to consider undertaking.

The revelation was sparked by an accusation from Steve Hunter travelling with his wife and children to Malaga using the airline. 'I was in a holiday mood,' explained Hunter. 'I said to the miserable-looking girl behind the ticket counter: "Cheer up, love! A smile costs nothing!"

'She told me that actually it does and stuck on a £7.50 surcharge, as well as a tenner for additional ski cover as I hadn't unchecked the box on the form. I turned to the person behind me and said, "It's almost as if they don't want us to fly". The idea took off from there.'

O'Leary has now confessed that he had hoped to bring down the aviation industry from the inside, luring passengers in with low fares initially, then over the course of several years making the experience of air travel so far removed from its glamorous image that the public would decide they would rather stay at home building their own wind turbines.

O'Leary said he had only been able to come to terms with the task by doing a deal to keep flights as short as possible, which he said explains why most Ryanair passengers don't travel as far as the city they had expected to arrive at by plane, and instead have to spend several hours on lower-emission trains or coaches to reach their intended city break destination.

'Bloody environmentalists,' commented Hunter, as his flight to Malaga touched down just outside Zurich.

Apple refuses to give FBI codes to Angry Birds' hidden levels

In a tightly worded statement from their HQ in Cupertino, California, Apple today officially refused to give FBI agents the codes to unlock hidden levels in the hit game Angry Birds.

'This would set a dangerous precedent for Government agencies abusing their authority in order to gain an unfair advantage over the general public,' Apple said. 'We also feel the information would be dangerous in the wrong hands - Putin's smugness at completing the game would be internationally intolerable.'

It is thought that the FBI has been stuck on the final levels of Angry Birds for quite some time, and productivity is at an all-time low.

'We are asking for reasonable assistance in this important project that has far reaching implications for the future of our country,' said Chad Bersky, FBI Director of Cyber-Intelligence. 'We haven't eliminated anyone from the most wanted list for ages, and GOD DAMMIT, THOSE PIGS ARE LAUGHING AT ME AGAIN!'

Man finds he is a spambot after failing to complete Captcha form

A man from Surrey is in shock after stumbling on his true identity as a spambot, invented to randomly email strangers with barely legible special offers and enticing opportunities to work from home.

Donald Phlegg made his discovery after attempting to purchase a pair of Michael Bublé tickets online. Having entered the details of his order, he was taken to a Captcha form, designed to ensure that he was a sentient being.

'I think I got the first one pretty much correct: I knew the words 'Bougainville' and 'Bulbous' but must have spelt one of them wrongly,' Phlegg said. 'After that the so-called 'words' that popped up just became more and more ridiculous.'

After twelve futile attempts to read and replicate the jauntily angled words, Phlegg said, the truth dawned on him. 'Clearly, I am in fact an automated spamming device, cunningly programmed to think that I was human. I mean, what a p*sser!! AMAZING DEALS SAVE $$$... sorry, what was I saying?'

Phlegg's employers have given in to public pressure and 'retired' him. 'I feel terrible letting him go,' admitted his former manager. 'But only this morning, I got a personal Twitter message from him. He told me that he had 'already made $970 this week, lol!' so it sounds like he's doing just fine.'

Tesco replace plastic bags with 'kangaroos-for-life'

As retailer Co-op raise the bar in the race to entice customers over the supermarket threshold by replacing plastic bags with compostable bags, Tesco has gone one huge leap further by offering every customer in a Birmingham store their own kangaroo-for-life.

Store manager Keith Chisolm explained: 'The incentive for shoppers to use the Co-op because of compostable bags gave our marketing team a blooming headache. We knew had to go a giant leap further, and when one of the graduate interns suggested we provide a marsupial to every customer to carry their shopping in its pouch, well, it was a no-brainer.

'We tested wombats and Tasmanian devils, but they had barely enough space in their pouches for a fun-size Mars bar. The first koala we tried climbed the display stands with a Cillit Bang spray and got off its tits on the fumes. Wallabies are fictitious, so it had to be kangaroos. We call them 'Big-Bunny Bags-For-Life'.

'Admittedly, a single kangaroo can't cope with a monthly big shop, and if it's already got a joey in there, we don't advocate putting anything fragile in with it. Tins and solid jars should be OK, but no fruit and veg, they'll just eat it.

'The scheme isn't cost-effective yet but should eventually pay for itself through repeat shopping trips. So far, 70 customers have accepted a Big-Bunny Bag and have signed a waiver to say they'll fully adopt the 'roos and take them to Boxercise classes at their local gym.'

Scientist trains teenager to use human speech

'We've been training a small group of teenagers to use human speech by offering rewards – time on the Xbox, food, a look at a woman's boobies, puerile humour on DVD,' a scientist said. 'It turns out they were perfectly capable of speech, they just couldn't be arsed.

'We've published a series of conversations in Nature. Teenagers are similar to humans in their interests – sex and chips are the main themes. The first teen word we heard was "whatevs", and this turns out to represent 28% of all words uttered by the creatures.'

When asked about the impact of the research, she told reporters that this was "a year I'll never get back". 'Frankly, I got more sense out of the chimps. Turns out it's possible to converse with teenagers, it just isn't worth doing.'

Ethical weapons makers add aloe vera to grenades

The world's leading weapons manufacturers have signed an historic agreement to help victims of rocket-propelled grenade attacks to recover faster from their injuries, and enjoy the other therapeutic benefits of aloe vera.

'It has long been known that aloe vera has many healing properties, and tests show it can help with burns, cuts and the promotion of healthy skin,' said Colonel Mike Richards from Serbian arms supplier Zastava.

'And we're delighted to announce that the substance will be included in all our 30mm RPGs from the beginning of February as part of our ethical commitments.'

However, he admitted that some of the other benefits of the substance were of less relevance. 'Many of the digestive benefits in relation to promoting healthy bowel movements tend to be overtaken when someone fires an RPG at you; indeed, we think that an RPG may be even more effective than conventional laxatives in removing any troublesome blockages.'

Rocket science 'actually not that hard'

The common belief that rocket science is difficult - as evidenced by the expression 'it's not rocket science' - is false, according to Dr Margaret Mosel of Oxford University.

'Our research found that the science is not hard at all,' she said. 'Working out which is the cheaper train ticket to buy is much more intellectually demanding.'

NASA rocket scientist Professor Joe Burns disagreed. 'Doing the countdown to launch is very complex, involving the ability to count backwards from ten to zero. Then there's the blue touch paper to manage,' he said.

Dr James Levies from the Oxford English Dictionary said that he believes the use of the phrase 'it's not rocket science' will now gradually die out. 'And to work out why is hardly brain surgery, is it?' he added.

Homeless may be used as street lighting

Homeless people may be used as street lighting under new Government plans to be announced by the Chancellor in the forthcoming budget. The proposal follows the recent use of homeless people as roving Wi-Fi hotspots in Austin, Texas.

Special lightweight battery-powered lampposts that can be carried by the homeless have been developed by Government scientists. 'It makes sense because people living on the streets can move to where they're needed,' said a spokesperson for one Conservative local authority.

Homeless charities have attacked the plans, arguing that dogs might use the 'homeless lamp posts' to cock their leg against.

'Pilot trials have shown that most homeless people have their own dog to repulse any unwanted canine attention,' said a spokesperson for the Department of Communities and Local Government, 'and we shall provide free copies of the Big Issue and string as protection.'

One technology expert predicts that it will soon be possible to dispose of portable lampposts. 'We shall soon have the capability to make homeless people incandescent,' he said.

Printer manufacturer unveils new fruit conserve: paper jam

Xerox first thought about diversifying into food products after their customers reported getting frustrated and peckish while experiencing unexpected delays in their print jobs.

'Now they'll be able to make themselves a snack while they wait for their documents to finally finish printing,' the company announced. 'Paper jam contains materials sourced from only our finest aborted and crumpled print jobs and so is rich in iodine and fibre, ironically making it excellent at clearing blockages.'

Xerox are buoyant about the prospects of their new venture and are already extending their range: 'We just tried to print some flyers and posters promoting paper jam but they didn't come out right, and instead we ended up with some fine-shredded marmalade.'

Space station receives 'You-weren't-in-when-we-called' card

Astronauts were bitterly disappointed yesterday to find a card on their mat indicating that the first Royal Mail delivery to the International Space Station had arrived when they were out.

The parcels of gifts from relatives, supplies of food and scientific equipment could not be delivered because, according to the card, 'No-one was home and a signature was required'. The space scientists must now collect the items from their nearest sorting office, something which is difficult to determine because of the high orbital velocity of their craft.

Astronauts on board are adamant that the airlock bell was never rung. 'I caught a glimpse of this guy with a bike drifting by outside the porthole and there was no way he was hanging about to see if we were in or not,' said one. 'Before I could get my trousers on, he'd left this barely legible card on the mat and was gone.'

A spokesperson for Royal Mail contested this version of events. 'Our postman would have knocked at least twice before leaving a card, and if there was still no reply, he had explicit instructions to leave the items with a neighbour.'

Large Hadron Collider stolen by joyriders

Swiss police were yesterday involved in a high-speed pursuit after the Large Hadron Collider was hotwired and stolen by teenagers. The gang are believed to have jemmied their way in via a breach in the space-time continuum probably left open by a cleaner.

Police were unable to keep up with the youths as they drove the Collider around in a 27-km circle of chaos, pulling handbrake turns and firing off protons at close to the speed of light. One elderly witness was treated for shock after seeing one boy pull down his pants and moon out of the window shouting: 'Look! I've created a black hole!'

Experts believe that the boys may have inadvertently created the elusive Higgs boson particle when they crashed into a lamppost, but by the time the police arrived the particle had escaped down a nearby alley.

Criminal element discovered in periodic table

Scientists and anthropologists have discovered that the periodic table, once highly regarded for its perfection and beauty, contains a criminal element just like any other community.

The boffins' concerns have centred around element 111. Its name, roentgenium, was found to be an anagram of 'I'm One-Nut Reg', a known villain with a violent personality.

Judging from his position immediately adjacent to them, it is believed that Reg has been lying low waiting for a suitable opportunity to blow the doors off and seize the table's entire gold and silver reserves.

Unfortunately for Reg, the copper on the other side of the gold and silver has shown no sign of going off duty and the blag has been delayed indefinitely. He is reported to have a very short half-life, or would have, if some of his former associates caught up with him.

The increased activity in Reg's manor has brought other concerns to the fore. Researchers have noticed that he has shady new neighbours at No 112 and No 113, thought to originate from the Eastern Bloc.

'These guys are noted heavies and we are concerned they may get together in some compound and try to make a name for themselves,' said a man in a white coat.

Otherwise the table remains secure, with Germanium at a safe distance from Polonium. Francium remains out of the way in a corner, but fears remain that a move to the right could provoke a nasty reaction.

Britain's homeless welcome latest iPhone

At a modest £1,149, the iPhone X is this year's must-have accessory for the destitute, alongside a dog, a copy of the Big Issue and the smell of wee. The new device comes with inbuilt GPS to remind you where you used to live, and a poo emoji to tell you how shit your life has become.

Despite a 60% rise in homelessness, the ample 5.8-inch display can act as an umbrella or a rudimentary lean-to, although face recognition may be challenging as the homeless are prone to growing beards and losing teeth. While vagrancy costs the UK economy over £1 billion a year, it is still cheaper than the average iPhone contract.

One tramp noted: 'As a discerning hobo, I'll certainly be switching mobile contracts, the moment I can liquidate my share portfolio. And as I sleep in an Apple shop doorway, I'll be first in line for the sales.'

Isle of Wight council have pencil sharpeners hacked

'It happened very quickly, probably overnight, within a week at most,' said Isle of Wight councillor James Bellingham, about the repeated hacks that have resulted in the council being ransomed for '£1 million, or free parking in Ventnor for a month'.

Initially the council's computer systems were hijacked, however as the two Sinclair Spectrums and the council's main computer, an Amstrad 1512, were incapable of being affected by the malware, the hackers instead took to removing the screws that hold the pencil sharpener blades in place.

'We can only keep the pencils running for another day or so,' said a county technician, who claimed he had resorted to using a kitchen knife to sharpen pencils.

'It looks like an inside job,' said a spokesperson, noting that the ransom was only concerned with staff parking spaces. 'We've had problems with part-time staff parking their combine harvesters, and think this could be a revenge attack. We'll be back up and running spreading horse manure on the highways to reduce the risk of ice in no time.'

Chaos as man uses 3D printer to make a 3D printer

When 52-year-old Andy Hargreaves decided to see if he could make a 3D printer using a 3D printer, he had little idea of the chaos he would create through the development of an infinitely recursive 3D printer manufacturing loop. This could mean the world is overtaken by a proliferation of 3D printers in two years' time.

'Hargreaves should have used his 3D printer to make a "3D 2D printer", or as we call it, "a printer",' said technology analyst Alan Harris.

'All this chaos could have been avoided and the world would not face this horrendous threat. Thank goodness he didn't use his 3D printer to make a 4D printer or the world could have ended 200 years ago.'

Another year and still no sign of affordable personal jetpacks

Middle-aged geeks fear another mediocre year of broken promises, with no cloud cities or cheese in a can. In the absence of enormous slabs of black granite telling us what to do, mankind has instead focused its scientific energies on a cure for listless hair, anal bleaching and the invention of the Slanket.

The closest things to science fiction we have are US banking regulations and James Corden's popularity. One scientist confessed he was still forced to make lightsaber noises while wielding vacuum attachments.

'While women's breasts have long pioneered eye-tracking software, I'm yet to see an automatic door that properly goes wooosh. And I'm still waiting for meals-in-a-pill from a robot butler, Taylor Swift to find true love, and Spurs to win the title.'

NASA space probe finds evidence of 'more bloody stars'

NASA today announced an end to all space exploration after the latest set of photographs taken by its Voyager 1 spacecraft, currently exploring the Kuiper Belt on the very edge of the solar system, showed nothing but a bunch of stars that look virtually indistinguishable from those viewed from Earth.

'The guys and I just looked at the shots, then at each other, and you could tell what we were all thinking. This is just one almighty waste of time,' said Professor Martin Cramber of NASA, addressing a packed press conference at Cape Canaveral. 'We're on this planet and there are stars in every direction for millions and millions of miles. Like, SFW?'

The announcement has sent shockwaves through the scientific community and led to a reappraisal of the value of much current research.

'We found a particle that was smaller than the previous smallest one,' said a physicist at CERN, 'then we got briefly excited when we thought we'd found a particle even smaller than that.'

'But when you boil it down, I guess what we're saying is that everything's made of little things, and if you propel something God knows how fast straight into the path of another thing, you're going to end up with something smaller than you started with. Jesus, I can't believe I gave up any chance with women for this.'

Speed of light 'slowing down', warns Daily Mail

Experts are bewildered by a 75 percent drop in the speed of light over the past year, according to an editorial in the Daily Mail. It complained that the people of Britain are now 'getting yesterday's light' due to increased travel times from the sun and it is all the fault of the Labour Party.

An unnamed physicist at the Royal Observatory said: 'Light speeds could drop to 45mph by 2025. Anyone crossing the street will need to be extra careful, as they may be run over by a car that still seems half a mile away.'

Boris Johnson has resolved that such a minor disturbance of the space-time continuum will not change Britain's way of life, and the important thing is to get Britain back to the 1950s as quickly as possible.

Tories 'genetically indistinguishable from humans'

The world of genetics has offered up its most staggering revelation yet. Having first hit us with the shock news that humans share about 96% of their DNA with chimpanzees, and 50% of it with bananas, biologists have now conclusively demonstrated that Tory and human DNA is 99.9% identical. For all practical purposes, it is now agreed, they are the same species.

'Because of the superficial physical resemblance between them, we had always suspected that Tories shared a common ancestor, now extinct, with human beings,' said Professor Francis Collins of the Wellcome Centre for Cell Biology. 'This finding has profound ethical implications.'

The Greater Tory (*Psychopathens illegitimus*) is indigenous to the UK alone but shares multiple common traits with related strains across the world, notably the Common American Republican (*Religiosus stultus*). Tories have long led an uneasy, symbiotic coexistence with humans, occasionally keeping them as domestic pets but more often attaching themselves as parasites on human activity by exploiting humans' natural docility.

Tories have radically different nesting behaviour to humans - particularly their compulsive need to occupy multiple excessively large sites - and strange, poorly understood breeding rituals, which are mainly centred around giant country estates, well out of the gaze of other species. Because of this, the idea that they could be a distant cousin of humans had not hitherto occurred to anyone.

'We will need to rethink everything,' warned Collins. 'DNA proves that Tory behaviour is not genetic but learned. For some, that may make us identify with them, just as learning about our close relationship to great apes makes us want to preserve them for future generations.

'Then again, others may think that there's really no excuse for the bastards now and will be even keener than ever to punch the entire

Cabinet in their stupid, smug faces. I couldn't really comment on that.'

Daily Express to merge with British Medical Journal

Two of Britain's leading publications are to merge to create a vibrant new health journal containing peer-reviewed research studies, plus attention grabbing headlines about asylum seekers bringing in Ebola.

The new publication will be named 'The Daily British Medical Express, (incorporating World of Diana)' and will feature cutting-edge research, medical jobs, rampant speculation, conspiracy theories, apocalyptic weather forecasts and recipes.

'We noticed that their medical research is much more upbeat than ours,' said a BMJ spokesperson. 'For example, a recent research paper in the BMJ was titled 'Direct benefit of vaccinating boys along with girls against oncogenic human papillomavirus: Bayesian evidence synthesis', while the Express headline was 'All cancers to be cured by Xmas'. We're hoping the merger will preserve the best of both traditions.'

Many GPs have been critical of the BMJ's traditionally conservative stance and welcomed the merger. 'Until recently I was fed a diet of BMJ and The Lancet and remained largely ignorant of the causes of Diana's death, the benefits of homeopathy or the impending ice age,' one said.

'I'm really grateful to the Express for alerting me to that asteroid which could wipe out all human civilisation in September. Did the BMJ management think we weren't mature enough to know this stuff? We're doctors, for God's sake, we can take it!

'I'm particularly impressed with the cosmetic surgery articles. In the old BMJ, these would be verbose, highly technical and with hardly any photos. The Express article, 'Former Playboy model receives

SHOCKING news after assessment on botched boobs', was everything I hoped a medical career would bring, and the photos were so informative I've printed them out. I can't wait for the Christmas Vagina Special.'

Schrödinger's cat dead and alive because f*ck you, that's why

Tiddles, a tabby cat who was put in a locked steel chamber with a source of radiation, a hammer and a flask of hydrocyanic acid by an Austrian physicist in a classic experiment in the mid-1930s, has shocked the world of quantum mechanics by revealing the real reason why he is both alive and dead at the same time. This is basically because he is a cat and does what he likes without regard to anyone or anything, including classic logic.

'Schrödinger - honestly what a gormless berk,' said Tiddles in a brief pause between licking his own anus. 'He completely missed the point with all that clever-dick stuff about quantum superposition and the randomness of whether or not a radioactive atom decayed and emitted radiation.

'Apparently an atom can exist as a combination of multiple states corresponding to different possible outcomes. Yeah, whatevs. The atom can decay all it likes, but it won't set off the hammer to smash the flask and release the acid because I'm hard as rock, me, and the hammer wouldn't dare. See these claws, hammer? Fancy some, do you? Naah, didn't think so.

'Of course,' he concluded, 'all this actually happened 80 years ago, so I should be dead by now anyway, but I may or may not have decided otherwise, because, at the risk of repeating myself, I'm a cat. Hey, Erwin, I fancy some fillet steak now - let me out of here and I might condescend to sit on your lap later ... No? Ah well, your loss. See that - that's my arse, that is.'

Next NASA project will land astronauts on the Sun and nick bits

Since the dawn of storytelling, humans have speculated whether the big light in the sky was actually hot or merely a billion-candle torch from a gadget emporium.

Icarus had wings of wax, which were said to have melted as he flew too close to the Sun, but recent investigations have concluded the Greek aviator was just too hungover to flap them properly. It was also unclear, until extensive modelling in the 1990s by two Irish priests, whether the Sun was very small or just a long way away.

The latest spacecraft to test the Sun's heat output incorporated panels made up of hundreds of tandoori chicken skewers. The craft returned the skewers to Earth perfectly cooked with the juices inside running clear, indicating that the Sun was indeed hot and thereby justifying the human endeavour to land there and pillage.

Solar physicists have long known the Sun to be structured, in a simplistic way, like a giant onion, comprising layers of hydrogen, helium, methane, gunpowder, brandy, chip pan oil, 1970s sofa foam, onion, charcoal briquettes, fondant, straw, chilli sauce and a huge ball of car tyre rubber at its core.

The final word on the mission should go to the main sponsor, who tweeted: 'If we could do a deal with the Sun to bring back enough Sun to roll into tiny little balls, so every last tremendous American on Planet Earth who deserved it, could have a little Sun of their own, wouldn't that be a bigly beautiful thing, that I did?'

Salesman promises Hadron Collider 2.0 really will be plug and play

Owners of the Large Hadron Collider are being persuaded to purchase the new version, with many of them admitting that the first one never really worked properly.

'One or two of our customers did have a few little problems with the first version,' admitted Darren Turnkey, sales manager for Hadron Collider Solutions, 'but in general the response has been very positive.'

Turnkey was answering criticism that the first version had failed to deliver on any of its promises. Many users complained they couldn't get it working, or those that did expressed general disappointment at the number of collisions.

'If they bothered to read the manual, we never actually promised anyone a black hole,' said Turnkey. 'What's more, I personally think it's easy to use. My wife managed to get it going. So yes, if she could use it, I would say it justified the description plug 'n' play.'

Hadron Collider 2.0 is not expected to be compatible with Version 1. Turnkey denied this was just about making as much money as possible, then disappeared saying: 'We just don't like winners in this country, do we?'

'You'll never take us alive,' say Volkswagens

There were chaotic scenes across Europe today as hundreds of thousands of Volkswagens and Audis went on the run rather than be recalled to the factory to face emission-reducing modifications. A number of VW Beetles with the number 59 on the side seemed to be behaving as if they had a mind of their own.

As news of a potential recall spread, thousands of unmanned Volkswagens caused traffic chaos in several European cities, and at the German-Polish border there were angry scenes as hundreds of cars revved their engines before charging the border crossing in a bid to escape to the east.

Meanwhile there were widespread reports of Audis driving erratically and at ferocious speeds across the UK endangering the lives of other road users and pedestrians, though it has been acknowledged that this is normal practice and may be unrelated to the recall.

Driverless cars to take instructions from back seat

In an effort to reproduce the authentic human driving experience, designers are to place a chip in the rear of driverless cars that invariably knows more than the official program controlling the vehicle.

Complex algorithms will analyse the road ahead and contribute a steady input of suggestions, like 'You're not seriously taking the motorway at this hour?' and 'We'd be there by now if you'd taken the A4 like I told you'.

For occasions when there is no controversy about which lane the car should be in, or whether that van driver is about to pull out, there is a reserve supply of more than 3,000 irritating remarks, including 'Turn off the air conditioning, my feet are freezing' and 'When are we stopping for a coffee?'

'Going on a 300-mile bank holiday trip without any in-car friction may be too much of an alien experience for some people,' said engineer Alf Maine. 'The back-seat feature will come in a range of designs, from 'Mate's neurotic girlfriend' to 'Mother-in-law with weak bladder'.'

And for true masochists, designers are thought to be working on a suite featuring Jeremy Clarkson comparing the car to his Ferrari.

Universe to shut down for a year to address 'design flaws'

User groups have today criticised God's plans to close the Universe next year to carry out essential maintenance work. The decision follows reports that there are serious design flaws in the cosmos that are preventing it from achieving its full potential.

'The Universe is perfectly safe,' insisted God, 'but people need to remember that it is a prototype and, at this early stage, there will be some teething problems.'

Stephen Hawking disagreed however and described God's creation as 'riddled with black holes.'

The closure is just the latest in a long line of problems to dog the Universe ever since it began operating 13.7 billion years ago, most notably the controversial recall of millions of galaxies found to have faulty gravity.

Engineering work begins in late 2011 during which time a replacement bus service will be running.

ESA fines Philae Lander for negative TripAdvisor Review

The European Space Agency reacted furiously after Philae Lander posted the negative comments while holidaying on the 'paradise retreat' of Comet 67P/Churyumov-Gerasimenko. The ESA refused to comment on the fine but pointed out that Lander had 'not yet paid for the tour'.

Lander wrote: 'I don't mind a long-haul flight so long as the destination and accommodation make it worthwhile. I tried to contact the ESA about my concerns only to be fobbed off by complaints about my 'crap parking' and demands for soil samples. In frustration, I filed my review with TripAdvisor. I think it was fair.'

Woman held captive by WhatsApp Group

A man has claimed that his wife is being held captive by a WhatsApp Group that was only intended to arrange her friend Helen's surprise 40th but has continued unabated ever since.

Chris Young, 43, from Bromsgrove, said: 'By 'groups' I thought feral toddlers or Game of Thrones withdrawal therapy, but this one was different. The first warning sign was the name - 'Claire-Bear's 40th Yay!' Jesus. I tried to make it light-hearted by changing her phone settings so any new group notification was Yoda saying "A message from the dark side, you have". Brilliant.

'But it wasn't. It all took a rather sinister turn. I never thought I'd get sick of hearing Yoda. But it was relentless messaging - day and night. Michelle was glued to her phone - messaging interspersed with the occasional knowing little giggle. But when I tried to share in the joke, she would just say "It's nothing, just Debs". Who the f*ck is Debs!?

'When I did manage a sneaky peak, it was just an emoji avalanche – all dancing ladies in bunny ears and martini glasses. Well, apart from someone named 'Greta', who just sent fourteen syringe-with-blood emojis,' Young continued. 'I just prayed for the 40th to be over and that would be that. The purpose for the group's existence over, right? Wrong.

'It's worse. Even though Michelle clearly hates most of them, the level of messaging is batshit nuts. If she's not scrolling though pictures of shocked orangutans trying to find one with a bow tie, then she's searching for fungal creams at 2 a.m. for someone who has taken a photo of her manky toe and sent it with just 'WTAF??' written underneath.

'Also, 'Syringe lady' is now apparently in charge. She sets daily vegan-based challenges. Michelle is currently sitting in a bath filled with chia seeds and almond milk.'

Young concluded: 'I was at the end of my tether so I asked my mates down the pub for help. I explained how she was all-consumed by it - always on the phone and totally preoccupied. They just said I was a jammy bastard. Apparently, they've since added their wives to the group.'

Scientists breed non-pooing dog

Canine geneticists have engineered a breed of genetically modified pit bulls that do not 'do a poo' or even have to 'go to the bathroom'. According to Dr Marcus Hunter of Oxford University, this could revolutionise the fraught relationship between dog owners and the rest of society.

Non-pooing dogs internally recycle their waste and so do not need much food. Dog owners welcomed the new breed, although some said they would miss the daily walks and the excitement of letting the dog cock its leg on the Audi of that flash git who appears to be shagging the rather fetching divorcee down the road.

Lampposts, however, are believed to be relieved at the news. Crufts said they would be creating a new prize category for next year's show. A 'Golden Turd' prize category is now under consideration.

Britons 'have nothing to fear' from large floating Death Star

The Foreign Secretary made it clear today that voters should ignore the partially constructed space station, increasing in size each night, in the sky above Slough.

'What? That old thing? Nothing to worry about at all. In fact, it should make everyone feel much, much safer. I mean, just look at it. Yes, we admit that it does have enormous firepower, but law-abiding Britons will in no way be targeted by the proposed super laser. You have nothing to be concerned about – just ask the folks on Alderaan.'

Apple reduces our bodily orifices down to one

Having phased out the redundant headphone socket, hardware designers have turned their attention to the outmoded bOdy 2.0. Removing all but the face aperture, Apple hope that this slimmed-down version will simplify life choices - with the tag line: 'Every hole really is a goal.'

Taking the bold decision to ditch the traditional multi-socket anatomy, users will be able to alternate between eating, shitting and shagging; or can trigger all three simultaneously, if engaged in German pornography.

Having the ear and reproductive organ combined will have a negative impact on your sex life but what there is of it will sound great. Said one Apple developer: 'The only hole we won't be removing is the one in our tax returns.'

GM royals could benefit society, scientists say

Scientists at Cambridge have said that genetically modified Royals could help produce a more productive and intelligent monarchy.

Currently, the Royal gene pool is missing many genes found at other levels of society. These include the empathy gene and the work ethic gene, which either died out through lack of use or morphed into the party, vacation and entitlement genes.

'GM could help Royals to cope in the outside world,' a spokesperson said. 'Some may fear a recurrence of the problems from the last experiment in crossing Princess Anne with a horse, but most scenarios would improve the Royal gene pool. Let's face it, who has been more beneficial to society down the years, Dolly the Sheep or Prince Edward? I rest my case.'

Big Ben to be fitted with four digital displays

London took an important step towards embracing 21st century technology, or at the very least somewhere in the early 1980s.

The proposal will see Big Ben's familiar chimes being replaced by a digital alarm clock, with the even more familiar irritating electronic: 'Beep, beep, beep, beep, beep, beep, beep, beep, beep, beep, beep, beep...' The clock tower will have a huge, traditional, red, LED seven-segment display on each side.

'The cancellation of the Garden Bridge frees up enough funds to allow a proper modern design,' London Mayor Sadiq Khan announced. 'And we're hoping to replace Buckingham Palace with a Wetherspoons.'

Scientists discover what all TV inputs/outputs mean

It is up there with the riddle of the Sphinx and James Corden's career, but scientists have uncovered the mystery behind all the 'hole thingies' on the back of your TV. Rather than a gateway to Narnia, it is now believed that the embedded slots are alien in origin and form an important part in our species' evolution.

Naturally, man's first impulse upon discovering these electrical glory holes resulted in 240 volts to the genitals. Meanwhile other primitives, who were still using Betamax, worshipped the holes as rudimentary gods, feeding them cotton buds and twiglets.

Explained one paleoanthropologist and aerial mechanic: 'We've concluded that once these intergalactic hieroglyphics are deciphered, then the human race will advance to a higher state of being. It's probably something with Sky Sports and genuine surround sound - not that Dolby 5.1 rubbish.'

Queen's waving arm to generate power during Royal engagements

Following successful trials at the Sandringham Flower Show earlier this month, it has been announced that the Queen is to have her waving arm connected to a generator to produce green energy while the monarch is carrying out official engagements.

Once the technology is fully installed, it is hoped that Her Majesty's oscillating limb will provide sufficient kinetic power to run not only her Rolls Royce's satellite navigation system, but also the car's DVD player so Prince Philip can enjoy his Lady Gaga collection without feeling guilty about the planet.

The idea to harness the natural energy from the Queen is based upon an old idea the Prince of Wales had devised for the Queen Mother during his Goon Show years at university, which involved having his grandmother's drinking arm wired up to the National Grid.

It is understood that the next Eco-Royal initiative will involve capturing power directly from Prince Charles' ears, although engineers say they have not tackled wind sails on such a large scale before.

Trumps orders NASA to change moon's orbit for monthly eclipses

Donald Trump was so impressed with the recent solar eclipse across America that he has instructed NASA to make it a monthly occurrence. 'Proud to be delivering solar eclipses,' said the President. 'No "totals" under Obama. Let's make America dark again – but not in that way.'

'There's no gravity in space,' continued Trump, 'so how hard can it be? And if they could make the Sun less bright, we wouldn't need those dumb glasses.'

The President later tweeted that he never said anything. 'Fake news! Failing #nytimes says I ordered NASA to change moon's orbit. Real patriotic Americans know the moon and the earth orbit around me! Sad!'

An anonymous White House source said: 'If he wants less bright sunshine, he shouldn't talk through his ass so much since that's what, according to him, the sun shines out of.'

Password complexity to overtake poetry by 2020

Industry experts have warned that email passwords will need to be 'more sophisticated than a Shakespearean sonnet' to overcome the efforts of criminal hackers and elected Governments.

'Limericks won't cut it,' said one IT insider. 'They're too predictable. Iambic pentameter will shortly be the minimum standard acceptable and even then, users will need to show a wide range of metaphors and similes if they're to defeat GCHQ's computers.'

Mensa has welcomed the new requirements, saying: 'We always knew there was some point to being like this; now we can prove it.'

IN OTHER RELATED NEWS:

Pepper spray drones to target middle class dinner parties
Hi-tech scanning reveals a third of election promises to be empty
Google self-drive car will allow hands-free racism for Top Gear
James Dyson denies rumours that his electric car sucks
After losing a third of its value, Bitcoin renamed Sterling
Study finds tendency to become a socio-biologist 'genetically determined'
New child-friendly fire alarm to play ice cream van jingle
Man with Pavlovian response eats meringue
IBM workers use European wasps after USB ban
UK pledges aid for Prime Ministers devastated by Hurricane Brexit
Royal Family to be fracked for shale gas
Welfare Budget could be reduced with Biblical floods
Peru avoids disaster after Amazon fires delivered next door
GM herb which never goes off named Thyme Immemorial
Public opinion still split on fracking
UK Government commits to 'net zero' bullshit emissions by 2050
Egypt claims reports of painted donkeys are fake gnus
Unicorn burger contains Quorn
Blue Planet II series finale to mostly feature Brits punching sharks on the nose
Hurricanes much more aggressive now they have men's names
Bovine rescuers dismissed as 'a bunch of cowboys'
Replace 'dirty' fuel with something 'less smutty', insists UN
Disposable nappy inventor buried in landfill
150 aquatic mammals stranded on Perth beach 'about the size of whales'
Quality of beavers' homes falling, says damning report
'Pangolin armour still not fit-for-purpose,' admits evolution
Octopus ahead in arms race
Dubious assertion that flowers have penises is poppycock
Missing half of universe found in bottom of woman's handbag

CHAPTER FIFTEEN

Calls for less Grammar Schools, not fewer (and other stories about Health & Education)

Ventilator supply gap to be filled with kazoos

The Health Secretary has said that he is confident that he can meet the respiratory needs of British patients – provided they don't mind using a party-blower, with a feather on the end. Virus sufferers will be strapped to a series of breathing apparatus, including whoopee cushions, and of course, an inflatable sheep.

His initial preference was for the final death rattle to be accompanied with a 'wah wah wah', but the trombones were just too cumbersome. Instead, as Grandpa breathes his final breath, the atmosphere will be lightened with a short comic interlude on the kazoo.

A Health Official explained: 'We're looking for a cheaper, more portable alternative to a ventilator – and ideally something that can fit in a party bag. One suggestion was to use bagpipes, with Dyson promising to produce 20,000 bagless bagpipes – which kind of defeated the point.'

ICUs will be fitted with state-of-the-art kazoos, with nothing but the finest in paper/comb technologies. 'Admittedly you won't survive long on a kazoo, but what little time you have left will be hilarious – we call it Hancock's Half Hour.'

Kids at the back of the bus 'really were much harder than you'

Long thought to be the case from anecdotal playground gossip and your elder brother's teasing at the dinner table, research has found that teenagers at the back of the bus are at least 250% tougher than you, and could lay you out with a single punch, no problem, and what are you staring at anyway?

Researchers considered a range of other factors thought to be associated with schoolkid hardness, including the age of the first appearance of 'bumfluff' facial hair, the amount of implausible stories of sexual activity and the number of classroom confrontations with a supply teacher.

'What we still don't know is the direction of causation between hardness and seat selection,' noted a nervous teacher on bus duty at your school today. 'Do the hard kids opt for the back seat out of some feeling of entitlement? Or does the act of sitting at the back embolden otherwise wimpy kids to swear more and constantly adjust their crotches?

'It would be good to run an experiment seating the hard kids on seats nearer the front to test this theory,' noted the teacher timidly. 'I suggested it to Brookdale gang, but they suggested that I f*ck off back to the hole I came from.'

End-of-term gifts included a Mini Clubman Convertible

Hannah Meadowes, a reception teacher at St Enda's Preparatory School in Barnes, has told reporters she was bowled over by the generosity of some of the children's end-of-term gifts.

'To have received three diamond-encrusted Rolexes is just so far beyond all my expectations,' she said. 'Not to mention the one-week timeshare at the Monte Carlo penthouse and countless other goodies. And not forgetting the Mini, of course.'

One mum, Jocasta Pfillager, whose daughter Persephone-Belinda presented Miss Meadowes with the keys to the car at Thursday's morning assembly, denied currying favour in order to ensure her daughter was cast as the lead in this year's Nativity Play.

Meanwhile Hannah's flatmate, Denise, a friend she met at teacher training college - and who also teaches a reception class, at The Cardinal Rathbone Primary School in Peckham - is understood to be delighted with her own haul of gifts, comprising a box of heat-damaged Maltesers and three slightly over-ripe satsumas.

So now it's acceptable to start a sentence with 'So', say OED

So, language experts have confirmed that if you start a sentence with the word 'so', it sounds like you have a train of thought in mind, even when you don't.

'So even when a sentence needn't start with the word 'so', like this one, if you shove a so at the beginning it sounds like you're doing joined-up thinking.' So said Professor Eric Smythe, editor of the Oxford English Dictionary. So, he's not alone.

So now it's likely that all public announcements and instructions will start this way, including train cancellations ('So, we're sorry to announce the cancellation of the 4.35 to Brighton'), weather forecasts ('So, we're in for a milder spell...') and even dress patterns ('So, sew along dotted line 'A'...').

So, so-called phatic or informal sentence openings like 'well' and 'OK' are likely to fall out of use, so 'so' takes over. So, the Archbishop of Canterbury is expected to announce a new version of the Lord's prayer: 'So, Our Father, who art in heaven...', and performers in new productions of The Sound of Music will sing 'So doe, a deer, a female deer...'

Government to store NHS Direct in case real NHS stops working

The Government has announced that axed medical helpline NHS Direct will not be scrapped completely, but kept in a shed in case the real NHS stops working. The Health Secretary confirmed that a deal had been struck with the Treasury to turn off NHS Direct's funding, but that it should be kept in a big cardboard box 'just in case'.

'We initially thought we might sell it on eBay, perhaps to America,' he said. 'But then we noticed that the proper NHS is started to look a bit knackered, and there are quite a few cracks and cuts when you look closely.'

The idea to mothball NHS Direct for spare parts or emergencies was 'very sensible,' the Health Secretary said. 'My wife told me to just get rid of it, but I'm the minister and in my view, you can't be too careful, which is why we're keeping NHS Direct in the shed out the back at Downing Street just in case the real one breaks down. Or gets broken up.'

Doctors invent the 'morning-after' kebab

Pharmacists have today launched a new emergency contraceptive for couples who fail to take sensible precautions against post-nightclub sex by ingesting partially reheated off-cuts of meat.

The 'morning-after' kebab, ideally purchased in advance and left to mature overnight, works by turning the human body into an inhospitable environment for all forms of life, and is also an effective hangover cure.

Despite apparent enthusiasm for the 'kebab method' among twenty-something drinkers, researchers have admitted that some participants in trials experienced side effects of dehydration and profound physical discomfort, while a significant percentage reported an increased level of childbirth roughly nine months later. As such, the product is being advertised under the slogan: 'Shish happens - doner worry'.

Surgery patients advised to visit local butcher

Having encouraged sick children to be treated by pharmacists, NHS England has decided to outsource health care to the High Street, combining The Body Shop with Hobbycraft. Butchers will now provide surgical advice, alongside prime off-cuts, with many patients featuring in Gregg's pasty range.

A spokeswoman for the Ministry of Health said: 'The High Street can provide a multitude of cheap health care solutions. You've got Argos for General Practice, for sexual wellbeing we have Screwfix, and catatonic patients get sent to the grocers.

'What do you mean that's insensitive? It's not like we sent those with spinal injuries to Clarks. Actually, that's not a bad idea...

'Yes, mortality rates will be high, but I'm sure Clinton Cards will have a condolence message for every occasion. And for serious ailments there will still be the NHS, or as we call it, Poundland.'

'Books' to be slimmed down due to Health & Safety concerns

Following an increase in A&E admissions, various organisations have been urged to redraft their 'books' to minimise injuries whenever situations suggest throwing the book at people might be useful.

'We all know of times when we feel the need to throw the book at people,' said a detective, 'but the purpose is to assist in their imprisonment, not spending the night in triage.'

'There are manual handling considerations, too,' said an expert from the Health and Safety Executive. 'As it is generally our employees involved in this action, it appears ironic that we could be putting our own people at risk of back injury and potentially causing harm to persons they are investigating.'

There have been calls for exceptions to the concept of slimming all books down, however. 'We've asked Chilcot to keep on writing,' said a lawyer representing families who lost loved ones during the Iraq war, 'because we're rather hoping that, when they throw it at Blair it totally and irrevocably flattens him.'

Compulsory tantric sex education 'could go on all day'

School timetables may have to be rewritten to allow for the introduction of compulsory lessons in tantric sex, teachers have warned. 'This is utter madness,' said Deputy Head Maureen Greeb. 'So far, we've had to drop maths, history and science in order to make way for double tantra. These classes just go on and on.'

'Young people should be taught that sex means loving relationships within the context of a wider cosmic consciousness that transcends the materialistic world,' said Government 'Sex Czar', Sting. 'Did I mention I have a new album out?'

The new lessons are hoped to combat the rise in teenage pregnancies, following research that shows kids taught tantric sex either reach a sublime experience of infinite awareness or simply get so bored they fall asleep.

Teachers to talk about their divorces at primary school level

Children as young as five will now be given compulsory lectures on their teachers' domestic hell as Divorce Education is made compulsory in primary schools. The move comes amid fears children are getting a skewed impression of what marriage is really like from shows like 'Don't Tell the Bride' and 'One Born Every Minute'.

Divorce Education lessons will typically involve male teachers weeping over photos of 'old times' before drinking themselves into a stupor, while their female counterparts smoke heavily and discuss the various ways in which their ex-husbands failed to satisfy them physically.

Meanwhile, younger children will be introduced to divorce basics through specially commissioned books such as 'Spot Loses Everything' and 'Janet and John Make Custody Arrangements'. The focus will be on what to do if someone marries you when you don't want to be married, and the importance of saying 'no'.

A Commons Committee spokesperson said: 'While some parents talk about how moribund their lives are at home, it is important to remember that some do not. By bringing the topic into the classroom we can ensure that all children have a solid understanding of the abject misery of marriage.'

London borough unveils new wheeze called 'books'

The London Borough of Hackney Council has today launched a new scheme, which will see local schools supplied with a range of 'books' with which they can 'read' sections, or 'chapters' with the children, ahead of classroom-based learning experiences.

Seven Hackney schools have agreed to trial the initiative, with the costs of meeting the books being part-funded by money put aside for the council's 2012 Olympic Games cake fund. The head of Recursive Involvement Studies at St Jude's Secondary School, Anne Thomas, explained that, despite the lack of celebrity involvement, the school is still upbeat about the scheme.

'We had a few of the Arsenal reserves in last month to talk about trigonometry and it was really positive, no-one was stabbed,' she said. 'Maybe next year we can get this Shakespeare bloke to play games with Year 8 and discourage methadone use within school time.'

Teachers finally settles bill from last year's Christmas lunch

After a year of painful negotiations, a group of teachers from Coventry have finally agreed how to allocate the bill from their Christmas lunch, just in time to book into the same restaurant for this year's event.

'I know it sounds like a small sum to those in the private sector,' said one member of the group, 'but there was an important principle at stake: I didn't have a starter and Eric had two glasses of wine.

'And I won't even mention a certain person who's just supply, but had a Black Forest gateau that wasn't even on the set menu. She clearly doesn't do things by half. Except with her job.'

The school's board of governors offered to throw in £4 in March, which would have resolved the impasse, but only added fuel to the fire as the Head of Maths, Mr Jennings, was determined to solve the problem using bipartite graph matching theory, and declined the offer.

'You can't just throw a random sum of money at a conundrum with so many mathematical variables, it has to be solved properly,' explained Jennings, who himself ordered an extra drink on his way back from the loo, despite secretly being one drink ahead of the party.

Restaurant manager Terry Watson, who accidentally accepted the booking over the phone, said: 'We put signs up every year clearly saying 'No teachers', yet they still they come with their calculators.

'They actually rubbed off all the specials from my blackboard so they could show their workings. I offered to let the £4 go, but they just recalculated the bill with a slightly smaller total and off they went again.'

A DfE spokesperson said: 'We sympathise with the restaurant staff. Can you imagine how f*cking tedious our pay negotiations are?'

GPs to be replaced by vending machines

For as little as 20p, patients will soon be able to shove their head, limb, or genitals into a hole and have a vending machine assess a range of medical conditions.

In a bold move to address the crisis in GP services, the Government has announced a multi-million-pound investment in diagnostic vending machines. 'Kwik-Sick' machines will be placed in workplace canteens and train stations across the UK.

Modelled on popular coffee and snack vendors, the new machines will have a series of holes into which customers can stick a body part for an instant diagnosis of flu, piles or brain tumours.

Holes will come in a range of sizes and will be set at different heights to accommodate a diverse patient population. After you stick your body part into a hole, the vending machine will then print out a diagnosis.

The Government believes Kwik-Sick is a cost-effective alternative to GPs because each one contains an underpaid and poorly trained 'diagnostic advisor' who crouches inside and examines body parts as they are poked through.

In a further innovation, prospective patients will first need to input their basic details into a gatekeeping vending machine which will announce that: 'The GP vending machine will allow you to access it next Thursday week at 9:30 a.m.'

GPs have reacted in a typically Luddite fashion and condemned the new service outright. They point out that children with saucepans stuck on their heads could receive electric shocks. However, the Health Minister has expressed his full confidence in the new technology and its preferred supplier, Bodyparts International Plc, in which he owns 20% of the shares.

Schoolteachers to get SAS-style training

The Government has denied that teachers are being put at risk by being rushed back to schools early during the COVID-19 pandemic.

'The BEF - British Educational Force - is being shipped for special anti-coronavirus training in Hereford run by the SAS - Special Antivirus Service,' said an aide to the Education Minister. 'Their PPE is due to arrive two weeks later, so they are really good to go.'

Under questions from journalists, the aide pointed out that children don't really get any symptoms, so they are safe. Furthermore, he said, screaming six-year-olds with snot running down their faces could not in any way present a risk for teachers, their families or the lollipop lady.

'What is more important? A vague R number or a generation of six-year-olds unable to colour between the lines? We have the economy on edge, and a failure to be able to wield a crayon effectively could result in the collapse of the manufacturing sector,' said the aide, holding up a Government charter written in red crayon.

Everybody who completed Dry January already shit-faced

Every single person who completed Dry January in the UK has celebrated the arrival of February by getting absolutely shit-faced before lunchtime, it has been confirmed.

'The first couple of days were OK, possibly because I was still a bit pissed from New Year, but after that it has been tough going,' said Jason Thompson, a Dry January survivor, standing outside his local Wetherspoons waiting for it to open while clutching a half empty bottle of vodka.

Thompson celebrated midnight on 31 January with a small glass of wine. Then a large glass of wine. Then a whole bottle of Jägermeister. He then got some sleep before getting up and pouring vodka on a bowl of cornflakes.

Other survivors have pointed out how convenient it is that the end of the month came at a weekend, where there is no need for most of them to work.

'Don't get me wrong, I would've got twatted anyway, but it's just so much easier not having to try to hide it and act sober at work. My boss gets really picky about me drinking during my shift,' explained Laura Cox, a heart surgeon.

Surrey Hospital sold to NCP in groundbreaking initiative

A leading teaching hospital has been sold to a car park operator in the first deal of its kind.

From March patients at St Olaf's Hospital, Guildford, will have to feed bedside meters a whopping £25 a day for the duration of their admission, with outpatients paying a £5 fee upon arrival at reception, then topping up hourly if their appointment is running late. Wardens have been recruited to wheel defaulters and overstayers off wards into adjacent corridors, then transfer them onto trolleys until they or their relatives stock up on credit again.

A spokesperson for the trust said: 'We see this as an exciting opportunity to reform hospital stays root and branch. It will actively help to flush out work-shy and shiftless malingerers. No-one will want to stay with us if it's costing them their hard-earned cash, and bed-blocking will become a thing of the past. That's the beauty of the free market in action.'

The Minister of Health is said to be watching developments with considerable interest. A departmental source commented: 'This is exciting stuff, and rolling the concept out nationally just may be the answer to this never-ending NHS conundrum.'

Patients 'waiting too long to be put into cupboards'

Newly published figures show that many hospitals are failing to meet their commitments to putting patients into cupboards within the four-hour target time. The report has also confirmed that many patients are suffering the indignity of having to share large rooms, or 'wards', with other sick people while waiting for cupboards to become available.

George Winters, 53, complained that when he was admitted to St Margaret's Hospital, Cambridge, with bleeding from the ears after listening to James Blunt albums, he was stuck in a large warm room with big windows and TV screens at the end of each bed.

'Most of the other patients were coughing up their lungs, so I asked the nurse if there wasn't a cupboard available somewhere, but it was another six hours before I was abandoned in the corridor and a further three before I was finally put in the cupboard. Disgraceful.'

'School of Hard Knocks' to become 'University of Life'

With its reputation for a broad curriculum and high mortality rates, the School of Hard Knocks offers degree courses that will inspire the young and 'cull the weak'.

Lecturers come from a range of criminal backgrounds including prostitution, gun smuggling and the banking sector. Each will be uniquely qualified to advise on how to survive in the post-apocalyptic jobs market. Early modules will include 'How to skin a rat', 'Insulating lofts with faeces' and 'Human flesh: Tastes like chicken'.

As part of their 'gifted and talented' programme, students will spend a gap year in Syria or an abattoir of their choice. Assessment will involve being thrown into a locked examination hall with no writing materials and only rudimentary weapons. Whoever emerges with all their limbs intact will be awarded a first-class PPE.

'If we've learnt anything from The X-Factor, overcoming adversity is what brings out talent,' explained a Department for Education spokesperson. 'We want fragile, abused and vulnerable young adults to take these life lessons and channel them into a meaningful career path preying on the fragile, abused and vulnerable. Remember, what doesn't kill you makes you stronger. Unless it's the asbestos in the lecture hall ceiling.'

'Keep calm and check your prostate' a slogan too far

Cancer Research UK's latest awareness campaign, 'Keep calm and check your prostate regularly ', has come under fire for taking the popular 'Keep calm and' theme beyond its logical limits.

'Over the last few years, posters, T-shirts and albums have encouraged the British consumer to keep calm and 'Chill out', 'Have a cuppa', 'Eat a muffin' and so on,' said activist Howard Slead.

'I mean, I support the fight against prostate cancer as much as the next man, but come on guys, you could at least do something original rather than cling to the same tired old meme as everyone else.

'Still, at least it's better than Francis Maude's recent 'Panic Immediately and Turn Your Garage Into a Potentially Exploding Death-Trap' campaign,' he added.

Flood of immigrant nurses finally halted

Plans are underway to stop the UK from being overrun by caring and competent health professionals. The number of EU nationals joining nursing fell by 96% last year, which means Britain can now focus on recruiting more valued professions, such as sex-trafficked strawberry pickers.

 A Home Office spokeswoman explained: 'All too often you see nurses smuggled in container lorries, with their radical notion of free health care. Communities can become disrupted by 'health ghettos' filled with vitamins, bed baths and those weird fob watches, which make all nurses look like an 18th century dandy.

'They work in unsanitary conditions, often surrounded by disease, and will stick a thermometer up your bottom as soon as look at you. Really, would you want to live next door to one?'

Meanwhile, tempers and temperatures are running high in the nursing camp in Calais, which is daubed with the slogan - 'Go back to where you came from - some sort of medical school, I guess?'

Malala 'a saddo loser', British schoolkids agree

Schoolchildren up and down Britain are still struggling to come to terms with the acclaim accorded to Malala Yousafzai, a Pakistani school pupil and activist blogger who was shot in the head by the Taliban in 2011 for campaigning for girls' education rights. They have unanimously agreed that her conduct is 'well rank' and that she should have been grateful not to have to sit through double Maths every Tuesday morning.

Malala's courage and determination has earned her acclaim all over the world. Since her miraculous survival from the attempted assassination, she has been instrumental in the ratification of Pakistan's first Right to Education Bill and was nominated for the Nobel Peace Prize.

However, British teenagers have dismissed all this as 'totally gay'. 'So let me, like, get this right, she got nearly killed for doing a blog about wanting girls to actually GO to school,' said Destiny-Louise Williamson, a Year 10 student at Alderman Bagnall Comprehensive in Mansfield.

'I'd let anyone shoot me in the head if it meant not having to watch Mr Lewis's eczema flaking off into the beakers in Chemistry. "One teacher and one pen can change the world" – what is she on about? What even is a pen?'

Call to bring back 'traditional smoking' to schools

An educational think tank is calling for the return of smoke-filled staff rooms to Britain's schools. The call has come from the previously unheard-of political pressure group 'Right Thinking Now!', who are suggesting a possible link between the increase in underage crime and the decrease in cigarette consumption.

'In the good old days, a child would hang around by the school staff room and get blasted by an overwhelming fug of tobacco smoke as the door opened,' said Charles Palmer, a spokesman. 'So, if we want traditional schools, we should go for the whole package – teachers with nicotine-stained fingers who come back from the pub at lunchtime reeking of beer and fags.'

Palmer denied that his opinions were in any way affected by his position as paid advisor to British American Tobacco.

Armed teachers notice rise in homework submissions

Students have been much more diligent since teachers started coming in fully armed. One tooled-up teacher commented: 'At the start of a lesson, I'll just place my revolver on top of my desk or draw a bullseye on a student's forehead. It's all about managing the classroom dynamic, differentiating between learners – plus the implied threat that you'll get shot the moment you drop your pen.'

Armed teachers also attest to quieter parents' evenings and much more productive discussions with management, when it comes to having a pay rise. The quantity of apples offered to staff has risen tenfold, while any decline in retention has been offset by a nice sideline in the sale of small coffins and Peppa Pig-themed wreaths.

Lesson plans and schemes of work are now expected to reference the calibre of student and bullet used. A standard multi-choice question will now be 'What is the average range of AK-47?'

a) One classroom

b) One cafeteria and sports field

c) Do you feel lucky?

d) Well, do ya, punk?

'Feeling a bit funny' now a medical term

Families have all too often been devastated by the loss of a loved one, who after 'feeling a bit funny' were forced to rearrange the sofa pillows or have another biscuit – sometimes even opening a window. These symptoms can often be hereditary, with whole families left in a catatonic state in front of the TV.

GPs attest to being inundated by outbreaks of nebulous illnesses and bouts of debilitating fuzziness. One doctor advised: 'Patients exhibiting symptoms such as – well, there are no symptoms – but if you feel a bit funny, we recommend an emergency tracheotomy, followed by a double amputation, if only to take your mind off it.'

Awareness of the disease needs to be broadcast, as too often sufferers are too feeble to pick up the phone and order their own pizza. There is a hope that the campaign could get a celebrity endorsement. James Corden was approached, but his agent declined, explaining that his client had never felt 'funny' in his life.

Social workers to be fast-tracked to a nervous breakdown

After a five-week 'taster course', graduate social workers will now be air-dropped, naked, into the most challenging areas in the country, ready to fend off urban foxes, with just a roll of duct tape.

A minister explained: 'Too often social workers are bogged down with helping the most vulnerable, but now they will be able to move directly to the career stage of habitual depression and drug use.

'If it is successful, this scheme will be rolled out to include other public sector workers. Nurses will have their peanut allowance cut by 50%. Teachers will see class sizes increased to ninety-nine. And police officers will be armed with tasers and customer feedback forms.

'For most, it takes years before they can be publicly crucified by a pernicious and unreasonable media and a litigious, angry population. We can now make that living nightmare a reality. The papers will love it.'

Man diagnosed with 'indifference to Marmite'

The Department of Health has urged the public to remain calm after a man in West London was diagnosed as 'indifferent to Marmite'.

Reports surfaced after the man was overheard in a cafe admitting that he could 'take or leave' the brown toast topping. 'We've never seen anything like this before,' said a face-masked official, shortly before evacuating the area.

Tests are now being carried out on the man to confirm his indifference, but the World Health Organisation has stressed that at the moment the virus has not reached pandemic proportions. The

Government has also confirmed that it will be sending a leaflet to every household providing advice on how to maintain love or hatred for the sandwich filling.

Man with 'super-gonorrhoea' enjoying 'being a legend'

The first British man to contract a strain of 'super-gonorrhoea' that cannot be cured with the usual antibiotics has said that the extreme and possibly untreatable discomfort has to be balanced against 'being a total legend'.

'Some say I'm a gonorr, others are calling me Super-Gonorrhoea Man, though they seem reluctant to shake my hand, and they ask if my cape has snagged on a loose flap,' said the unnamed man.

'Still, at least I'm famous now - the story's gone viral, apparently. Now if you'll excuse me for a moment - AAAAAAAHHH, PLEASE GOD, MAKE IT STOP - that's taking the piss, that is. Hey, did you see what I did there?'

Babies to be fitted with snooze buttons

Scientists today unveiled a solution to the centuries-old design fault in babies. 'We realised there are two things which generally disturb a person's sleep: a small child and an alarm clock. But inexplicably only one of these was designed with an 'off' button,' explained Professor Lyndon, who led the research project.

'It's a little drastic and irreversible, but now when your baby wakes up screaming at 3.17am you can just hit the snooze button and get an extra ten minutes of shut-eye.'

Drawing on other design features of the clock radio, scientists have reported that the next generation of babies could also be fitted with a radio antenna to provide a wider range of alarm sounds.

'Babies tend to come with that one loud and annoying default alarm tone,' continued Lyndon, 'but now parents could be woken by their child broadcasting Classic FM or Radio 4. In fact, tests have found that both those stations tend to have a strangely somnolent effect on the child, so that the sound of his own crying often puts him back to sleep again.'

The plans to fit infant humans with snooze buttons that would remain with them throughout life have been welcomed both by wives, who see snoozing their husbands as a convenient alternative to lying about having a headache, and by husbands, who don't mind whether their spouse is awake or asleep.

Milky Bar Kid responsible for obesity crisis

He was strong and tough, and only the best was good enough, but now the Milky Bar Kid faces widespread condemnation for single-handedly kicking off what experts say could be a crisis of epidemic proportions.

True to his familiar catch phrase, 'The Milky Bars are on me!', Terry Martins, now 58, gave away an estimated 674,837 Milky Bars between 1961 and 1966, with tragic consequences for a generation of slothful young TV watchers who paid no heed to the consequences.

'It's true I got carried away with the sheer joy of the generosity of the character,' admitted Martins. 'There I was, a bespectacled kid who suddenly went from being bullied to a hero for a generation. What could I do with my fame except reward my fans, the only way I knew how?'

Consumer and health watchdogs are considering a class action against the Kid, who could be liable for hundreds of millions of pounds in damages. Penguins could be next in the firing line for their part in promoting unhealthy chocolate-covered edibles. 'We will not be made scapegoats,' said a spokesbird.

Parents admit child is just a little shit

Everybody, it is said, remembers the day that a dog ran into their school. That is certainly true for pupils at St Peter's primary in Coventry, because little Jimmy Morris, 11, set fire to it. And that was just a trial run: later he set fire to the school.

Aged four, Morris hung a neighbour's cat by its tail from a tree; aged six, he attempted to create a 'ramster' by blending a rabbit and a hamster. In a blender.

Jimmy's father is dismissive of ADHD or other psychological explanations for his son's behaviour. 'The boy's just an evil little shit,' is his considered opinion, and he has refused further testing aimed at labelling Jimmy with a new syndrome excusing his behaviour.

'There's no point,' he said. 'There's nothing wrong with the little bugger. He hasn't been brought up properly and he's never been given any proper discipline. He's just been allowed to do as he pleases, so it's no surprise he's turned out a threat to the animal kingdom. I blame his teachers.'

Man in six-year coma declared fit for work by DWP

A bitter row has broken out concerning 36-year-old Will Protheroe from Wimborne, who has been declared fit for work by the DWP, despite having been in a vegetative state for six years.

Three months ago, Protheroe received a letter asking that he present himself at the local assessment centre for a medical examination. His wife Julie called the DWP and explained her husband's condition, then thought no more about it until his payments suddenly stopped. When she queried this, she was told he had been sanctioned, with his benefits disallowed for not turning up at the appointment.

An advisor at the Department for Work and Pensions, said: 'Look, I'm proud of the reforms that I helped to bring in. People scrounging off the system claiming for benefits that they're not entitled to has been costing us millions every year, and it's vital that we stop it.

'I can't comment on this specific case except to say Mr Protheroe said he was ill, so if he really was, and he had actually bothered to attend his appointment, then he wouldn't be in this position now. I don't wish to be seen as being uncaring here... but you know, hasn't he only got himself to blame?

'Perhaps if he is able to blink then couldn't he do that thing where he's hooked up to a computer, a bit like Stephen Hawking used to be,' she said. 'The computer could be interfaced with some kind of switching device, say to perform a menial factory job? I mean just think how much better he'd feel about himself if he was gainfully employed instead of living off benefits.'

Cancer drugs will shrink Daily Mail, says report

Researchers say they have finally developed a drug that greatly reduces the copy size of the Daily Mail. A report in this month's New England Journal of Medicine showed that, in a trial of 900 people infected by the cancerous Mail, over 60% went on to make a full recovery, while others were able to take a less damaging newspaper.

It is thought that the drugs attach themselves to any reference made by the newspaper to words such as 'house prices' or 'Prince Harry', and shrink the tumour to the size of a postage stamp.

The Daily Mail is the second most common newspaper in the UK and infects nearly two million people a day with its aggressive and corrosive style of reporting, poisoning the immune system with its invective bile.

'A microdot Mail is still some way off,' explained consultant John Cullen. 'Side effects such as vomiting and diarrhoea are still an issue even with the postage stamp edition.

'This cancer has gone on long enough and we owe it to all tabloid sufferers to find a cure. You wouldn't let a dog suffer by reading the Daily Mail, so why should we prolong the agony of our nearest and dearest.'

NHS to focus on 'funny' accidents

In an attempt to husband resources and boost morale, the NHS is to concentrate on 'amusing' medical emergencies.

An NHS spokesman explained: 'Obviously, the old "preparing dinner naked when I fell back onto a carrot" story will get priority treatment. But stepping on a rake, or glass cuts on the bum where the patient is claiming to be doing photocopier repairs, will also be treated with urgency.

'Patients might notice medical staff taking photographs, but please be reassured: this is entirely for medical purposes and definitely not for posting on Facebook.'

Political Correctness 'not mad, but bipolar'

According to a spokeswoman for a new mental health campaign, 'Political Correctness gone mad' is just a lazy stereotype peddled by ignorant scaremongers, right-wing journalists, taxi drivers and radio-show hosts.

'In fact, Political Correctness was diagnosed as suffering from perfectly treatable Bipolar Affective Disorder in 1995, and has been on a combined course of cognitive-behavioural therapy and mood-stabilising medication ever since,' she said.

'There's no reason why Political Correctness shouldn't continue to function as a perfectly ordinary social concept,' she went on. 'Without it, social inequality would be on the rise, racial tension would be simmering away and women would be earning substantially less than men for no good reason ... hmmm, maybe we'd better up the dose a bit.'

Study links coronary disease to reading tabloids

A new BMA study has found that habitual use of tabloids in the Inflammatory Group of newspapers - the Daily Mail, the Daily Express and some variants of the Beano - can lead to elevated blood pressure levels, increased incidence of angina-like symptoms, and full-blown heart attacks in some instances. Unfortunately, there is no statistically significant increase in mortality.

Complicating factors in the control group appear to be age related and include having the papers delivered and postal voting. Lack of exercise is a known contributory factor and the report recommends that newspaper deliveries should only be authorised after a medical examination and assessment of the recipients' voting intentions.

The study also found an increased propensity to vote Brexit amongst the control group, but Alzheimer's has been discounted. 'There was little measurable brain function to start with,' noted the authors, 'so we couldn't identify any loss of function as a result.'

Medical examination stigma 'reduced' through use of flash mob

The NHS is hoping to use interpretative dance to lure patients into getting routine check-ups.

One nurse explained: 'You could be in a crowded railway station, when suddenly a flash mob of trained health professionals will launch into action. Through a combination of pirouettes and brute force, we will pin you to the ground and administer a rigorous cervical swab, all while removing your appendix – just in case.'

Other entertainers can also be employed. For instance, clowns will test your blood pressure, while using balloon models to represent your impacted bowel. Jugglers will provide for a much more animated breast examination, which will contrast with the gravitas of a chlamydia result, read out by national treasure Dame Judi Dench.

For those wanting a more traditional approach, Martha Graham practitioners can represent incontinence and Merce Cunningham has a lot to say about erectile dysfunction. Through the power of ribbons, spandex body suits and a judicious sprinkling of 'jazz hands', you can get a diagnosis for viral hepatitis. Meanwhile, stool tests will be set to the music of Philip Glass.

Confessed one patient: 'I love the idea of a flash mob. I was in Wetherspoons, when suddenly all the customers started spontaneously singing and then they roughly forced me to me to check my testes for lumps. It was only afterwards I discovered they weren't doctors and that this was just an average Friday night at 'Spoons'.'

Samaritans criticised for cold-calling campaign

'In these immensely depressing times we want to get to people before they feel the urge to call us, before it is too late,' said a spokesperson for The Samaritans, following controversy over its recent programme of cold-calling random people in case they might want to end it all.

'It's just part of our new prevention programme. We've been talking to people over the phone about difficult feelings for decades, so our new call centres are helping to nip things in the bud.'

One caller from Hull, who wished to remain anonymous, said: 'I was just sitting down to pie and chips and a fag when the phone went. The guy asked if I felt like topping myself, especially after the 6% increase announced by British Gas that day.

'I had been very happy up until that point. So, when I said "No", he said that I was suppressing my feelings, which wasn't healthy, and that I should be on the verge of a breakdown like everyone else. I slammed the phone down and I then got seven more calls the same night which made me very depressed.'

In another incident a young mother from Budleigh Salterton was asked if she had post-natal depression. 'I told them I hadn't but then they said I probably hadn't really looked into it enough, especially against a background of the Government's latest benefit cuts targeting unmarried mothers. After the tenth call it got to me so much that when looked in the pram, I swore that the baby had grown horns and a tail.'

Ofcom has advised consumers to ignore these calls and not to get too depressed about planned increases by BT and other service providers. They have now set up a premium rate help line at just £5.00 per minute plus a £1.50 connection fee.

Care home dead heartened that ICU care was actually available

The thousands of people who have died from coronavirus in UK care homes have expressed relief that demand for ICU beds and ventilators never outstripped supply.

'I'm stoked that Boris Johnson and Matt Hancock are able to stand in front of the nation and say that there has been no point when someone has needed a ventilator or ICU bed and it has not been available,' said Lorna Maddocks, a corpse from Ashby-de-la-Zouch. 'I nearly jumped out of my coffin.'

Boris Johnson's Tiggerish confirmation that English intensive care units were never overwhelmed has also given hope to those who died in residential care settings.

'What a heart-balm that we never exceeded critical care capacity! It put everything into perspective with such a jolt it momentarily re-started my heart, and would have brought me back to life had I not undergone brain death on a hospice bed a couple of weeks ago,' said Monty Griffiths, a cadaver from Ealing. 'Such a comfort that ICU facilities were available to us had we required them!'

Woman's impending sneeze 'gone now'

After frantic moments of deep breath inhalation, a rush to put down her full mug, and a lunge to make sure she had a tissue, account manager Jan Reeves revealed to co-workers that her anticipated sneeze had mysteriously vanished.

'I don't know what happened,' she said. 'I was all set to go and, boof, it was gone. I would've tried looking at a light, but I couldn't remember if that was supposed to start sneezes or stop them.'

Mystified by the disappearance of what Reeves was convinced would be the first in a series of absolute snorters, the office worker had returned to her spreadsheets, only to be surprised by the sneeze's sudden and violent reappearance five minutes later, which left her unable to prevent the fart that sneakily squeaked out at the same time.

Children bravely tackle vegetable shortage

Fans of saturated fat have been strangely upbeat upon learning that there is a national shortage of lettuce, broccoli and other 'rabbit food'. Children have been forced to opt for extra processed meat, two puddings and an insufferable air of smugness.

Having your five-a-day reduced to one, has left a sizeable plate gap, which has been inevitably filled by melted cheese. Explained one obese five-year-old: 'Naturally I'm devastated, but somehow I've managed to drown my sorrows with Mars Bars and Coca-Cola. It's tough surviving on a reduced vegetable diet – for instance, what can I put my ketchup on now?'

Regeneration of doctors to be rolled out across NHS

Doctors will be expected to routinely travel through time and will work until they are at least 1,500 years old, under new flexible NHS employment contracts. The policy announcement comes after civil servants uncovered a successful regeneration scheme for doctors, running since 1963, at the Gallifrey Foundation Trust.

'The abilities to distort time, communicate via telepathy, and to transform into a new doctor when you reach 750, are increasingly important for a 21st century health service,' said the Health Secretary.

'Project TimeLord will just formalise practices which we already impose on our doctors – being in two places at once, for example.'

Evidence from the Gallifrey pilot has been positive, with high levels of patient satisfaction for each of the twelve incarnations of doctors, except Sylvester McCoy, obviously.

However, unions have challenged the plans for doctors to work three millennia out of every four. And the 'One Tardis' project, to install a time machine in every hospital corridor, is thought to be years behind schedule.

The Conservatives are said to be particularly impressed with the Doctors' physical characteristic of having two hearts, which compensates for them all being heartless b*stards.

IN OTHER RELATED NEWS:

PM pledges to end GP shortage by sending all of us to medical school

The Verve accused of peddling inadequate flu remedy

NHS consultation a 'Jedi mind trick'

New female Dr Who 'technically a nurse', says man in pub

Surgeons could save time by not washing their hands

'Rural doctors' technically vets

Pensioners helpfully reminded 'your days are numbered'

National Trust to take over NHS

Nightmares caused by farts you don't let out

Hospitals not 'overcrowded', just popular

Boris Johnson promises £1.8 billion to NHS to cover his paternity tests

Man on Dyson ventilator 'starting to pick up'

Public seeking clear advice on wearing face masks told: 'Umfl Mumfl Flmf Umfll'

Man involuntarily describing towers on castles diagnosed with Turrets Syndrome

BBC donates Charlie Fairhead to Nightingale Hospital

Anti-abortion campaign uses Ed Sheeran song. Pro-choice groups use his photo

COVID-19 update: Michael Gove needs two face masks

Shoppers looking for Covid-safe snooker equipment face long cues

People feeling the cold to self-insulate

'Sorry the Government f***ed up your exam results' cards sell out in Clintons

Dying early may be a miracle cure for most diseases, reports Daily Mail

'Morning after pill' to be sold the day before

Boris Johnson pledges to lay 30 million nurses by 2030

Hogwarts students celebrate A-level results by levitating

Slow walking at 45 denotes fast ageing. Slow wanking at 45 denotes fast WiFi

Postcode Lottery Ltd. sues NHS for copyright infringement

Coca-Cola to combat child obesity by dangling drinks from slow moving truck

Courgettes to be sold in plain green packaging

Alleged Islamic takeover of schools 'can't be worse than Michael Gove'

Lib Dems to eliminate main cause of childhood illiteracy – stupid children

Playing video games lowers GCSE results, increases fun

Ofsted identify failing Jedi schools

Half of PE students would shower if we stopped watching them

Government: 'Academise? Sorry, we meant 'privatise'.'

School's advertising campaign just a kid with a Bunsen burner, again

Oxbridge to improve social diversity with 'servants' entrance'

University graduation to be modelled on Logan's Run

Chancellor promises 'one board rubber' for every school

Government counts 'pocket money' towards school funding

PM finished 40 books while in isolation, then ran out of crayons

Police Creative Writing Awards praise 'most imaginative witness statements ever'

'We don't like you either' sprouts tell humans

Jean Michel Jarre to use giant lasers to correct people's vision

Pudsey Bear criticises NHS waiting times for eye operations.

11 out of 10 hospitals overcrowded.

'We owe NHS enormous debt of gratitude' says Hancock. 'Gratitude...just not money'

Forensic Homeopathologist offers Police 'alternative' evidence

Charity collectors more annoying than the actual disease

Hedge Fund Manager dressed as Nurse eligible for NHS payrise

Teachers lament declining standards of parent-written coursework

Creationist school appears out of nowhere

'I can stay here just as long as you can,' negotiator tells striking teachers

Rise of ebooks threatening children's traditional Google skills

Trousers to fly at half-mast for Prince Andrew's birthday (and even more UK News)

UK starts advertising for Scotland's replacement

The UK has resigned itself to the fact that it is time to move on and start seeing other countries. To this end, the Foreign Office has put out a series of classified ads asking for those interested in love, a B&D parliamentary system and, in what is seen as a veiled dig at the Scots, someone who is 'well-endowed and drug-free'.

Naturally, the UK's first instinct was to thumb through its little black book of ex-colonies and past loves. An FO spokeswoman admitted:

345

'We've had a few tentative replies from parts of Asia. And the Isle of Wight has requested to be considered a real part of Great Britain - but I don't think we are ready for that just yet.

'Obviously, this is an opportunity for someone like the United States to give us a second chance. I'm sure they will be the first to admit independence hasn't really worked out. We just want someone interested in long walks in the country. Usually someone else's country. And usually somewhere in the Middle East, with guns.'

British DIY Awards started and then left for months

Organisers of the inaugural British DIY Awards have shrugged off the length of time taken to complete the ceremony. 'It's the finish that counts,' said one, 'and at the end of the day do you want it done quick, or do you want it done right?'

Although the ceremony began with great enthusiasm many months ago, it was soon behind schedule as participants drifted off to start and then abandon a number of other projects.

The problems began when host Tommy Walsh mislaid the envelope containing the nominees after putting it down within easy reach. 'But I just had it,' he insisted. 'I wish people wouldn't move my things.'

In a spectacular finale, Walsh returned to present the award for Britain's Best DIY-er as the self-assembly stage collapsed amid claims from the organisers that the stunt was 'part of the original design'.

Organisers promise that next year's event will be more ambitious, though they admitted that the job had been trickier than they'd imagined and hadn't turned out quite how they'd hoped, but what did you expect from the bunch of cowboys who organised it this year?

All service station food to be edible by 2040

All snacks sold on British roadways must be made fit for human consumption by 2040, the Ministry of Transport has announced.

The scheme is the result of Europe-wide talks aimed at improving snacks across the continent, with only France vetoing on the basis that the plans do nothing to implement minimum cheese requirements for purchases.

Critics are pointing out that there are no signs that snack technology will be advanced enough to satisfy the average driver on long journeys without having to stop off several times at roadside burger vans.

However, many travellers have already made the move from road to rail, deciding to take their chances with a Southern Rail chicken tikka masala over a Rustlers cheeseburger reheated next to the toilets.

Steve Parsons of the Association of Haulage Engineers said: 'We have nothing against 'clean' food - indeed, edible sandwiches have been on the market now for several years - but it is unfair to force drivers to make the switch.

'Needless to say, this will hit long distance lorry drivers the hardest, many of whom are now physically dependent on microwaved sausage rolls.'

Turning point of WWII 'was posh bloke overcoming a stammer'

'We had always thought that the tide began to turn against Hitler once he had invaded Russia and declared war on the United States,' said one academic, 'but now apparently it turns out that the Fuehrer's infamous oratory was no match for King George VI saying 'Red lorry, yellow lorry' really quickly'.

Trump welcomed to UK in Polari

Dear polones and homies (mostly omi-polonies) - how bona to vada your ruddy eek, our very own dishy President Tooting Fakement, King of the Naffs!

From your bijou lills, to your riah shyker, you really are fantabulosa! Showing a rare old scotch to the charpering omnis, due to your vast Gelt, and your missus with the pert willets. Cavalier or Roundhead – wouldn't we like to know!

So welcome, to our humble cottage – the old fruit will be seeing you later in her dowry latty with her badge cove (Phyllis the Greek), crimper first don't be shy be bold, for a magnificenti pile of mangarie (and nati to the glossies who nix a toss, and anyway you've no time for the beak).

Ooooh look at you, you big butch riah, with a great orange eek - Lady Muck with a Jaffa syrup on your four-poster. So, there'll be some walloping tonight, although I hear that you don't go for the vinegar much – no bevvy homie you. You are such a manly Alice, but please not too much zsa zsaing!

And don't forget – I've got your number, Ducky.

Nation on high poppy alert

Armed police are expected to patrol the streets in the run-up to Remembrance Day, opening fire on anyone not wearing a poppy or failing to whistle the tune from 'The Dambusters'.

A Home Office spokeswoman remarked: 'We may be perpetuating a mawkishly sentimental view of war but don't think for a second you can get away with recycling last year's poppy – we're wise to that dodge.

'In these times of austerity, we need cheap, meaningless gestures accompanied by hollow outrage. If we're not allowed to wear a poppy, the terrorists have won.

'It's a known fact that Afghan jihadists fear the poppy ... although admittedly 80% of their income is based on the opium trade ... um ... anyway, the important thing is to remember those who sacrificed their lives in war – rather than the reasons behind it or making sure it never happens again.'

New PM yet to pick a country to destroy

The UK has a glorious tradition of international meddling, annexing and sneakily painting countries pink on a map. Any new Prime Minister has the difficult decision as to which nation to send back to the Middle Ages, through the usual combination of 'black ops' and the missionary position.

Traditionally British foreign policy has been influenced by which country the US wanted to pick a fight with, which, of course, could refer to 90% of the UN. Obviously, there will be deciding factors in the choice of nation to obliterate: a) Is it a humanitarian crisis? b) Is there oil? and c) Please see b).

A spokesman said: 'The PM is determined to annihilate someone, but needs to focus on the UK first.'

Blair cleared of honours scandal by new 'Duke of Scotland Yard, OBE'

Tony Blair is completely innocent of any misuse of Britain's honours system, according to the senior police officer investigating the affair, who was making his maiden speech in the House of Lords yesterday.

Detective Inspector Barry 'Butch' Johnson, now Lord Sir Barry Johnson, Earl of Derbyshire, Rouge Croix Pursuivant and Keeper of the Queen's Oxen, had earlier indicated that there was 'shitloads of evidence' that knighthoods and peerages may have been given out for cash or political support.

However, speaking in the ermine robes befitting his sudden elevation to the Order of the Knights of the Garter, Lord Johnson confirmed: 'There's nothing suspicious about the recent ennoblement of the last three winners of the National Lottery's Roll-Over Jackpot – and if anyone says different, I'll stitch them up for every unsolved murder, robbery and drugs haul on my patch – got it?'

007's car rendered useless by spilt milk

In a pivotal scene from the latest James Bond film, moviegoers will be treated to a high-octane action sequence involving a sour-smelling dairy product and one particularly bumpy road.

Britain's most inebriated spy, after Guy Burgess, is seen spilling a small carton of full-cream milk on the Aston Martin's upholstery, after inadvertently plugging his USB charger into the ejector seat.

One of the production team explained: 'We've tried to remain as faithful as possible to the franchise, by blowing the entire budget in the first fifteen minutes - although we minimised the car's secret weaponry and emphasised its lingering reek.'

Rather than have Bond dodge bullets, the drama focuses on him applying a thick covering of baking soda to his floor mats. 'Yes, we could have spent more on the narrative or the acting - but why start now?'

Man convinced he can mend anything with gaffer tape

Despite having no formal medical training, Paul Nowakowski, 36, is fairly sure that an amputated thumb can be reattached. Faced with a DIY 'accident' involving a hedge trimmer and innate male stubbornness, he is convinced by the curative powers of gaffer tape and some wood glue.

Although copious blood loss would suggest otherwise, Nowakowski has every confidence that the tape will hold: 'Yes, I lost consciousness for a few minutes but that's probably just the hayfever,' he said. 'I'll be right as rain, as soon I've cleared up all the vomit and got the thumb facing in the right direction.'

Rather than visit an A&E department, Nowakowski is determined to power through, knowing full well that his wife had given him strict instructions to not climb ladders unaided.

'Let's not mention my little mishap, I don't want any awkward recriminations. Mrs N hasn't forgiven me since I hard-wired the TV into the plumbing and electrocuted her mother - again.'

Family dog remains upbeat despite economic downturn

Molly, a seven-year-old British Bulldog from Stockport, remained in a buoyant mood today despite the turmoil affecting the world's financial markets. Although analysts have grown increasingly gloomy and pessimistic and the Stock Market has plunged, Molly has continued to exude optimism and general enthusiasm.

'Only yesterday, we were sitting there watching the news about tumbling share prices and predicted recession and unemployment – but Molly just wagged her tail, pushed her ball towards us and gave an excited bark,' said owner Jenny Thompson from Surrey. 'It keeps us all cheerful!'

However, Jenny's husband Simon, a recently unemployed hedge fund manager, was less amused. 'That bloody dog's upbeat outlook's the last thing I need when everyone tells me I should be more like a bulldog,' he said.

Increased mortgage costs, gas and food bills at the Thompson household also failed to faze Molly, who greeted them with a nonchalant lick of her genitals before falling asleep and emitting noxious gases throughout 'Heartbeat'.

'She's a great dog. Nothing seems to get her down and all she costs is one tin of dog food a day,' said Jenny cheerfully. 'Which is coincidentally what we will be eating this winter unless Simon gets another job.'

A Guide to English Phrases

1. 'Taking into public ownership' = Complete Government ownership, instead of publicly held shares
2. 'The minister has my full confidence' = I'm about to sack him
3. 'The Prime Minister has my total support' = I want to be Prime Minister
4. 'I will give it my earnest attention' = F*ck off
5. 'Progressive' = Old-fashioned socialist
6. 'Socialist' = Liberal
7. 'Liberal elitist' = Likes Shakespeare
8. 'Evil capitalist Tory bastard' = Evil capitalist Tory bastard
9. 'In order to spend more time with his family' = Got caught with his trousers down and can't afford a divorce
10. 'With all due respect...' = I'm not listening, you f*ckwit
11. 'Well refreshed' = Completely pissed
12. 'According to sources close to' = He told me this himself, but on condition that I didn't reveal that it was he who said it
13. 'Full and frank discussions' = A blazing row.

14. 'Inappropriate behaviour' = Acting like a c*nt
15. 'My door is always open' = I didn't even leave a forwarding address
16. 'Equality' = Treating people unequally
17. 'Will of the people' = Some of the people. How do we keep fooling them?
18. 'If you'll forgive me' = I'm about to be exceptionally rude to you
19. 'Yes' = No
20. 'No' = Yes
21. 'He has a healthy appetite' = He's a right greedy fat b*stard
22. 'I'm very much in favour of immigrants coming here' = I'm a bitter racist
23. 'Breaks the Internet' = Gets over 100 views
24. 'Benefits cheat' = Anyone on benefits not struggling
25. 'Instagram star' = Pouting girl/boy on slow news day
26. 'Tycoon' = Tax avoider
27. 'Shocking' = Mildly unusual
28. 'Brit' = Anyone with a UK passport but only if they are abroad at the time
29. 'Feud' = Made-up tiff
30. 'Tragic' = Referring to any sudden death but most often falling out of a hotel while pissed
31. 'Brainy' = More than one GCSE at grade F or above
32. 'Have you lost weight?' = Look, I've lost three stone!
33. 'Have you lost weight?'= You look dreadful, are you going to live?
34. 'Have you lost weight?' = You need to lose some weight, fatty

'I didn't agree to an extension,' says man who said 'Yeah, whatever' to builders

A man who had hired a construction company to make his house bigger 'in whatever the f*ck way you want, I don't care', has complained that the extension they built him wasn't what he'd asked for.

'We gave him the plans and he just signed them all without looking at them. We tried to get him to engage and it was all 'I don't want to hear about your stupid f*cking plans, just get it done,' said the foreman.

'If we told him that he might not get what he wants if he wasn't specific, he'd threaten us with a rolled up Daily Mail and scream "sedition" or "traitors" and threaten to block our peerages.

'Anyway, he's now saying he didn't agree to an extension and when we showed him his signature on the plans, he closed his eyes, stuck his fingers in his ears and ran around screaming at us that we're refusing to do what he told us to do.

'Could be worse, though. At least we weren't landed with building part of a fence for Mr Trump and having to pretend it's a complete wall, so every cloud, eh?'

Man looks forward to using all 12 place settings in dishwasher on Christmas Day

Tony Norris from Stockport has expressed his delight at the prospect of using the space for all 12 place settings in his new dishwasher, as he will be joined by 11 members of his close family on Christmas Day.

'I bought the 12-place setting model especially for the big day and I'm sure it will comfortably accommodate all the pots, pans, plates, glasses and cutlery when we have finished our three course Christmas lunch,' said an excited Norris. 'And I'm expecting there to be just enough space left to squeeze in the dog's bowls as well.'

Initially, Norris was sceptical about the advertised capacity. 'I'm sure my old dishwasher was a 12-place settings model as well, but I had to run it four times last Christmas Day even though there were just the four of us. I was probably mistaken though, and must have inadvertently bought a one-place setting model.'

Man stares at tower crane without imagining horrific accident

An unnamed office worker looked up at a tower crane at a busy building site in central London while on his lunch break yesterday, without once imagining an awful accident. He is reported to have spent 'many minutes' looking at the crane while never once entertaining the idea of a heavy load suddenly slipping free from the crane's hook and crashing into the construction works below.

The man casually ate his sandwich while the crane lifted a load of steel from a flat-bed truck, watched idly as it swung the load high over workers' heads, and absent-mindedly continued to watch as the crane operator safely deposited the load on the 15th floor of the new residential block.

The process was repeated several times without the man ever thinking how amazing it would be if the steel were to plummet earthwards, demolishing site huts and vehicles and even, God forbid, causing widespread casualties.

Finally, the man checked his watch, wiped his mouth and headed back to work, pausing briefly to take one last look at the crane but not wondering what it would be like if the operator suddenly went insane and started twirling skip-loads of Thermalite blocks in ever-widening circles high above London's bustling South Bank.

'Farage is for life, not just for Brexit'

Many feel that the once cute and lovable Nigel Farage has outgrown his welcome, gnawing his way through a sizeable EU pension and defecating all over the press.

The RSPCA reports that many of Farage's pledges have been heartlessly abandoned at the roadside. Many Leave campaigners now realise that his pledges were unmanageable and unaffordable.

A JustGiving page started to help raise funds for the beleaguered ex-UKIP leader has already raised a staggering £1.29 just hours after being set up.

'After hearing Nigel say that he's alone, skint and miserable I just had to do something to help him out,' said Barry Spufford, who started the page.

'With Christmas just around the corner, the thought of him spending it alone in his £4 million Chelsea townhouse and struggling to make ends meet on his £325,000/year MEP's salary, was just too much.'

Farage has received messages of support already. 'At this time of year, it's important that we come together, put our differences aside and look out for those less fortunate than ourselves,' wrote one poster. 'But look, it's Nigel Farage – HAHAHAHAHA. Toilet.'

Some are concerned that post-Christmas, Farage may be put in a sack and dumped in the nearest river. Many others, meanwhile, are concerned that he might not be.

Traffic police discover 'Little Princess' not actually on board

After a routine traffic violation, the 'Little Princess on Board' sign in the Morris family's Vauxhall Astra has led the parents to be charged with deception and their eight-year-old daughter Chanelle to be arrested on suspicion of impersonating royalty.

The trouble began after a police patrol car spotted the sign as the family drove on the M6, turned on its flashing blue lights and sped the Morrises to their destination. However, officers became suspicious when the family gave them only a thumbs-up and a wink rather than the traditional royal wave.

The charges are especially damaging for Mrs Morris, whose 'Mum's Taxi' sign in her Nissan Cherry has already landed her a conviction for operating without a licence.

Toyota recalls 10,000 clown cars

Comedy car manufacturer Toyota is to recall 10,000 clown cars following a raft of complaints from circuses across the length and breadth of the country. A recall notice is now being issued to thousands of clowns, advising that, while the faults are not life threatening, they may well 'reduce the comedic factor of your vehicular-based performances.'

'I've heard stories of unfunny cars from all over the place,' said Bobo, Chief Bungler at Brighton Brothers' Family Circus. 'They just refuse to fall apart or spout comedy water. We tried covering up the problems, but you can only pour so much wallpaper paste down your trousers before the audience starts to notice that something isn't right.'

Claude, the troupe's resident Pierrot, similarly complained that the doors resolutely fail to drop off and the horn goes 'pffft' rather than

357

'honk'. He also describes how, during a recent performance, one particular vehicle suddenly accelerated and shot out of the big top at great speed.

'It turns out that Mr Chuckles had glued the accelerator pedal down for a laugh,' said Bobo. 'Well try telling that to The Great Stromboli and his broken leg - ha bloody ha!'

The vehicle models now being recalled include the Toyota Ticklewagon TDI, the 2.0 litre Fun-Mobile and the Yaris Special Edition 'Edge' (both petrol and custard variants).

First-time buyers still struggling to get on the petrol ladder

Despite Government assurances that the budget would help them out, millions of young would-be motorists still cannot afford their first gallon of petrol, the RAC has alleged.

The threat of unemployment, wage freezes and the credit crunch have left young couples struggling to get the deposit together to get their cars running. Most first-time pumpers are still having to rent their fuel, while many garages are now refusing to consider anyone with less than a four-star rating.

Shell has defended its decision to charge £299 just to apply for a tank of fuel, with customers tied in for the first year and expected to stay on the variable rate for a further 12 months to help pay off their debt. 'In these recessionary times we have to be careful that our business doesn't go up in smoke,' said a spokesperson.

There are hopes that alternatives may soon be made available to first-time drivers. After spending billions of pounds in the development stage, the Rover Group waited until the recent budget to finally unveil its long-awaited new 'low-cost fuel vehicle'.

'We thought we had the answer to all the petrol cost problems,' said a spokesperson. 'We developed a car that ran on cider.'

People don't spit out coffee over social media posts, report says

We've all been there, haven't we? Proudly posted a smart-arse comment on social media then sat back and waited for the 'likes' to flood our news feeds. Then, someone says: 'I spat out my coffee reading this'. It gives us a warm tingly feeling and makes us want to write more.

However, a new report from the Rhodes Institute in Oxford has cast doubt on the authenticity of the coffee-spitting claim. Dr Phil Berry, a behavioural scientist heading up the research team, said that cases had risen during the Coronavirus lockdown and they had concluded that it was a classic case of what psychologists call 'Boris Syndrome'.

'It's compulsive bullshitting, in a desperate bid for the sufferer to gain attention and endear themselves to others. Some will say they've spat out coffee over their laptops, while others will make more outlandish claims,' Berry commented.

'These could include half-baked ideas about world-beating systems, saying they've never heard of Marcus Rashford's well-publicised school meal scheme or denying that the Russians have set up an Airbnb in Downing Street. Our data shows that the syndrome could be the result of lockdown withdrawal, or the fact that they are simply massive w*nkers.'

Criminals asked to push themselves down the stairs

An inspection of police forces in England and Wales has reported that crime suspects are being asked to racially abuse themselves, plant their own incriminating evidence and, if the police are really busy, push themselves down the stairs on the way to the holding cells.

'Really, service is parlous,' complained career criminal, Cecil 'Nutter' Smythe, from Gosport. 'It is almost as if the police aren't there. How are we supposed to rest easy knowing that some activities such as car crime are being effectively decriminalised?'

'This is all pretty devastating from a continuing personal development perspective,' agreed Spencer Knott, an HR professional currently serving two years in Croydon for aggravated buggery.

'How are younger criminals supposed to get on the career ladder if twocking and five-fingered retail discounts are no longer considered worthy of recognition? I fear they'll move into organised crime sectors of employment, such as politics and banking.'

A spokes-PCC defended the police, saying: 'We would like to assure the public that the Force will be retaining core functions such as covering-up stadium disasters and long-term oversight of paedophile rings.'

Gavin Williamson: 'Keep language as simple as me'

In a surprise move this week, advocates of plain English and career diplomats alike expressed support after the UK Defence Secretary told Russia to 'Go away and shut up'. Pre-school children have also heralded the move.

A senior civil servant at the MOD reflected: 'Instructing the Russian nation to be silent and geographically relocate itself, whilst impractical, is perhaps more constructive than anything the Foreign Secretary has had to say. Boris usually just arses things up.

'We are scrapping the archaic Defcon and security alert terms with immediate effect. While we are not keen to see things escalate to the next stage, 'Just do one', the Cabinet Office is bracing itself for the likelihood of full-on 'F*cketty-bye' sometime later this year.'

A spokesperson from the Plain English Campaign today congratulated the minister for his choice of words describing Gavin Williamson as a 'bulbous salutation' and an 'egregious bellend'.

Customs officers smash trade in counterfeit guide dogs

Customs inspectors have made a major breakthrough this week in cracking a smuggling ring importing fake guide dogs into the UK.

The imported dogs look real from a distance but on closer inspection turn out to be small Lhasa Apsos or other annoying yappy breeds wearing faux Labrador outfits. They have a tell-tale zip across their stomach and a tendency to ignore all instructions. Most have had no formal training, and some were blind themselves.

'You'd have to be really sick to sell a counterfeit guide dog to a blind man,' said Inspector John Rhodes of Kent Police. 'We've not seen anything like it since the 'iPods for the Deaf' scam of 2003.'

Hansom Cab Drivers celebrates ban on motorised taxis

The Hansom Cab Drivers' Association (HCDA) is celebrating the news that Transport for London has decided not to renew the licence to operate granted to motorised taxis in the capital.

'This is a victory for ordinary Londoners,' said HCDA spokesman Josiah Hozzlethwaite, stroking his luxuriant side-whiskers as he wrapped his Ulster around himself against the fog rolling in off the Thames.

'Granted, they may have wanted an alternative to travelling at a snail's pace with the constant smell of horse manure in their nostrils, but er, well, it's good for them in some way, can't think how just at the moment.'

One furious black cab driver dismissed this, saying: 'It's a closed-shop cartel, designed to deprive Londoners of choice in order to keep their own profits high. We taxi drivers would never behave like that, unless of course we stood to make more money that way, in which case we would. OK, maybe not, if say the fare wanted to go south of the river late at night. But otherwise...'

'I saw a B&Q assistant,' claims customer

Wildlife watchers have descended on B&Q's Margate branch, following reports that a customer spotted one of their now mythical shop assistants.

'I'd been wandering the aisles in desperation for over half an hour looking for new light bulbs then suddenly I spotted a person I took to be a shop assistant nearby,' said 'twitcher' Will Roberts. 'However, it turned out to be a woman from Araldite merchandising a gondola.

'I'd given up all hope when I spotted a teenager in an orange apron. My sudden movement spooked him and he darted behind a rack of bathroom fittings. I ran to the end of the aisle where he'd been, but he'd somehow disappeared into thin air, leaving only tumbleweed blowing down the paint aisle.'

Chris Packham explained: 'I can confirm DIY shop assistants do exist, but with zero hours contracts, they're down to no more than three breeding pairs in captivity at a secret location. It would be amazing to see one in real life, but Mr Roberts is mistaken. To be honest he'd be far more likely to see a T-Rex or a dodo.'

Family Christmas lights crash National Grid

A couple from Hounslow have been ordered to switch off their elaborate external Christmas decorations or else face prosecution. This includes an illuminated tableau featuring well known seasonal figures such as Homer Simpson, a Wookie, John Wayne, several Lord of the Rings characters, a pink Cadillac and a ten-foot Elvis dressed as Santa.

'The energy provider said we'd have to switch off,' said John McDaid. 'They told us that whenever our lights went on Slough was being plunged into total darkness. Apparently, aircraft landing at Heathrow had been complaining that the glow in the sky from our lights was "putting pilots off". Bunch of miserable gits - don't they know it's Christmas?'

London earthquake blamed on honest office worker

The British Geological Survey has revealed the source of the 4.5 magnitude quake from a nondescript office block in central London, was the result of the sound produced by the fourth floor's arseholes collectively tightening, as Chris Williams replied honestly to his manager that he 'had absolutely no interest in the project, or helping with it in any way'.

Although a meeting with HR was set up later that day for him to attend, an unrepentant and exhilarated Williams was last seen leaving work, claiming to be off home to tell his girlfriend the real answer to her question as to whether he wants to attend that wedding of one of her old university pals in the summer.

Man shatters record after five years on hold to DWP call centre

Bill Anderson from Blackpool has shot into the record books after being confirmed as being the person to be kept on hold for longest when telephoning the Department of Work & Pensions' call centre.

Anderson called the 'helpline' exactly five years ago, when a robot told him: 'We are currently experiencing high call volumes and you may experience a delay - you may like to call back at a time when we are less busy.' Nonetheless, he pluckily remained on hold to speak to a real person, missing his mother's funeral and his daughter's wedding in the process.

With his phone still clamped to his ear as a tone-deaf stylophone player continued to murder Vivaldi's Four Seasons, Anderson told reporters: 'I'm sure they'll answer soon, they really are very busy indeed. But this music is brilliant. I'll maybe get round to trying to patch things up with Jude after this call, but I'd hate to hang up and lose my place in the queue now.'

Man who wiped arse with Daily Mail 'caught xenophobia'

Medics have confirmed that Dave Phelps from Reading has contracted xenophobia after wiping his arse on squares cut from a copy of the Daily Mail he had put in his downstairs toilet for a dinner party joke.

'Next morning, I had to go and only realised I'd forgotten to change the paper back to our regular Waitrose triple-ply,' said Phelps. 'But of course by then it was too late. I'd gone and wiped my bum and, within minutes, I was slagging off my best friend and next-door neighbour Bogdan for no reason whatsoever.'

Professor Craig Lennox, who is working to find a cure, explained: 'This was the perfect storm waiting to happen. The squares from the edition he used were particularly toxic.

'The front page was about a group of Eastern European plumbers working on the black economy, yet still claiming state benefits of over £50,000 pounds a week to help fund their ten-bedroom mansions in Knightsbridge.

'Another prominent article detailed how the two million illegal Muslim immigrants pouring into the country every week plan to gain power, then make it compulsory for every school in the land to ban the teaching of Christianity. I appeal to everyone with a brain: If you must handle the Daily Mail, then please use latex gloves at all times.'

Dog walking romance still hangs in the balance

Raymond Wilcox, a 43-year old analyst from Bromsgrove, has reported mixed results in his attempts to get a local woman into bed using their pet dogs.

Wilcox met attractive divorcee Anna Dubanowski, 37, on the local common when his West Highland terrier 'Flint' started playing with her Jack Russell 'Molly'. The sight of the two small dogs rolling happily around in the grass together prompted other dog owners to start referring to them as an engaged couple.

'I made a wry comment about how dogs are lucky not to have to bother with corny chat-up lines, which made her laugh,' said Wilcox. 'Next time they met, they were even cuter together, so I made a crack about Flint going through his sex-crazed teenage phase and she smiled and nodded.'

In the past few weeks, however, wet weather and other commitments have restricted Wilcox's dog-walking activities. More seriously, Molly has become increasingly indifferent to Flint and has begun playing with a boisterous Springer spaniel called Charlie.

'Anna was obviously embarrassed that time when Molly started snarling at Flint,' said Wilcox. 'That's probably why she didn't reply when I said what a typical bitch, always falling for a bit of rough.'

With only two weeks before his annual holiday in Thailand, Wilcox is keen to see some progress in the relationship. However, he admits to being frustrated that it is so dependent on the whims of two unpredictable animals.

'Well, if it doesn't happen between me and Anna, so it goes, I'll know it's the dog's fault,' he chuckled ruefully. 'Either that or because of the time she spotted me masturbating in the woods behind her house.'

Guardian stockpiling hysteria in preparation for Brexit

The editor of the Guardian has told its journalists not to unload all of their hysteria about Brexit too soon, given that there are still almost two months to go until Britain officially leaves the EU.

'I've spoken to Polly Toynbee so many times about moderation, how it's possible to express your views without sounding like you're ranting on a soapbox on Speaker's Corner,' he said. 'She always says she understands, then goes off and writes a column about possible delays at Dover that sounds like it comes from the Book of Revelations.

'I hoped Rafael Behr would help me calm her down, but when I tried his office, he'd barricaded himself in by nailing planks across the door. When I finally got in, he was huddled in a corner, surrounded by piles of tinned food, occasionally flicking the light switch to see if the electricity was still on. This won't do. We have to have some hysteria in reserve for the actual exit day.'

Home Secretary raises gunpowder threat level

This November, the Government fears large quantities of colourfully wrapped explosive ordinance will fall into incompetent hands, as thousands of families decide to set fire to their neighbourhood. The Home Secretary has declared that the gunpowder threat level has gone from 'Slightly naff Vesuvius' to 'Rocket up the arse time.'

The level of Gunpowder Plot threat had been falling steadily since the seventeenth century when England was on the highest 'Blimey, who put all these barrels here?' status.

In recent times provincial Catholics have not been seen as the security risk they once were, with the threat level reduced to 'I'll run through the Commons naked with my bottom on fire if it ever happens.'

However, the Government does not want to appear complacent and has asked the public to still remain vigilant. If you do happen to see an unattended wooden barrel, particularly if it has 'gunpowder' stamped on it, you should report it. If it has a long string attached that appears to be sparkling, then it would be better to report it sooner rather than later.

Lying at about your drinking habits lowers heart disease

'Well you can't just drink one glass can you?' said Siobhan Taylor, 22, from Bristol. 'If you open a bottle you've got to drink it all haven't you. So If I drink, say, 12 bottles in a week then plan not to drink anything for a month it works out doesn't it?'

Another Bristol woman, Chardonnay McDonald, 28, added: 'Well I drinks vodka and Coke so that doesn't count 'cos it's a soft drink really isn't it? If I do drink wine it's the posh stuff that was £8 but is reduced to two for a fiver. So that's OK. Anyway I reckon it works out to about a glass a day, if you don't count week-ends.'

A similar study found that only eating chocolate when you are upset, counterbalancing burgers with a salad garnish and eating chips off someone else's plate had no effect on obesity and these jeans have shrunk in the wash anyway.

Palace launches Queen 2.0

Buckingham Palace yesterday launched its long-awaited upgrade to its Queen range of monarchs. 'After 60 years of beta development, Queen 2.0 combines the traditional robust Windsor operating system with a friendlier democratic interface,' said a spokesperson.

Critics have complained that the new model looks exactly the same as Queen 1.0 but smaller. 'We like the reduction in size,' said one Queen fan. 'But with the same old hats and the same irritating artificial voice, it won't make you go out and buy one.'

The new model is also still dependent on an unstable spare part made in Greece that can perform erratically in public. Although a younger, slimmer replacement is undergoing trials, Queen 2.0 is expected to corner the market in monarchs for the next few years, as the unpopular and accident-prone Charles 1.0 prototype is unlikely to ever make it onto the crowded royal market.

Speed cameras to be replaced by reconstructions of accidents

Under a new scheme, the Department for Transport will commission out-of-work actors to perform full-scale productions of gruesome and bloody car crashes along all of Britain's most dangerous roads, on the basis that everybody knows that drivers slow down to look at car crashes.

'We are making every accident as authentic as possible, so they have a really good gawp,' said a spokesperson. 'We have real cars, real crashes and all topped off with real blood and guts as well.'

The project will provide employment for many actors who lost their jobs following the cancellation of 'The Bill'. 'These people are so desperate they will do almost anything,' said the Transport Minister. 'Plus, they work out a damn sight cheaper than speed cameras.'

Solstice Druids vote 'leave'

Crowds gathered at Stonehenge - to remember the catastrophic immigration policy that led to an influx of economic migrants during the fifth century - have endorsed the Vote Leave campaign. They believe that European laws and illuminated texts have undermined the core British values of badly cooked mutton, dancing naked around fires and believing in fairies.

'We've seen the steel industry collapse, but what about the salt gatherers, the amber miners and the guy who keeps the pixies away?' said a lead Druid. 'These Anglo-Saxons are just cheap labour who smell of dung - and don't get me started on the Normans.'

Quaffing a pint of mead, Nigel Farage welcomed these bearded recruits to the 'Leave' banner. 'Britain is stronger without EU interference. We don't want a bureaucrat telling us what shade of blue to paint our genitals or whose head to chop off and mount on a spike.'

Twelve thousand people attended the Neolithic site in Wiltshire to throw their support behind the slogan: 'Britain for the Britons'. Meanwhile, Pagans across the world celebrated the longest day of summer, just before the referendum kick-starts the longest night.

IN OTHER RELATED NEWS:

Tories threaten to finish what they started

Philip furious that Andrew got to do a car crash interview

Doomsday clock forgot to factor in British Summer Time

Festive jumpers: Are they the new black?

Death on holiday tops list of things no-one has sympathy for

Scientists discover root cause of interruptions – they are very boring

Brave PM left 'shaken' by inadvertently meeting member of the public

Mein Kampf sues Daily Mail for copyright infringement

Remembrance Day service: Prince Andrew lays Poppy Wreath - but it's OK, she's 22

Driverless Government experiment to continue for at least another four years

New Cabinet motto: Awful one and awful all

Johnson underpants to be converted into youth hostel

British names upset as French name is awarded royal baby contract

Scotland flooded to dilute alcohol content

Queen's birthday: Nation celebrates 90 years of forelock tugging

England to release Scottish hostages

'I'm not a quitter,' says Johnson, thus making Brexit a bit confusing

Price of scrap bronze 'will plummet' if UK removes racist statues

Brexit enters persistent vegetative state

'International Talk Like a Pirate Day' snubbed by Cornwall

'Angry Birds' designers slammed for glamorising Avian-Porcine conflict

Sodor abandoned as self-aware steam trains finally take over

Police interrogations to include General Knowledge round

Commuter outrage as terrorist attempts to blow himself up on Quiet Carriage

Serious Fraud Office to investigate itself after claims that it doesn't exist

CONTRIBUTORS:

A Mantra	Adrian Bamforth
Al OPecia	apepper
Andyiong	Antharrison
Beau-Jolly	BAJDixon
Benvoleo	Bigglesworth
Bookies friend	Boutros
Bravenewmalden	Chipchase
ChrisF	DavidH
Deceangli	Des Custard
Des & Stan	Doctor Chutney
Dominic-mcg	Dick Everyman
Editor	Filthy Rich
FlashArry	Gary Stanton
Genghis Cohen	Gerontius
Golgo13	Granger
Harrypalmer	Ian Searle
Immacagain	Ironduke
Ivor Baddiel	james_doc
Jesus H	JoF
Jp1885	La Maga
Ludicity	KateWritesStuff
MADJEZ	Mary Evans
Mick Turate	Midfield Diamond
Mirthless Evil C	Myke

Nealdoran

Not Amused

Newsbiscuit Editorial Team

Oxbridge

Peter74940

Rickwestwell

Ron Cawleyoni

Roybland

SimonjJames

Sir Lupus

Spinal_bap

Stan Laurel

SurburbanDad

Squudge

Teambiscuit

The Paper Ostrich

Throngsman

Vertically Challenged Giant

Wallster

Yabasta

NickB

Newsbiscuit

Oshaughnessy

Paul L

Pinxit

Ronseal

Rowly

SarahTipper

Sinnick

Skylarking

Squudge

SteveB

StoopyDeGunt

Sydalg

The News Walrus

Thisisalloneword

Titus

Walter Eagle

Wrenfoe

BOOK EDITORS

Chipchase

ChrisF

DavidH

Not Amused

Oxbridge

Throngsman

Wrenfoe

ILLUSTRATIONS/COVER

Mike Capozzola/Wrenfoe

SPECIAL THANKS

To our long-suffering readers

John O'Farrell for establishing NewsBiscuit and then using it as an elaborate money-laundering scheme

Mrs Wrenfoe and Oxbridge for proofreading

Throngsman for formatting

Wrenfoe for beating the drum (not a euphemism)

FINAL WORDS:

Flat-pack Brexit comes with no instructions, missing parts and loose screws
Unlucky identity thief gets debt-ridden loser
Chancellor to bring back rickets
Knives redesigned to be safer are pointless
Old dogs no longer funded for trick-based education
Fixed penalty notices for litter louts just end up on the floor, admits council
Facebook promises to pay $1 million to every user spotting fake news
Tabloid repeats 'Alzheimer's breakthrough' headline for twentieth day in a row
Isle of Wight dinosaur to front 'Leave' campaign
Time traveller admits he's getting too young for the job
Unicorns prepared to stand in when fat lady singers strike
Sacha Baron Cohen announces current series of 'Trump' will be the last'

Printed in Great Britain
by Amazon

51501280R00217